REMNANTS:
SEASON OF WONDER

REMNANTS: SEASON OF WONDER

BOOK 1 IN THE REMNANTS SERIES

BY LISA T. BERGREN

BLINK

Lisa invites you to join her and other Remnants readers
on the fan page found here:

Facebook.com/RemnantsSeries

You can also learn more about Lisa Bergren and the Remnants
Series by connecting with her online:

www.LisaBergren.com
Twitter: @LisaTBergren
Facebook.com/LisaTawnBergren

And check out *Remnants: Season of Fire*
when it releases winter 2015!

BLINK

Remnants: Season of Wonder
Copyright © 2014 by Lisa T. Bergren

This title is also available as a Blink ebook. Visit www.zondervan.com/ebooks.

Requests for information should be addressed to:

Blink, 3900 *Sparks Drive SE, Grand Rapids, Michigan 49546*

ISBN 978-0-310-73564-9

Cover design: Brand Navigation
Cover photography: Fotolia, iStock
Interior design: David Conn

Printed in the United States of America

14 15 16 17 18 19 /DCI/ 20 19 18 17 16 15 14 13 12 11 10 9 8 7 6 5 4 3 2 1

We disappeared the same day we arrived. Even our neighbors couldn't tell you where we'd gone.

Children of subversives, we were born in different territories, but every one of us emerged on the seventh day during the seventy-seventh Harvest after the Great War. And every one of us carried the Ailith Strain.

Our coming was foretold for years. The elders spoke of children who could change the future, change the world, just as the planet teetered on the edge of darkness. Born on the prophesied day with birthmarks in the form of a crescent moon, they knew us immediately. Swaddled and screaming, we were spirited away by those who hid us, trained us, and kept us safe until our time came.

They poured their lives into us. Some died to save us.

None of us knew where the others were, but we knew we were not alone. We could sense one another, even from afar, and the need to be together was like a slow burn, intensifying until the Hour was reached.

And now we, the Remnants, protected by Knights of the Last Order, have gathered.

We are warriors, set to right so much that has gone wrong.

Called until we breathe our last … to save the world.

CHAPTER
1

The elder likened the Hour of our Call to a tidal pull, the first birthing pangs of a pregnant mother … but to me it felt like a scream building inside. Excitement and glory, swirling in a ball within my chest. Electrifying. Mobilizing.

I sat up straight in my bed and looked out the window. Through the mists that plagued our planet even during the season of Harvest, I could see the dim glow of a crescent moon. Our mark. The Maker was calling us to rise, to gather, to begin at long last.

At last. At last. Was I truly ready?

Part of me felt it was perfect. The culmination of everything I'd dreamed about and prepared for. Relieved that the wait was over. That it was finally beginning.

Part of me felt unready. So. Not. Ready.

Slipping from my bed, I forced myself toward my clothes and strapped a dagger to my calf, yanked my long johns to my waist, then the ratty long-and-loose brown trousers I wore every day. I reached for my bra-band and tee, followed by a dark blue, long-sleeved woolen shirt, knowing the day would be cold, as it always was. I stared hard in the mirror while brushing my dark hair. Mom always loved this shirt on me. Said it brought out the blue-green color of my eyes.

Mom. Dad.

I swallowed hard, against the lump in my throat. I couldn't think about them — not now. It was as if we'd already been pulled a distance apart in that waking moment, making me longingly glance over my shoulder in their direction from the other side. They'd know it too. At least, I hoped they would. It would make our parting one of destiny. Bittersweet, but sure.

By the dim light of the moon, I put on socks and laced up my boots, then stuffed my hairbrush, toothbrush, box of baking soda, several changes of underwear and socks, another T-shirt, a cami, and thick sweater into my backpack. I tugged on a long, oilskin coat, strapped on my sheath, then reached for my sword on the wall — which had been there ever since I was a babe in my protectors' arms — and slid it into the sheath on my back.

The wall looked curiously blank without it, and I took one last, slow glance around the room I'd had my entire childhood. Some of the warlords' kids still grew up with images of Winnie the Pooh or Beatrix Potter on their nursery walls, I'd heard. Characters from precious books my mom and dad had read to me from tattered pages, making up the story for me when a section had been lost. I pondered that for a second, the idea of a pristine room, clean and freshly painted.

But I'd always been destined for this, this night among nights. A girl with a sword on her wall from birth.

Mom and Dad were outside my room. Dad lit one of the

candles on the wall and then turned to stand beside Mom. They appeared drawn and tired, fear lurking in the lines of Mom's face, but with encouragement and love fighting it back. Dad looked at me with compassion, and was first to pull me into his arms. "You are brave, Andriana. Capable," he whispered. "What a privilege to be a part of preparing you for this moment. Go. Go and make us proud."

"I will," I said, suddenly choked up, feeling the loss within him, the pain this was causing, as well as a fierce sense of pride. "Thank you, Dad. Thanks for ... everything." I tried to memorize the warm feel of his embrace, the last I'd likely ever have from him. Because we were going away.

Most likely very, very far away.

That was when I felt my first pang of panic.

Mom pulled me into her arms next. She was shorter than me, but she still felt strong. In her, I sensed the tearing too; the grief, as well as a measure of fear. "I'll be okay, Mom," I said, swallowing hard, trying to convince myself as much as her.

"You'd better," she said with pretended threat, hugging me harder then pulling away to put a delicate hand on either side of my face. "We raised you to do nothing but this, Andriana," she said, staring into my eyes, willing me to understand, to remember. "You have what you need within you to do what you must. The Maker saw to it. In him you will find strength and courage and direction. Remember that." Her head shook back and forth a little, as if she were arguing within herself, reassuring herself, like she wanted to say more.

"I will, Mom," I said. I embraced her again, and then turned toward the door, feeling an Ailith — someone like me, born with the strain that destined us to be either Remnant or Knight — even before we reached it. We could all do that — know when another of our kind was near. But this one felt special to me. More known than the others. *Ronan.*

I opened the door to my tall knight, his finely muscled arms bulging out from a sleeveless shirt, worn despite the night's chill that made his breath fog before his face. Ronan's fingers twitched nervously over the hilt of the dagger at his waist, making me seek the deep shadows beyond him. Normally, he was steady regardless of what we faced, but tonight even the air around him was tense. His green-brown eyes met mine and he gave me the barest of nods, then slicked back his long dark hair from his face. "They're coming. They feel it too," he whispered, too low for my parents to hear.

The Sons of Sheol. The dark ones. The elders had warned us.

He reached past me to shake my father's hand with both of his own and then embraced my mother, as if they were his family, not mine. Even though they'd never met — by careful design — and never would again. "You've served the Maker well. Thank you. She will be safe with me."

In his arms, Mom broke. "Do take care of her," she managed to say with a strangled voice, nodding quickly and forcing a smile, even as her lip began to tremble and her shoulders began to shake. As if that would make me think she was fine. I reached out to hold her hand.

"With my life," he said tenderly, backing away so she could see the pledge in his eyes. So kind to my mom, it made me catch my breath. "Andriana is strong," he said. "But together we will be even stronger."

"May your words be true," Dad said.

Before I could nod in agreement, a shiver ran down my

back. My eyes met Ronan's, and together we searched the bank of dark trees that lined our village of twenty homes.

"What is it?" Mom whispered.

"They're coming for us," Ronan hissed. "We must be away."

Never had we felt our enemy this close. A few times, they'd entered the Valley, scouting, but never come this far...

"Go, Andriana," Mom whispered, tears running down her face. "Dri, go," she said, but her body and tone screamed at me to stay. *Stay!*

I looked back at her, tears running down my face as well, fear for those I loved almost immobilizing me. We were trained to battle the dark, born for it, in a way. My parents were not. And never had our enemy come this close to our village.

"You must go too, now," I said. "Into hiding. Far from here. Far from anything that ties you to me. Do not wait. Do you promise?"

"We promise," Dad said. "Go."

Mom nodded as Dad wrapped his arm around her shoulders.

Comforted, I quickly pulled them to me one last time, kissed their wet faces, then turned to take Ronan's offered hand. He was immediately in a full sprint.

Directly toward our oncoming enemies.

I fought the urge to pull my hand from his as we ran into and through the forest. But there was only one reason my knight would head toward them. "You brought the bike?"

"Just over the hill," he grunted. He'd often stashed his dirt bike in a copse of aspens, waiting for me at the forest's edge to escort me to training. There were times over the years I'd felt him near, keeping watch, even when I hadn't expected him.

It'd made me smile, warmed by his presence even a thousand feet away. His fierce protection. The first day we'd met, on our decade-and-second birthday, he took my hand in both of his and stared into my eyes, and I'd learned the full meaning of the term *bonded*. Training together every day since had only strengthened our connection. Now, in the early hours of our decade-and-seventh birthday, we moved out to claim our inheritance, our birthright as Ailith warriors. Finally, finally fighting back against the dark that threatened to overtake us.

We ran crouched over, feeling the rising pressure of fear within our chests entwining with the warm pull of the Ailith's Hour as we hurried across fallen logs and through brush.

Ronan abruptly stopped by a huge tree and pulled me up short, then tightly against his broad chest. I remained as still as I could, panting, as he edged his face to the left, slowly, ever so slowly peeking out. He straightened and sighed, closing his eyes in frustration. His arm around me tightened. "Scouts," he whispered, close to my ear. "Two."

I couldn't believe it. We'd felt the Call but an hour before. Had the Sheolites somehow known the Hour was upon us? And if we couldn't get to our meeting place — if the Sheolites managed to capture or kill us — what then?

Oh no. No, no, no. We didn't go through all this, do all this ... My parents sacrificed so much ... I shifted, wanting to tear after these spies like a banshee, but Ronan held my arm. As if he knew I'd want to rely on myself rather than the Maker. I shook my head and closed my eyes and tried to concentrate as our trainer had taught us. To hear the Maker in my very breath, focusing, remembering we were not alone.

A minute or so later, a mudhorse — bred for our rainy, wintery conditions — snorted, and I visualized the rider in a wide saddle atop it, a mere five feet away. I listened intently for the second, but heard only silence.

Ronan looked down at me and I nodded. If we were to escape and not be followed, if Mom and Dad were to be safely away, these two had to die. Our trainer had warned us. There would be no skirmish with these dark knights; it would be a fight to the death. The Sheolites' charter had always been to seek out and kill anyone with the high gifting. Ronan tapped me on the shoulder and pointed with two fingers, directly west. He wanted me to run as bait. Before my heart had time to drop, he took my hand and lifted it to the hilt of my sword, and I smiled. While I would play the rabbit, any wolf that chased me would soon find this rabbit had teeth.

I set off immediately, running as fast as I could toward Ronan's favorite place to stash his bike. I tore through the brush like I was in a blind panic, just as our trainer had shown us. Making plenty of noise so they would follow, and so Ronan could cut them down from behind. Though as I crested the next hill, with no sound of pursuit behind me, I turned and faltered.

Because clearly, no one was coming after me.

My heart sank. *Ronan.*

Could he defend himself against two of our enemies at once? I turned and ran back through the brush, slowing as I reached the first hill, hiding beneath the wide, broad leaves of a fern as I searched for him in the crescent moon's light. I could see and hear nothing. Our forests had long been devoid of birds and other creatures, hunted out a century before, but the mudhorses had been right there, stocky, short, strong, snorting in the misty night. *Right there.*

I could make out the dark outline of the big tree where we'd paused. But nothing else.

The silence was liable to send me into sheer panic, my heart now pounding more from fear than from my running. Had they managed to take Ronan? Or gone the other way?

I turned to the left and pushed through huge ferns before I ran right into the flank of a mudhorse and fell back. The creature whinnied and shied away, then reared, but as I struggled to rise, her rider leaped from the mount's back to me; nothing but a terrifying, flying shadow, growing larger by the moment.

I moved without thought, whirling low and into a defensive stance. And the shadow became flesh and blood as he descended, directly upon the upturned point of my sword. He came down so hard and fast that he was fully impaled before the sword slowed his momentum, but he was still largely atop me. He reached out to grip my throat, his fingers cold, even through the long gloves he wore. I felt his chest heaving for breath against my pinned arm, and I pried at his strong fingers before he groaned then gasped, the sound raspy and wet with death.

He took one last breath and seemed to freeze, his hand still on my neck. I shuddered and pushed and pulled until I could scramble, crab-like, away through the soft, loamy soil of the forest, then to my feet. I stood there, trembling, trying to absorb the fact that I'd killed my first enemy. I lifted my sword and warily turned in a slow circle, wondering where the other was. Where Ronan was.

But then I heard it. An enraged scream. The metallic clash of swords. Six, seven strikes. Another guttural cry. Then silence.

I forced my body into motion, running toward them,

sweeping through the great, wet ferns, desperately hoping I was in time to help. What I found was Ronan in a clearing, rising above another body, wiping his lip of sweat and wearily sheathing his sword. I ran into him, practically tackling him in my relief.

"Easy there," he said with a gentle laugh, panting while settling an easy arm around me. "Whoa, you're shaking." He turned fully toward me, dropping his sword and placing both hands on the sides of my face. "Andriana, are you all right?"

"Fine, fine," I said, pushing his hands away, embarrassed by my weakness. What had I thought we were training for? Day after day? I swallowed hard. "What happened?"

"They didn't take the bait."

I thought I saw a flash of white teeth as he smiled. I loved the way he smiled, like he was in on the best of secrets. It made me smile too. But then I sobered. "Ronan, they must've *known*. They knew our break-and-bait plan as soon as I set off."

"Yes," he said, grabbing my hand firmly again and pulling me along. "They didn't even think of going after you. Or ... they figured that if they teamed up on me, brought me down first, they could get to you next."

I let him drag me forward even as my mind raced back over his words. *They didn't even think of going after you.* "They got to a ... They got to a *trainer*?"

"Maybe," he said, never pausing. "Worse, an Ailith." He let go of my hand, leaving me to trudge behind him as if he needed a moment to digest the idea of it himself.

I tried to swallow, but found my mouth dry as I stumbled after him. If they'd gotten to a trainer, how much did they know? Of our skills? Our tactics? Of us? Such thoughts were foolish, however. There was no way they got our trainer. He was too good, too strong. And he would've died protecting our secrets, as he always said every trainer would.

But had they captured one of our fellow Ailith? On this night of nights? I slowed to a stop, feeling the slip of mud beneath my boots.

"Hey," Ronan said, pausing to turn toward me. "Don't worry," he said, reaching up as if he wanted to touch me, then thinking better of it and dropping his hand. "We fought 'em off, didn't we? And we'll learn new tactics. This is just the beginning, Dri."

Just the beginning. His words echoed through my mind.

This was the first night. The first hour.

But if this was the first hour, what was yet to come?

CHAPTER 2

I clung hard to Ronan's waist and leaned with him as we curved up the old remains of a road on the dirt bike. I leaned my head between his shoulders in the V formed by the swords on his back, closing my eyes, inhaling the scent of oil and leather and dust, feeling the taut muscles of his torso tense with each turn. The blowing strands of his dark hair, tied in a ponytail at the nape of his neck, tickled my cheek as the wind blew past.

I knew I wasn't supposed to feel the way I did. Ronan was my knight. My guardian. Nothing more. Anything more than kinship was expressly forbidden among the Ailith, and our trainer had drilled it into our minds from the start.

For a long while, we'd been nothing but brother and sister, companions learning to defend, to attack, to intuit, to respond. Learning the ancient words by heart, the process of meditation, the use of every weapon. But last year, as we practiced at what our trainer called "hunter and prey," I'd managed to come upon

Ronan from behind. More silent than ever before, refusing to let my soft boots betray me. Just as he sensed the Ailith in me was near, I'd pounced, leaping onto his back, laughing in victorious glee.

He'd been rising, and managed to grab me and pull me around. But my weight upset him, and we tumbled far down a mossy, fern-covered bank, over and over again. When we came to a rest at the bottom, laughing and groaning, Ronan was above me, his arms on either side of my body. I could see it now, in the moonlight, as if I'd returned to that place. His face a foot away, his hair coming loose from its tie in a dark, shining wave. I moved to get up but he held me still, staring into my eyes, not laughing as I was. I paused, confused, wondering what he was up to, if he was claiming Hunter when he'd clearly been Prey. It was only as he slowly leaned toward me, searching my face as if he were asking permission, I knew.

He was going to kiss me.

But I'd ruined it.

Laughed in panic. Squirmed away.

"What are you doing?" I sputtered, scrambling to my feet. Half-angry, half-exhilarated. Brushing off my pants and examining a new tear in an effort to do anything but reach out and pull him to me again. To kiss him.

"I was just checking you out, making sure you were okay," he'd said, turning so I couldn't see his face. "Let's go."

I sighed at the memory and repositioned my arms as we rounded another corner, closing my eyes, appreciating the chance to be this close to him again with excuse. Because since that day, he'd not tried again, even though I'd given him more than a few chances. It was as if in that moment among the ferns, he'd decided to do as our trainer had taught him to do. To give his life for me, if necessary. To love me more than himself. But never to *love*-love me.

My heart ached at the thought of it. In admiration of his inner strength, fortitude. And in misery that he'd never be mine in a way that I wanted so much.

No one could know. Ever. What would they do to me if they found out? To him? Because it wasn't an Ailith's path to marry, mate, bear children. Our task was bigger. Greater.

We were born to save the world and all that. I gave my head a little shake, hearing our trainer's words, spoken every time we met. *You were born to do as the Maker bids. To fight the dark. To fight for the light. To save the world, one step, one person at a time.*

We reached the end of the road as the moon crested above us, and parked beside the rusting remains of a train track that cracked and twisted as if some giant had reached down and cut it short.

"You sure this is the right place?" I whispered when Ronan cut the engine.

"Somewhat," he said, getting off. He moved over to the old train tracks, and I saw what made him cautious. The metal had been harvested, most likely cut and hauled away as fodder for cave-housed bullet factories.

I tensed in tandem with Ronan as he rose. Because the war-lords who still bore bullet-bearing weapons were a different breed altogether. Could there be some of their rank so close to us? Right here, in the Valley? Ronan moved ahead of me and lifted his chin, searching the dark silhouette of the mountain ridge above.

My heart was pounding. Not from fear — from the grow-ing presence of Ailith. Strong and true, almost as if our hearts pounded in unison. "Feel that?" I whispered, trying to cover my excitement.

"Yeah," he said, still studying the ridge. He took my hand and squeezed, and I looked up to where he seemed to be staring. And saw the figure of a man. Slowly, the man raised his right arm, his hand closed in a fist. Greeting us. Welcoming us in the way of the Community, as our trainer had himself.

"This way," Ronan said. I followed him, even though I knew he was guessing. But his guess was as good as any. As we rounded a boulder, four men surrounded us, emerging from behind other rocks.

"Peace," said one, even though he held an automatic weapon and I could see two swords strapped across his back, as Ronan wore his. "You are expected."

I felt Ronan take my hand. There was no mistaking these men as our own, but he was taking no chance we'd become separated again. He pulled me after him in a way I was coming to expect, even when we slipped through a slit in the mountainside, entering sheer darkness at an angle. At times the crevice became so narrow, I wondered how Ronan managed to squeeze through. Ahead we glimpsed light, due to torches lit along the wall. I welcomed their glow, but it was something else entirely that beckoned us — the warmth of it pulling us to its edge like a warm fire after a cold, wet trip.

We passed pair after pair of guards, many of them bearing guns of all sort — automatic rapid-repeaters as well as ancient rifles, pistols. My mind whirled, trying to make sense of the fact that I knew not one of them — when I thought I'd known most in the Valley. But I paid them little heed as Ronan and I fought the urge to break into a run, so eager were we to reach them ... our brothers and sisters.

The other Ailith set my senses on alert, but the Community drawing close to them was like nothing I'd ever experienced anywhere else. With them even near me, I felt whole. Awake. Known ... more *myself*. More excited and at peace, all at the same time. It was like being back at home in the village, but better. More like being with a hundred brothers and sisters instead of only Mom and Dad and a few of our neighbors. I wished my parents were with me to meet this extended family. All awaiting us, welcoming us.

We could hear the murmur of voices, and as we emerged through the last bit of tunnel, a cheer went up. I froze, and Ronan turned back to me, but soon he was looking up and around as well. Around us, in a tight, steep beehive of an auditorium carved from the rock, forty or fifty elders sat clothed in robes. I'd never been with so many people all at once in one place. And never with people so *old*, many of them with gray or white hair. They stood, clapping slowly, with big, exaggerated movements, faces alight, as if they gained strength solely by the sight of us.

On the floor, three young people turned to face us, and I immediately knew two of them as Ailith. We reached to grip arms with each of them and they welcomed us. A dark, stocky guy introduced himself as Vidar, all big, white teeth against olive skin as he smiled into my eyes. Bellona, his knight, flipped her long brown braid over her shoulder as she reached for my arm. She was a couple inches taller than Vidar, my height, and didn't smile, but I didn't care. Given our encounter with the Sheolites, I figured the more tough warriors who joined our side, the better. And while she acted gruff, I knew her as sister as soon as our eyes met. It was like a knitting, a connection within the heart. A *knowing*, as surely as I knew Vidar as brother.

The last was Raniero. "Niero, they call me," he said, sliding his arm into mine, every nuance of movement embodying ease, peace, utter assurance. He was beautiful, powerful, massive, and yet as graceful as a dancer, and I think I had to tell myself to shut my mouth when I felt it drift open. "Or you can call me *Sir*," he said, the hint of a smile behind his dark, knowing eyes set in tawny skin. *Ahh*, I thought. *So here is our leader.* He was older than we by a few years, and ... not Ailith. I didn't feel the same pull in him. And yet he was special — unlike any other person I'd ever met, and so clearly bearing authority that I fought the compulsive urge to kneel. He unmistakably belonged with us, Ailith or not.

My eyes followed him as he moved on to greet Ronan. Niero was predominantly Asian and African, with tight, dark curls that he wore closely cropped to his head. Just a couple inches shorter than Ronan, but more elegant force than brute strength. Some would call him the perfect example of man — the crossroads of all our ancient cultures in physical form.

Out gleaning once, among a long-abandoned village, my dad and I'd discovered a pile of colored books in flimsy covers. "Magazines," Dad had called them, picking one up. Half had long been penetrated by mildew and mold, disintegrating in our hands, but I'd squirreled away a few. They were filled with people in odd clothes — people from the olden days. Smiling, clean people, in bright homes. The words did not tell one story. They were like little stories, a page or two long, and addressed things like dating, job hunting, eating specially prepared healthy meals. Things they did in the olden days.

As I watched Raniero over Vidar's shoulder, I decided he reminded me of the men pictured within those ancient magazines, tending to bright green grass — *lawns*, they called them, according to Dad — or hovering over a smoking *grill*. Or showing off a crisp shirt that would never have been usable now, as it would soak up rain rather than warding it off.

But unlike those men in the magazines, who often looked harsh or cold, Raniero seemed to be the kind of guy who invited everyone in and so ended up with a house full at all times but who yet somehow managed to scrape out enough soup for all. The kind of guy who convinced you to do things his way, and made it seem like it had been your idea all along.

I breathed a sigh of relief. With him beside us, I immediately felt more ready, more qualified, even as we left behind our parents and trainers. And as I watched the others, I knew they did too.

"Ailith warriors, welcome to the Citadel." My eyes moved to a wide chair in the middle row of the auditorium, where a man of seven decades lifted his right hand in a fist to quiet the chatter around him. Gradually, the entire hall grew silent as everyone copied his gesture.

Ronan turned to him in deference. "So, we are not to wait? For the others?"

"It has not been disclosed where they are, or when they will arrive, or if you are to go in search of them," said a gray-haired elder, a woman of perhaps six-and-five, at the man's side. "But we all recognize the Call, do we not? I imagine they do too, regardless of where they rest this night. It is our prayer that they are in other pockets of Community, receiving their own blessing until you all are united."

We all nodded. Every hair on my arms and legs, as well as my neck, seemed to be rising.

In that moment, the air felt energized, as if the Maker himself was present, flowing about us, around us, *through* us in spirit form. I glanced toward Vidar and he was grinning. He felt it too. The warmth. The presence. We all shared a moment of silence, looking at one another, Ronan and I last. This ... this was *the* moment, the time, the culmination of what we'd all awaited. It was stunning, really. On one hand, I felt unready, too young for that asked of us — we'd not yet celebrated our second decade, still three seasons of Hoarfrost and Harvest away. On the other, I knew we could not feel any more ready.

"Kneel, Ailith," the man said, taking a wooden box from the woman and slowly climbing down the steps. "Alternate Remnant and Knight before me. Kindly remove your coats and sweaters. Your arms must be bare."

We did as we were told, aided in removing our outer garments by elders who respectfully took the jackets and long-sleeved shirts and sweaters from us and set them aside. Clothes were of significant value, and I tensed until I saw that mine were but five paces away. I shivered in the chill, glad for the warmth of so many bodies. Even though we were in the season of Harvest, it was still chilly in this fortress carved from stone. Again, I glanced around. How had they managed to create this place, especially without anyone in the Valley finding out? How long had it taken? Decades? Centuries? There was a sense that those here had been born within the Citadel's walls. Maybe they had.

A table was brought forward, and I saw the older man carefully, reverently open the wooden box. "These bands were forged the night the Ailith were born." Behind him, a line of women stood waiting. The hair on the back of my neck stood up again as the air buzzed with excitement. *Joy*, I decided. *Promise. Hope.* Had I ever felt such a thing? In such purity?

The Maker, I thought. *This is what it is to be surrounded by the presence of the Maker.*

The elder pulled out the first item, and I gasped as he raised it upward as if dedicating it. For the bands were crafted with the design of an eternal knot, one wrapping into another — in silver and gold — each band an inch wide. Worth a thousand harvests. I'd never seen a hundredth of such precious metal, as it was the currency of the richest traders, often the only thing they'd take for a sack of meal, salt, grain. And there was little to go around — most of it in the warlords' hands, melted and placed in bricks for their coffers, or adorning the inner sanctums of their palaces.

The elder handed the object to the first woman behind him, then reached into the box. And pulled out another. I couldn't help it; I gasped again as he lifted it to the ceiling, muttering, as if in prayer, then handed it to the second woman and reached for another. With the combined wealth that appeared to be in that box, we could rule a kingdom.

As each woman received an armband, she came to kneel to the right of a Remnant or stand to the right of a Knight. When there was someone beside each of us, the old man spoke while slowly circling around, head bowed, arms folded behind his back. "You were chosen whilst still in your mothers' wombs, and trained from the day of your birth on. The tasks you face ahead are grave indeed. The future of our people, of the world itself, rests upon your shoulders."

I glanced up to watch him, his watery eyes narrowing, the loose flesh on his face folding around a frown. "But you go with the power of the Maker within you. These armbands are the symbol of his eternal connection with you and everyone in Community. Regardless of what you encounter — what terrors, what strife, what trauma — trust in that." He looked up to meet my eyes. "Trust in that."

He pulled to a stop between Bellona and Ronan. "My young friends, here it begins. Remember that you have the power of the Maker within you to do what you must. He shall not abandon you, no matter how dark the night."

"Remnants and Knights of the Last Order," Raniero said, standing in the center of our circle, "place your right hand on your comrade's shoulder. While each of you exhibits the beginnings of a unique, high gift, tonight, through tongues of fire, you become marked as one." I swallowed hard at his warning tone, as well as his words *tongues of fire.* I placed my hand on Ronan's shoulder, then felt Bellona place her hand on mine. Across the circle, I looked into Vidar's brown eyes. He was a Remnant, like me. What was his gift?

Vidar's eyes never wavered, and there was no trace of humor in his face now. "No matter what happens, sister, you keep your eyes on me," he whispered. "It will be good, what comes. I'm certain of it. There is only good here; hope, light, *promise.*"

I nodded once.

At our sides, each of the elders unclasped the armbands on a delicate hinge and held them open, like jaws ready to clamp down around our biceps. Four in all, for Bellona, Ronan, Vidar, and me.

"And now the power that was, that is, and is to come is invited here, among us," said the sage elder, nodding. He lifted his aged face to the concave stone ceiling. "Long have we waited for this day, Maker. We commit these Ailith kin to your care, to your call."

Every inch of my skin felt tingly, my hair raised and surges running through my body from head to toe. Vidar could feel it too; I saw it in his eyes. The Knights? I dared not look to the side. Vidar began to whisper the words with the elders, and I did the same, feeling the power of each one as we called upon the Maker.

"Maker, long have you been forgotten among our people. But now you shall be known again. Come and abide with the Ailith. Work through them for your purposes. Seal them with your power so that they might combat those of the dark. Preserve them, Maker. May it be as you promised. May it be so . . ." As the Community continued to repeat *may it be so*, I could see the flames rising around us, licking up toward the ceiling, interlinking across it, warming the auditorium until it actually felt hot. Filling us, heating us from within. Making us almost unbearably hot now. *Tongues of fire*

With each successive refrain, an elder clasped shut the armbands of those around me.

I felt Ronan shudder and gasp. As if time had slowed, I saw Vidar's mouth open, his eyes widen in pain. Felt Bellona's hand shudder just as I received mine.

I stared hard at Vidar, wanting to seize what I saw in his eyes and hold on to it. For in them was wonder. Overwhelming wonder. Glory.

Against searing pain.

Bright light seemed to flood the room, blinding me. And yet my heart surged simultaneously with such joy — such sheer, breathtaking happiness — that I could not think of the pain or of my blindness. It filled me to a place of overflowing, until I thought the feeling must be actually taking shape and oozing from my very pores. That I might be swelling with it all, a rising flood wave about to crest and spread out onto opposing shores.

And then, when I thought I couldn't possibly feel anything more, I felt . . . nothing.

CHAPTER
3

I came to a moment later, held firmly in Ronan's arms. I glanced down and knew the armband was more than just clasped shut around my arm in a perfect fit. It was seared into my skin. One with it. As if it had been made for me alone. And somehow, I knew that it had.

The elder kneeled before me, as if waiting for my eyes to focus on him, and then gave me a smile. "Good. Very good, Andriana. You will likely feel pain the most, for your gift is of empathy, which your trainer surely helped you discern. From here on out, you shall feel every emotion thrice as intensely as before — both good and bad. Even another's emotion shall become your own, whether it be sorrow or glory. Because of this, others will be drawn to you, because you connect with them in a way that is beyond most of us ..." He shook his head. "This will allow you great access but also put you in greater danger, because those who wish to rule this world will recognize the power within you."

I swallowed hard. So it was both really, really good and really, really bad. I knew it was an honor. The Maker had chosen me, and chosen this day to fully reveal it. But given that thousands upon thousands exhibiting the high gifts had been executed in the Trading Union since the Great War, hunted down by Sheolites originating in Pacifica, having my own high gift become more recognizable was … concerning.

The elder struggled to rise, and two women helped him complete his task. He turned to Vidar. "And you, son. What is it you felt in the moment of sealing?"

"Joy. Peace," Vidar said, mouth half open and working as if he sought the right descriptors but couldn't stop. "Love. Hope. L-light? Light. I *felt light* in and through me. Around us." He looked around, eyes wide, as if wishing he could recapture it.

"Indeed, yes," nodded the old man, chin in hand, eyes smiling. "For you have the gift of discernment. From here on out you shall have a clearer sense about those cloaked in darkness as well as those open to the light, even at a distance. Tend to your gifting and it will serve you and the other Ailith in time. For you all will need every edge you can gain against the Sheolites." His smile faded at the dreaded name. He whispered the last of it, as if uttering the word might evoke them from the very crust of the earth.

"So, uh, *my* trainer didn't really talk up the pros and cons of this gift thing," Vidar murmured out of the corner of his mouth to me. "Did yours?" I smiled.

"But do not rest in your gifting," said the elder, shaking his finger at him. Clearly he hadn't overheard Vidar. "For your gift shall make you all the clearer their enemy. It shall be you, first, they wish to destroy. For you shall warn your brothers and sisters in every battle."

"Boo-yah," Vidar said with a satisfied nod, folding his arms before his chest and lifting his chin. "Let 'em come."

The elder shook his head and shared a long look with Niero, then back again. "There is no place for bravado among your ranks, young Vidar. Courage, yes. But do not get ahead of the Maker."

Vidar's face settled into a very serious expression. His arms fell to his side, and he nodded, lips pressed together.

"Now, rise, Remnant and Knight, and circle 'round with Raniero."

Vidar, Ronan, Bellona, and I stood up, and dutifully wrapped our arms around the others. The elders from above us came and placed their hands on our shoulders, and others beyond them on their shoulders, until the entire floor was filled with those of the Community, each laying a hand on us or those closest to them.

I smiled as joy again pervaded my heart, surrounded me. So pure. So right. A glimpse of the afterworld itself. At least the afterworld as I hoped it would be, as the elders depicted it.

At our center was an old woman. She lifted the remaining bands from the chest and turned in a circle, looking each of us in the eye. "Your first task is to find the other Remnants and their knights. A healer, a seer, and one of uncommon wisdom should be among them. Together, you will find increased strength and protection. There are two others — each with miraculous powers " Her delicate, gray brows lowered and she shook her head. "It is unclear to me whether they still live or have been hunted down."

We stared at her. Was she a seer too? And was it possible? That some of the Remnants were already dead, before we'd even begun?

She handed the precious bands to Raniero and he tied the bulging satchel to his wide belt, as if she had said nothing out of the ordinary. As if he did not now carry the wealth of a nation.

"Where do we find them?" Niero asked.

"Along the path toward your ultimate goal, in freeing Kapriel," she said. I puzzled over the name, even as my heart-beat picked up over this mention of our task. "The Maker shall reveal them to you in time."

Raniero bowed his head a moment, chin in hand. "Seek within," he said to us. "Ask the Maker where we are to go in order to find your fellow Ailith as well as free our prince."

"Our ... our prince?" I sputtered. It was a moment before I realized I'd done so aloud.

Raniero looked up at me, and a slow smile spread across his face. "Yes. Pacifica seeks to subjugate us all. Our prince will unite those who can fight against it. But that is but one portion of our mission. First and foremost, we go where the Maker leads, and do as he asks of us."

I blinked, slowly, but an overwhelming sense of truth settled around me. This was part of our call? To be Kapriel's rescuers as well as his guard? "But who imprisoned him? Where is he?"

"That is unclear; rest in what you know and allow the remaining to be revealed in time." The elder shook his head grimly and raised a finger. "But do not try and free him until you have gathered the other Remnants."

"We must be at our strongest," Raniero said, nodding, understanding what the elder had left unspoken. "Together in body and spirit. So now let us be about our first task — finding the other Ailith by asking the Maker to reveal to us our first steps."

We did as we were told, as our trainer had taught us:

closing our eyes, calming ourselves, centering on the Maker. The room became silent as the Community joined with us.

But I didn't like what practically shouted to me in response.

I sucked in my breath and blinked rapidly. Zanzibar? *Impossible.* I furtively looked around, hoping I hadn't really heard anything, as the word alone struck fear in my heart and mind at the same time.

Niero looked right at me. "Tell us what you heard, Andriana," he said gently.

"Zan-Zanzibar," I said, clearing my throat, wondering if they'd all think me crazy. "She's in Zanzibar." *She.* I didn't know where that came from either. "Our healer."

But Vidar, Bellona, and Ronan were all nodding at me, in solid, grim assent. As if they'd heard the same thing. It scared me, this strange, spooky commonality, this intrinsic understanding. Almost as much as the thought of going to Zanzibar. All our growing-up years, we'd only heard stories that made it seem like the last place we wanted to go. Ever.

"There is no place for fear, Ailith," Niero said, easily reading it in our faces. "Guard against it. The presence of fear denies the power of the Maker and invites the enemy to use it for his own purposes. And where the Maker sends us, we are to go in complete trust. We have been called." He put out his hand, using the leading phrase our trainer had always used.

We all placed our hands atop his. "And we shall answer," we said as one.

"So, they couldn't have tossed us an easy one first, could they?" Vidar said, hiking up the straps of his old military backpack, speaking just loud enough for Niero to hear. But our leader ignored him, trudging forward as we had throughout the night. The sun was just beginning to rise, casting the mountains around us in a rosy glow through the mist. "Couldn't it have been just some Mudhorse Weed," Vidar went on, "close to the bank? You know, since this is our first time and all outside of the Valley. But no. We get to go and retrieve *our* healer from among the sickest kingdoms in trader territory. *Zanzibar.*" He let out a long, slow whistle.

"I suppose if we wanted easy, we should've ditched the call," I said, readjusting my own pack as I walked alongside Vidar, all the while studying Niero's back, just beyond Bellona ahead of us. Ronan brought up the rear guard, and I could feel him listening in. "But that would've about torn me apart anyway, ignoring it. How about you?"

"Yeah, yeah," he said, tucking his thumbs to relieve the pressure of his shoulder straps. All five of us carried many supplies — items that would gain us acceptance among the traders. For if we gained acceptance with them, we'd likely gain access to any village, outpost, or kingdom in the Union. If they helped us secure safe-passage papers, that was.

"Are you wondering what's inside these packs, like I am?" Vidar whispered over his shoulder. "I mean, it must be good."

I shook my head, staring at the path before me. "I'm trying not to think about it. Otherwise, I might be tempted to run away with it."

"You and me both, sister."

I wasn't joking. My mind ran rampant with possibilities and settled on canned corn, something I'd only had once. Sweet, delicious yellow kernels, popping in my mouth, juicy with a taste I've never had since. *The path* ... I reminded myself, staring at the trail that led us lower and lower. Soon we'd reach the mouth of the Valley, the only home I'd ever known, and see the desert sprawling before us, no mountains in sight for miles. How did one know where they were without mountains in sight?

I dropped back a few steps until I was next to Ronan. I sensed no fear in him, only excitement. I'd long felt in tune with him, but now I *really* felt his emotions, as if they were my own. He'd always wanted to see what was beyond the Valley. He was finally getting his chance, and he was fairly bursting with energy.

"Hey," he said, looking down at me with a small smile. "Need me to carry your pack a while?"

"I'm all right," I said, shifting the straps again. Truth was, the flesh around my armband burned more than the flesh beneath the pack's weight. The elders had rubbed a healing ointment on our skin, and then coated the band itself with a mixture of dirt and oil, making the precious metals look cheap, like tin, in the end. They knew there were many ahead that would gladly cut our arms off for the metal alone. We'd welcomed the thick grime, as well as our long-sleeved shirts and sweaters. I partially resented the band and how it might endanger us, and I partially loved it, feeling like a crowned royal with something so extraordinary upon my person. My mom had had a gold locket, once. She traded it for food one harsh, desperate Hoarfrost when I was little. No one I knew had owned anything so precious since.

They'd given me films for my eyes, delicate material that turned my blue-green irises brown. I hated them, feeling like I wanted to scratch my eyes out one minute, wiping away agitated tears the next. But there were many places ahead that viewed women as a commodity, and since brown eyes were the norm, any other colors were apparently prized. "The last thing you want is to end up in the harem of Zanzibar's warlord," said an elder, handing me the colored films again when I tried to hand them back.

I shuddered when she said it. I'd heard the stories, knew the truth behind them. Three families had disappeared from the Valley when they'd gone on a journey to trade and wandered too near the walled city. Simply disappeared. Children my age, those I used to play with. Mothers and fathers. One grandfather. Gone. The story went they were taken for the women, the others likely killed. Which was apparently why Ronan didn't have to disguise his true eye color. The men of Zanzibar treated their women as property — something to be obtained, traded, kept.

I had no idea where the elders had found the films. But it made my mind go wild with possibility about the packs on our backs again. If the Community's reach allowed them such lenses, what else might be traveling with us? Ancient survival instincts kicked in, making me want to break and run, keep my precious stores for myself. If Mom and Dad had had such gifts, how much different might our lives had been these last years? *Perhaps I could sell my films too.* I smiled at the thought.

"They don't suit you," Ronan said, seeing me wipe my watering eyes again. "I'll miss your true color while it's hidden away. But you'll get used to them soon enough."

"Easy for you to say," I said resentfully, ducking my head so he didn't see me smile over his partial compliment.

"And if they keep you safe — "

"I know, Ronan, I know."

"You'll stay close to me, right? With what's ahead..."

"Right by you," I promised.

He smiled down at me, his expression like a gentle hug, and I gave him a small smile in return.

As we walked, we found out that Vidar and Bellona had narrowly escaped two other Sheolite scouts at the Hour of our Call.

"How'd they know, boss?" Vidar tossed out in Raniero's direction. "How'd they know to be here, in the Valley, at that time?"

Niero turned and walked backward, his dark eyes flicking from one to the other of us. "The Sheolites have never been far from our valley's door. They routinely sent scouts, seeking you out, and I, aided by your trainers, routinely denied them. But last night, when you were revealed, when they could fully sense you as Ailith, we could not be everywhere at once." A small smile tugged at the corner of his full lips. "Rest assured, we were busy taking care of many others." With that, he turned and continued walking, and I stared at the twin, crescent-shaped blades on his back, imagining them at work cutting down our enemy. Was it thanks to Niero that we all reached the Citadel at all? How long had he been our silent guardian?

"Wait," I said, hurrying forward, past Vidar. Niero glanced over his shoulder at me, then turned forward again, never pausing. "So you ... You knew our trainer? Is he well?"

"I know not. His mission is completed. He was to relocate immediately, as were your parents."

I swallowed hard, disappointed that he couldn't reassure me. And at mention of my parents, I frowned. If there had been so many Sheolites in the Valley last night

I slowed, and Vidar nudged me with a playful smile. "Chin

up, sis. We have deserts to cross. Enemies to slay. Horrific cities to explore. Impossible missions to accomplish."

"You're the one who is impossible," Bellona grumbled, frowning from me to him. I felt her motherly concern and knew I must look scared, stressed. "Can you please shut up?"

"Ahh, you'd miss the sound of my voice, Bellie, if I did," Vidar said cheerfully.

"Don't call me that," she growled.

And Vidar tossed me a wry grin. Clearly, he knew just how to agitate her.

We eventually reached the mouth of the Valley at noon and stopped to eat. Dried meat, along with Mudhorse Weed — long, slimy grasses we competed with the beasts for, but we ate ours only after it'd been dried by the fires and salted. The horses gladly waded in, chewing the wet cud like the moose of old. The meal ended with a single slice of dried orange from some distant land. I'd not had one for years and took tiny bites of it, letting it reconstitute and melt across my tongue.

"Pine needle tea," Niero said, offering me a cup. "Keeps us well. Guards against the Cancer, as well as the Scurves."

I accepted the tea, but what I wanted was another slice of orange from the few he had left in his hand. And secretly, I hoped that as an Ailith we'd be granted additional shares in the days to come. *Maybe this Call won't be all bad*, I thought, sitting back and popping the last of my slice into my mouth. *Though who am I fooling?* I thought, daring to look Ronan's way. There wasn't anywhere else I could possibly be. The thought of him leaving, going without me somewhere ... Well, it was pretty much impossible to imagine.

And yet for all our years of training, this was the longest period of time we'd spent together. We'd had nights in which we trained. Afternoons. Mornings. But not all through a night and into a day. And it felt good, so good, to be with him that long. To know we didn't have to separate soon. As if we were escaping, getting away with something. Even if we were heading into the lion's den.

"What's a lion's den?" I said to Ronan, the words running back through my mind. It was a phrase I'd heard my dad say forever, and I knew it meant danger. But I didn't understand the image itself. "A place the lions rested back in the olden days?"

Ronan shrugged.

"Yes. Often a cave," Niero said, from ahead of us.

I nodded, a little embarrassed by my naïve question. At least I knew what a lion was, having read about them as a child, as they'd long since vanished from the earth. But Niero was kind in his response; no judgment in his tone or words. For all the education afforded me as an Ailith — from birth onward by my mom and dad, intent on the task — it had been mostly reading and writing and arithmetic. Critical thinking. Pre-Great War history, seven generations past, from a basic children's book yellow with age and long parted from its binding. From that time forward they'd taught me oral history, as best they knew. There'd been precious few sources on the wildlife that once roamed our earth before the bombs fell and destroyed so many or eventually choked them with poison. Fewer resources still on geography, none of which my parents could ever lay hands on, forcing them to teach me from what they could remember.

New-ancient books made their way to our home every week, spines long gone, as well as many of their pages. A few encyclopedias — the *F*, *I*, and *N* volumes, the only ones we had. Nonfiction books on politics and society, biographies of people — scientists and politicians and leaders and philosophers, good and bad. But my favorites were novels; the only downfall was that so many were ragged with age. It was more aggravating to turn the last page and yet find the story was incomplete, the ending long since torn away and lost. Still, I could not keep from reading about proper young ladies in a land called England, girls among the sun-dried, swaying grasses of a place named Africa, or men in uniform fighting on great sailing vessels across massive waterways called seas. Anything I could read, I read. And when the stories ended prematurely, I did as my parents did with me as a child — I finished the end how I saw fit, in my imagination.

I smiled, remembering my treasured books as we moved out again and began walking behind Niero in pairs, then single file. On and on we walked. And by midafternoon we left the trees of our youth behind us and were surrounded by a vast land filled with short, clumpy grass and sand thick with the drizzle falling from the sky. The sand stuck to our boots and slowed our progress. But it didn't matter to me, because I was amazed and in no rush. Never in all my life had I seen such wide, flat land, spreading out in so many directions. Over and over again, I turned in a full circle, trying to comprehend such sprawling *openness* when I had always been surrounded by the inclines of the Valley.

Niero bent and brushed back some grass, took ten paces, and bent again. He'd picked up a trail, which led us to the deep ruts of a road moving south.

We'd found our road to the trader camp.

They saw us coming, even when we were tiny dots on the horizon.

Niero looked through a long tube he called a "looking glass," and when he saw my expression he handed it to me.

"Close your other eye, so you can see better," he said, standing close enough to wrap his arms around me from behind and twist two dials at the center, bringing it more into focus. "Let me know when you can see it."

"There," I breathed, as two circles became one, clear view. I was aware that Ronan hovered at my other shoulder, and I felt a wave of strange emotion from him, but I was distracted by seeing what I could through Niero's collapsible tube, dropping it from my eye to view what I could normally then comparing it to the looking glass's perspective again. "That's amazing," I said, handing it back to him. The trader guards appeared a hundred times closer when peering at them through the odd tube.

He quickly folded it back together and shoved it into his pocket. "Follow my lead," he said over his shoulder. The mud-horses and guards gradually drew closer, guns casually slung across their arms as they came up beside us, passed by, and circled around, constantly moving even as we instinctively gathered in a group, backs together as we'd been taught. If attacked, we would face our enemy to our front and protect our brother or sister's back. But Raniero had not drawn the crescent-shaped swords strapped across his back. So neither did we.

"You got papers?" said one camp guard on horseback, edging past me, so close I felt the horse's flank brush past my shoulder.

"I have what I need to see your boss," Niero said, staring

dead ahead, not turning to watch the man. He carefully pulled out a map and opened it. "You are of the Nem Post, aren't you?"

"Who's asking?"

"Raniero of the Valley."

"So, Raniero of the Valley," the man said, his eyes flicking over to me, Ronan, Vidar, and Bellona. "What is your business?" His eyes stayed on Bellona, and he kicked his horse in the flanks, edging nearer to her, looking her up and down, then flicking over to me. "You trading women? My boss isn't interested but I know—"

"They are not for sale today," Niero said idly, as if we might be tomorrow. "They have not yet completed their second decade."

"Now age has never been an obstacle for us before." He leered at me.

"We have other goods. Take me to your boss. I will discuss it with him."

"You ought to rethink it," said the man, now admiring Bellona. "Fine, sturdy stock as these ..."

I felt the gathering rage within Bellona. If she broke, attacked them, we'd be done before we started.

The trader looked over his shoulder at Niero. The man was weak within. Playing a role, not exploiting true power. I felt his hesitation, barely concealed. "Don't care what you got in those packs. Girls like these would be worth a year's pay in—"

I broke our circle and faced him, edging in front of Bellona before she gave in to her fury. "We are not for sale, and you feign authority where you have little," I said steadily. "Now do as my boss has asked and take us to *yours. Now.*" It pained me to use his weakness; I felt his inner wince and flush of humiliation. But I knew it was the only way to stave off the confrontation almost upon us.

Surprise registered in his eyes. He was well past his fourth decade — or perhaps only appeared that way. And my words seemed to slice into him. His brown eyes widened and he lifted his hands. He forced out a thin laugh. "I take it back," he said, staring at me, and I felt his hatred then, his fury and humiliation. "Woman-flesh is only valuable to those who buy if said woman-flesh knows her place."

I felt Bellona move behind me and glimpsed Vidar casually reaching out to grasp her arm.

"Ha," croaked the man, catching Vidar's movement too. "There you go, man. Show yer woman her place." He turned his back on them, resting in his companions' ability to guard him. Displaying power to try and show me I was wrong. Trying to retrieve some of his pride. We let him complete his drama, even though every one of us would have paid a whole gold coin to see him in a ring with Bellona.

"C'mon, then. You better be worth letting into camp, or the boss won't feed us tonight."

We continued our trek forward, the three men on either side of us casually riding their mudhorses as our legs grew rubbery with weariness. We'd walked through the night and most of the day, the longest I'd ever walked in my life, even after years of training.

"Let me have it now," Ronan said, pulling the pack from my shoulders before I could complain. Bellona didn't ask to carry Vidar's, and I felt a little guilty about it for a time. But mostly I felt relief as the ache spread from my neck down to the center of my back.

"So that one's yours?" said the nearest trader, edging near Ronan while looking over at me.

"Yes, she's his," Niero barked. "Now leave her be."

I bit my lip as my face flamed with embarrassment, not daring to look at him or my knight. So this was what we'd be forced to? Cowering behind our men? *That won't sit well with Bellona*, I thought, catching her clenching her fists and sharing a look with Vidar.

But then we were entering the post, a gathering of tents shielding the traders from the constant rain and wind. I knew from my education they could survive under tarps instead of behind stone because traders had what every warlord and villager wanted: goods. The guns upon every shoulder and in every holster — plus the backing of kingdoms who wanted them in place — kept the marauding Drifters away. To take on traders was to take on at least one kingdom that backed them. Which didn't keep them entirely safe, but most of the time …

A couple of the guards carried rusty old rocket launchers, hoisted on their shoulders. At least I thought they were rocket launchers. I'd only seen them in our trainer's drawings. My gaze shifted to the horizon. What were they prepared to defend themselves against?

People came out as we passed, following our every step with weary, steady eyes. Men, mostly. When we reached the largest tent at the center — twice as high and five times as long as the rest — we paused. "You can leave your weapons here," he said, gesturing to a wooden barrel and a guard standing outside the tent entrance, apparently on duty. "My compatriot will make sure they don't walk off while you're with Tonna."

We did as he asked, gradually filling the barrel with our assorted weapons: Niero's crescent blades, Vidar's halberd — along with two pistols I didn't know he carried in his belt — Bellona's bow and quiver of arrows, and an assortment of swords from the rest of us. I knew that each of us kept hidden daggers upon our person, unwilling to go in completely unarmed. We waited for several more minutes on our escort, whom we could hear murmuring inside.

Finally, the guard reemerged, and behind him, his boss.

I looked to the right, so she wouldn't recognize my surprise and read it as disrespect. She was short as she was wide, with dark skin and slitted eyes, and she walked right to Niero, not looking at the rest of us. She recognized him as leader. "Name's Tonna," she said, offering her arm.

"Raniero of the Valley. Niero, to my friends."

"They grow 'em tall in the Valley," she grunted, looking up at him and then each of us. "But there's not much up there other than people, right?"

"Just the right number, as far as we're concerned, Harvest to Harvest. We've been gleaning. Found a stash in a forgotten village we'd like to trade," Niero returned. "Care to see?"

"Sure, sure," she said. "Bring it in." She turned and we followed her through the flaps of the tent. I took in what was inside. To one side was a curtain — her own private area, I decided — and I could just glimpse a cot and blankets. An oil lamp. Books. A bundle of incense beside a tray with a small portion slowly burning, sending a tendril of sweet smoke into the air. Beneath the table was a wide, shining, copper tub. My eyes lingered on the tub, suddenly aware of the layer of the grime on my skin, as well as my own stink.

Before us on four tables were a stack of blankets that reached shoulder high, sacks of what I guessed were rice and oats, as well as baskets of dried pears, bags of dried apples, and lye soap. She made a dismissive gesture and her men set to work, placing the goods to the side, making room for our packs.

"Not many venture from the Valley to trade," she said, folding her fat arms across her ample chest.

"Not much to trade," Niero said evenly.

"There was a family that came by last year," she said, lifting her chin, appraising him. "They had some decent items. Perhaps there is more up there than you say."

"That family never made it back," Niero said. And it was then that I knew they both spoke of the clan that left my village. "For most of our people, it's safer to remain at home."

Tonna appraised the group of us, then shrugged and waved to the table. "Let's see what you have."

Niero went first, unpacking in a steady, assured manner. Twelve cans of sardines, the labels torn and faded. Six boxes of thread. Twenty skeins of wool. And a contraption with all the letters of the alphabet on small black keys.

She grunted, running her fingers over them. Pressing one. A small metal arm sprang upward and slammed against the roller. "Well, I'll be. You have any ink in those packs, Niero? Or paper?"

"Sadly, no," Niero said.

"Pity. But a typewriter's a novelty, sure enough. The warlords would love it."

"I thought so."

She gestured for my pack, and I unloaded it. I felt her eyes on me, studying me. She was wary of me, for all her casual, in-charge manner, and I worked to do nothing to make her warier, moving methodically. Inside my pack were more skeins of wool, twelve cans of soup, and ten more of something called tuna fish. My mouth watered and I wished we'd sat down and

45

had at least one feast before carrying on. Surely these traders wouldn't have missed a few cans from each of our packs.

"Tuna. Haven't seen this in ages," she said, picking up one. She glanced over to Niero. "Where were you gleaning? This is quite the haul."

He gave her a slow, knowing smile. "Well, if I told you that, I'd lose a bit of my trading power, wouldn't I?"

She smiled back, her small eyes practically disappearing. I thought her to be about five decades. And she liked Niero. That was good. That was really, really good.

The rest did as I had before them. In the end, two whole tables were full of our goods. Soft cloth, perfect for diapers. A pack of bone needles, tiny and sharp. Two women's dresses that looked a hundred years old yet finer than anything I'd ever worn in my life. Five sweaters, meticulously woven. Cans and more cans of food — so enticing I didn't dare to read their labels, fearing I'd discover corn and try and steal one. A radio; another enticement for the warlords, even though any radio towers had long been dismantled or destroyed or abandoned. Three shiny silver discs that Niero called "CDs." Neither he nor Tonna had the device to play them, but they were pretty, casting iridescent rainbows under the candlelight.

Tonna's eyes surveyed the bounty and flicked back to him. "What is it you seek for your goods, Niero?"

"We seek safe-passage papers. From kingdom to kingdom. In turn, we shall return to you every time we draw near, bringing you more goods."

She stared at him, puzzled. "What business would you of the Valley have in the kingdoms? Your people have avoided the warlords since you retreated to your godforsaken mountains and trees and rain." She looked up and around at us again.

"That other clan came through here and never returned. You all appear in good health, a feat in itself these days. Is it best not to simply remain in your Valley and come and trade with me on occasion?"

Raniero said nothing for a moment. Then, "We have our reasons for seeking entry."

Slowly, she crossed her fat arms and peered up at him with squinty eyes. "The warlords grant us passage through their gates for one reason only: to trade. Should you or yours" — she paused to glance over the rest of us — "decide to pursue *other* activities, they'll come after me." She pointed a thumb to her chest. "You'll tell me where you're going and what you're after, or we're done here."

"We're heading to Zanzibar," he said without hesitation.

"Zanzibar. After …" Tonna's eyes moved to Bellona and me again. "Best leave them here with us while you go. That city is no place for a woman, whether or not she's reached her second decade." She huffed a laugh. "Even I barely get in and out unmolested."

"We're going after a girl in there. She's probably in hiding. And we go together."

Tonna cocked her head and cast a shrewd eye upon him. "Only a few places to hide in Zanzibar, as a woman. Places a gentleman wouldn't go. Or maybe I've misjudged you," she said, a slow smile curling up her round cheeks. She was missing two teeth on the bottom; the rest were yellow.

Niero paused. "We shall find who we seek and depart."

Tonna considered him, then cast calculating, greedy eyes over the goods. She sighed and threw her hands upward. "It is not for me to protect you from your own idiocy. I can grant you safe passage in. But you'll likely not get out. Not once they see these girls — or the one you seek. You will burn my passage papers upon entry, and when you get back to me, *if* you get back to me, I shall give you new ones. Do you understand?"

She waited until Niero nodded, then turned away and looked to her man at the door. "See them fed and give them bedding for the night. In the morning they leave." She disappeared behind her privacy curtain without further word.

Apparently, we'd been dismissed.

CHAPTER
4

I awakened in the middle of the night, my flesh cold even with several blankets over me and the heat of the others in the tent.

Rage. It radiated from my chest, over my shoulders, and down to my fingertips, making them tremble. I blinked, clutching the blankets to my chest, trying to understand where it was coming from. Why I was feeling it in another. I sat up and saw that Vidar was rising too. But it wasn't coming from him . . .

Raniero.

I saw him by the door of our tent, peering outward. Swiftly, I slid from beneath the blankets and padded over to him, hugging my arms to me, feeling the chill in my arm cuff and putting it together with Vidar's troubled expression.

"What is it, Niero?"

"A Sheolite tracker is terribly close," he whispered. "An old enemy of mine. One of their elite. Do you sense him?" He stepped aside and turned to awaken the others. But the rest were already rising, apparently awakened by the growing chill in their armbands as we had been.

"Who is it?" Vidar whispered, rubbing the cuff on his arm as if it pained him as mine did me, trying to see.

"I don't know," I whispered back. "I don't see anything." There was nothing but darkness, the camp still. Had Niero seen this tracker? And if not, how had he known him? He did not have an armband as we did.

Agitated, Vidar left to pace, muttering to himself.

Ronan slid up behind me, staring out the slit over my head. We both held our breath as a powerful-looking man in a long, hooded red cape rounded a corner twenty paces away. He was far taller than the scouts we'd encountered. I felt the burst of alarm in Ronan as he took hold of my shoulders with gentle hands. "Get to your sword, Dri," he whispered, the hint of a tremble in his voice. "This is no ordinary scout."

I felt foolish, needing him to tell me. Again … after Niero's warning. But even as I heard Vidar quietly sliding his pistol from his waistband to my right, I found the Sheolite too intriguing to look away from yet, even as he continued to approach. If he was our enemy, shouldn't we know more of him? The man walked to the tent directly across from ours, reached for the flap, then paused, turned, and stood straight with shoulders squared, looking over at our tent and then around. Slowly, he pulled his hood back, as if straining to hear better.

I stilled, knowing he was far more visible than I. He was about Ronan's height, with brown hair pulled into a long braid, like the scouts we'd taken down the night before. I reached out, trying to sense him, but only felt a frigid sensation, like placing a hand on metal in Hoarfrost. I instinctively retreated, concentrating on the light, the warmth of Community, Ronan, standing again behind me. The stranger frowned in puzzlement and gradually turned away. When he faced the torchlight in full, I saw what I thought were amber eyes, and the effect was jarring for some reason. A shiver of fear ran down my spine, and at the same time his head jerked back to stare directly at the slit of our tent's flap.

He went on staring, almost directly at me, and I heard the soft inhale of Ronan's breath, felt his alarm. But we stayed stock-still, not daring to move. Fearing he'd see. The other four in our group mirrored our alert, total stillness, and the combined alarm in the tent made me want to scream. I had to do something

Bewildered by my own daring, I reached out again, trying to move past the cold wall that separated me from the Sheolite. Over the last day and a half, I'd become accustomed to easily reading my companions, as well as the guards of Nem Post and Tonna herself. Why was this one so different? He was as difficult as Niero, and the murderous rage I felt within our leader tonight had been the first I'd been able to read him. Maybe I was breaking through some barrier. I narrowed my eyes and concentrated. There. *There* ...

It startled me, the utter void within the tracker. I concentrated harder. Was he too distant? Did I have to be close enough to touch him? Or did he truly feel no emotion at the moment? Even those utterly at peace *felt* peaceful to me.

The man stiffened, and looked left, then right, then to our tent again. Someone called him from inside, but still he paused.

A hand clamped down on my arm and pulled me roughly away. I narrowly kept myself from crying out. But it was Niero, facing me, frowning down at me with his back to the tent entrance. "What are you doing?" he whispered harshly.

Despite his anger, I also felt a wave of protection from him, as if he were shielding me.

"Me? I, umm … *Nothing*," I said, deciding on anger as defense.

"That," Niero said, lifting a thumb over his shoulder, in the direction of the other tent, "is an *enemy*. Do not experiment with your gifting on them," he said. "You endanger us all."

I felt the heat rise up my neck to my face. Endanger the rest? That hadn't been my plan. Only to —

"*Andriana*," he said, shaking me a little. "There's no excuse."

"I-I'm sorry," I whispered. "I didn't mean … I only wanted to … Oh, whatever!" I shook my head in agitation. Truthfully, I didn't know at all what was going on. Other than a massive headache crawling inward from my temples.

Ronan grimaced at the two of us — clearly dismayed by all our movement and whispers — then slowly returned to watching our enemy, his movements like liquid, as our trainer had taught us to move, in order to avoid detection. A second later he whispered over his shoulder, "He's inside."

Just as he was turning away, our own tent flap opened. I gasped, and Niero turned to block me. Ronan fell into a stance I knew well — it was designed to protect me from the new arrival. Bellona did the same with Vidar.

But it was merely the Nem scout we'd first encountered in the desert, the one atop the mudhorse. He stared in surprise at Ronan, then the others. "Time to go," he whispered loudly, his grin ghoulish in the near-dark. "Tonna says these new arrivals are looking for you. Bluffed her way through and set them up right across the way."

"Who is he?" Vidar asked, stepping past Bellona.

"Didn't say. But I haven't seen a tracker cape like that, other than over near the borderlands. Castle Vega. Usually they just send their scouts." He perused us all with renewed interest. "What'd you Valley-folk do to garner such interest?"

"It's none of your business," Raniero said, turning to strap his bedroll to his pack. Was he avoiding me on purpose? Blocking me? The rage was gone. In its place was ... nothing. It still surprised me that someone could do that, when most everyone else I met seemed to be an open emotion-book. What didn't he want me to know?

The scout hooked his thumbs into the waistband of his breeches. "Exactly what I was thinkin'. It bein' none of my business and all. But I tend to remember things if I don't have a gold coin to distract me "

Niero whirled and strode over to the man. The guard's face went white. With only inches between their faces, Niero fished out a coin from his pocket and handed it to the man. "You will forget we were here."

The man, looking chastened, hurriedly nodded and nervously grabbed the coin.

"Tonna couldn't have found another tent?" Vidar said, tying up his bedroll.

The man tried to smile, feigning ease, but I could feel his fear as clearly as if I could hear his racing heartbeat. "Only two guest tents at Nem Post."

"Pack up," Niero whispered toward me, seeing I wasn't moving. "Quickly."

"Shouldn't we wait? Until they're asleep?" Bellona asked.

"No, he's right," Vidar said, and I felt the nauseating foreboding that ran through him. It made me regret searching his emotions as I swallowed bile. "The safest thing is to be away. Fast."

We did as he asked, and were on our way out before sixty

seconds had passed, stepping as lightly as possible. Raniero stood between us and the tent flap of our enemies, arms wide, gesturing us past, and again I felt an overwhelming sense of protection. When I looked back at Ronan to make sure he was behind me, my pack brushed against our canvas tent, making a loud, scraping sound. At least it sounded loud in the relative quiet. I cringed, paused, wondering if we were betrayed, but Ronan grabbed my arm and pulled me forward. We gathered at the stables a hundred paces away, where five mudhorses awaited us. Two finer horses, with a red blanket across their backs, were tied in the corner. "Tonna expects these mudhorse mares back, with more promised goods," the man said, looking up at Niero as he placed his hands on the horse's reins.

"She'll get them."

We rode out, eyeing the horses tied outside the corral. They were far taller than any mudhorse we'd seen, and I noticed their red blankets were edged with black tassels at their flanks. I wished we were on Ronan's dirtbike, which could easily outrun any horse. But the Community had only had two, and there was no guarantee about fuel along the way. At least we weren't on foot. Unlike those near home, the trails to and from the Nem Post were worn deep from countless mudhorses before us, and thus harder for enemies to track.

We rode through the dark watches of the night and only began to breathe a little easier as the sun rose to our east and there still was no sign of pursuit. The sun steadily made its climb through the mist and up into the clouds. On occasion, it broke through in lovely rays. That was what distinguished Harvest from Hoarfrost: broken sunshine. Come Hoartime, all we saw was gray from morning until night, and trees encased in white. As the clouds parted and rays of light once again streamed across the green desert before me, I smiled, taking my first deep breath in what seemed like hours, and lifted my face to enjoy the slightest warmth upon my skin. All the while the mudhorse walked on, my body swaying from one side to the other in its rhythm.

"Hold," Niero said, lifting his left hand in a fist. He slipped off his horse before it came to a complete stop and pulled out his looking glass. As he slid out the long tube and stared back in the direction of Nem Post, we pulled our horses to a stop and slid off too, stretching. My thighs and butt hurt from the hours astride her back.

"Anything?" Bellona asked him after several long moments.

"No," Niero said, frowning, staring backward even after he'd taken the glass from his eye.

"You look upset they're not after us," Vidar said with a laugh.

"Not upset. Confused." Niero put his hands on his hips and looked to the rays of the sun over his shoulder, then over to us. "Either the Maker has granted us protection or that Sheolite tracker has lost his edge."

"I'd take both," Vidar said, smiling.

"Don't assume either," Niero said. He turned to the land ahead of us and peered through his looking glass again.

"You said you knew that Sheolite," I ventured. "That he was an old enemy. From where?"

"It's a long story," he said, in a manner that made it clear he didn't want to tell it.

I bit my lip, refusing to give in to the curiosity that burned within me. When the time was right, he'd probably tell us. I studied his broad shoulders and narrow waist, trying to put all the broken pieces of knowledge I had about Niero together in my head.

"Do you see Zanzibar?" Ronan asked, breaking the silence.

"Yes," he said. He slid the tube's cascading pieces back together, compacting it, and glanced up at Bellona and me. "Bellona, pull your braid up, under your hat. Wear the brim low. Andriana, how far forward can you pull the hood of your coat?"

I pulled up the hood on my oilskin coat, reluctantly drawing my head inward from the sun and confining my face to shadow.

"Good," Niero grunted. "Keep it that way. The guards in Zanzibar's towers will likely have far more powerful looking glasses than this one. And the last thing we need them to know is that we travel with women. They'll likely discover it once we're there — let's not give them time to formulate a plan."

We mounted and moved out again, figuring we'd reach the desert city by nightfall. If we didn't, they'd lock the gates and we'd have to camp until morning. My breathing became tight at the thought. Did I prefer to risk the bands of marauding Drifters or the men of Zanzibar who traded in women?

Niero pulled back and rode beside me and Ronan, as if he sensed my unease. As much as I begged my parents to tell me of the city, after our neighbors went missing, they'd refused to share any more detail. *There is time enough for you to learn of the evil about us, Andriana.*

I plunged through my hesitation. "Niero, why is it that Zanzibar has so few women? Why must they trade to get more?"

He didn't look my way. "They knew they were in trouble after a few generations. But still, even after these long years, they choose not to resolve it." He spoke as if I already knew their past. "Such is the obstinacy of men."

"Is it because they are cruel to the women? Do they beat them until they run away?"

He turned his keen eyes on me, and his lips parted in soft understanding. "You were never told?"

I shook my head. "They did not wish to … did not wish me to …"

"Your parents were protecting you in another way," he said softly, reverently.

I nodded.

He sighed and took a deep breath. "The time of protection is over. As an Ailith, you are a woman grown before your time, already past your second decade as the Maker sees it." He looked up ahead to the horizon, where I could barely see the walls of a city, tiny in the distance. Like a solitary, rectangular mountain.

"Zanzibar was established toward the end of the War, her people thinking that in fleeing other, larger cities for her smaller confines, all would be spared. To a certain extent, they were right. When the bombs came, she was ignored. But given that she was a walled city with limited space, and given the relative health of her people, her leaders instituted a strict birth policy. One child per family."

"But the Cancer reached them, as it did everyone, right?" Ronan said, from my other side.

Niero nodded. "And as with everywhere else, in that first wave more men died than women. Male children became more prized than females, and the girls were routinely drowned or left to the elements." He said this with no trace of emotion in his tone, but his face looked pained.

"In three generations, they ran two males to each female, but they chose to continue their policy, only allowing their population to grow to sustainable levels by trade. And part of the trade became women."

Ronan snorted in disgust. "Because they still favored the male babies?"

"Yes," Niero said. "The Cancer continues to plague Zanzibar. And now, in this city, it takes more women than men, making women more valuable than ever."

"How many?" Ronan said. "How many of her men have passed their second decade and are still without mates?"

Niero paused for a telling breath. "That is unclear. But some estimate it at many as three-quarters. And they have ceased to care whether a girl has yet passed her second decade. Many are far younger. They fight like rabid dogs over them all."

I felt sick inside at his words, and we were all silent for a long while. But it was good to know. Good to be prepared. There was a reason Tonna thought it best for us to stay at Nem Post. A reason Mom hadn't wanted to tell me everything ...

"How is it that our healer remains hidden, unclaimed?" Vidar asked. "A healer and a ... *woman*?"

"Perhaps she is not," Niero said. "She might be the bride of the Lord of Zanzibar himself. All we know is that we are to free her of this cursed city and have her join us, so we shall do just that."

I glanced at him in alarm. He couldn't be serious. If she were the lord's lady, we were to ... what? Walk right up to the palace and ask if there were any healers about? It was madness. Even the Maker wouldn't ask such a thing of us. He wouldn't want us to die before we started.

Right?

We reached the gates just as they were about to close. We pressed into the rush of perhaps three hundred people who gathered, many herding goats or cows. Niero led us as deeply into the center of the throng as possible. By the time we reached the entry, the warning bells were gonging, so loudly it reverberated in my chest, and the massive gates — thirty feet high and three feet thick — began to swing shut. Guards hurriedly glanced at papers, barked names, took in faces. But the one who waved me past was more interested in my horse than me, running an admiring hand over her well-muscled flank as I paused beside him.

"Looks like Tonna's marking," he said, checking the mare's brand and looking over at me. I ducked my head deeper beneath my hood.

"They are," Ronan intervened. "We spent the night at Nem Post and she lent them to us."

The guard laughed and lifted a brow in alarm. "Then you'd best be about her errand." He signed our papers and immediately moved to the family behind us, swiftly entering with a flash of Zanzibar's mark upon their shoulders — the tattooed outline of the three-tiered fortress, which graced every citizen of the city. The man was perhaps four decades, his wife, two; there was a baby in her arms. Beyond them were ten people, the last who'd find entry this night. And in the distance, I still did not see the Sheolite tracker. Had Tonna sent him in a different direction? A draft of fear washed through me. What if she had sent him toward the Valley? Or if her wretched guards had betrayed us ...

Niero stopped by a blind beggar and slipped a coin into his upturned hand. "Where might we find a safe inn and stables for travelers, friend?"

"Safe is a matter of perspective, friend," he returned, biting the coin. Clearly pleased, he said, "Try the Bricklayers Arms.

Head left, and after two blocks turn right. You'll find it there-abouts. Tell Percy I sent you and he'll give me a bowl of gruel come morning."

"We shall," Niero said.

We readily found it. Niero took two rooms at the small inn, and we traipsed up winding, narrow stairs to the fourth floor. The smoke and spoiled scent of the long-unbathed filled our nostrils, making me slightly sick, even in the face of my own stench after two days' hard journey. I prayed that there'd be a window we might open for the night.

At home in the Valley, we'd bathed a couple of times a week, steaming in a sauna cave until we sweat, rubbing pine needles across our skin, then jumping into the river that flowed beside the village in order to lather our hair with poke weed or Sweet William. For a couple of months we'd had lye soap, but it left our skin dry and itchy, and we'd returned to the Sweet William and its sweet, spicy, clove-like scent. Where was I to find a bath now? I'd have even welcomed a basin of clean water and a bar of lye at that point.

I looked over my shoulder and saw Vidar peering anx-iously down the stairs, Bellona waiting beside him, face trou-bled. "Vidar?" I said, my longing for a bath quickly forgotten.

"This place," he said, shaking himself and looking up to our leader. "There are enemies here, Niero," he whispered.

"There are enemies everywhere," Niero said calmly, step-ping toward him. "The trick is for you to discern when our enemies are alert to *us*." He clapped Vidar once on the shoul-der. "I wager they're not yet, right? At least I hope ..."

After a moment, Vidar nodded slowly, his face still grimly intent, as if listening.

"Good," Niero said, casting a long look down the empty

hallway behind him. "You and Bellona will be in here," he said, opening the first door and tossing Bellona the key to the tiny room. "Ronan, Andriana, and I'll be in here," he said, moving to the next.

We followed his instruction without comment. I dared not look at either him or Ronan, certain they'd see my cheeks flame in the wall sconce's light. It made sense that my knight would be with me at all times. That Bellona would be with Vidar. It made sense for any Ailith who was true to her vows; at least for any girl not falling for her knight, or knight for his charge.

Only Niero's presence gave me room to breathe. Had he sensed the undercurrent of risk? Otherwise, why had he not chosen to bed down in Vidar and Bellona's room?

Niero dropped his small pack to the floor and untied his bedroll, unfurling it between the two musty straw ticks on the floor. I did the same and put mine at the foot of one of the ticks, rather than atop it. I knew such things were the breeding grounds for Cancer. Or at least fleas. I looked up to a high window and stifled a groan. It looked long shut, impossible to open. A wave of nausea passed through me. Again, I hungered for the clean, thinner, lighter air of the Valley, far from me now. Terribly far away … Down here the air felt thick, and in it I felt sluggish, stifled, almost as if I were slowly suffocating.

"I'll see if I can find something for us to eat," Niero said.

"You don't want company?" Ronan said, wearily kneeling on his bedroll.

"Best not to," Niero said, his eyes brushing past me. With that, he was out the door.

I flopped to my back, nearly delirious with the joy of being still. Flat. Free of my pack. Even if it was in this horrible building.

My mind whirled with all that we'd seen and experienced since we left home. I felt as if I were in one of those eddies in the river; running upstream, circling around with the current, then riding up again.

"Here," Ronan said, tossing me a canteen.

I saw it in time to catch it and unscrewed the lid, wondering where he'd spied a clean well. I drank deeply and then lay back down. "I don't think I've ever been this tired, Ronan."

"Me neither. And we've just begun to follow the Call."

We both closed our eyes. I might've slept, must've slept, since Niero seemed to arrive seconds after he left, carrying two loaves in his hands.

"Bread," Ronan said, incredulous. "I think it's been years since I had bread."

Niero smiled as he handed one to Ronan and the other to me. "That's the good part of traveling to wealthy cities, even if we risk our lives to do it. They have access to Pacifica's wheat traders," he said, lifting a bite in the air and tossing it into his mouth.

I had no idea how far the wheat in this bread had traveled to reach my tongue, or where Pacifica was, really, or how old the bread might be. But it mattered not. The flakey dough melted in my mouth and eased down my throat.

"There's more," he said, handing a brown-wrapped item to Ronan. "Meat. Fresh. Or at least freshly cooked."

Ronan unwrapped a large slab and took a slow, tentative bite. He smiled even as he chewed. "What is it? Horse?" The only meat we'd ever had was dried horse and occasionally, mutton.

"Bison."

"Never heard of it, but it's good." He rose and handed the

red, barely browned slab to me. I tore off a chunk with my teeth and chewed and chewed, experimenting with the taste of the beast's juices sliding through my mouth. I wasn't sure if I liked it as well as Ronan did, but my hunger forced me to take another big bite before passing it to Niero.

Bellona and Vidar walked in and sat down against the wall, already chewing.

"So ... do we go after the healer tonight?" Vidar asked, mouth full.

"At least for an hour. Stop at a few taverns. See what we can find. Andriana, you and Bellona will need to stay here. We will — "

"What? No!" Bellona said, lowering her half-eaten loaf of bread. "If he goes, I go." She hooked a thumb in Vidar's direction.

"And I don't go without Andriana," Ronan said.

"You'll all do what I tell you," Niero said, as unperterbed as if we were discussing sunset. His black eyes flicked to each of us. "Whatever I tell you."

Ronan opened his mouth to speak and then shut it. I frowned. Did I yet trust Bellona as much as him to watch my back? We Remnants were as thoroughly trained as our knights. But we'd trained with *our* knights. For years. We instinctively knew one another's tactics, pacing.

"We are one now," Niero said. "Yes, Knights still pledge to give their lives for their Remnant. But we must learn to move as a body. Giving and taking. Flexing to accomplish the most. And in this moment, that means using different tactics to accomplish our goal here. If Bellona and Andriana are discovered *as* women here ... Please. Trust me in this."

We all stared at him. Then Vidar filled his quick mouth

with a bite and the rest of us followed. Concentrating on chewing rather than arguing.

■ ■ ■

Bellona reclined on Ronan's bedroll, which irritated me for some reason. So I closed my eyes or looked up at the ceiling, examining the paint peeling away from ancient timbers while trying to think of anything but her on Ronan's bed. I wished he were still here with me. Without him I felt even more antsy than before. Vulnerable.

"Where'd you grow up, Andriana?" Bellona asked.

I looked over, and in the light of an oil lamp saw she was on her back, ankle across the other knee, playing with the end of her braid. She was big and tough. But she was beautiful, in a way. A long, straight nose. Strong chin. High cheekbones. She reminded me of a Greek or Roman statue I'd seen once in an ancient book.

"Let's sleep, Bellona. Aren't you tired?"

"Beyond tired, yeah." She took a deep, long breath and was quiet for such a long time, I thought she'd taken my suggestion and dropped off. But then, "Though aren't you curious? All four of us, out there in the Valley. All these years. Never knowing one another, just now coming together. Did you ever know about the Citadel?"

I shook my head.

"Me neither. Aren't you wondering if we all had the same kind of ... I don't know ... start?"

I considered her words. Sensed she wouldn't let me rest until I gave her a little something. "I had a mom and dad who protected, taught, prepared me. Did you?"

"Two different sets. The first I loved, but when I was five they were killed, and I was moved to the Valley. The second set weren't ... the best." Her eyes shifted to me, clearly wondering if mine had died too.

I frowned. Her parents had died? I knew they promised to protect us to the death. For the first time, I wondered if I too had others. I could remember way back. But who was to say that as a baby, a toddler. "My mom and dad raised me," I said at last. "From birth." I was pretty certain.

"Brothers and sisters?"

My eyes widened, stunned by what her words could mean. "No. You?"

"Five."

"I thought our parents were discouraged from ... from ..."

"Procreating?" she said with a scoff. "Uh, yeah. They risked a lot to do it. My parents risked my brothers and sisters, had a Sheolite come hunting, like what happened for my real parents."

In our villages, most men and women married on or shortly after their second decade, and before their second-and-five. Any babies had to be born by their third decade; after that they simply didn't seem to come. But I had long been told none of that was for me: No falling in love. No betrothal ceremony the Harvest before my second decade. No wedding on the first full moon of Hoarfrost. No settling in as husband and wife. No babe in my arms.

None of that was the Ailith's path. But it had been for Bellona's mother.

"Were you there?" I whispered. "When he came for you?"

She rose to her feet, an easy roll and jump, and went to hang on the sill of the high window, looking up to it, even though she couldn't see through it. "The Sheolite scout was female. And yes, I saw her. My mother was fighting her, and losing, my dad already dead. An elder in our village intervened. Had she not heard my mother's cry, I would've died with my parents. She gathered me up and rode all night to the Valley. And then I was with my family—the only one I ever truly knew. I don't remember much more of my first. Only that . . . never mind."

I felt the pang of loss within her, despite her gruff *never mind*. I considered her second family, then, and growing up with such a number of children. In the village, there was one family with two children. Another with three. All the rest had one, the most that the majority of families felt they could support. I'd never seen a family as large as she described—with six children, counting her. "How'd they feed you all?"

"My dad was a good hunter. There's still a good number of squirrel where we lived. He was wicked-good with an arrow."

I digested that. I hadn't seen many squirrels in my part of the Valley. "Did he teach you?"

"Yeah. The elders didn't want me to carry a bow," she said, reaching for an arrow from her quiver and fingering the pointed tip. "Said it'd draw more attention than a sword, and not be as effective in close combat." She smiled softly. "I'm a decent swordswoman, but as an archer? I'd say I would've made my father proud."

We were silent for a time. "Do you miss them, Bellona? Your family?" When she didn't answer, I rushed on. "Because I'm missing mine. There's so much . . . So much I didn't say."

She didn't answer for several breaths. Wariness filled the air between us, then a decision to risk, then pain. "Yeah. My littlest brother, mostly. He called me Nona. I really miss him."

I said nothing, only tried to forget the ache in her voice, so different than I expected. So different from everything I'd decided about her, and an ache that awakened my own longing for home. For my parents. For the Valley. For home. For the familiar.

The men returned in time, unsuccessful, having gathered no information on our mysterious healer, and we all gave in to slumber until sunup.

Come morning, Bellona and I insisted on going with the men, given that more women were reportedly on the streets.

"Perhaps if they are willing to feign belonging," Niero said, looking at me and Bellona.

"Bellie's a little tall for me, but I'll take her," Vidar joked, giving his guardian a sly look.

Bellona hit him, hard, on the arm. "Because I'll keep your neck from a sling."

"Only after I save yours," he said, wincing as he rubbed his arm.

Bellona shook her head and rolled her eyes.

"Can you do it? Play the part?" Niero asked them, no trace of humor in his eyes. "The belonging? Convincingly?"

Bellona stared hard at him. "Fine," she said at last, throwing up her hands.

Niero looked to me.

"Done," I said, never daring to look Ronan's way. I only knew I didn't want to be left behind. Whatever it took. And there was something within me that said if we were together, we might have a greater chance of finding our healer.

"All right. Let's go," Niero said. "Place every knife you have on your person. Vidar, your pistols in your waistband, but as last resort only, got it? Go to the halbert or sword first. The guns will draw more attention."

"Got it."

"Bellona and Andriana, you will walk behind your companion as the women of the city do. Behind the man, hand on their right hip, matching their stride."

"The old ball and chain," Vidar said. "Isn't that what they called it back—"

"Quiet, or I'll make you quiet," Bellona bit out.

"Fine, fine," Vidar said, raising his hands. "You really ought to give me a chance, though," he said, following her out, back to their room. "My people make fine mates. Passionate, spirited, good cooks "

"Vidar, you've never made me a decent meal in your whole miserable decade-and-seven," Bellona said, her voice fading into the next room.

Ronan smiled at me and lifted a dark brow, laughing silently. I couldn't help but smile with him. *It won't be hard for me to pretend*

"Let's go," Niero said, sliding his slicker around his shoulders—and over the crescent-shaped blades at his back.

I put on my oilskin cape and waited, but both men turned to me and then glanced at each other.

"Uh, Andriana," Ronan said. "You need your hair down. They wear it that way here."

I paused. Back home, the only time I untied my hair was for bathing. "Very well," I said, pulling out the tie at the end of my braid and loosing it into waves.

Ronan stared at me a second. "Good," he muttered, biting the corner of his lip. "But more like this." He reached forward and lifted my hair, letting some fall over my left shoulder, some over my right. His fingers against my scalp sent shivers down my neck and shoulders, and I swallowed hard, staring up into his eyes. He drew a little back, as if he sensed our connection too, and then his eyes searched my face so intently, I forgot to breathe. Belatedly, he seemed to recover himself. "Right?" he asked Niero, looking over his shoulder. "She looks the part?"

"I changed my mind," Niero said grimly, reaching forward to take my hand. "Your knight will trail you, making sure you're well guarded. But it will be *my* hip you hold." He looked back at Ronan, daring him to complain. But to complain might be to admit that he'd seen something between us.

Had he?

"Come," he said, pulling me out the door. We walked past the others, and I did a double take when I saw Bellona, looking so … feminine with her hair falling across her shoulders in shining waves from her braid. Again, I thought her beautiful. In a classic sense. Did I look the same? So very different than before? Was that what had surprised Ronan when he saw me? Made him pause?

"What's this?" Vidar asked. "Lover's quarrel?"

"Shut up, Vidar," Ronan said.

"Oh, right. The jealous lover, then."

"Shut up, Vidar," Ronan and Bellona said together.

"All right! Apparently your parents didn't read you the classics. Of Latin love? Shakespeare? Danielle Steele? Hey, did you people not sleep as well as I did last night?"

We ignored his questions, hurrying down the stairs, through the empty pub below, and out into the crowded city streets.

Niero put my hand on his hip and began walking, assuming I'd catch on. After an awkward start, I caught the length of his stride, matching it. It was an odd custom, this. But they were right — only women literally attached to their mates were on the street.

Since we didn't have any direct clues as to where the healer might be, we decided we'd canvas the city, waiting until we sensed her as we sensed one another. We had no idea if it would work. Maybe it was only an anomaly we shared from growing up together in the Valley, but it was all we had. Vidar led, because we hoped he'd sense her even before the rest of us did. Ronan trailed behind Niero and me, as instructed. I dared to look back at him, and he gave me a worried shake of his head. Because Niero might see? Or because it was not allowed here?

I bowed my head and tried to catch glimpses of other women as they passed. Most were in long dresses, not in pants as Bellona and I were. But there were just enough dressed as we were to make us passable. Ronan had been right though. If I hadn't had my hair down, we might've been stopped right away.

We moved methodically through the city, circling using the widest street first — the broad Market Street — with its shops and noblemen's homes on one side, the city wall on the other. Patrols of six men in blue capes and broad-brimmed hats, and armed with rifles, passed us every fifteen minutes. Finding and sensing nothing of our Ailith sister, we moved to the next one in, Second Street.

By noon we'd made it as far inward as Sixth Street, which was lined by crumbling hovels that housed men that made me feel sick to my stomach with their lustful intentions.

"What's your pleasure, brother?" one called to Niero from a doorway. "Fine womanflesh at your side. Do you wish for another? Or a trade?"

"Inhale once," said another dark merchant, sitting down

on the front steps and blowing out a mouth full of smoke with a sick grin on his face. "Just once, and all your troubles melt away."

I looked nervously back at Ronan, trying to get a read on his emotions. But all I gathered was his grim nod that seemed to say, *It's all right.* Even while it felt like anything but.

Vidar abruptly stopped and bowed his head, hands splayed out at his side.

"Brother?" Niero asked him after a moment, seeing two men leave the last house selling women and enter the street behind us.

The emotions around me were becoming steadily unbearable for me too. *Pain. Fear. Desperation. Sorrow.*

Niero studied us both, then turned to the men, speaking to them over my shoulder. "Where does Zanzibar take your sick? Those with the Cancer?"

The men paused, their faces contorting in confusion. "We have no Cancer. By decree, the ill are tossed out the gates."

I sucked in my breath. They did not even bother to see them through their illness? Into the afterlife? And what of those with lesser illnesses than the Cancer?

The men stared at us. "If you have no business on this street, you should leave," called one, opening a knife and flicking it closed, over and over.

"Agreed," Niero said cheerfully, striking out again. In the wrong direction. I knew it as soon as we passed the sewer grate and my armband began to almost *hum* in odd fashion, waves of vibration that moved up my shoulder.

"Niero, wait," I whispered, gesturing casually to my armband. "Why would a healer stay in a city without illness? She wouldn't. She must be in hiding. Or imprisoned ..."

His dark eyes searched around and spied the grate as well. He shook his head a little and stared into my eyes. "You don't think . . ."

"Let's pass another and see what we sense. Deeper. On Seventh."

He clearly didn't like my suggestion. If we'd seen what we'd seen on Sixth, what would we discover in the very heart of the city?

CHAPTER
5

Ronan drew closer as we entered the next street, Seventh. Here no one walked alone, and we — in our relatively fine clothes compared to their rags — stood out even more starkly. But our cuffs vibrated with such loud urgency, I feared they might actually begin to be audible to others.

She was close. She had to be. The metal at my bicep was practically hot as a stone by an open fire.

We examined every face we passed, paused at each doorway.

But it was at each grate that we had the strongest sense of her presence.

Niero looked back at us for confirmation and we all nodded. He bent and grabbed hold of the metal crossbars, shook it loose, lifted it, and set it aside. After peering downward and looking both ways, he pulled a small black tube from his pocket that emitted a beam of light once he pressed a button and leaned deep into the chasm.

What was this? I wondered in awe, drawing back in surprise. Never had I seen such a thing.

"What's down there?" I whispered to Ronan.

"It's a sewage tunnel. It takes the foulest of the foul and washes it from the city." I wasn't sure what *foul* meant, but from the smell, I could guess.

Apparently satisfied, Niero flicked off his light tube. "I'll go first. Then Vidar and Bellona. Andriana and Ronan last." He bit down on the light tube, grabbed hold of the far side of the hole, and swung downward, hanging for a moment to steady himself before dropping with a soft splash. I grimaced at the thought of what we'd be trudging through. But at least the constant rain would keep it all moving ... Although there'd not been any rain today. It surprised me. No rain? I didn't think I'd ever spent a day without at least some rain upon my head. This, if anything, was good reason to miss it. Sewage.

The others dropped into the tunnel, and I was clambering down to sit and grab for the far edge when Ronan made an odd sound in his throat.

"Andriana!" Vidar cried at the same time, staring up at me with urgency, hand atop his armband.

I glanced up and down the street, and what I saw kept me from looking away. The Sheolite tracker—the elite one from Nem Post—stood fifty paces away. The man spread his feet wide and faced us, delight etching his cruelly handsome features as his red cape stilled behind him. "The high gifts have long been forbidden," he cried. "You are under arrest!"

"We do not answer to you," Ronan said, striding toward him, drawing a sword from his back.

"You will. We rule these lands, Ailith." He raised his arms

to his waist, his fingers crag-like, and pointed to us as he opened his mouth.

What emerged were the makings of nightmares. Such a high-pitched wail, so full of pure agony, that I covered my ears and hunched forward, gasping, almost falling into the tunnel. It felt like he was slicing my eardrums with his call, stealing my very thought, my ability to think by inserting pain, sheer *pain. Death. Despair. Loss. Fear.*

From the corner of my eye I saw Ronan drive toward the tracker.

The tracker ceased his hellish call and pulled out an odd weapon — a double-tipped sword with a handle in the middle. He slid one foot outward and raised it parallel to the ground, preparing for my knight's attack as if he had all the time he needed.

Ronan screamed, yelling at me to go, I thought, but it was as if I'd been deafened by the scream and I heard him from far away, as if his scream was but a whisper. He drew one of his swords from the back, followed closely by the other.

I looked down, and Niero was there beside Vidar, both desperately gesturing for me to jump. "Now," Niero's mouth formed, every line in his face demanding obedience. "*Now.*"

In a daze I took the far edge, and allowed one last glance at my knight — who was now striking the tracker while the Sheolite turned in a swirling wave of blood-red cloth — and did as I knew Ronan wished. *Get to the others. Find relative safety.* I eased down, the floor farther down than I anticipated, then dropped. Niero caught me, turned me to his side, then gripped my hand and ran down the tunnel, toward one side of the mucky stream. As much as I couldn't seem to hear, my sense of smell seemed unfortunately whole.

We'd done our business in a small hut outside our home, as others did in the village. Even as they did at Nem Post. But here in the city, it seemed that everyone's most private business ended up in the sewer tunnels.

These were the dim, distant thoughts I had as Niero dragged me forward, following Vidar and Bellona. It was better than my desperate wonderings over Ronan, and how he might catch up once he dispatched the tracker.

If he dispatched the tracker.

I preferred thoughts of sewage here, and where it would ultimately go.

The farther we got from the battle, the more my hearing returned, and the more the cuff at my arm warmed me again, even against the chill of the underground tunnel.

"This way," Niero urged when I hesitated, looking back. "Ronan will follow." He pulled me onward and I reluctantly followed.

At a Y in the tunnels, we turned right, rushing forward. And at the end we spied two men, standing beneath the pointed ends of a raised grate, light cascading down around their shoulders, swords in their hands. Vidar slowed, Bellona with him. Niero and I stopped behind him.

"We have nothing to fear from them," Vidar breathed, a slow smile spreading across his face. "They are like kin to us."

"Subversives, here in the bowels of this wretched city," Niero whispered in wonder. "The Maker be praised." He stepped between Vidar and Bellona and went to the men, while I hesitated, staring down the long, silent tunnel behind us. Ronan still wasn't coming. And if the tracker found us here, could these two stop him? They'd clearly once been fearsome. But now they were of six decades and frail unto the point of death. Bent. Thin. With gray beards.

"I am Raniero. Of the Valley," said our leader, offering his arm.

"Raniero of the *Valley*," said the longer-bearded one on the left, as if that answered some long-asked question in his mind. He accepted Niero's arm and glanced at his companion, then back to our leader. "I am Clennan. And this is Tyree."

"We are searching for one of our own, brother," Niero said. "A healer."

Clennan's lips clamped shut and he stared hard at Niero, searching his face.

"Our elders sent us here, for we are to free her of this loathsome place."

Tyree shared a grim look with Clennan.

"You are too late," Clennan said. "Tressa was taken from us a week ago. Arrested for trying to purchase medicine, but mostly for being unregistered and unmated."

Raniero frowned. "Did they discover her high gifting?"

Clennan's eyelids, hooded with age and sorrow, lowered further. "I don't believe so. But her crimes are already enough to send her to the gallows at sunrise."

"Oh, that won't work," Vidar muttered with a soft, mirthless laugh, grimly crossing his arms. "That won't work at all."

I didn't laugh with him. I was thinking about how the scouts had come to the Valley. Anticipated our bait tactic in the forest. Then the tracker's arrival at Nem Post. Had Tressa betrayed us, as well as those in the Citadel? Told them of our ways? Our training?

"Come," said the man, looking over his shoulder and into the dark tunnel. "You shall be safe ahead. We'll speak further there." He turned and we followed, running a bit to catch up with his surprisingly long, strong strides.

"There is a tracker behind us. A Sheolite," Niero said, glancing backward.

Clennan faltered and appeared shaken. He reached out and wrapped spidery fingers around Niero's arm. "You led him here? To us?"

"It was not our intent. He found us only as we slipped below the streets. He's one of the elite. Do you understand what that means?"

The man nodded gravely, took a deep breath to gather himself, and continued walking. "Sethos. It has to be. He's sought us for years and has come close to Tressa, sensing her gifting. But we taught her how to evade him." His brow furrowed and his pace seemed to increase. I hurried behind him, thinking over his words. He spoke as an elder. Like one of those in Community. "At least we'll have the night to make plans," he said. "He won't get past the grate ahead."

But then neither would Ronan. The thought of him separate from us, alone for the night in this horrible city, terrified me more than this temporary separation. "B-but our man. A knight," I sputtered. "He was fighting the tracker. Defending us." *Defending me.* "We need him with us."

"He'd best hurry," Tyree said with concern, still walking. "We are directly below the city gates here. When the sun sets and they close the entry, this metal grate comes down here as well, sealing the sewer tunnel."

I glanced up to where he pointed — at the rusted, pointed ends of the heavy grate. "You cannot," I said, reaching out for his thin arm. "You cannot shut it! Shut it against the tracker if he comes, but not our man!"

"It is out of our hands," Clennan answered, gesturing upward as Tyree had. "They determine the moment. You either remain on this side" — he looked up to a slice in the stone above us — "and wait for your knight. Or you come to this side," he said, taking a step past a groove in the floor, "and we shall tell you all that we know of our Tressa."

"Just do not stand directly beneath it," said Tyree, stepping quickly to the other side. "It's killed many a rat."

We heard the city bells that signaled sunset. It was happening.

I stared into the depths of the dark tunnel and willed Ronan to arrive. *Ronan, come on!*

Niero took both of my arms in his strong, gentle hands and drew me slowly backward. To the other side as the bells continued to toll.

"No," I said, wrenching away. "Didn't you say we were to stay together?"

"Ronan is a knight. He shall find his way to us, if he yet lives. Stay focused. A fellow Remnant is sentenced to *death*. We must get to her, Andriana. We need her. It is the Call."

I stared at him in horror, his words rolling through my mind again and again. "If he yet lives?" I said, disliking the screech in my own voice. The panic.

The bells ceased and yet continued to echo down our tunnel. "Ronan! Ronan, *run*!" I screamed.

"Andriana!" Niero growled. "Be quiet!" He grabbed hold of my arms again, facing me this time, and dragged me to the wall on the far side of the slot. I stared at the ceiling, scared that the grate would come crashing down at any moment. But Niero was shaking me, bumping my back up against the cold stone, making me focus on him. "You are forgetting yourself,

Remnant. Forgetting yourself! Listen to me. We have one Call. Nothing can get in the way of it. Nothing!"

"It has begun?" whispered one of the tunnel dwellers in awe, Clennan. He fell to his knees. "You are also of the foretold?"

His companion dropped to his knees too, ignoring the muck. Both raised their hands in prayer, lifting their faces to the sliver of setting sun that streamed through the crack of pavement above, and invoking the name of the Maker.

My inward spinning came to an abrupt halt, a draining whirlpool, now a cistern. Tears welled and streamed down my face as they continued to pray, their words and tone like a song in my heart, bringing to mind the elders at the Citadel surrounding us, and the beauty and intensity of the presence of the Maker. Reminding me of our own Call.

But then we heard the *thunk* of the gates come together above us and then the metallic slide of a second beside us. Dense and heavy, it began slowly descending and gained speed until it slammed into a slot in the floor, sealing Ronan off.

Separating us.

I felt it as keenly as if a knife had been shoved into my belly. *Ronan, Ronan, where are you?*

I pushed Niero away, and he let me go. I hurriedly rubbed my wet cheeks and eyes with the backs of my hands as I tried to think, then rushed back to the grate, wrapping my fingers around the cold, rusted steel. *How to get to him, how to get to him* ... I stared into the gathering abyss of the tunnel, listening hard, but no sounds of footsteps came our way. Was it possible? Had the tracker killed him?

But if that were so, wouldn't the tracker be in pursuit himself, even now showing his face again?

Or had they each accomplished their task and killed the other?

My eyes strained in the low light, hoping I'd see him coming, hear him coming.

"Andriana," Niero said, placing his big hands on my shoulders. His tone again was gentle, assuring, even if weary. "Ronan shall find his way back to us. It shall take more than one Sheolite to bring down your knight."

"But he wasn't just any tracker, Niero. He opened his mouth and let out such a shriek—" My voice broke and I brought a hand to my chest. "It was the sound of the dead and damned."

"This is why the elders brought you Ronan," he said. "He can defend you when our enemies prey upon your gifting. He is strong where you are weak. He is your shield. Trust the Maker. Wait and see."

"What if he returns to the inn? Looking for us?"

"Then he will see that we did not return. He'll come back to the tunnels tomorrow to search for us."

I took steps I did not feel, my mind solely on Ronan's eyes, his secretive smile, the way he'd looked at me that morning, his fingers in my hair. But as we walked, my vibrating armband forced my attention back to the present. To what was ahead. To the task.

As we entered a wide room, blessedly devoid of sewage, I felt the presence of the Maker as I had not since we left the sacred chamber within the Citadel. But the sensation made no sense to me, given who we'd found. The walls were lined with beds, four high, and on each one patients looked our way, or rose up on one elbow. Many cried out and groaned in monstrous pain.

And yet all managed to look upon us with favor. Welcome. Peace.

"They all have it?" Niero asked, turning in a slow circle. More than fifty men, women, and children lay around us. "The Cancer?"

Our guide nodded soberly, even as we instinctively drew a step back. All but Raniero. The old guardian considered him carefully. "Tressa cared for us here. For a long while her father worked for the office of health, and he knew who would be taken the next day. He managed to squire these to safety, and tended to them here with his daughter. Until —" His voice broke. He wiped his nose with the side of a crooked finger and looked away.

"Until they suspected him as a subversive," said the second man. "And killed him as they had her mother."

"And you, brother?" Niero said. "You have the Cancer."

"Had it. I seem to be on the mend," he said, lifting frail hands.

"She healed you?" Vidar asked.

"She said the Maker healed me. As he heals us all, in this life or the next."

"As is so," Niero said with a dignified nod.

I wandered from one bank of beds to the next, wondering how a girl our age had managed to do all this. Each one had the essence of an Ailith, like they wore it as a perfume. From her touch? It was this that had drawn us, that made our armbands hum with recognition. I reached out and touched each hand that reached for me, though I was no healer. Did I have something yet that I could give them? Comfort, I decided, smiling into one face and then the next. "The Maker sees you. You are not alone," I said, squeezing a small girl's shoulder. "He shall see you to wholeness."

She smiled, looking almost angelic herself, until pain

contorted her tiny face and she cried out. Fear, I felt in her. Agony. Like tiny echoes of the tracker's screech in my ear.

"In the next world, when we go to be with the Maker, there shall be no more pain," I said, bending down to look into her eyes. "There will only be peace. Restoration."

She nodded, weary tears in her eyes as she clung to my words. I forced myself to move on, past a man of perhaps four decades who almost vomited, he coughed so hard. Making me think of another I'd known until just past my first decade.

The Cancer had come in waves in our village and others among the Valley. It came in two forms: a twisting of gut or a siphoning of breath. Here, it seemed the same. But at home we'd done our best to see our people through it and on to the afterworld. Here in Zanzibar, they were cast out, sent into hiding or directly to their deaths. And yet in spite of our dedicated, loving care for those of our village afflicted by the Cancer, never had we seen one rise again, as Clennan and Tyree had. My hope soared, thinking of the good we could do, getting Tressa to others afflicted. How much more powerful could her gift become once she wore the Remnant arm cuff? Once she was one with us?

"Who is Tressa's knight?" Niero asked the men. "A Remnant is not without a Knight of the Last Order. Who did the Maker raise up?"

"Killian," said Clennan, glancing in sorrow from Tyree to Niero. "But he left when she was arrested and we haven't seen him since. We fear the worst."

"No," Niero said, looking over to us. "We won't believe that yet. We seek not one now, but three. Ronan. Tressa. And her knight."

CHAPTER
6

The streets of Zanzibar grew fiercer at night, few but those with ill intentions out and about. But still we followed the guardians of the sick out and upward. We emerged through a disguised entrance in the back of an apartment — an entire wall that looked like our outhouse back home, except with crumbling plaster and stone. I tried not to think of anyone sitting there, seeing to their private business. But I had to admire the ingenuity; never in my life had I seen something so clever. Once it was in place, you'd never know it was an entrance to a hidden alcove for the healer to attend the sick.

Bellona and I had braided and tucked our hair again, preferring to disguise ourselves as men at this hour rather than as wives. And it made us look, collectively, more fearsome, we decided, observing men coming our way electing to enter a nearby door or alley rather than pass our group of six.

When a patrol came toward us, we edged into a busy place called a pub, the men surrounding us as if we were only there to imbibe, taking shots of the clear, liquid fire they sold within. The men about us, long gone in their senses, smiled as we passed, waving at us as if we were old friends as they simultaneously ordered another small glass. They laughed boisterously and yet then were quick to take offense, clearly not in their right senses.

We slipped out behind the patrol after they'd passed, glad to know exactly where they were, rather than be surprised by another. But they led us directly to the eastern edge of the castle's gates, toward the Lord of Zanzibar's sprawling abode. We split from the patrol and clung to the gathering shadows, perused the wall climbing five stories above us. Our armbands began to warm and we shared a look. She was here.

"There," said one of our elderly guides, gesturing upward in pain. He clutched a hand to his chest and leaned back against the wall that bordered Market Street. I understood then: he loved her as a daughter.

High above us, a woman in a simple white gown was chained, her arms spread wide. The clouds opened and it began to rain at last. Torches were set all about her, and in the sputtering light we could see she had dark red hair and ivory skin. With coloring like that, she must have been twice as challenging to hide in Zanzibar

I took a step forward and looked up, her presence calling to me, as ours did to her, apparently, for she looked down at us then back over her shoulder. I shivered, thinking about being where she was, so high up. I'd never liked heights. Try as he might, our trainer had never fully trained that fear out of me. If I were up there, on the edge of the wall … My stomach did an involuntary flip. "How are we to free her from such bonds?" I asked. Could I even manage to climb up there if I was on a mission?

"You won't free her," said a voice from behind me.

Niero and Bellona both drew swords as a tall man with blond dreadlocks emerged. But he left his weapon in place. "Because I'm going to do it."

Vidar barked a laugh.

"You're late," the blond man said. "We could've used your assistance and your swords." He edged past Bellona's tip. "A week ago."

"Yes, well, the Maker sends us when and where he pleases," Niero said, offering his arm even as he refused to accept any offense. We knew this stranger to be one of us, felt it in the core of our gut. Ailith. Just as Tressa was, above us. Our armbands hummed, echoing our unmitigated joy, our strange sense of reunion with unmet relatives.

"Killian," the man said, offering Niero his arm. As Killian brushed a coil of his shoulder-length dreadlocks away from his dark eyes, I bristled at his manner. Cocky. Brash. Edgy. If the elders had chastised Vidar in all his good humor, what would they do with this one?

Niero gripped his arm in greeting. "Tressa's knight. We knew you must be close. I am Raniero of the Valley."

"Our captain, I presume?"

"If you accept my leadership," Niero said, studying him. I noticed, then, the deep shadows beneath Killian's eyes, the drawn look. He'd clearly had some sleepless nights.

"Accepted," Killian said, giving Niero a slight bow as he released his arm.

"Forgive me, brother," Niero said, "but I'll need to see your mark. Just to be more than certain."

Killian considered him a moment, then casually lifted his woolen shirt, loosened his belt and folded down the edge of his trousers to show us the crescent moon directly above his right hipbone. Exactly where ours were.

"Sorry. One cannot be too careful."

"Understood." His eyes shifted up toward Tressa.

Niero made the introductions to the rest of us and inquired if Killian had seen Ronan about, or heard any word about him or of Sheolite trackers.

Killian shook his head, and his eyes slid over to me. "This is your knight he speaks of, woman?"

I swallowed an irritable retort. *My name's Andriana. Did you not just hear* — "Yes."

"Then he shall do everything he can to get back to you."

"Agreed," Bellona said. "If he yet lives. Once we knights have bonded with our Remnant, nothing can keep us from our task."

"You always say the sweetest things," Vidar said dreamily, hand over his heart. She crossed her arms and rolled her eyes.

"Please," I said, ignoring Vidar's humor, still pained over Bellona's words. *If he yet lives.* She said it as if she didn't care. And Vidar responded in kind. "Let us not speak with anything but of hope about him. You are with me on this, yes?"

One by one, they all gave me a sober nod. Then Niero looked to Killian. "What's your plan to free her?"

"I've tried ten different ways of breaching the castle walls, and this is the only way left to me. I'm fairly adept at climbing, but I have lacked a diversion ..."

I volunteered immediately, knowing exactly what would distract the vast majority of those in this city. I knew Bellona would never be willing — it would hurt her pride too much. But a part of me thrilled at the thought of striking out, hair down, without a man to lead me in this wretched city. I was all wound up inside, a coil of irritation and fear and loss.

"Are you certain, Dri?" Niero asked, pulling me aside.

I stilled. Only my parents and Ronan called me that. But I nodded quickly. "It will feel good to do something tonight. It will be okay. I promise," I said. "Our trainer did his work well. I am adept with the sword."

"See that you are." We went through the plan one more time, and as he spoke I touched each of my weapons. The sword on my left, so that I could draw with my right. A dagger on my right. Two more in my waistband, a third at my calf.

"You really think you can do this?" Vidar asked him, as Killian shouldered a heavy, long coil of rope. "Simply climb up there and save her? How will you get her back down?"

"The Lord of Zanzibar has seen challenge from outside the walls aplenty. But do you know how long it's been since he's been challenged from within? *Years.* They grow complacent, lazy in their power," he said, thrusting his chin upward. His eyes narrowed as he saw two soldiers taunting Tressa. The only thing we heard from that distance was the faintest of laughs, but I could see Tressa's wince. I hadn't seen such fair skin as hers ever, really. Did it come from living beneath the ground so much?

"Get me close enough with my pistols, and I'd take care of them," Vidar said.

"No. No bullets. If they know we have bullets, they'll be twice as apt to give chase," Niero said.

"Really, Niero," Vidar complained. "Do you have to take the fun out of everything?"

"Ready?" Killian asked me, ignoring Vidar's antics, his eyes not leaving Tressa.

I bent over and ran my fingers through my hair, scrunching

it, giving it volume, then stood up quickly so it flowed around my shoulders.

Vidar laughed. "I hope Zanzibar is ready. For her women are rising in the prettiest of ways." Bellona hit him in the belly with the back of her hand and I smiled as I heard the soft *ooph* of his escaping breath. "What? What did I say? I meant it as a compliment!"

His voice faded behind me as I turned the corner and walked confidently down the street. Strutting, really, my pace long. Carefree. As if I were but a girl just past her first decade, skipping into the forest. As if I weren't walking directly into the lion's den, I thought with a grim smile.

I saw them coming, torches raised, but didn't slow my pace. A patrol. I had to stop them, distract them, keep them from turning the corner, and hopefully draw the attention of those above as well. With grim pleasure, I saw them falter from their measured march, frowning as they saw I was coming directly at them, not stepping aside. A woman alone, without her mate.

They were nearly upon me. I sensed their outrage, as well as their fascination as I walked directly between them, splitting their group in half. They sputtered and found their voices, yelling at me. One grabbed me and I pulled away. My action enraged him, and his face pressed into a snarl. "Papers, woman."

"I have no papers," I said, sweetly smiling up at him.

His mouth dropped open. "No papers ... What's your name?"

"The Maker knows my name."

"She's mad," said one. "The Cancer, probably. I've seen it before, taking the brain — "

I smiled at him, waiting, waiting for them to understand.

"Nah, she's womanflesh from Sixth, wandering far afield."

Lust. I shivered at the recognition of it within him, wanting me.

"Her clothes are too fine," said another, touching my coat in admiration. *Coveting.*

I slapped his hand away and turned, pulling my sword at the same time. I waved at one, then another, lazily jabbing at them as if I was unfamiliar with the weapon.

The soldiers cried out, half in dismay, half in delight. *Surprise. Challenge. Desire.*

"The desert flower stings!"

"Bah. Take her down," said the captain. "We'll toss her into the dungeon and sort it out come daybreak."

They separated, and that was when I finally saw him. Ronan, held between two burly guards, head hung as if injured, blood dripping down his face. But his eyes met mine for one split second and I knew *joy, blissful hope.* He was not as injured as he feigned. But he needed me. Needed me to free him.

"You go after her, Jarno," said one. "It's your turn. And even you could take this mark."

Jarno, a big man with a bigger belly, scowled at his companion, clearly not appreciating the jibe. He pulled his sword and edged it along mine. "All right. That's enough, woman. Come along."

But as his sword reached the center of mine, I twirled my blade around and sent it flying over the heads of the others. The others hooted in surprise and laughed. Even the captain snickered under his breath. High above us, we heard the calls of other guards on top of the wall, saw that they drifted toward my section of the wall. *It's working. Even their eyes are on me. Go, Killian. Go.*

The captain shook his head and waved two others in after

me. I dropped my sword at their approach, making them relax and think I was giving up, then slammed my left fist into the first man's face before turning and roundhouse kicking the second into the other, sending both to the ground. I tried to ignore the throb in my left hand. Had I broken a finger? Two? But worse were the echoes of the soldiers' pain and dismay I felt reverberate within me, something that had never happened before. I gasped against the emotion, tripling my own sensations.

Anger. The others pounced on me, their laughter fading, and within moments the captain grabbed my arms and wrenched them behind me. I lifted my legs and kicked off the nearest man, sending him to the ground, unbalancing the captain behind me as well. We fell backward. The captain roared in frustration as he shoved me off of him, then rose and pulled his sword.

I bent over, reeling not from battle but the continuing, rising wave of emotion around me, layered and pulling, weighing me down like nets over a fish. Desperately, I reached for my sword and staggered to my feet.

The captain advanced on me and I knew what he felt then too. *Hatred. Humiliation.* He stalked closer, bringing the point of his sword toward my chest as I struggled to bring my own sword up to meet his.

I glimpsed Ronan, free of one man, battling another with the first man's sword.

Ronan!

We can't finish this too soon. With two of us we're moving too quickly. Killian needed a few more precious minutes of distraction. Idle distraction. A woman alone, fighting like a man. But now my knight was with me, and even though I feared our timing, I could not shove down the shriek of gladness in my heart.

The captain moved toward me, and I backed up, fearing

what I felt inside him more than his sword. It was my experience that humiliation made men the most difficult foe. He rammed his sword down at me then, and I narrowly parried his strike. He didn't pause, whirling to whip his sword at me again, trying to eviscerate me across the belly.

Except I knelt low and heard his sword *whoosh* past my head.

His humiliation doubled, engulfing me like a dark cloud, and he let out a cry of rage and rushed me then, ramming me with his shoulder against the brick wall with his body, stealing my breath for several precious seconds as he backed away to raise his sword and finish me.

Soldiers above us called out an alarm.

Bellona was beside me then, blocking the Zanzibar's captain's strike inches from my chest, plunging her dagger into his belly while Vidar and Niero easily dispatched the rest of the Zanzibar patrol to their dark afterworld. As one, alongside Ronan, they turned and prepared for the next patrol rounding the corner, running our way.

Six more men. Others would follow, responding to the alarm.

"I do hope the Maker blessed this Killian with speed," Vidar said, standing beside Bellona.

"We must surprise them," Niero said grimly, facing the patrol and eying the guards above. "Continue to distract. We charge." He led us forward, letting out a battle cry.

And after a second's hesitation, we followed.

CHAPTER
7

Together, we dispatched the next six, the last falling with some effort. Only Bellona was wounded, a slice across her belly that she seemed to largely ignore.

Actually, the *others* dispatched them while I stumbled about, mostly on the edge, my mind and heart a swirl of emotion. *Loss. Fear. Fury.*

Niero turned toward me and grabbed hold of my arms again, this time not in anger but in concern. "It'll be okay, Dri," he whispered in a pant. "Once we're out of here, you and I will find a way to manage it."

He knew. How did he know? I wondered dimly. But the thought of it was again lost in the flood tide of emotion, threatening to sweep me away.

Ronan had his arm around Bellona, holding her up. She pressed against the wound, blood oozing between her fingers. "It's all right," she said faintly, fighting to control her breathing. She slapped Vidar away, as if his attention embarrassed her. "I'll be fine."

Vidar straightened, concern coming off him in waves, but his eyes moved up and over her shoulder. "Look!" We followed his gaze.

The chains that had once held Tressa were empty. Killian had done it. But could they make it to our meeting point?

We could see patrols charging toward us from both directions.

"Uh, Niero?" Vidar said. "The next part of the *mapo divino*? Now would be a good time ..."

"This way," a voice said from the shadows. Clennan, from the tunnel. "Come with me."

We had little choice. We turned and ran after him.

Ronan took my hand and I winced, pulling away because it was the hand I'd used to pelt the Zanzibar soldier, but my heart again surged with gladness. He was alive. Well enough, even if he had blood caked at his brow and ran with a limp, obviously in pain. He was alive. Alive!

He did not return my grin, only looked grim. Because of the pain? Confusion over my pulling away?

We turned a corner, then another. We could hear the patrols behind us. Closing in.

Our guide rapped on a door on Sixth Street and it opened. I wanted to shield my eyes from what I saw. Half-dressed women. Men passed out in a cloud of smoke. But they opened like a doorway of humanity and then closed in behind us, wordlessly shielding us even as we moved through another tiny trapdoor into the next building, then slid down a chute to the tunnels.

We ran through a hallway and emerged back in Tressa's hall among the sewers. The room erupted in quiet cheers.

We'd made it. I couldn't quite believe it. By all rights, we should be dead. Outnumbered. Outpowered. *Maybe not quite outpowered …*

Tressa brought her hands to her lips as she watched us enter, one after the other. Killian stood behind her. "My brothers. My sisters," she said, tears streaming from her eerily blue eyes. "How I've waited for this. Longed for this."

"Tressa of Zanzibar," Niero said, standing in front of her. "We have come for you. Are you ready to receive your Call?"

"I received it days ago," she said, blue eyes shining. "But I am ready for what you are to bring." She was truly beautiful, with auburn hair that waved around her shoulders, that pale skin, and big eyes. Nothing about her seemed sharp or dangerous, only soft, welcoming. She wore no weapon. How had she remained hidden all this time? Remained safe? In a city so hungry for women exactly like her?

There was no answer but the Maker. *And Killian.* My eyes slipped to her knight.

"We have little time," Niero said. "We must be away while we still have cover of darkness. Kneel, Ailith Daughter, with your Remnant kin. Stand behind her, Ailith Son, with your fellow Knights." Bellona eased Killian's coat from his shoulders and we knelt in a circle, feeling stronger by the moment as we smiled at everyone who formed it.

Niero returned with two armbands, nodding toward Clennan. The man reached for them, mouth agape as they glittered in the lamplight. I'd almost forgotten how mesmerizing they were without the protective covering of oil. Niero gave him a quiet word and gestured for the second man, Tyree, to come near. They moved to Killian and Tressa's right, waiting on Niero.

Niero proceeded with a ceremony, within the pit of Zanzibar, and I felt my armband hum with pleasure, glory.

The bands were clasped around our sister's and brother's arms. Tressa let out a soft sigh of pain. Killian cried out, sounding almost enraged. And then the lamps about us — only three flames, far smaller than we'd had in the Citadel — grew high like massive bonfires, flooding the room with light, washing us all with the beams, stealing our breath with the heat.

In a moment it was over, the lamps returning to their normal inch-high, dancing flames, as the fifty around us stared with wide eyes. I knew their surprise and wonder as my own.

But as Tressa rose on Killian's arm, she was not the only one to be set to rights. One by one, those afflicted with the Cancer sat up, rubbing their chests and bellies. Confusion, joy, and hope surged around me, taking my breath as surely as the flames had a moment before. I turned in a slow circle. Could it be?

My eyes settled on the little girl that I'd spoken to earlier, who'd been in such agony. She now sat up on the edge of her cot and swung her legs back and forth, face lit up in delight.

"My belly," Bellona said, lifting her shirt to show us the wound sustained minutes ago, now but a harsh, red line in her white skin. I might've thought I'd imagined the whole thing had not crusty, dry dark blood remained around it.

"My fingers," I said, gazing at my left hand, suddenly recognizing the pain was gone.

"And my leg," Ronan said, leaning hard on it, looking almost angry, he was so confused.

I saw Niero smile. "And so it has begun. Our healer has become one with us. And leaves those she loved whole behind her."

"Not all are to be left behind," said the first man from the tunnel, straightening his shoulders. Clennan. "I believe we are to go with you." He gestured toward Tyree. "We have much to tell you. There is much yet for us to do."

Tressa and Killian confirmed his words with a nod, and Niero seemed to accept their word without question. But Vidar cast me a wide-eyed look. Apparently I wasn't the only one worried that these two aged men could keep pace with us.

"We must get clear of this place," Bellona said, voicing my own thoughts. "Are you in good enough health to travel with us?"

"I hope so," said Tyree. "For if they find us here in Zanzibar, we shall meet our death anyway."

"Why?"

"We are the protectors of your new Ailith kin. I raised Tressa and Tyree raised Killian, right here in the city," he said, "when their own parents were killed."

"Understood. But Clennan, why did you not train Tressa to wield a weapon?" Niero said gently, his eyes shifting from Tyree to Clennan and back again. "It was the charter of every Ailith protector."

"He did," Tressa said, taking a deep breath and shaking her head. Twists of auburn hair moved around her shoulders. "It is only that I cannot bear to inflict pain on another. Perhaps as a healer, it is not within my blood."

"The warrior is within every Ailith's blood," Niero said dismissively.

"No," I said. "She tells the truth." I had to let the others know of my ... incapacity. Warn them that I could help, but might not be ultimately reliable. "In battle this night ... Something's transpired with my gift since our own ceremony within the Citadel. Now I feel every emotion around me. It's almost as if it's physical, Niero. And once blood is shed or pain is felt, it's as if I feel that pain as well."

Niero's eyes narrowed.

"Well, *that* was not foretold," Vidar said with a humorless laugh, clapping Ronan on the shoulder. "You're going to have quite the task ahead of you, brother."

Ronan shoved off his hand, concerned eyes washing over me, trying to think through the information I'd given them. Bellona stared hard at me, disappointment edging her eyes. Tressa gave me the pained look of a sister who knew my frustration, but she seemed to have accepted it. Even before we arrived. Before her reception as an Ailith, sealed with the armband. Her look of understanding irritated me, and I glanced away.

I didn't want to be understood. I didn't yet understand it myself.

"It is all right," Niero said. "Our sisters are as the Maker intended them to be. We must trust in their gifting, even if they cannot be the warriors we imagined. And I will seek ways to aid them in managing it."

"There is more than one way to be a warrior," Tressa said gently.

Niero's eyes searched hers. "Agreed. I shall look forward to seeing how that might come to pass, sister. But for now we must escape this city. Before they find us."

"We have much yet to say," said Tyree.

"And you shall say it," Niero said. "After we are free from the reach of the Lord of Zanzibar. Because something tells me he won't appreciate the fact that we've stolen a prisoner sentenced to die from his own castle walls."

"You'd be right on that count," Killian said. "If they catch us, our death shall not be swift. It shall last days."

I shivered, my mind too readily comprehending what he could mean.

Ronan slipped his big hand around mine as they discussed options for our flight, our clasped fingers hidden by the folds of our long oilskin slickers. I hoped my face did not betray my surprise. But what I felt from him was *courage. Hope. Faith.*

While there was a part of me that hungered for *love*, I'd take what I could get, even if it was only my dearest friend trying to ease me back to comfort and peace. I dared to give him a quick, smiling glance, and his eyes — those beautiful green-brown eyes I loved so much — smiled back at me. Could he feel my emotions? They sang within me, but the predominant one was *gratitude*. With *gladness* a close second.

I wanted him to hold my hand forever. I wanted to feel this connection with him, this blessed communion of emotion for days, weeks.

But Niero was already on the move, picking up his pack. Urging those so recently healed of the Cancer to find their way back to their homes and families. "You must not tell them of what you've witnessed," he said, raising a finger and slowly looking each one in the face.

"Why not?" cried a boy. "It's a miracle!"

"Yes, why not?" asked a young man past his second decade. "Why not shout it from the city walls? Such glad news has not been heard in generations!"

"Because we must not yet be discovered," Niero said, glancing around at us. "There is much to do before our enemies are certain that the Ailith are on the move. And talk of Tressa's high gifting will only fuel their fires of interest." He looked back to those around us. "Please. I beg you. For our sake, keep silent. Because our work has just begun. There will come a time when we will want you to share it. Just not yet."

Slowly, each nodded. And I saw Tyree and Clennan share a satisfied look.

In the end, we had to leave Tonna's stabled mudhorses behind. There weren't enough of them to carry us, and the guards would be paying far too much attention to those who exited the city anyway. Even though they were on heightened alert, with stealth we managed to draw near; upon Niero's hushed "now," Bellona and Killian took down a pair of guards with arrows, each deadly sure in their target. The men fell out of sight, and we froze and held our breaths, waiting for a shout of alarm. None came, and the seconds passed swiftly, each a moment closer to the next patrol along the wall. Killian heaved up an iron claw, and loops of rope disappeared up and up.

I was already finding it difficult to breathe. Ronan took my arm and pulled me a few steps away. He reached for my other arm and leaned in close, his forehead nearly touching mine. "You can do this, Andriana," he whispered. "Just keep your eyes on me. Pretend we're in the trees again."

That was how our trainer had tried to wean me of my attachment to the ground — sending us high into the swaying cedars, in the wind and rain. To the top of a mountain ridge, again and again. Each time, the way I managed to keep moving, to not seize up in terror and refuse to move, was to keep my eyes on Ronan. Every handhold and foothold he took, I took afterward.

"Without pause," Ronan whispered. We both knew Niero was looking back at us, the others already climbing the rope.

"Without pause," I whispered back, my voice tight and strangled.

Ronan took my hand firmly in his and went to the rope. He grabbed hold of it as high as he could, lifted himself up, and pulled up his knees, letting the rope interlace through his feet. Using the break-and-squat method we'd been taught, he pushed upward and repeated the movements. I made the mistake of looking above him, to Tressa just clearing the edge. And Bellona rising, nocking an arrow and letting it fly. She looked down at us, urgency coming off her in waves.

"Dri," Ronan said. "Come on."

Niero edged nearer to me and took my hands in his, then placed them high up on the rope, still covering them. He looked into my eyes. "You can do this, Andriana."

And in that moment, I thought I could. Courage seeped into me. I moved mechanically, falling a bit behind Ronan, but comforted by the fact that Niero was beneath me. I had the distinct impression that if I fell, he could reach out and grab hold of me, save me. *But don't think about falling, Dri. Nothing but the next squat. The next reach. Follow Ronan. Keep your eyes on Ronan.* Sweat beaded on my brow, ran down beside my nose. I felt the salty taste of it on my lips as I licked them, swallowed hard, and reached again. In minutes we'd reached the top of the forty-foot wall, and Ronan reached down to grab my wrist and pull me the rest of the way up. Then he reached for Niero. The others were already going down the other side; only Bellona and Vidar were still atop the crennel-lated walkway, each peering the opposite way, waiting for the dead guards to be discovered. "Go, *go*," Bellona urged.

I know Ronan couldn't see my expression in the dark — the nearest torch had been extinguished, which might draw its own attention any second — but he knew me. Wordlessly, he took a second rope and fashioned quick knots, panting so hard

I could feel his breaths wash over me. "What are you doing?" Niero hissed. "We don't have time for this."

"Go," Ronan said. "We'll be right after you."

I heard the thrum of Bellona's bowstring and looked up in time to see a soldier fall on the short stairwell of the next tower. His companion began to cry out, but her next arrow sliced through his neck, effectively silencing him. I gulped and then swallowed down the bile rising in my throat, dimly aware that Ronan was sliding a loop around my leg, and then the other, pulling it up to create a seat then wrapping the belt around me.

"As entertaining as this is, we really should be off," Vidar quipped.

I had no more time for delay or complaint. Ronan didn't whisper a "Ready?" warning or anything. He just shoved us off the edge. I clung to him, my fingers digging into his back, knowing I must be hurting him yet unable to do anything else in my terror. My heart was pounding so painfully that I wondered if it would explode. Right here. Along the wall of Zanzibar. My companions would have to leave my dead body behind, or carry me along in order to leave no evidence of who had breached the high walls.

The rope shuddered and I swallowed a scream, concentrating on Ronan, the comforting smell of him. A smell I'd known for years. Of pine and leather and a musky, manly sweat. I pulled in closer and put my head under his chin, my nose against his sweater, trying to convince myself that I was back home. Just doing an exercise with our trainer. Not on the brink of disaster. Or on the perilous edge of endangering not only myself but my precious Ailith kin too. Only that thought kept me clenching my teeth and my lips closed.

At last, at last my feet touched soil and my knees gave way.

I would've fallen, a limp, pathetic mess, but Ronan held me up. He took hold of my arms as Bellona and Vidar and Niero joined us. Niero wordlessly unknotted my rope cradle and slid it from my legs. And then we began to run, waiting for the shouts, the bells, the arrows.

But none came.

When Clennan and Tyree had to stop, I leaned over, hands on knees, panting, struggling not to fall all the way to the ground again. The wall was far behind us now. I'd faced my worst fear and made it through.

Correction, Dri. Ronan and Niero bodily hauled you over the wall. Deep within, I knew that had it been up to me, I would've found another way out. Or died trying. Anything but go up and over ...

"What in the heck was that?" Bellona said, lifting her chin. I could see her outline five feet away, in the dim light of the waning moon. But I didn't have to see her face in order to make out her resentment. She walked over to me. "What in the *heck* was that?" she repeated. "You could've gotten us killed!"

Ronan edged between us. "Back off, Bellona," he whispered, his tone carefully tempered.

But she didn't look away from me. "Are you incapacitated by heights? Is that it? If so, it would've been good to know *before* we were facing off with a kajillion enemy guards."

"I know," I murmured, forcing myself to rise and square my shoulders. "I'm sorry. There was no time."

"Next time," she said with disgust, leaning closer, ignoring Ronan's hand in a V at the base of her throat, preventing her from actually touching me. "*Make* time. Saints, those *old* guys made it over easier than you." She whirled around and looked at the rest of the group. "Any others with a phobia we should know about?"

The group was silent, stricken by her anger but understanding it too.

"I'm not super fond of spiders," Vidar said, all white teeth in the dark.

"Vid," Bellona warned.

"I'm serious. Eight legs? That's downright freaky." I could see his deep dimples in shadow.

"*Vid*," Bellona repeated. "You want to talk serious? *Any* weakness among us weakens us all," she said, shaking off Ronan's hand and brushing past my shoulder.

"She's right," I said, in barely more than a whisper. "I might endanger you all."

"There's not a one of us who doesn't have a weakness," Niero said, placing his warm hand on my shoulder as I took a shaking breath. "You've done well, Andriana. And you too, knight," he said to Ronan. His dark eyes moved back to me. "But you must lean on the Maker to show you the way through this fear, Andriana, as you would any others."

"This isn't like any other fears," I whispered faintly.

"Ah," he said. "Isn't it?"

He moved away from us then, leaning down to retrieve a canteen from his pack, which he then passed around. Vidar cracked a joke, hoping to lighten the mood, and soon we were walking again, all of us eager to put as much distance between us and the dark city before the sun rose.

"Why hasn't an alarm still not sounded?" Clennan asked, voicing the question on all of our minds.

"He won't like it," Tressa said. "The Lord of Zanzibar. He'll see it as an embarrassment. We'll have wounded his pride. And made ourselves a very powerful enemy."

"That's all right," Vidar said. "We came, we saw, we scurried away into the night. No need to ever go back there, right, Niero?"

Niero remained silent.

After a beat, Vidar said, "I don't suppose it's in you to lie to us once in a while, is it, man? A little fib once in a while might make our way easier. We won't hold it against you, I swear."

"Yeah," Niero said. "That's not how the Maker made me."

Vidar sighed audibly. "Sometimes honor and integrity suck."

I didn't care why no alarm rang that night, really, only felt deep thankfulness that grew the farther we got from the dark city's wall. We padded at an even, steady pace, the old men lumbering, farther and farther behind, but with ragged and yet determined breaths. We continued on through a deep, incessant, drenching rain and the bone-deep chill of pre-dawn. As the sun began to lighten the skies to the east, Niero paused at a ravine and urged us down and into it, fearing that even though there were miles between us, the guards on the towers of Zanzibar might see us through their looking glasses and come after us. "We'll never outrun them," he said. "Our best course is to hide through the day and resume our journey come nightfall. The rains will wash away our prints."

"We hope," Vidar said under his breath.

We followed along the ravine, seeking to discover a cave to shelter in. But while we did not find a cave, we found a curious rusting metal construct.

"What is it?" I asked, as Niero put his hand on the open, ragged edge. The top of it was three times as tall as he.

"A transport, from the War," said Tyree. "I'd heard there was one out here."

As it began to rain again, Niero shrugged and said, "I call it sanctuary," clambering in.

We all hurried inside, as even our oilskins had become soaked in the constant rain. On the walls were the rotting remains of belts and cushions on top of a metal bench. Chairs, I decided. The partial skeleton of one soldier still hung against a sagging chest belt, as if strapping him in for eternity. I hurriedly looked around for others. Vidar and Bellona were already in the front, where I could see small, dirt-encrusted windows. "Two more up here. Looks like they died, never trying to get out."

"I don't understand," I said. "How? How'd they get here?"

"It was a war plane," Clennan, said, comprehending by our expressions that we did not recognize his words. "In the olden times, there were huge machines that flew in the sky. Planes," he said, thrusting his flat hand forward, "and helicopters, which had the power to hover as well as fly forward. They were part of the country's defense. And her offense as well."

We of the Valley shared confused looks. We knew of the War, of course, and had read of such machines. But this was lost history rising before our eyes. We'd seen other old machines in the ancient, abandoned villages when we'd gone out gleaning. Cars. Dishwashers. Boxes I'd heard called *computers*. But never anything that flew in the sky. Where had the rest gone?

As we sifted through the old plane, looking for usable supplies and finding them long-since stripped — by Drifters, most likely — we spread out our bedrolls along the benches and laid down to listen to our elders share what they knew.

"What more do you know of the War?" Tyree said.

"I know that it began, far to the East," Niero said.

Tyree grunted, taking a seat as if the action pained him. "There was severe unrest. Radical thought. Terrorists, they called them. Governments fell. Others rose. As did ancient rivalries."

"Both sides vowed to never be taken," Clennan said, eying Killian.

"Vowed to fight to their death. Vowed to see their own nations destroyed before they fell to their enemies," Tyree said.

"Which they did," Clennan said.

"It was all destroyed," Killian put in. "Every major city. They unleashed toxins that set the Cancer free, washing through the populations of those that had survived the bombs, destroying them from within. And then it evolved and seemed to stay with us, in us, rising again and again in every generation."

Tressa winced, even though this history was clearly known to her. But I sat still, enrapt. I'd known of the War — of the time when all changed and our people fled into hiding — but little else. Why had my parents not told me? Had they not known either? This part of history was not in the books we'd read; it was passed from one generation to the next in story.

"The climate had changed decades before, making things all the more tumultuous. First a long drought, which weakened us from within — setting one kingdom against another due to fighting over water. Then the Great Wet that we still know of today, though, to my eyes, it seems to be lifting." He shrugged. "Still, crops failed from lack of rain, then from drowning. Animals were hunted to extinction. Some bodies of water became riddled with a brain-eating parasite, so even those surrounded by water became fearful of drinking it. And the Cancer ..." He shook his head. "For several generations, those who lived thought they would be the last of their kind."

We were all silent for several long moments, trying to absorb such horror.

"So is it true? Are we are all who remain?" Bellona said. "What of the others who once lived beyond the Desert?"

Tyree shrugged. "I've heard tell that there are others still across the Great Seas. Pacifica purports that she protects us all from them, and maybe she does." He lifted his thin shoulders in a shrug, hands splayed. "Zanzibar trades with her, as do others. And she must not suffer the Great Wet, because we get wheat, salt, and fruit from her trader trains. Stores no other kingdom can deliver as of yet. Clearly, there are still people there. And from what we can gather, that is where most power emanates. Zanzibar and other kingdoms all bow to that one in the west."

We stared at him in fascination. All my life, I'd known of those in the Valley. Those in the Desert, and to our east, the Plains. But he spoke of land much farther away — land we'd considered lost to us. Diseased, or flooded. He spoke of what my protectors had called the Coast and beyond it, across the sea. Cities that had supposedly been lost to the bombs, by his own description. Had they become livable in recent years? Resurrected from the rubble?

"It is from brothers and sisters who came to us from the salt caves, and farther West, along the Great Sea, that we learned of something you must know," Clennan said.

"A young man came to them in the salt caves, fleeing from a very dark enemy," Tyree said, picking up the story. "He served a man named Kapriel, but Kapriel was arrested and sent away, years ago."

The four of us from the Valley stilled at the sound of this name. Kapriel — as in our Kapriel? Our imprisoned prince?

"Some say he was killed, but others say he yet lives," Clennan went on.

"Who sent him away?" I managed to ask.

"One who calls himself the emperor of Pacifica." He gave me and the others a grave look. "It is a troubling place, Pacifica. On the outside it appears prosperous, clean. Indeed, it seems as if it would be our united goal to be more like them. But the darkness runs deep in that city, and in a different way than in Zanzibar." He shook his head, as if he dared not speak further about it.

"We have heard of a man named Kapriel," Niero said casually. "On what charges was he arrested?"

"Because he was a threat," Clennan said, shaking his head. "His high gifting is great indeed."

"His gifting?" Vidar asked.

"This young man, Kapriel, was born on the seventh day of the seventy-seventh year," Clennan went on, ignoring Vidar's question, staring at Niero.

All of our eyes went to him in alarm and awe and he smiled gently in return.

"He is Ailith?" Niero barked in confusion, his own dark eyes narrowing. "Why did our own elders not tell us that?"

He shook his head and shrugged his thin shoulders. "I do not know. Perhaps they weren't aware of it. But there is more. He was one of two."

As we waited for him to go on, my armband stilled. Twins rarely survived in our village. Perhaps this other had died. Clennan seemed sincerely grieved.

"His twin, Keallach, took a far different path," Tyree put in for him.

"Keallach is his *twin*?" Vidar asked. "And an Ailith too, then." He let out a low whistle.

"Even now, the empire of Pacifica has grown to five times the size of Zanzibar," Clennan said. "And Keallach is her ruler, claiming the title of emperor because 'king' was not enough. He is the one who had Kapriel arrested."

I frowned. An Ailith on the throne? How could this not be good? Even if he'd arrested his brother ... could we not get to him, help him see his destiny?

"Pacifica appears to be beautiful. Pristine," Tyree said. "But she rots at her core, just as Keallach rots at his. He could not abide by his father's wishes for the brothers to share the throne, and burned with jealousy over Kapriel's growing fame. He said it pained him to do so, but for the sake of the people, no division could be tolerated. And with his brother seeking the old ways, proclaiming the need for the high gifts to be restored, Kapriel was decreed a subversive and taken away."

We were silent.

"Is he dead?" Niero asked at last.

"No one knows. As deep as Keallach's hatred goes for his brother, there is an equal amount of love. We believe that Kapriel still lives, but is imprisoned where no one can find him."

"He is ruled by Sheol," Niero stated, more than asked. "This Keallach."

"Yes," Tyree said, nodding. "It is subtle, the evil one's presence within Pacifica. Sheol's ways are not unlike mold, stealing in spore by spore. Overtaking other life in subtle, insidious fashion. It is from there that the Sheolites originate, seeking out and murdering those with the high gifts."

Niero rose and paced the length of the plane and back,

chin in hand. "Is there a way for us to retrieve Keallach from the brink? Help him before he is fully deviant?"

The old men looked to each other and then shook their heads, their eyes blank. "We know not. But he appears determined to find you."

Niero paused a second and then continued to pace. I studied him, trying to read him and failing. It wasn't that he felt nothing; his emotions seemed too deep for me to reach. "The Sheolite," he said. "They arrived in greater and greater frequency in the Valley. The trainers and I could barely keep them at bay."

Tyree nodded gravely. "Keallach has had them hunting for the Ailith for some time, for he and his brother were raised, as you were, by those who told him of the ancient prophecies. His parents knew they were special, and as twins potentially twice the Ailith ruler the people had prayed for, if serving together."

"Until Keallach killed them," Clennan spat out.

We sat, stunned. He'd killed his own parents? Those who taught them the ways of the Community? To fight for right?

Worse, he'd killed his brother's parents too.

"It was that action that made Kapriel draw his sword against Keallach. And it was then that Keallach had Kapriel arrested."

"But he had him arrested, not killed," I pointed out.

"And instead of the ultimate Ailith kings sharing the throne, we now have the ultimate Ailith enemy," Ronan said, talking over me. "One who knows of us."

"And those trackers he sent after us," Vidar said, running a hand through his still-damp hair, slicking it back from his dark eyes. "I don't suppose they have a thing for red hooded capes, do they?"

Tyree lifted tired, hooded eyes to meet his. "Red is the royal color of Pacifica."

"I'm afraid there will be more, if you've been recognized," Clennan said. He looked to Ronan and me, clearly remembering our words in the tunnel and fearing the worst.

The tracker's scream still echoed in my mind. "We were clearly recognized," I mumbled, feeling somehow guilty, responsible for betraying myself as Ailith. The tracker had known his death call might immobilize me, strike me at my core. Tried it out, as a test to see if we might be those he sought. "He escaped, right?" I said to Ronan.

He nodded once, pain in his expression as well as his heart. Did he not know that I was only glad that he survived that encounter?

"These brothers," Niero said, still pacing. "Something must be off. They were born with the mark, as the Remnants and Knights were?"

Tyree shrugged. "One would presume so. But we know not. You now know all that we do."

"And born with gifting?"

"Again, that might be assumed. There is talk of sorcery. Keallach passes his high gifting off as a low gift, which is allowed. Kapriel's man had no idea how deep the magic goes. But he can move objects with his mind."

"And Kapriel?" Vidar pressed.

"He has some control of natural elements."

Killian let out a low whistle. "Twins with miraculous powers, dueling it out. That oughta be interesting."

"How could Keallach turn away after the Call? Why would he resist it?" Tressa asked.

"Perhaps he prefers to hold on to the power he knows versus the power that might be," Clennan said tiredly.

"We need to return home," Niero said. "To the Valley. To convene with the elders and find out what they advise."

We all nodded soberly. His plan seemed right. Like it was exactly what we were to do.

"At least this Keallach has no armband," Vidar said, crossing his muscled arms in smug satisfaction. "We only began to experience the full force of our gifting after our presentation." He patted his cuff and grinned around at us, but we did not smile back. Because we deduced what Vidar had not yet.

If Keallach learned the armbands were a source of power, a connection to the Maker's power, he'd seek to retrieve one from Raniero's leather bag — or from any of us.

At any cost.

And at that moment, I was not the only one who felt the shiver of fear, like it had washed in from the dark seas itself.

CHAPTER
8

We slept through the day and skirted Nem Post during the night, knowing we could not face Tonna until we had more supplies to give her — especially since we were not returning her mudhorses. We slept through the following day, taking shelter from discovery between the wet dunes, wrapping up in our oilskins to combat the blowing sand and rain that fell harder as we neared the mountains. We resumed our journey come nightfall, reaching the Valley's mouth as the sun broke free beneath the cloud layer, illuminating our beloved mist-covered mountains.

"It will be well," Niero said when I voiced concern over Tonna's wrath. "We burned our safe passage instructions, as she wanted. And she got more than the worth of the mudhorses in those packs. Trust me, she'll be glad to see us again. Especially if we arrive with more supplies in hand."

"Even if we continue to bring Sheolites behind us?" Ronan asked.

Niero frowned and looked to the setting sun at our backs as we entered the Valley at last. I inhaled, glad, so glad to smell the scent of pine and loamy earth. *Home.* All around me, the Ailith felt relief, bone-weary from our journey and battles, anxious for what was yet to come.

Niero seemed to sense it too. "Be at peace, sisters and brothers. The Maker shall sustain and restore us here. Here, we will seek and receive the counsel we need."

■ ■ ■

When we finally arrived, I collapsed within the elder's sanctuary deep inside the Citadel, sleeping for what felt like days. I'd come close to waking, then fall back into dreams that seemed to pull me under.

At last I awoke, recognizing anxiety in my room, and sat up straight. Fast.

"Oh," I breathed with relief, seeing Ronan, brushing my hair sleepily out of my face. "You scared me. I thought …" I rubbed my face. "I thought something was wrong."

"Hey, Dri," he said, straightening himself. He'd been sitting in a chair by my open door, his head in his hands. Keeping watch over me?

I rubbed my face and eyes again, squinching them up and opening them wide in an attempt to focus. "What a relief to be free of those stupid films," I said, eying the case beside the bed with disdain. "I hope the elders don't send us anywhere else where I need to change the color I was born with." I yawned and stretched. "After all, if Tressa can go about Zanzibar with those blue eyes of *hers,* I figure I can manage with mine. Right?"

"Yeah, but look where that got her. In chains on the wall."

His words were light but his tone flat. I tensed, trying to discern what I was feeling. He opened his mouth as if to speak, but then clamped his lips shut. He was stressed, and full of sorrow. It became like nausea in my own belly.

"Hey, hey," I said, flipping back the covers and swinging my legs out. "What? Did I scare you? Sleeping away the week? What time is it? What *day* is — "

"Dri."

I stopped chattering and stared at him.

"Dri, I have bad news." He rose like he was eight decades old and walked over to me. He sank to his knees and took my hands in his own. Then swallowed hard. "Dri, It's about your parents. Dri, I, uh … They were … they were killed while we were away."

I searched his face, the face I loved so much, my heart oddly twisting into confusion and hate. That mouth had opened and spilled terrible words. Horrible words.

"No. They left. Right after us, they were going to leave."

He stared at me, stricken. "They didn't make it."

I was dreaming. I had to be dreaming again.

Dimly, I turned and began pulling my trousers over my cotton long johns, then pulled on my sweater over my cami. The blue one that Mom always said brought out my eyes. I had to go and see her. Dad too. End this nightmare. Prove to myself it was only that — the stuff of night terrors. I'd had dreams like this for a long time, starting around the celebration of my first decade. So real that I often had to prove to myself that they'd only been a dream in order to dispel them from my head and heart. See for myself the doll hadn't been thrown into the fire. See for myself that the foal hadn't drowned. Now, see for myself that my parents were fine. Right as rain, as my dad said.

Right as rain right as rain right as rain right as rain …

"What are you doing, Dri?" Ronan asked, misery and exhaustion coloring every syllable as I passed him.

"Going home. I've got to see them." I pulled on a pair of boots and then reached for my oilskin on a hook by the door as Ronan neared me.

"Andriana," he said, grabbing my arm. "Did you hear what I said? Dri, they're gone. They're not there. You can't go."

"Stop it," I said, brushing off his hand and walking out of the room, then down the narrow hall — a crevasse in the rock.

He matched my steps. "You can't go there," he said again. "A tracker may be about. Waiting on you … It could be a trap."

I paused and studied his face. It all felt *so* real, this dream. My heart shuddered and then pounded, sending a jolt out to my fingertips and down to my toes. But I'd had such waking dreams before. Dreams that were even more apt to stick with me for days. And this was one I didn't want to live with.

I simply needed my little mom to hug me. Dad too. Get folded between them in a family embrace. Forget I'd ever had such visions. Heard such wretched words. Dreamed such dreams.

I strode forward, past Vidar and Bellona. Past Tressa and Killian, Tyree and Clennan. Almost past Niero before he reached out and grabbed my arm. "What are you doing? Where are you going?" He asked it more of Ronan than me, staring at him with accusation.

I looked back, watched as Ronan ran a hand over his brown-black hair, shining clean. "I tried to tell her. She refuses to believe me. She thinks it's a dream. She's gone through so much, felt so much. Slept so long … I don't think she's even fully awake now."

I stared at him in growing horror. This dream was becoming too realistic. "No," I whispered, pulling loose from Niero's hand and backing away from him, shaking my head. "No."

"Andriana," he said, hands out, advancing slowly, as if trying to capture a wild mudhorse. "I'm so sorry. Let us help you, sister. Let us hold you through this pain."

"No! No!" I cried, turning to run.

I tore out of the residence wing, through the gathering hall — now wide and empty, deep in shadows and feeling anything but holy — and slipped through the narrow crevasse, out into a day heavy with drizzle. I scrambled down the rocks, past the startled guards, and to the shack that held one of four dirt bikes. *They'd obtained others. From where?* I wondered idly. I turned the key and fiercely shoved down on the kickstart, willing it to roar to life, just as my fellow Ailith emerged above me, shouting, with Ronan in the lead.

But the engine caught, and I released the clutch as I twisted the throttle, narrowly avoiding the road's edge and speeding down the mountainside. I went so fast, leaning around the corners, that I felt the gravel and mud scrape against my boot. Soon enough, I could hear the other bikes coming down the mountain in pursuit.

It didn't matter: I had to get home. To the village. To Mom and Dad. They'd promised to escape. To leave, right after me, when we sensed the Sons of Sheol drawing so close.

So close so close so close so close so close …

Someone in the village would tell me where they'd gone. I just needed someone, somewhere, to tell me where to find them.

I reached the bottom of the mountain and made my way down the valley, then into the woods that led to the place I'd lived my entire life. But the closer I got, the colder I felt. Waves of an emotion I had a hard time defining seemed to enter and exit my body like a dagger to my belly. I actually let go of the throttle and then twisted it again each time it happened.

I didn't bother to hide the bike in the woods, as Ronan had done day upon day, week upon week, when we met for our training sessions. I drove right up to my house, noting that there was no smoke coming from the chimney. *Good*, I thought with some relief. *See there? They're gone.* Just as they'd promised. *Somewhere safe*, I told myself, as I stepped off the bike and walked to the doorway. If the neighbors couldn't tell me where they'd gone, maybe the elders would when I went back. But since I was here, I'd take a look around. One final good-bye. That last night had been so rushed

I heard the other bikes' engines in the distance across the field, and I hurried to the door.

The frigid emotion sliced through me again, making me double over. I frowned, gasped for a breath. Forced myself forward, through the front door swinging open on creaking hinges. Paused when I saw blood spattered across a wall that Mom had so meticulously whitewashed with a ground stone paste she made every year.

Always white always white always white always white ...

Eyes wide, I followed the shock of red — a broad, streaking trail along the white wall — into the living room. My breath came fast, loud to my own ears. I dared not breathe through my mouth, only my nostrils, afraid I might scream and not stop.

Because the wall where Dad had kept the swords and other weapons was empty. I stepped over a sword, blood dried in streaks and spatters on its blade, then past a flail and a battered shield. In the corner, near the kitchen, there was more red splattered against the wall, then a pool of blood that spread five feet across the stone floor. Flat stones that Dad had laid, one by one, when I was small.

I could remember him on his knees, sternly telling me to stay away from the mortar and off the wet floor, even though I wanted to play with it. Later letting me put a handprint in a corner section.

I moved on what felt like wooden legs to that far corner, seeing another pool of blood, then a heavy, wide streak, as if someone had dragged themselves over to it.

My knees crumpled beneath me as I studied the floor. Because across my childhood handprint, so tiny, was another, bigger, etched in blood. Not large enough to be Dad's, but more like ...

Mom.

I rocked back and forth, screaming within, the ache so loud, stretching so wide within me, I couldn't let it loose. And only as my Ailith sisters and brothers entered my childhood home did that cry find voice in a keening wail.

Because I'd finally named the cold emotion that had threatened to break me in two, ever since I entered the home I'd known all my life.

Despair.

CHAPTER
9

Ronan tenderly picked me up and carried me from the house that now contained both sweet memory and horror. He wept with me, great tears sliding down his face as he walked down the wide dirt road, between the abandoned houses, to the end of the village. At the river, at the water's edge, he knelt and rocked me, my head tucked beneath his jaw. Rocked me and rocked me and rocked me as we wept together.

Gradually, my tears were spent, and I gasped, hiccupping as I tried to regain the rhythm of normal breath. I then realized the Ailith stood guard. Niero, Killian, Tressa, Vidar, and Bellona formed a perimeter around us — Vidar with a rifle, Bellona with her bow, the others with swords. Even Tressa.

Vidar's eyes shifted back and forth, wary. "They are not here," he said to Niero in a low tone. "It's just a Sheolite shadow that I sense now, all that remains of their passage."

"Agreed," Niero grunted. "But we best continue to keep alert."

"Why?" I asked Ronan, searching his face, knowing he'd tell me the truth. "Why'd they kill my parents?" It made no sense to me. Even though we'd feared for them, we knew it was us they'd be after.

He hesitated, resisted, looking at me with pain from beneath his long, dark lashes.

"Tell me, Ronan."

"Dri, it's best — "

"They wanted to know where you went," Niero put in, turning and crouching before me. "Your parents had almost escaped — "

"Do you really think this is necessary?" Ronan asked.

Niero put his hand up to my knight, still looking at me. "The villagers said your mother went back for something. They were caught then."

I frowned at him. Wanting him to go on. Wanting him to stop. Yet understanding I had to know it all. I looked up to Ronan. "*Tell* me." I didn't want to hear it from Niero. I wanted to hear it from the man who'd understand best. Who loved his parents, as I loved mine. Where were they? What did they look like? Were *they* safe?

He licked his lips and swallowed, looking up to the nearest house, then back to me again. "The neighbors said they were tortured, Andriana. One, then the other. The Sheolite scum used them against each other. Tried to use their love for *each other* to get the information they sought. But they refused to betray you. Until the end, they were your protectors."

"Where did they take them?" I asked, swallowing hard. "Their bodies, I mean?"

Niero shook his head. "No one knows."

"Why take them?" I asked, my voice strangled. "Maybe

they're not dead. Maybe they were just wounded." I looked around at my friends, and they only looked back at me with sorrow and pity. It was madness. I knew it was madness. No one could lose that much blood and survive. No one.

New tears rose and flooded over my lips, running down in twin streams, mixing with the rain falling from skies that seemed to echo my sorrow. And again Ronan held me close, rocking me for several minutes.

At last, Niero intervened. He reached forward and grabbed my arm, stilling our momentum. "Enough."

Ronan frowned up at him. "She just found out, Raniero."

"I said it's enough," he said, more gently. "Come, Andriana. Rise. For we are not people of despair. We are people of the promise."

I looked back at him, half wanting to stay nestled in Ronan's arms. Safe. Cared for. And half wanting to do as my leader asked. Seize upon the strength. The hope in his words.

Reluctantly, I reached out and clasped arms with Niero, and he helped me rise on shaking legs. He stood there a moment, letting me gain my strength, holding me steady. But as a wounded warrior, not a woman in need. Not as Ronan had held me . . .

"You shall never forget them," he said, looking down and into my eyes with compassion.

"I shall not," I said, and though tears fell once more, this time my chin was held high.

"They died to serve you and the Maker."

"As I would live to die," I said.

He nodded, seemingly pleased by my words, hollow as they felt to me. But I discovered that once spoken they formed a sort of empty vessel within my heart, a vessel that gradually filled with each breath I took. Filled with the hint of faith. A trickle of trust. A whisper of hope.

His dark eyes stared into mine, as if willing strength into me. "You were chosen. The path is long. And it does not end here."

"It does not end here," I repeated, grinding out the words.

"The elders have spoken," Niero said, eyeing the rest of the Ailith over his shoulder. "In the morning, we leave to see if we can find this servant of our Kapriel and discover more about his brother. If the elders are correct, then we have much to do in preparation."

We returned to the Citadel, and I curled back into my bed, my blanket over my head as I feigned sleep, knowing Ronan would keep prowling the tunnel, keeping watch until he knew I was resting. Half an hour after I'd curled up and remained still, I sensed him ease away and knew where he was going.

To check on his own parents.

They were likely far away, safely escaped. Surely the other three Ailiths from the Valley would've told me if they'd lost their protectors too. But the idea of being able to see my village, my parents as I'd left them just days ago, set me to weeping again. I cried and cried, wiping my tears and snot on a soggy handkerchief that Clennan had given me.

Why? I asked the Maker. *Why, why, why, why, why? They'd given their lives to serve you. To serve me. Was it not enough? Was it not enough?*

Weary of my own internal tirade, I sat up and threw back the covers. Bellona looked over at me from her post in the hallway. Standing guard, I guessed, in Ronan's absence. I sighed and blew my nose again, quickly brushed out my hair, and wound it back up in a knot before exiting my room.

"Andriana, wait," she said, following me to the right, down the narrow, curving tunnel.

I was determined to explore the Citadel. Move. Do anything but think and cry any more. So I didn't respond. She could come, she could stay; I didn't really care. And that utter lack of emotion — that apathy — spooked me and made me start tearing up again. I hurriedly wiped my face with the long sleeve of my sweater.

We stood to one side, pressing ourselves into the rough stone as two armed guards passed us. They gave us a long look, clearly curious, but then hurriedly looked away when they saw my tearstained face.

We entered a large room with a massive round table and twelve stools, all carved from stone. I exited through it, found another hallway, this one lined with what appeared to be twenty dorm rooms, possibly to house the guards. In each section of the Citadel's labyrinth, dripping candles and torches lit the way, and there were open ventilation shafts carved through the cliff face at regular intervals to bring in fresh air. I wondered why we weren't colder than we were. Even in Harvest season, especially with the steadying climate of a cave, it should be cold underground, and yet in here, it felt rather ... temperate. Almost as warm as it had been in Zanzibar.

I walked farther and noticed old bells of all sorts were interlinked by chains along the wall. One pull would sound the alarm in hallway after hallway.

"Andriana," Bellona asked, still behind me, "where are we going?"

"I just want to know what's up here "

Appeased, she settled back into silence, perhaps as curious as I to see the upper reaches. We climbed round after round of stairs, and passed armories filled with machine guns and rocket launchers and crate upon crate of bullets — obviously meant for defense of the Citadel. More dorm rooms, these appearing empty. Room for hundreds. More meeting rooms. Kitchens.

Up here it was warmer, and I wondered again how they heated a fortress buried so deep into the mountain. But then I smelled it: sulphur. My eyes traced the wall and I saw the clay pipes and some telltale drips that painted the gray stone green and blue. They were pumping hot mineral water through the pipes, throughout the entire structure. It was ingenious.

I tiptoed past a massive steel door that looked capable of withstanding a bomb, and down a narrow hallway that led toward small alcoves that exited out and behind giant boulders, surprising chagrined soldiers who kept a sleepy watch. It seemed the boulders disguised the men's location from below, appearing as outcroppings of the mountain itself. But judging from the view from inside, with the soldiers' mountain of firearms, no one would be capturing this mountain with ease. I had no idea how long the elders had been collecting individuals willing to defend the Citadel, but those who'd already arrived appeared to be ready to go down fighting.

At last we hit an alcove with no soldiers on it, and I moved around the boulder barrier.

"Andriana," Bellona said in irritation, taking my arm and going in front of me. I allowed it, too weary, too beaten to argue. She did a sweep of the area and then I moved forward, looking away so she wouldn't see me roll my eyes. After all, who would be coming after a Remnant, here, in the heart of their own fortress? Or perhaps she was edgy because she'd accepted watch duty from Ronan and felt the added responsibility.

Or maybe she felt sorry for me. Orphaned now, as she was once, my parents gone.

I leaned against the short barrier, forcing myself to look down, to think about a fall. The cliff dropped a good fifty feet below before hitting another ledge — I could see a few armed guards among the boulders below — and then dropped again for a thousand feet. Higher, so much higher than the Zanzibian wall, than the towering cedars of the Valley I'd been forced to climb. I welcomed the familiar terror, the sickness in my throat, the tightening of my chest. Anything, anything to think about other than my parents. Even this old, familiar panic was better than that pain. The rain clouds directly in front of us had dumped their load and were disappearing as we watched, steadily lifting, gliding past. I closed my eyes and absorbed the sensation of nothingness below my boots, the sensation of utter space all around me, after the cramped confines within the mountain city behind us. Felt my belly clench. Knew my breath was coming in short pants.

"What are you two doing up here?" Niero asked, standing on a rock up and to my right. I gasped and felt a wave of vertigo, seeing him standing there. One half step shy of that fall.

How had we not heard him climb up? Or seen him when he came out beside us? It was as if the clouds had deposited him as they dispersed.

"Whoa, Niero, what are *you* doing?" Bellona looked angry and a bit pale, which made me smile a little. Hardly anything got her upset besides Vidar's teasing.

"Don't like heights either?" he asked, his tone mildly curious.

"I don't like taking careless risks," she clarified, leveling a gaze at him.

Niero smiled, then picked up a pebble and flicked it over and off the edge, watching it fall. Was this an object lesson? An attempt to show me how to conquer my fear by modeling complete trust, or something? I looked away from him, but could feel his eyes move to me, could feel his gentle, probing, insistent summons.

I sighed and finally met his gaze. But I shivered at what I saw. His eyes were so wise, so keen. So full of peace and confidence, as if they held a thousand years of knowledge rather than his two decades. I sat up straight and studied him, feeling the first emotions I'd felt from him, really — besides the rage against Sethos — and the first emotion since despair had so wracked me.

Concern. Care. Hope. And something I just couldn't quite put my finger on.

"Niero, are you sure you're not Ailith?"

He smiled and looked out to the clouds. "Yes. I'm sure."

"And you are not a knight?"

"Not of the Last Order, no. You Ailith are unique. But we are all called to this task before us." He jumped down to the alcove, landing beside me, and then gestured for me to come closer. "You may leave us, Bellona. I will see Andriana back to her quarters."

She left without further word, but not before I read the odd twining of relief and resentment within her; she liked being off duty, but disliked being cut out.

We stood in silence for several minutes, side by side. Then he asked in a soft tone, "Are you doubting your Call, Andriana?"

I watched as the clouds swirled before us, still clearing to reveal portions of the mountains and then gathering again. "I'm doubting everything right now," I mumbled. "May I have permission to do that?" I asked, glancing at him, eyebrows raised. "A day to mourn my kin? The people who loved me most? Roil around in the torn bits left to me before I allow the Maker to weave them back together? Do I get to be *human* for just a day?"

"You may do what you wish. But you are called to more."

The feelings flooded back. Irritation. Rage. Sorrow. Fear. Confusion.

I turned toward him. "Can you not just leave me be? At least until morning?" I said, tapping against his hard, broad chest.

He was immovable, standing there, taking it. Looking down at me with nothing but compassion and love and understanding, which made me all the angrier. Now, of all times, he was allowing me to read him? Because why? He felt sorry for me?

"Do you know what it is to lose someone, Niero? Someone you loved with everything in you?" I asked, feeling tears stream once again. "Someone who loved you just the same?"

He didn't blink. The muscles in his cheeks twitched. "I do," he whispered.

I felt the breaking within him and it drew me, that shared moment of understanding. I was in his arms then, enveloped, cradled, held, which both choked me with gladness and frustration. I shoved weakly against him, but found him impossible to move. He didn't release me and, after a bit of flailing, I gave up.

"Do you know what it is to lose your memory?" I asked, forcing the words past my tightening throat, leaning my cheek against his shoulder. "The core of who you are? My parents, Mom and Dad, they held me," I said, gripping him now, clinging to him. "Held me as a baby. Watched me walk, talk. Eat.

Laugh. Cry. Play. They taught me my first everything. I don't remember those firsts. I don't," I said, shaking my head, knowing I was babbling. "They held me, Niero. *Held* me. Loved me. All they did wrong was love me, protect me, prepare me. And for that, they're dead."

I melted then, shuddering through my sobs. And just as I felt my knees would buckle and I'd fall, he pulled me tighter, as if willing his strength, his courage, his *hope* into me. My armband hummed and its warmth spread through me, as if responding in pleasure to his presence. He held me not as a lover, but as tenderly and fiercely as a mother caught standing in a storm with her bundled newborn. And in his grip, my weeping ended, my tears dried, my heart lifted.

I squirmed and he let me loose, but not entirely away. I looked up at him, staring into his dark, lilting eyes again, trying to make sense of what I'd just felt. "What ... Niero, what was *that*?"

He gave me a small smile, but kept a grip on my upper arms, looking intently into my eyes. "Andriana, your parents were the first to love you, but they will not be the last. You are seen and loved by the Maker, as he loved your parents even before you were even born. He will see you all reunited in time." He paused, waiting for me to nod. "Trust, Andriana. You are not forgotten."

"Dri?" I looked up and saw Ronan in the doorway, relief sliding across his face at finally finding me.

But still Niero held on to me, never looking at Ronan, and waited until my eyes returned to his. "Andriana, no matter how it feels — and hear this well, because it is most important for you — no matter how it *feels*, you must rely on what you *know*. What you've been taught by your protectors, your elders, your fellow Ailith. In the battle ahead … Andriana, it will be vital. Do you understand me?"

I hesitated. So much about my mind and heart was becoming centered on how I felt. Feelings dominated my every waking moment, especially since I received the Ailith armband. I couldn't simply turn off my feelings, could I? Wasn't he asking the impossible?"

"Raniero, you've made your point," Ronan said, coming closer, using his full name as he'd taken to doing when he was agitated. "Let her go now."

"Andriana …" Niero said, clenching down on my arms, ignoring him. "Tell me. Tell me you've heard me."

I looked up and stared into those old eyes in a young man's face. What did he want? Why the intensity?

"Yes, yes, I heard you," I said.

"Good," he said, dropping his hands, still looking at me as if he wanted to will his thoughts into my own mind. "Good."

CHAPTER 10

We left at daybreak on the four dirt bikes, with packs of new supplies to trade.

"You have enough petrol to reach Nem Post, no farther," an elder said. "We've heard reports that someone's running petrol north of the salt caves. It will be a handicap, this need for fuel. But they are much faster than your enemies' horses."

"Unless they manage to find dirt bikes too," Vidar said, waggling his eyebrows.

"They are good machines and cost the Community greatly."

A blind elder of perhaps eight decades stepped closer, hanging on a man's arm. "As you travel, the Maker shall speak into you. Advise you as you go to find your fellow Ailith, as well as prepare the way for our coming king."

We stilled. Her words thrilled us. The hope in them, the promise. A king?

"We are to send the Maker's people to the Valley as we go?" Niero asked.

"Send them if they are in danger," she said, "or if the Maker urges you to do so. If they are safe where they are, prepare them to follow and support Kapriel and the one who is to come. That is what the Maker has told me."

I thought about what she told us. How Tyree and Clennan knew they were to come with us. As we did too. I hoped the others we came across would be as obvious.

"May your path be swift and sure," said another elder, taking Niero's arm, then mine, then Ronan's and onward. "Know you are not alone. The Maker travels with you. And while you may be far from us, know that our hearts are with you. We shall pray for your protection, your direction, without ceasing."

We rode as pairs on the dirt bikes, Vidar and Bellona on the first — Vidar driving, since we were relying on his gift of discernment to lead us away from any Sheolites — Ronan and I on the next, Killian and Tressa on the third, and Niero on the last.

The Sheolites who'd murdered my protectors had apparently left the Valley, tracking us outward. Even now, I hoped they were in Zanzibar, still seeking us there, rather than in the desert. Hopefully the Lord of Zanzibar would keep refusing to admit his walls had been breached, and they'd search and search, finding only Tressa's empty hospital below ground.

We reached Tonna's Nem Post by noon, marveling at our speed, but the tradeoff was the dirt and mud that coated our hair, skin, and clothes as result of debris thrown up by the bikes that went before us. I could tell that Ronan tried to avoid the spray, often steering the bike to one side of the road or the other rather than directly behind Vidar. But before we left the Valley's narrow trails, we'd been pelted repeatedly.

We paused and waited for the guards to approach on their horses, knowing if we drove right in they were liable to shoot.

Niero looked to Vidar, then back to the tent camp. "Sense anything?"

Vidar frowned and shook his head. "Just a hint. Another shadow. I don't think there are any Sheolites there now."

"You people have a lot of guts coming back here," said a guard who continued to eye me and Bellona like raw mudhorse steaks, even covered in our filth. "Ever since, Pacifica scouts have been here like a plague. Every day they ask if we've heard word of or seen travelers who've been to Zanzibar and back." He eyed us all, grinning as if he had us. "Their description sounds pretty much like you folk."

Niero looked forward, to the post. "Any scouts or trackers here now?" he asked evenly. I wondered how he did that — appear unmoved — when my own heart was pounding.

"Four left this morning, heading north."

My heart pounded. North. We hadn't seen anyone, but around noon, Vidar had led us away from the main Trader trail and through a long, ancient, now-dry riverbed. Had they been what Vidar sensed? It could mean they were heading north and east, into the Valley. I prayed that there were enough guards posted to fight off warriors like the Sheolites, that the Maker would warn them too. I shuddered, remembering the scouts that had attacked us in the forest the night of our call, and the tracker in Zanzibar. Our training had made us feel safe, with an extra layer of protection. But if our fellow Ailith — Keallach and Kapriel — had received the same instruction, and prepared their soldiers to counter our defenses, then how safe were we? The Nem Post guard had no idea how dangerous those scouts were to us; perhaps because his own foul heart resonated too easily with them.

"We need to speak to Tonna," Niero said.

"I don't see the mudhorses you owe her," he tossed back, shifting the gun in his hands.

"We've brought other supplies she'll be interested in."

"We'll see about that. Tonna's none too pleased about the trackers. And without the horses —"

"Just be about your business," Niero said. "And pass along our inquiry to Tonna. We will wait here."

"'Be about your business and inquire,'" he mocked. "Aren't you the uppity one?"

Niero waited him out, staring at him benignly, and the man finally turned his mare and casually moved back to the post on the back of his mudhorse, leaving the three others to guard us.

We waited for long minutes in the rain, but at last a flag was raised. We'd been permitted entry.

I sighed in relief. Because there was one main thing we needed from Tonna — petrol. Our fuel gauges were all hovering on empty. Or lower; Vidar's engine refused to start when we moved forward, so we all turned off our engines and walked the bikes forward.

She waited for us in the space between her tent and the others, arms crossed, her eyes squinting in a deeper glare the closer we got to her. "Do you have any idea how much trouble you've caused me?" she asked Niero.

"I beg your forgiveness, friend," he said.

"Yes, well, let's hope you've come as traders rather than beggars." She looked down at his bike and then slowly took in the others. "Yamahas," she grunted. "Did you bring these as replacements for my mudhorses?"

"Now, Tonna," Niero said with a patient smile, "you know you received more than enough from our packs to pay for the horses, passage, and more."

"Did I?" she said, raising brown brows in irritation. "I'm not so sure."

"I am," he said, pushing the kickstand out and perching the bike at the side of Tonna's tent. "Now, should we conduct our next deal or shall we be on our way to Tah Post?"

"You know as well as I do that you don't have the petrol to get there," she said. "You carry empty cans, by the lift of them. Best come in and we'll see if we can come to a deal. Can't give you shelter, though," she said over her shoulder as we followed her in. "If they find you here, I'll lose my trader permits."

"That's all right. We intend to cover some miles before nightfall," Niero said. "Can you tell me more about the scouts and any others who have been asking after us?"

"Yes. The first arrived the night you were here. Then scouts, every day, all originating from Pacifica," she said, taking a seat on a table. "You wouldn't want to tell me why they're hunting you, would ya?"

"No," Niero said, with another disarming smile.

"Figured. They were closedmouthed about it too. I'm just trying to figure out how people of the Valley have gotten Pacifica so upset. Each kingdom in the Trading Union keeps to her own. Why do they care about you?"

"That is the question, isn't it?" Niero said, taking his pack from his shoulders and beginning to unlace the top.

Tonna grunted. "Well, if you aren't going to trade information, you surely'd better be carrying valuables I want."

After Niero waved his assent, I pulled out of our pack bundles of dried mushrooms, wild onion, and garlic, their smell so rich and so quick to fill the tent, it made me remember the soups Dad used to make. Thoughts of him made me sick with longing, and the memory of yesterday's despair made my eyes burn. I ducked my head and bent in to dig for more, not wanting anyone to see. There was mint, asparagus, and Mudhorse Weed. Tressa had twin oil-burning lamps fashioned from sheep horn, a woven blanket — softer than anything I'd ever felt — and twelve skeins of wool.

Vidar shook his head, lifting Bellona's heavy pack off her shoulders. "Sheesh, what'd you do to the old man that he hates *you* so much?" he grunted to Bellona, wrestling out one piece of heavy machinery after another and setting them side by side. I had no idea what they were. Did Tonna?

"I don't know," Bellona said, rubbing her shoulders. "But I'm going to feel the ache from their weight for a few days."

The day's trail had been grueling enough, with the bumps and dips and swerving. I couldn't imagine holding on to Ronan and carrying such a heavy pack all day. My admiration for Bellona increased.

Niero pulled a small, heavy chest from his pack and set it down with a *clunk*.

Lifting a brow, Tonna reached forward and unclasped the latch, opening the lid. Slowly, she opened it, and I think we all inhaled sharply at the sight. For inside were fifty or more gold coins, all with a woman's head on the front, in profile, wearing a crown. Tonna cast a wary eye up at Niero and reached for one, lifted it to what remained of her small, yellow teeth, and bit on it as her eyes greedily washed over the rest.

Niero smiled then. "You see, Tonna. It is good to do business with us. We wish to trade for petrol. But we also wish to purchase safe-passage papers again. Papers for *anywhere* we wish to go."

CHAPTER
11

In the end, Tonna wouldn't write our safe-passage papers for beyond the Wall. Only among the Trading Union, outside of Pacifica's border. She'd looked at Niero as if he were crazy when he'd mentioned Pacifica. "You know they're out for your blood, right?"

"Clearly," he'd returned.

She'd just shaken her head. Niero told us he took what he could get, figuring the Maker would show us a way beyond the Wall and into Pacifica once we got there.

We drove for hours along the tattered remains of a long, straight road, through expanses of land devoid of anything but the occasional red stone butte, eroded by rain and wind. Here the rain fell, bringing green to the red soil that stretched for miles. All of us kept searching the horizon for other dirt bikes or the big vehicles Tonna warned us the Drifters favored, ready to move to higher ground if necessary. But it wasn't until we'd crested a long, slow rise that we saw a town below, hugging the edge of a river that carved its way through the desert.

Niero motioned for us all to pull over to one side of the road, and we stood there, drinking from our canteens, filling our dirt bikes with one of our extra tanks of petrol, and watching for any signs of life below.

"Think anyone's there?" Ronan asked Niero, as he pulled his scope down from his eye.

"I see a few goats. That means there must be a shepherd hiding nearby."

"Probably jumped inside at the sound of our engines," Vidar said.

"Wise man," Bellona said, "if there are Drifters about." She flipped her thick braid over her shoulder.

"There's someone else there," Tressa said, looking down at the town. "Someone I need to see."

"Need to *see*-see?" Killian asked, bending his dreadlock-covered head to get a better look at her face.

She nodded softly, never looking his way. Her expression was a little eerie — distant, almost ethereal — and in response, Killian's hard edge softened.

We all took another look at the small, ancient gathering of buildings. Ronan reached for Niero's scope and peered through it. The town was like countless others among the Trading Union — roofs blown off, walls down, streets overgrown with bush and tree. It wasn't a post or settlement. Other than a few goats, it looked abandoned.

"It could be a trap," Vidar said. "Drifters waiting on us to come in and glean, then springing out to nab us."

Raniero continued to look down at the town, arms folded. "Any of you sense true enemies?"

I shook my head and so did the others.

Niero turned and straddled his bike. "Only one way to find out for sure," he said with a smile, putting his goggles on again. "Tressa, you drive your bike. Same with you, Andriana. I want your knights able to access their weapons with both hands if necessary."

We did as he said, following him down the road at a slower pace than we'd been going, this time with Vidar and Bellona bringing up the rear. I concentrated on following Raniero's back wheel, rather than my growing fear of a potential trap. If Tressa was right and we'd been called to this road in order to come across the remains of this town, so that she could heal someone here, then would the Maker himself not be keeping watch over us?

We finally reached the ramshackle town. Old, rusted, corrugated metal on one roof — half peeled away — waved in the wind, making a terrible screeching sound. Most of the buildings were crumbling adobe, only a few with more than two standing walls. Niero pulled up a hundred feet from the only one with a roof and we alongside him. In seconds, all of us could all be away. But now we fanned out in a small arc, checking out the town. I could see the remains of an old, massive cannon — still pointed to the sky — at one end, in the middle of a crumbling wall that once circled the ancient weapon. We'd seen others. At one time, they'd protected their townspeople. Until bombs were dropped with vapors that carried on the wind, killing those that didn't even see it fall.

Vidar pulled out a small toxicity reader from his belt, and we could hear the static and warped signals as he waved it over the ground in front of him. For more than a hundred years after the bombs, huge spans of land had been unlivable — or proved deadly to those who tried. "Decent," he muttered. "Not perfect. But decent."

"Hello in the house!" Niero called, pulling his goggles up to his head again. "We mean you no harm! Is anyone there?"

A goat turned the corner and stood there, chewing long stems of sage.

I glanced behind us, up the road. How had the goats remained unclaimed if there wasn't a goatherd nearby?

The door slammed open and an old woman appeared. "You get on!" she yelled, waving a rifle about. "Get on outta here unless you have goods to trade for cheese!"

Ronan and I shared a look. Cheese?

"We have goods," Raniero said. "We intend no harm, friend. We are about the Maker's business."

"Yeah? Which maker?"

"I think you know of Whom I speak."

She gaped at him, and I could see for the first time that her eyes were milky white. "You move on! I'll have no trouble over such talk! Go. Go!"

"But I am to heal your eyes," Tressa said, stepping forward.

"Eh?" she asked, the folds of her face gathering in confusion. "What's that you said?"

"Your eyes," Tressa said, taking another step. Killian followed, just to her right. "The Maker wishes to bring back your vision."

The woman stepped out from under the shade of the roof, and I could see she wasn't as old as I'd thought. She appeared to be only six decades, but she looked weathered, as if they had more sun here than rain. Perhaps they did, I thought idly. "You witches? Warlocks?" she called, waving her gun again. But this time with a little hesitation.

141

"No, friend," Niero said, glancing from the old woman to Tressa and back again. "Today you will know the power of the Maker. For he wishes to bring you back your dearest gift — your eyesight — through Tressa, who has the high gift of healing."

She lowered her rifle, considering him and Tressa and Killian as they drew near, the rest of us hanging back so she wouldn't feel overwhelmed. Her mouth fell open. "You tell the truth," she said, staring up at Raniero with eyes such a pure opaque they looked like pearls. Her mouth went a bit slack. "I've been asking and asking the Maker "

"And he has answered you," Niero said, taking her elbow when she looked as if she might faint.

"Oh," she said, bringing a freckled hand to her chest. "Oh! But not me, sir. Not me. You must heal my grandson."

Raniero looked to Tressa in confusion. But she shook her head and nodded at the old woman.

"You first, friend," he said, gently. "Then we shall see about your boy." He looked back at us. "I'm not sure how long this will take. You and Andriana take up position where you can see to the north," he told Ronan. "Vidar, you and Bellona go back up the hill and keep an eye on the south." With that, he disappeared inside, leaving us to do as we were told.

Reluctantly, we left them, feeling ill at ease in separating, but with clear orders. And with the little town on a low part of a long saddle, it was wise to get to points we could watch. I started the engine and Ronan slid on behind me. I liked the feel of his legs lining mine, the bulk of his body behind me. I only wished he would wrap his arms around me as I tended to do around him whenever I was on the bike. Instead, he sat rigidly upright, only his hands upon my shoulders, as if he feared touching me. That wariness I felt … Was it me? Or our strange surroundings?

I resisted the urge to pretend to falter, to alarm him into reaching forward and holding on to me. *Quit it, Dri.* I had no business fantasizing about such things. No business at all. But with him so close, how was I to keep from such ideas? *Help me, Maker ... Make me strong where I am weak.*

I clamped my lips together and drove as straight as I could, around potholes and over breaks, to the northern hill where Niero wanted us stationed. Once there, I pulled to the side, glad to see that there were a few boulders. With luck, we could gain some shade from the sun that seemed intent on keeping clear of the drifting cloudbanks. Ronan got off, and I used the toe of my boot to push the kickstand into place. I shielded my eyes and looked in a long, slow circle, as he did. The only living things we saw were the three goats beside the house, and in the distance, Vidar and Bellona standing on the ribbon of battered road.

"Strange country, huh?" Ronan said, crouching and picking up a handful of the black substance that had once held the road together.

"We're a long way from home," I said.

"They called this road a highway."

"Yeah," I said. I'd seen the sign too, rusted and upside-down on a post. "They used to crisscross the country."

He looked down the length of it, squinting. "I wonder how many are left, this intact."

"Guess we'll find out. I mean, at least about some of them." I rubbed the back of my neck and found it sweaty, and shrugged out of my oilskin jacket, draping it over the bike. Then, still finding I was warm, I pulled off my sweater, leaving just my T-shirt beneath. I hurriedly straightened it out, feeling my cheeks heat as it lifted up my belly, flashing bare skin. My eyes flicked over to Ronan to find out if he'd seen.

Face muscles tight, he quickly looked away from me and rose, walking around the width of the boulder. To what? Get away from me?

I sighed and leaned against the side of the boulder, raising my face to the sun. The heat of it wasn't intense. It felt good, warming my skin and arms. I looked down at my armband and wished I could clean off the grime and see it again as it was meant to be — a jewel of interwoven metals. But even in its diminished state, it was pretty impressive. I fingered the edge, noting my healing skin at the edge. I tried to get a fingernail between it and the skin and winced. A tiny drop of blood formed where I'd pulled.

I lifted my eyebrows. Apparently, the Maker wanted us to never be without our cuffs. They'd become part of us.

Ronan finished his walk around the rock and saw what I was doing. "Yours fused like mine?"

"Yes. Don't you find it a bit ... odd?"

"I'd say *everything* about our lives is a *lot* odd. The fact that we have jewelry fused to our skin and a friend who seems to think she can make the blind see is just the latest verses of the song." He grinned at me and then turned to pull off his oilskin, wiping his forehead of sweat. Then he yanked off his own wool sweater, and I spied more skin than I'd ever seen in fifteen seasons together. The flash of a flat belly. A broad, finely muscled chest ... the small hollow at the base of his neck, formed by a taut muscle and sinew ...

"Andriana?" he asked.

His Adam's apple bobbed and I finally met his eyes, then rushed to turn away in flushed embarrassment. "Yeah?" Had he really just caught me staring at his neck? Had I been that obvious?

"You okay?" he asked, coming closer, behind me.

"What? Yeah. Fine," I said, lifting a shoulder in a little shrug, daring to look over at him. His eyes were trailing down the length of my arm, and I felt the draw within him, the heat, pulling me back around. And in recognizing his draw for me, my own mushroomed. It so stunned me, overwhelmed me — the pulse of attraction between us — that I literally froze for a moment.

"Andriana ..." he whispered, lifting a hand. To touch me. To touch me!

"Hey," I forced out brightly, walking backward as he rubbed the back of his neck — as if that had been his only intent. "Did you see anything on the far side of the rock?"

"No, I uh ... It drops off in a valley over there," he said, following me, his eyes so soulful, so yearning, meeting mine for a breath. I paused, my feet feeling stuck. He shoved his hands into his trouser pockets. But the hope, the need, the want was so intense in that moment that neither of us seemed able to move. We simply stood there, staring at each other for one breath, two, three, four ...

"Maybe I, uh ..." he said, his voice cracking, "I, uh, I think I should go take a quick look again. You know. Over there. Scout it out."

Fear was rising between us. Terror. And yet it was welcome, like cool rain on this crazy desert heat. Stamping out the embers of a fire on the verge of igniting new timber.

"Sure, sure," I said. "Good idea."

"You'll be all right here, by yourself, for a few minutes?" he asked hurriedly as we finished our circle around the boulder and came out on the roadside again.

"I think I can manage lookout duty on my own."

He reached for my sword, in a sheath attached to the bike, and tossed it to me, keeping me at max distance. "Out here, you can see anyone coming for miles."

"Yeah. I can shout if I see anyone."

"Do." He gave me a brief, curious, searching look, then took off running, as if I might chase him down. I edged around the rock to watch him go, admiring the breadth of his shoulders and triceps as he jogged over and around the dunes with his twin swords crisscrossed on his back, heading toward the edge of a small canyon. I made myself turn back and do a long, slow sweep of the horizon again. Vidar and Bellona were sitting in the center of the highway, back to back, knees up. They weren't as lucky to find boulders beside their lookout point.

That was close. I let out a long, slow breath, fighting the urge to peek at Ronan again. We hadn't been that close to a *moment* for a couple of seasons. I'd almost decided it was all in the past, maybe even made up in my imagination. That there hadn't been anything then, and wouldn't be again.

But no. It was there. It was definitely there. And there'd been that second in Zanzibar when he'd had his hands in my hair ... Remembering it made my heart both surge with joy and squeeze in fear.

I looked up to the sun and became aware again of its intense beams. I didn't know if I'd ever been hot in my life. Was the heat possibly making us a little crazy? Unbalanced? I'd never seen this many consecutive minutes of the sun. To center my mind, I lifted my sword and did some stretches, making a figure-eight, turning and jabbing as if surprising an opponent, then abruptly turning and doing the same thing in the opposite direction. Panting, I turned the sword tip downward and rested my hand on the hilt.

I glanced toward the town below me, and the house in which Niero, Killian, and Tressa had disappeared. Back in Zanzibar, the healing had taken but a breath or two of time. We'd been here a half hour already. What if —

A scream echoed up from the town. A second later, the old woman ran out of the house, arms stretched out. She continued a long, terrified cry, turning in a slow circle outside, hands on her head. My heart pounded. What had happened?

Then she lifted her hands to the sun and dropped to her knees as my companions came to the door and followed her outward. Were they laughing? I wondered if I heard the light sound of it on the breeze. But the old woman was up on her feet again and running up the hill, directly toward me, the three goats following behind her, bleating as if they were complaining that she was abandoning them.

On and on she came, until Raniero caught up with her and offered her a ride, while Tressa and Killian mounted their own bike. They reached me in seconds, and I smiled at the utter joy I saw in the woman's clear eyes, now like warm, polished brown granite. She got off Niero's bike and ran past me, smiling and screaming again. But this time, I heard a name on her lips. *Ignacio.* Tressa and Killian raced after her, taking the same path Ronan had earlier.

"Andriana, where's Ronan?" Raniero asked in confusion. His frown deepened as he looked over my bare arms and spied the band.

"He, uh, went to scout that area over there," I said, feeling like I should've come up with another story as I sheathed my sword on my belt. Our leader wouldn't like it that my knight left me alone, even if I was armed and the only enemy in sight was a tiny brown scorpion, his tail curved into attack mode. But then he didn't know what had almost happened.

I strode after Niero, my feet sinking in the silky soil, sweat trickling down my back, trying to get an emotional read on him but getting nothing but a vague mix of frustration and glory. Anger at Ronan plus the joyful remains of being a part of the woman's healing? Why was he so much more difficult for me to read than the others?

I looked to my right and saw Vidar and Bellona already on their bike and headed in our direction, up the highway. Maybe if they reached us, Raniero would sense greater safety and calm down before he reached Ronan.

I ran down the path after him, knowing the other two would know where we'd left the road and follow. It appeared the canyon sloped downward on just the other side of the saddle. But when I reached the rise, I saw that it dropped quite a ways. A narrow path hugged the cliff to the right — apparently where the goats walked back and forth. I slowed and leaned hard to my right, wishing there were handholds, my heart pounding as much from the ground falling away beneath the path at a steep angle as from my exertion.

I could hear them before I reached them. But when I turned the corner, my mouth opened in surprise. Because a young boy of perhaps a decade was hugging the old woman as they turned in a hopping circle, eyes alight, laughing. And more animals than I'd ever seen hovered about — a hundred goats occupied every single crevice and foothold in the rocks in the narrow bowl of the cliff.

Their methods were clear. Her grandson tended the goats, far from the road, where she kept a few sacrificial animals in case the Drifters came through. As a result, the Maker had blessed them, granting them a growing herd that could sustain a whole village.

The old woman leaned down and the child put a small, brown hand on either side of her face, staring into her eyes. I could sense the wonder and amazement and praise within them without even trying. Perhaps it didn't take the gift to read such joy. After this kind of event, all I knew was that I couldn't stop smiling myself.

At last, the old woman paused, wiped the tears from her cheeks, and brought the boy over to Tressa. It was then that I saw the odd angle of the child's foot and knew why his own hopping had been with an odd gait. The foot must've been broken at some point and had healed poorly, at an angle that had to cause its own measure of pain. I looked back and forth along the narrow, treacherous trail that the boy followed each day to tend to his goats. It was a miracle he hadn't tumbled to his death long ago.

Tressa took the boy's bare foot in her hands and ran her thin, elegant fingers over the bones, over the skin stretched taut from the odd curve, across toes pulled into what looked like a painful arc. She closed her eyes, and the wave of compassion and longing I felt from her nearly took my breath away. But it was Niero's long, steady glance, what I felt emanating from him, that really captured me, encircled me, filled me. "Believe, Ailith," he said to us all. "Believe that the Maker, who spoke each of you into existence, can right that which has gone wrong in our bodies, just as he is about to in young Ignacio here."

My armband hummed, growing even warmer under the heat of the sun — or no, now from within. Vidar abruptly turned and stared hard at Niero, his dark eyes searching our leader from head to toe, his forehead wrinkling in confusion, eyes blinking rapidly, and again I felt a wave of an emotion I was trying to name in my heart —

Ignacio cried out as Tressa brought her other hand to his foot, closing her eyes and lifting her face to the sun.

"Ahyeeeee!"

The old woman cried out too, out of terror, even wonder, at the same moment the emotion from Niero and Tressa reached me as well, enveloping me as clearly as if I might be wrapped in a cocoon. Vidar was looking up, above us, to the edge of the cliff, eyes wide as if he could see something else, but all I could really focus on was the amazing sense of peace and love that was flowing from Raniero and Tressa and surrounding all of us.

And then it was done.

Ignacio yelped, his big, round eyes wide in his thin face. He smiled, his teeth spread in wide gaps. But my eyes were on his foot. Because there, in Tressa's hands, it was at the correct angle again, as it was meant to be.

And it was perfect.

CHAPTER 12

"hy do you stay here?" Vidar asked. "In this place, so far from any others?"

"We have been trapped for generations," the old woman, Zulema, said. "Beholden to the Drifters who come each week and bring us just enough supplies to make it through, and take everything else. Even my daughter and her husband. Ignacio's sisters too. They only left me Ignacio so that we could continue to make the cheese."

We were all silent a moment, stricken at the thought of repeated kidnappings and loss.

"But they haven't taken your goats," Bellona said at last, gesturing toward the canyon where the herd remained.

"Ignacio is good at hiding them," Zulema said proudly. "They're well aware that there must be more, for every week we give them a few to take with them. Though as long as we have a few ready for them, as well as rounds of cheese, they leave the rest alone. They call it a tithe."

"You are prisoners, in a way," I said.

Zulema's dark eyes met mine. She nodded once, and in the lines of her face I saw countless weeks, months, years of fear and trial, and a price extracted from her that was deeper than imagination allowed. Ignacio was clearly the last of her family. What had happened to the others?

"How long until the Drifters come to collect their next tithe?" Niero asked.

"Three or four days. We never know for certain. We are only to be ready, always ready," she said wearily.

Niero searched the skies, where gray storm clouds gathered. "Your time of captivity is nearly over, sister," Niero said. "Come the end of Harvest, we shall return to you and take you with us to the Valley."

"Wait?" she said, blinking slowly. "I don't think so. We must go now."

Niero dropped his chin and stared at her a moment. "I believe you are right, though it will be dangerous."

"Life is dangerous," she said. "But I have my eyesight and my little grandson a good foot, do we not? The Maker will see us through."

Niero smiled. "Gather a week's supplies and your goats and find the most hidden trails possible through the canyons until you reach the Central Desert. If you can avoid the Drifters and cross that flat land at night, you will enter the sanctuary of the forest by morning, and in the Valley our bretheren will keep you safe. There you must teach our people your talent in keeping such a herd alive."

"And growing," Zulema said proudly, sliding a crooked and age-spotted hand across Ignacio's shoulders.

"And growing," Niero said with a smile.

"I hope those goats like Mudhorse Weed," Vidar said, crossing his arms.

"Do you joke? My goats eat anything," Ignacio said.

"You must tell no one of what has occurred," Raniero said. "Speak not of your healing, nor of meeting us. Do you understand?"

Zulema and Ignacio nodded, their faces betraying their fear, confusion. I knew they wondered why they must keep such secrets — about wonders that had brought them such joy. But I also knew what Niero was after — our safety. If word got out about such signs and wonders, of Tressa's high gift, we might be mobbed by those seeking healing. Worse, our enemies would have no difficulty finding us.

"Travel at night. Not during the day," he said, touching her arm as if she were a treasured aunt, and frowning in concern. "When you reach the Valley, tell them that I sent you and you will be looked after."

"You tell that Jorre at Tah Post to treat *you* well," she said, sliding a baby goat into Niero's arms. "He used to be a friend, when we were free to trade." His pack was already full of rounds of her goods for us. If we could've taken them, she would've given us far more; the sense of freedom and excitement — *hope* — within her surged, making her more than generous.

Raniero smiled and turned to put the squirming goat in my arms. I wrinkled my nose at his gamey scent, but took hold, knowing how valuable he was. Tressa held another. Quickly, Ignacio showed us how to bind the kids so we could slide them into our packs, their little heads sticking out, so we need not fear they'd try and jump out.

"My goats are good animals," Ignacio said. "I hope they find good homes." His eyes trailed down to his foot, and he practiced rolling his toes and straightening them, staring as if he still couldn't quite believe it was true.

I laughed, looking at the small, pale round eyes of my baby goat before I hauled the arm straps over my shoulders. "Thank you for the gift of your goats, little brother." I straddled the bike behind Ronan and turned toward Ignacio. "Take close care of your grandmother."

"I will," he said solemnly. His face split in a grin. "My new foot will make me fast!"

■ ■ ■

Tah Post, where we found shelter late that night, felt similar to Nem Post, in that it was a tent village well guarded by heavily armed men. An unseen leader — the man Zulema had called Jorre — greeted Raniero in the privacy of his tent, and relieved us of both our baby goats and all our cheese. A servant showed us into a large tent to sleep for the night, and we collapsed on piles of buffalo skins, pulling others atop us as the chill of the desert night tried to infiltrate our bones.

But it was with some surprise I awoke to the sounds of children. Many children. Babies crying, toddlers giggling, older ones shrieking in play. I frowned in confusion, wondering if I was yet dreaming. I hadn't heard the sounds of children since I'd left my village. In the Citadel, I'd only spotted two, each about a decade old. No others.

Were there families here? Women? We were a day's ride from Zanzibar, close enough for raiders to come and take their pick.

I looked around at my companions. Only Niero was awake, the rest still wearily slumbering away. He was kneeling in morning meditation, his back perfectly straight, his face upturned, a hint of a smile on his lips. His eyes moved beneath the lids as if seeking, seeing. I looked to the others, aware that I was staring at him, reaching out to read him, and it felt like I was intruding into a sacred space, a place I should only go if invited. My eyes ran over Vidar, on his side, one arm curled beneath his head, the other atop it. Bellona, mouth open, breathing loudly. Killian and Tressa, curled toward each other and but a foot apart. And Ronan, his face twitching, as if encountering battle in his dreams. Perhaps I'd caught up more on my sleep while in the Citadel, and wasn't in such grave need of more. Niero and I might have to shake the other Ailith awake.

I sat up, flipping back the warm skin, and pulled on my sweater, then my boots. I slipped to the ground, to my knees, and stretched out my arms above my head, bowing deeply. *Thank you for this morning, Maker. I commit this day to you and yours. Live and breathe and move through me. Make my day your own.* I sighed and stretched and then rose, waiting for Niero to meet my gaze.

When he did, I lifted my chin toward the door, silently asking his permission to go and use the outhouse. He rose, already fully dressed, and led the way, apparently unwilling to let me go alone. As I stepped through the flaps of the tent, Ronan called to me in a voice heavy with sleep.

"I'll go with her," Niero whispered over his shoulder. "Rest." I felt a wave of emotion move from him to Ronan, and started. What was *that*? Reassurance? Peace?

Whatever the man was emoting, it was all it took for Ronan. In two seconds he was breathing so deeply he was almost snoring, and I smiled at his handsome profile, his dark hair — loosed from its customary band — in a shiny, deep wave beside his head.

"Dri," Niero grunted in irritation outside, any semblance of peace evaporating. I jumped, remembering myself, and bent to exit the short door, avoiding his eyes. "This way," he said, pausing to let two children, chasing one another, pass before him.

I smiled and watched them go, spotting the baby goat with others, then followed Niero toward three outhouses on the edge of the tents. "This is more a village than a post," I said. "There are *families* here? How do they keep the Zanzibians away?"

"The power of trade," Niero said, reaching one of three outhouses first, checking it for me before gesturing inward. "And a trader with a softer heart than is healthy for him. I fear he'll be overtaken." His dark eyes shifted over three little girls, skipping together, hands interlocked.

I closed and tied the door shut, wondering what he could mean about a heart too soft to be healthy. And afterward, as we paused by the stream to wash our hands and splash our faces, he began to tell me what he knew. "Tonna told me that Jorre has five wives," he said in a whisper, pausing as two children filled large earthen jars with water. I watched as they balanced them on their heads and padded off on bare feet back to their tents, even though their curious eyes said they wanted to stay with us.

"Five wives?" I whispered.

"Each were widows with children, wandering the Central Desert when he found them," he said, scrubbing his hands, picking dirt from beneath his nails, and scrubbing his hands yet more. "They would have been kidnapped by Drifters, or Zanzibians, and their male children immediately dispatched. As a trader, he keeps them all safe. Both the Drifters and the Zanzibians respect him too much, need him too much, to steal them away. So here he sits, a trader of the desert, in nothing but tents, with his ever-burgeoning family."

I frowned in confusion. It was against the ways of the Community to marry more than one person. We mated once, and for life. But how could I argue with what Jorre had done? I'd seen the depravity that faced women in the city. And all these little girls … I counted five, just within my direct view.

A big belly laugh greeted us as we shook our hands dry and turned back to the tents. "My friend, my friend," said a man, turning to Niero. He carried a thin boy over his shoulders and a babe in his arms. "I finally am allowed to greet your friends," he said. He was a huge man of about three decades, with rolls of fat at both his neck and arm, and a smile that displayed many missing teeth. He shifted the boy to the ground and passed off the baby to him, then folded me in his arms like we were long-lost family, kissing me on both cheeks, then clasping arms with Raniero. "I am Jorre of the Desert," he said to me. "Welcome, welcome. Forgive me for not greeting you all last night. I just got in from a trade run and was rather weary." He eyed the horizon and then Raniero. "With the sun coming up, it's best we keep our women hidden among the tents."

Jorre put a gentle hand on my shoulder and ushered me toward the tents again.

His overly familiar manner irritated me, even if he meant it as a kindness, and I squirmed away. "If we can get in and out of Zanzibar, I doubt that — "

"Andriana!" Niero barked, coughing, as if he were trying to hide anger and alarm.

I looked to him and abruptly shut my mouth when those feelings were confirmed.

"Please," he said to our host, as the big man turned keen eyes from me to Niero and back again. "Let me get Andriana back to the tent and we can then speak in private, Jorre."

"Certainly, certainly," Jorre said, studying me as if searching me, trying to make sense of who or what I was. He wasn't lusting after me — he apparently had all the women he needed in camp. What I felt from him was intrigue. Curiosity. As if I were a new puzzle for him to solve.

Niero took my arm and clamped down on it, pulling me along, clearly furious. For what? Standing up for myself? I wasn't some lost desert woman, looking for a man to save her.

He practically pushed me into the tent. The others stirred and began to sit up as I turned and faced Niero. "What?" I said, growing angry and confused. Scared I'd done something really wrong.

"We cannot have anyone knowing where we've gone. Or where we're going," he said, almost shouting at me even though he whispered. "You endanger us all, volunteering information like that," he said, pacing a few steps and then back, one hand on his hip, the other madly gesturing in the air. "How long would it take Jorre to connect the story of those who freed the healer in Zanzibar with us, here? Given Tressa's red hair? Your comeliness? Four men beside you? Aren't we already recognizable enough, without you waving a report of our history like a flag before you?"

I took a step back, confused. "I-I'm sorry. I didn't think — "

"No. You didn't." He heaved a sigh. "Look, Andriana ... All of you," he said, turning to the others. "We have to be careful. *Wise*. Jorre most likely suspects that we are the ones the Sheolites hunt. But now he knows. He *knows*." He lifted his hands to the roof of the tent, as if speaking to the Maker in silence. "Please. *Please*," he said to me. "Speak only upon permission when we're not alone, especially with people we do not yet know or know we can trust. Jorre manages to keep all these women and children safe through *trade*. And knowledge of us is a commodity."

"All right. *All right*," I said, feeling both defensive and humiliated as his words echoed in my mind. But also surprised. He thought me ... comely. Beautiful? Wasn't Tressa far more pretty in all her soft femininity and exotic red hair? But then I immediately chastised myself for such vanity. Who cared if he thought me beautiful or not? He was my leader, my brother. Nothing more. Making an observation.

But no one in my whole life had called me beautiful. The Community considered it low to exchange such compliments, unless one was in the most intimate of situations. Catering to our most base desires ...

"Stay here," he said, looking fiercely at me and then at all the rest, daring them to argue. "I'll be back in a little while."

With that, he disappeared out the door, and I noticed the children outside were now quiet and far from our doorway, as if they'd sensed our tension, and it had cast a pall over the entire trading post. Or had their mothers all drawn them into their tents, as Jorre had wanted?

"Well, this is going to be a good day," Vidar said, flopping to his back. "Way to start us out strong, Dri. Dad's all mad now."

Bellona and Killian smiled. But I didn't.

■ ■ ■

Niero returned and ushered us out to our bikes in the center of the post, now filled with petrol — the extra tanks on the side topped as well. Jorre's huge family and a fair number of the Tah Post gathered around to see us off. With that much petrol, we'd likely reach the salt caves. But would it carry us all the way to the Wall, if necessary?

"Take care, friend," Jorre said, clasping Niero's arm and then looking over at us, as if committing each of us to memory. "The Drifters have been thick between here and the salt caves, and I suspect you have extra enemies about." His eyes rested on me, Bellona, and Tressa. "Traveling with females won't help."

"We'll have an eye out for our enemies," Niero said. "Farewell, Jorre." He nodded toward Jorre's wives, then turned and passed by me while pushing his bike, and we followed. Jorre's many children — thirty or more — watched us in mute fascination, a gauntlet of dirty feet and running noses and shy grins, with two of them holding the baby goats. I reached out and rubbed the head of the nearest animal.

But my attention was on our leader. It unnerved me, the way Niero refused to look my way, speak to me. I told myself it was childish, that I'd simply messed up and he'd called me on it, but I still wanted the uneasiness between us to go away.

"I'll be right back," I said to Ronan, touching his arm and gesturing forward.

He nodded, understanding, as he straddled the bike. "Hurry."

I rushed past the others and up next to Niero. He was dressed in new oilskin pants — apparently trading for them the night before — and a brown turtleneck sweater that brought out the color of his eyes. "Niero, look, I'm sorry."

He glanced my direction then back, ahead to the open desert. The sun was peeking out again this morning, thick rays cast from holes in the cloudbank to the miles of clumpy grass below. "It's all right, Andriana," he said with a sigh. "You didn't know, didn't realize. Will you forgive me for reacting so strongly?"

I quickly nodded, feeling a measure of immediate relief.

"You must understand that it's my call to see you all

through this. To not only keep you safe, but to help you reach the Maker's goals. To keep you *all* safe," he quickly amended, gesturing to the rest of the Ailith behind us. "And if any of you threaten to endanger the rest, I'm liable to jump like that."

"It's a big task, keeping us all corralled," I said, fully recognizing for the first time what was before him.

He smiled. "Do you know that for years before the Hour arrived, I'd steal out to see you and Ronan, Vidar, and Bellona?"

I frowned in confusion. "You knew? You knew who we were?"

"Yes," he said, looking ahead again, a wistful smile on his face. "The Maker made it known to me that you were within reach. Once I had found you in your villages, I checked on you periodically. And alongside your trainers, kept you safe."

I considered that. That connection. I'd known he was older than we were. Or was he simply what the elders called an old soul? "Raniero, were you born with a mark too? Of the crescent moon?"

"I have my own divine mark," he said, looking into my eyes. "But your moon was imprinted upon my soul from the beginning. Born to serve you as much as watch over you, lead you. Serve the Maker alongside you, free our prince, and bow before the coming king."

"Thank you, Niero. For doing as they have asked of you. Your task ... it's big."

"I could do nothing else," he said with a shrug, straddling his bike, considering me. "Want to ride with me?" he said, gesturing over his shoulder. "I have room."

I paused, feeling caught again. "Oh, I, uh ... I'd best get back to Ronan."

He nodded, his face and heart unreadable again for me.

A sliver of loneliness, perhaps? Longing? I left him, and even though I was certain he didn't turn to watch me go, I could almost sense him imagining me walking back to Ronan, tucking my legs behind his, wrapping my arms around his waist.

"Everything all right?" Ronan asked me over his shoulder, his voice just audible over the roar of the dirt bike, as I did exactly that.

"All is well," I said, locking my arms around his tautly muscled belly.

"Good," he said, twisting the throttle.

As we took off west, heading toward the salt caves in hopes of finding the man who had been so close to Kapriel, and perhaps find out information that might help us free him, I thought more about Raniero. Of his call, unique from ours but different, in that he was not paired with either Remnant or Knight. Was it his destiny to always travel alone, in a way? Perhaps so that he wasn't unduly tied to any one of us?

My own sorrow over the thought surprised me. For there was so much ahead of us, so much asked of us, that it was unlikely any of us would manage to bond with anyone but others within our group. But here, now, holding tight to Ronan's strong body, I at least knew a deeper level of intimate partnership than Raniero would.

Even if Ronan and I hadn't ever kissed.

Come noon, we paused at the edge of a steep canyon to eat like starved wolves from our packs. Salted beef, a few strips of fish — which Niero had negotiated from Tonna's stores — dried apple, bread. We drank deeply and rested while Vidar and Bellona and Niero went to scout a way around the canyon, or at least down from the canyon's rim and up the other side. There was a trader trail nearby we were supposed to catch in order to reach the Hoodoos — tall, eroded cliffs that had the appearance of massive statuary — and the halfway point on our path toward the salt caves. But we'd somehow missed it.

I rambled after Ronan toward the canyon, but stopped when he continued to the very edge of the cliff, plopped down, and allowed his legs to dangle over an emptiness that descended for a thousand feet. Far below, we could hear the rush of the river, the sound oddly delayed from this height.

"Must you, Ronan?" I said, disgusted with his lack of care.

"Come," he said, gesturing me over to him. "It's exhilarating. Like standing on the top of Devil's Peak."

Each week, our trainer had forced us to carry heavy packs and climb to the top of the dreaded mountain ridge. We'd hated it, every step of the way. But Ronan had loved it, every time, when we reached the top, whether we could see the entire valley spreading out below us and our villages in miniature, and especially when we rose above the clouds and all we could see was a blanket of white below us. *He* loved it. I spent the whole time counting seconds until we were released to return to safer grounds.

"I imagine the ocean looking like the clouds had, from up there," I said, as I sat down behind him. "Remember Devil's Peak, when it was all clouded in and we couldn't even see the other mountains? That's how I imagine the sea. Like a vast blanket of clouds. Except blue."

"Hmm. Maybe. Think we'll get as far as the Coast?"

I thought about that. "I don't know. It seems terribly far off."

His dark brow rose. "I never expected to see the ocean." He

picked up a handful of pebbles and began tossing them into the canyon abyss, one after the other. It made my stomach jump a bit, watching them fall. "When the elders said we'd have a part in saving the world, I thought they meant *our* world. The Valley. Certainly not farther than Zanzibar."

I quickly looked at him in stark surprise, then cocked my head. "I guess I hadn't thought much bigger. I thought they were speaking of the Desert and Valley. Maybe the Plains. But never beyond the Wall."

"Why do I get the feeling," he said, tossing three rocks out, watching them for a second as if they were in a race, "that this will *continue* to unfold? Grow bigger. Broader."

"Maybe it's as the Maker wanted it. Maybe if we'd known it all in the beginning, we would have run away and hid."

"Saner people would still run," he said, with a jeering laugh. "Not us. Not the called."

I turned his words over in my mind. I found them vaguely troubling. More disconcerting was the vague sense of unrest, worry, fear I felt within him.

"Hey, I didn't mean anything by that," he said, lying down and stretching to touch my leg. "I'm just tired."

"Me too," I said. But my eyes lingered on his fingers, now running through his dark hair, pushing back a tendril that had escaped his tie and wanted to fall across one brow. When he'd touched me, I'd felt all his emotions tenfold.

"Dri?"

"Hmm?"

"What is it? You're looking at me strangely."

"Nothing," I said, shaking my head. What was this? When I touched someone, I knew their emotion all the more? It was if it became funneled, intensified. "Ronan, can I take your hand for a second?"

"Sure," he said slowly, clearly wondering what was going on. But he scooted closer and offered his hand. I slipped my fingers into his and closed my eyes. Emotions hit me like a battering ram. Confusion. Fear. The desire to protect. Desire itself. For me.

My eyes flew open, looking directly into his. He frowned and dropped my hand. "Dri?"

I hurriedly scrambled backward, crab-like, and then rose and turned, striding over to Tressa and Killian. "Tressa, may I take your hand a moment?" I asked.

"All right," she said, tentatively rising and offering it to me. I studied her, trying to get a read on her emotions even before we touched. Again I read fear, here in this new place. A longing to use her gift.

"All right," I echoed her, taking a deep breath, then placed my hand in hers. Her fear became like a black cloud around me, far more intense than Ronan's. And her longing to use her gift was like a hunger, a yawning chasm within me, growing wider

I gasped and dropped her hand, her emotions still filling me, like a dream hard to shake. "Quickly," I said to Killian, before I lost courage. "Would you mind? Take my hand for a moment?"

Killian reached out to me, as firm as if he were shaking my hand like men in the olden days did, rather than allowing me some intimacy.

He was wary. And irritated. And curious.

I immediately dropped his hand and stumbled backward, the combined emotions from all three threatening to make me feel as if I might explode. Ronan caught me, his strong arm around my waist. "Dri?"

"Wait—let me go," I said, pulling away from him, wincing as I registered *hurt* at my own words and action. I closed my eyes and lifted my hands, as if fending them all off. I took several deep, long breaths.

"There's something you should know," I said, looking dazedly at them, feeling worn. Behind them, in the distance, I glimpsed Niero, Vidar, and Bellona, all tiny figures. "I can read your emotions. But when we touch ... I can *really* read your emotions. It's almost as if ... they become my own."

Ronan glanced at me with confusion, then became alarmed as he looked sideways to our companions. I followed his line of vision.

Raniero, Vidar, and Bellona gradually grew closer, and we realized they approached at a dead run. Yelling at us, but impossible yet to hear. But then we heard Vidar's gun.

"Ronan ..." I said.

"I heard it."

He was shooting up in the air, something we'd never seen. Because ammunition was precious, and he had limited supply, and it would draw more attention to us. Make us more memorable. Niero had told him to use it only when there was no other recourse.

No other recourse.

Killian and Ronan slowly unsheathed their swords, waiting, completely still.

Raniero's mouth opened in a shout, but we couldn't make out what he said. He was waving at us as if he were angrily shooing us away.

"What's he want us to do? We're not leaving them!" Killian said, loosening his grip on his sword and then repositioning it. "Andriana, can you sense anything? Vidar?"

But then we all heard him.

"Get on the bikes!"

We hurriedly grabbed our packs and did as he asked. And that's when we saw it. In the distance behind our running companions, a massive dust cloud began to rise.

"What is that?" Killian asked. "A storm?"

I felt the first twinge of *glee* and *greed* from the cloud, and panic from our companions. Combined, it was like a sickness in my gut and I knew. "That's not a storm. Drifters!"

Our trainer had told us of the Drifters, people with no homes, who wandered from village to village along the desert floors. Pillaging. Gleaning. Taking everything they could from those they crossed. Demanding people join them, serve them or be left for dead. Men who had encountered Drifters had lost their weapons, supplies, and clothes, and been left without water, naked in the desert. "There was once an insect that roamed the earth in swarms," our trainer said, looking to the mountains about us as if he could see them, even though I knew he'd only been taught about them. "They were called locusts. These Drifters, they are like the locusts. Eating everything in sight, leaving you with nothing."

Tressa got on a bike behind Killian.

I started toward Ronan's bike but then diverted to Niero's, and started it up.

"Andriana?" Ronan said, alarm lacing his question.

"Judging from how fast our locusts are closing in," I said, "we won't have time to waste, waiting for them to get going." I slammed my boot down on the kickstart, willing it to turn over. And then kicked down again. It roared to life, and I revved the engine, making sure it would stay that way for a moment.

"Good idea," Tressa said, stepping off her bike.

"No, Tressa," Killian said, reaching out to try and grab her wrist. But she dodged him.

"This is something I can do, Killian." She got on Bellona's bike and shoved her boot down hard, the engine roaring to life immediately. Regret washed through Killian; I'd watched him teach her how to operate it himself.

Ronan's face drew together in frustration and fear as he looked behind us. I knew he was seeing what I had glimpsed— fifteen vehicles of some sort, near enough to take shape now, racing toward us terribly fast. "You stay close to us, you hear me? Right behind me, Dri. Right behind me."

"You too, Tressa," Killian said, obviously hating every single part of this plan.

I nodded. "C'mon," I whispered to our companions, now able to make the faces of drivers out among the first vehicles that were closing in behind. Handkerchiefs and masks over faces. I could no longer hear the rush of the river, far below. Only the roar of many motors, growing louder every second. "C'mon, c'mon, c'mon."

They were fifty paces away, coming so fast they seemed intent on running us over or hurtling over the canyon's edge.

Seeing how we'd prepared, Niero shouted something to Vidar and Bellona as he ran. Sweat dripped down their faces and soaked their shirts. Bellona broke toward Tressa, Vidar for Ronan, and Niero for me. Killian rode alone.

"Go, *go*, Andriana," Niero grunted before he was even on the seat.

Fear cascaded through me as I twisted hard on the throttle, rushing after Ronan as I'd promised.

CHAPTER 13

The Drifters drove us along the edge of the canyon at such speeds I feared we'd crash. They shouted and jeered. Shots from guns whistled past us. Out of the corner of my eye, I saw Vidar manage to reload his pistol and take aim, heard the crack of the gun, but still, on they came.

Another bullet whistled past our heads.

"They don't want to kill us. They want the dirt bikes!" Niero shouted.

I blinked rapidly, now directly behind Ronan, trying to watch where he was going, avoiding the obstacles he and Tressa did. The Maker had not brought us this far to die, had he? What purpose would be served if we died now?

"Focus, Andriana!" Niero said, squeezing me tight when we hit another hole and I barely recovered, the bike wavering erratically for a heart-stopping moment.

I shoved back my frustration. Did he think I wasn't

concentrating? Every moment of thought was on nothing but our way out.

"Think not of escape, but of the path," he yelled in my ear, over the wind, schooling his own tone into something calmer, less given to panic. I felt a wave of peace, centeredness, pass from him to me, so strong I almost let off the throttle. "The Maker shall show us the way."

I felt him centering in, meditating as we'd been taught, and I began to do the same, the way made easier by his touch. The road became more a series of unified elements, a path that led us forward rather than a barrage of threatening blocks. I refused to look again to the faces at my right, where I'd seen a vehicle — one with massive wheels that spit sand and weed up behind them, effortlessly bouncing over the rises and dips as it drew steadily closer. It almost became silent, as Raniero and I fell deeply in tune, as if we were flying on a slightly altered plane. We focused together on the path, only the path, gaining on Tressa and Ronan ahead of me while silently urging them to focus as we were, to remember the ways of the elders and our trainers and our parents.

I felt as if Raniero were almost growing behind me like a human shield stretching, rounding about me. I thought it was madness. The stress of the moment, the fear.

No fear, Andriana. Peace. Security. Strength. You are —

The crack of a gun went off — so close now that I thought it might be beside me — breaking me out of my concentration, breaking our connection, even as I felt Niero pull me close and then abruptly release me. "Niero!" I cried, letting go of the throttle, not thinking, in order to reach for him. Had he been hit?

The bike abruptly sputtered and died, wobbling, even as I

knew I couldn't hold Niero's dead weight against me with one arm. Unable to do anything else, I let him fall and slammed on the brakes. Niero hit the ground and rolled five times. I skidded to a stop and dropped the bike on its side, unsheathing my sword as I rose. I ran back to him as three vehicles shuddered to an abrupt stop around me, a good six or seven people piling out of each and jumping to the ground, surrounding us just thirty paces away.

The others chased after the other Ailith. Ronan hadn't yet looked back and seen that we were stopped. Silently, I thanked the Maker, begging him to see them to safety as the Drifters surrounded us. Even with the other Ailith by my side, I doubted we'd get out of this alive.

I hurried to Niero and reached down with a shaking hand to check for a pulse. But before I found it, he was coughing, waking, trying to focus on me.

"Niero," I said, half glad he yet lived, half regretting it. For surely people such as these would make us suffer before we died.

"Fo-focus, Andriana," he said, coughing, sputtering blood from his split lip, gripping my hand as if he knew now that I could read his emotions. "On the Maker, *not* on them."

I patted his chest, took a deep breath and rose, waving my sword in a slow, controlled arc above my head, ready for any of them to try and advance farther. They stopped twelve paces away, some of them staring at me in mute fascination as if they wanted to gobble me up, some of them with rank disinterest, as if they couldn't wait to shove us over the canyon edge and be off with my bike and supplies. I tried to concentrate on the ways of the Maker, to not give in to the swirling, threatening emotion around me.

Viciousness and animalistic. Primal. Their very emotion felt like blood lust.

No, Andriana. Focus. Concentrate on the Way. Of peace. Of promise. Of utter security, no matter how it seems. I closed my eyes a moment and searched my heart, willing it to stop pounding so I could hear, see what the Maker wanted me to do. And how.

A solemn man, barrel-chested and bearded, who emoted a cold distance — almost as empty as a Sheolite — pointed at three of his people, two men and a woman, then gestured toward me. "Take her down. But gently. She'll be worth a good amount, whole. Do you see those eyes?"

"Not to mention the body beneath 'em," laughed one.

I swallowed hard, then took a long, slow breath and placed my feet shoulder-width apart, turning slowly in one direction, then the other. I was careful not to turn fully around, striving to keep all three within my peripheral vision.

One lunged, and I dodged it and brought down my sword swiftly, striking his arm.

He screamed and fell away, and I fought for breath, feeling his pain like a sucker punch. I tried to do what Niero had urged me, but I was finding it nearly impossible —

The other two did not hesitate; one sent a sweeping, low kick at the same time as the other pressed in, striking with his sword again and again. I jumped, avoiding the woman attempting to take out my legs from under me. But then I was a half-breath behind as her companion came at me. He was swift and strong, and I narrowly parried each thrust and swing of his blade.

I knew the woman was about to kick me again, but I could do nothing but concentrate on my assailant with the sword. Not if I wished to hold on to my head. Even though his boss said he wanted me alive, this one seemed to thirst for my blood.

The female assailant's leg swung against my back leg, buckling it, and as I struggled to regain my balance, the man feinted right then punched me across my left temple. An explosion of pain ignited in my head and my vision swam. I circled around, my sword out, trying to ward off any of the Drifters. But the next blow from the woman took out my legs, and I fell to my knees, my sword tip sticking in the ground. I lost hold of it.

I reached for my daggers, immediately taking one in either hand. But even as I drew them and jumped to my feet, another man punched me in the kidney from behind. I arced, then bent over, gasping for breath against the pain.

"Careful, careful!" shouted the leader. "I told you, don't harm the merchandise!"

"What would you have us do?" bellowed the man, face in a grimace. "The wench is fairly rum with a blade."

"Just don't touch her face again," allowed the boss. "The Zanzibians like their dollies looking pretty."

I fought for breath, for the courage to rise again, to reach for my sword, but they'd closed in, Niero and I at the center of their ring. I stumbled over to his limp body, aware that blood was spreading across his shirt, and straddled him, a foot on either side. I crouched, ready for the first to come close. They might take us, in the end. But until they did, I would defend my brother as well as myself.

Two grinning men closed in, arms out.

"Now come on, dolly," said one, his lips buried in a bushy beard. "This will be better for you if you come along, peaceful-like."

"Better for *you* is more like it," I snapped.

"She's got fire, this one," said Bushy to his companions, and the others laughed. But my eyes were on the other one, tall and lean, eyes calm and calculating. He was far more frightening to me, in all his lithe, easy silence.

Holding one blade outright in my left hand to ward off Bushy, I flipped the other upside down in my right, and slashed in an arc toward Tall. He leaned back, and watched as my blade missed his throat by inches, then swiftly grabbed my wrist and twisted, forcing me to drop the blade. I didn't pause, moving as we'd been trained, over and over again. Unthinking. I shifted my weight and flipped, going with him as he pulled my wrist right and down. And brought my left leg up and against his head.

He was surprised, and the group around us hooted and laughed as he stumbled and went down, with me partially atop him. But the woman was back, then, and she punched me across the cheek. Black spots clouded my vision, and I wavered, even as Bushy grabbed hold of me and brought me against his chest, a wickedly sharp, thin blade against my throat.

My own chest heaved for breath, but I tried to stay very, very still. Already, I could feel the edge of the knife slicing my skin, the warmth of blood trickling down my neck. The tall man rose to his feet, eyes never leaving me.

The bearded leader looked at the woman and Bushy with seething hatred. "I said I wanted her *whole*."

"You saw it for yourself, boss. She's been taught to fight," she spat back, wiping her upper lip and panting. "I brought her down for you, didn't I?"

"She's not hurt in any way the right buyer would complain about," said a sandy-haired man of about two decades, leering at me in a way that made me drop my eyes.

"Ach. We can take her to the night dollies before auction," said another, waving a dismissive hand. "They'll cover her bruises with make-up."

"Or if she's of no use to you, boss, you can just give 'er to me!" shouted a short man from the back of the group.

The rest laughed at him.

"No," said the tall one, brushing off his pants as he edged closer to me, the first word I'd heard from him. "If anyone gets this dolly, it's me." His cool eyes raked over me, from head to toe.

The barrel-chested leader glared at them all, but was already turning away. "Bring her, and if the man lives, him too." He walked with weary steps to his earth-crosser. *Jeep*, I thought it read on the side. It had four massive wheels and two seats up front. A bar stretched along the top, and the others had stood in the back, holding on as best they could.

"Let's take his clothes, boss, and leave him for the buzzards," called Bushy. "He's shot, clean through."

I held my breath, waiting for the leader's response. He half turned and his eyes shifted between me and Niero, considering us, as if idly evaluating if we were worth more separate or together.

"No, bring them both. The man looks strong. He may live through the night. Maybe his people will pay a ransom. Or we can take him north. To the mines. Bind the girl and bring her."

The tall man and the woman held my arms as Bushy approached, grinning at me, his teeth surprisingly straight and milky white. He pulled a length of rope from his belt and quickly wound it around my wrists, tightening it until it bit into my skin, knotting it expertly. He leaned close, his fetid breath hot in my ear. "I like a dolly tied up," he said, then leaned back to look me in the eye. "Maybe I'll come around to see you tonight."

"Please do," I grit out. "I know ways to kill that don't require my hands or a blade but create exquisite pain."

He drew back a little, his brown eyes widening in surprise. And then he smiled again. He turned away, tossing his head as if he weren't threatened. But I'd seen the uneasiness in his eyes. So had the man and the woman, who both laughed under their breath.

I looked around, desperate for any glimpse of Ronan, Vidar, Bellona, Tressa, and Killian, but saw no one. And it appeared that half the Drifters had gone after them. Were they somewhere negotiating their own battle as I was? Had they been captured? Killed? The tall man shoved me forward, surprising me, and I lurched across the sandy soil. Two burly men grabbed hold of Niero, one under each arm, and yet still struggled to drag his bulk beside us to the vehicle.

The tall man picked me up and set me roughly in the back of the vehicle, and the woman got in alongside the boss up front. Grunting, the men tossed Niero roughly in at my feet, then climbed in over him, standing to take hold of the bar as the engine roared to life.

Grimacing at my trembling fingers, I leaned down to check for Niero's pulse. I drew back in surprise, studying his face. His heartbeat was steady and strong, not the thin, faint beat I'd expected. I went to my knees, intent on pressing down at the center of his bloody wound, hoping I could help staunch the flow. But Bushy savagely kicked aside my arm. "Leave him be!"

Another man, quiet and wary, intervened. He grabbed my arm and pulled me to my feet. "Here," he said gently. "You'd better hold on wi' us if you don't want to take a tumble."

I'd barely grabbed hold of the bar, between Bushy and this other, kinder man, when the boss put the Jeep in gear and tore off in a tight circle, heading back the way they'd come. It took everything in me to hold on, and several times I bounced off my feet, struggling to avoid coming down on poor Niero's body. *Hold on,* I thought, willing him to stay alive. *Please don't die on me. I can't get out of this alone!*

As we bounced along, I leaned the back of my legs against Niero's torso, searching for a sense of what he was feeling. To try and figure out if he was conscious at all.

And in that touch I noted pain. But moreover, a thirst for revenge. He was easier to read, injured as he was. As if the bullet had pierced the barrier between us.

I peered at his face intently, a tiny smile edging my mouth even as I struggled to remain in the Jeep and watch where we were going. I knew it'd be up to me to remember our path if we could somehow escape. But feeling the half-deadened emotions of the men around me all too clearly, I knew it'd be a miracle indeed.

Ten minutes later, we took a road down and into the canyon, and after slowing to make tight turn after tight turn we emerged on the canyon floor far below. High above us, the sun was fading, and I fought the sensation that it was taking my breath with it, leaving us down here in a red-rock grave. On the far side of the canyon, across the river, I spotted two boys about Ignacio's age with shepherds' crooks in their hands, watching us arrive at the bottom, approximately thirty feet below them. A small goat danced before them, then disappeared. They went after him as if we'd only been a passing interest.

Thoughts of Ignacio and his grandmother made me eye Niero again. If I could somehow escape and get to Tressa ...

could she save him in time? Despite his strength, he'd lost a great deal of blood and continued to lose more. The Jeep's floor ran red with it.

The river was wider than my village, and moving at a fast pace through this part of the canyon, turning white as it leaped over rocks and cascaded down the other side. Perhaps it formed a boundary line between territories, for I knew the Hoodites — settlers among the odd rock formations we had been told were called Hoodoos — were not far from here. Were the shepherd boys Hoodites? I felt a stirring of hope, which I knew was desperate, since they were but boys. But being seen by them made me feel like I wasn't quite so alone. So abandoned.

The Jeep lurched to a stop beside the river and the leader lumbered out, pausing beside me. "Bring her," he said. "Leave the man. If he dies, it will be easier to back up the Jeep and dump him in the river."

"But the blood, boss! The shirt's a ruin, but lemme save his coat!"

"Fine, fine," he said, tossing a hand over his shoulder. "Take his coat."

The others pulled me out of the Jeep as they set upon Niero, rolling him out of his coat, like scavengers picking on a carcass. My attention was forced to the massive cave before me, a place the river had probably carved for centuries before receding, leaving a wide, flat, sandy bottom and a decent amount of shelter from the rain. There were several fires burning, and I smelled the fish before I spotted them on skewers. My mouth watered, but that quickly disappeared when the foul stench of human waste and rot entered my nostrils next.

Two men sat in raised towers on either side of the massive cave, automatic weapons facing out. To guard them from what? Hoodite shepherd boys? The man who'd brought me to my feet in the Jeep now offered me his hand to get up and over the boulders that formed a barrier to the cave. I ignored it, choosing to make my own way, but followed him over to the nearest fire.

"Whatcha doin', Socorro?" cried Bushy. "She ain't getting any of our fish."

"Yeah, keep 'er skinny," said the woman with a lop-sided grin. "The Zanzibians like 'em skinny. They don' look so costly to feed." I stared at her. How could she speak of women like she did? And how had she avoided the same fate? But then I saw the boss grin and slap her backside, and knew. She belonged to him.

Socorro cast me a swift look of regret, then gestured to Bushy. "Quit your gripin'. I'm not giving anyone nothin'. Just lettin' her get warm. She's shaking all over."

"She'll need the fire," the leader allowed, "because we'll be having her coat too."

Two women pounced as if they'd been waiting on such word, and pushed and pulled me out of my oilskin. Even as Socorro yelled at them, they turned me over and pressed my face in the sand, so hard I worried I'd suffocate. I was abruptly released once they had the coat. "She has something on her arm, boss," said one, scurrying backward with my coat in hand. "Something hard."

The man's gaze narrowed at me as I spit sand out of my mouth, and again I was more scared by his utter lack of emotion than by the others about me with more challenging, dangerous — but at least identifiable — feelings. "Bring her to me," he said, waving to them.

I panicked, grasping at the man nearest to me, the one they called Socorro, who'd helped me a little. I felt bits of pity from him. Compassion. But mostly I felt grief, as if I was lost already to his mind. I tried to gather enough spit in my mouth to swallow.

The tall man and Bushy dragged me across the sand and we reached the side of the cave, where two, rusty chains came down from a metal circle inserted into the rock, high above. Two more from the base.

"What's on your arm, girl?" asked the leader, slowly brushing off his sleeve as if he wasn't really all that interested.

"A trinket. Worthless. A marking of my people."

"Not a receiver?"

"A receiver?" I said, fighting to focus on his face. "I-I don't know what a receiver is."

"Show me," he said, hands on his hips, his feet spread wide. He watched as they wrestled my sweater from me — my hair coming loose with it — then my long-sleeved shirt, leaving me in my T-shirt. I wrapped my arms around myself, feeling exposed, vulnerable, and already terribly cold as the sun continued to recede.

The leader frowned and walked over to me, lifting my arm in his big hand.

I could not bear to look as he perused the priceless band. Tapped at it. Turned my arm back and forth. "Well, it's not a receiver. Just a grubby adornment of some sort." He tried to slide it down, like it was an arm cuff, and I cried out.

He looked hard at me. "What the — "

"It's a tradition in the Valley," I said hurriedly. "The skin is seared, and the cuff adheres. It's, as you say, worthless. A bauble to remember a rite of passage."

He continued to stare, doubt lacing his eyes. "Everyone is to leave it be," he declared, a glint in his eye. "It's not worth much. But she'll look all the more enticing and foreign to the Zanzibian traders in a couple days if we leave it on. They favor such adornments."

For the first time, their chatter and action fully registered with me. They planned to steal my clothes and sell me as womanflesh. I thought of the dark streets at the center of that southern city. The sense of despair —

"What are you doing here, girl?" the leader asked, stepping forward to study me closer. "You and your friends? You're not of the Desert. You've been trained to wield a sword. Where are you from?"

"The Valley," I said. "We have safe-passage papers. Niero had them "

"Bah! I don't care what papers you wield. You're mine now. Your future is dependent on me alone. Where are you heading? For what purpose? This is what I wish to know."

I frowned. How was I to answer that? "We were headed to the salt caves," I tried, having no idea if it would help or harm, but too weary to think up a lie.

His eyes narrowed. "The salt caves," he said dismissively. "Nothing there but starving villagers. Your friends turned tail and ran out on you. Is that how people of the Valley treat their companions?"

I stared at him.

"Is it? Because that's how we Drifters do!" he said, with a sudden laugh that didn't reach his eyes. The others laughed with him, but the sound was empty of joy.

"Tell me, really, where you are going," he said, biting out each syllable and leaning down toward me. Greed and suspicion twined within him.

"Eventually north, for more petrol."

"For what purpose?" he asked, throwing up a hand. "You have two extra tanks on your bike that are still full. The only reason you'd need more is if you were headed to Castle Vega. Or ... Pacifica."

"We seek to build trade for our people," I tried, wary of the surge of bitterness I got from him at the mention of the city beyond the Wall. "Perhaps we could even trade with you. We got off to a rough start, but I'm willing to look past it for the right deal and safe passage."

He stared at me for a long moment, and then again let out a loud guffaw. The others laughed, uneasily, around him. "You have us mistaken for those others who gave you *safe passage*. We don't trade, girl. We *take*."

"Hey, boss!" called a man, from beside what looked to be their storage area. "There are three barrels of potato whiskey here!"

"Where'd those come from?" he called, half-suspicious, half-pleased.

"I don't know!"

"Well, find out!" he shouted, his eyes still on me.

He made a motion and two men took hold of my arms. They wrenched up on the chains until I was on the balls of my feet, and my arms spread out in a Y. I gasped. Then he came closer, so close I could feel his hot breath on my face. "When you're ready to tell me where you're really going, and why, I'll loosen your chains. Tie you so you can sleep rather than stand through the night. Until then, I have some potato whiskey to drink. Catch me before I'm too drunk to hear your call or we'll have to address it again come morn."

I watched him walk away and felt the self-pity rise within

me. A Vidar-like thought came to my mind. *So far, this Ailith thing is less than fun.*

My eyes shifted to the back end of the Jeep, no sign of Niero shifting or rising.

Never had I felt so alone. *Maker, where are you?*

Was this how it was to end? Me, sold into Zanzibar? I'd escaped the city once. But could I do it again—alone? If they'd followed Niero's instructions, all of Tressa and Killian's friends were long gone from the sewage tunnel. Clennan and Tyree were back in the Valley. A shiver ran down my spine, not from the damp of the cave or the nearby river or the falling rain. But from the possibility of returning to Zanzibar. Not as a warrior, strong among her sisters and brothers. But as a slave.

It was impossible. It couldn't happen. I had to escape. Or welcome death. Because I couldn't go there. *I can't ... I can't ... I can't ... I can't ...*

Thoughts of the womanflesh traders, Tonna's warning, even walking with my hand on some man's hip, bound to a mate as property, made me want to vomit.

I wondered if my friends had gotten away. If they searched for us or carried forth without us. We'd never discussed anything other than to go everywhere together. Though that had been Niero's plan. And he was here with me. Dead. Or could be still be alive? I was so sure I'd sensed that flash of vengeance within him ... but had I only felt what I wanted to feel?

One thing I knew: Ronan wouldn't leave me willingly. He'd be fighting, desperately trying to get back to me, free me. I'd been relieved when the other Drifters pulled in, having failed to capture the remainder of our group, and I concentrated on that emotion now. I watched as my captors pushed, shoved, jostled for more potato whiskey, a clear liquid they drank from cups of all varieties — cans, ceramic, glass, even what appeared to be hollowed rocks — downing more and more of it.

Ronan will come. The thought gave me strength.

And yet, if they couldn't find our trail, couldn't find the access point to the canyon high above, couldn't find *us*, what were they to do? While Ronan and I were inexplicably tied, and I knew the other Ailith on a deeper level of kinship, were we not all called to a higher task? Regardless of the cost to some of us, wasn't our collective goal more important?

No, they wouldn't leave me and Niero. Not without knowing we were dead first, lost to them until we were reunited in the afterworld. I knew it. *I knew it.* But then I feared the thought. If they came down here, were shot dead or captured with me, all in an effort to save me … If I was the cause of any of them losing their lives —

I pulled at my chains, wishing I could wrench them free from the rock above me. But as I tugged at them, I knew they wouldn't budge, even if they were old and rusty. And I felt the scream of panic within, as wide and all-encompassing as my grief when I first discovered my parents were dead.

It was that thought that brought me up short. Reminded me of Ronan carrying me, so tenderly, to the river's edge. Of Raniero, forcing me to rise. Of him saying that fear blocked the power of the Maker. Of him gripping my arms and making me promise I'd remember. To hold on to what I *knew* rather than getting lost in what I felt.

In what I felt.

I took a deep breath and closed my eyes, trying to grab hold of the tiniest tendril of truth, in the midst of all my feelings roiling about in my head and heart. Raniero had known something like this would come. He'd known. And while my gifting gave me an edge at times, it also left me weak, vulnerable.

Truth. Whispers teased me, like the very end of a frayed thread, refusing to move through the eye of a needle. *What truths do I know?*

The Maker sees me.

He does not abandon his own.

I am called.

He hears me.

Maker, hear me now ... Deliver me. Protect and deliver me ...

I dozed off or passed out for a time — I didn't know which.

I came to with a start, my eyes wide, shifting. But the camp had been drinking for a good while, judging from those who were down already, slumbering as if they might not wake for days. The remaining number played a game in which they each downed a gulp of whiskey, then took three steps along a line in the sand, then took another, dropping off, one by one. Two children, one who looked about his first decade-and-two, the other far younger, sat and watched the drunken adults — casting furtive glances my way — while moving about, scavenging food from the adults' hands like starving dogs. Perhaps they were but insignificant creatures among the Drifters. Just another mouth to feed until they were big enough to fight, bully, take. When they'd eaten their fill, they fell asleep, cuddled up together beneath a filthy blanket. The guards in their towers looked decidedly dazed as they stared outward with glassy eyes.

I studied the thirty before me, now like logs among the sand, snoring, blessedly leaving me alone, and found myself grateful for the discovery of whiskey. Even if it meant I'd be standing here all night. I selfishly wished Raniero'd been tied beside me; his presence would give me confidence and hope. I glanced into the dark, trying to make out the lines of the Jeep, but could see nothing but the wash of white upon the river, oddly a second off from the sound. Perhaps the cave

Niero, I reminded myself, trying to focus as my vision swam. My thoughts were all over the place. Unfocused. Might he be rallying? Could I rouse him if I could somehow break free?

I shivered in the cold. Beyond the mouth of the cave, it was raining. I twisted, looking for anything I might use to aid me, then up at the rocks and chains that tethered my blood-drained hands to them. A soft groan from the far tower drew my attention, and I saw a guard fall from view and tumble to the floor. Had he given in to the drink and the lulling sounds of the river?

His companion appeared confused, then disappeared too.

Hope surged within me even as I frowned, trying to make sense of what I'd seen.

I squinted, trying to see better in the gathering dark, given that the fires had burned down to embers. A man, mostly hidden in deep shadow, appeared between the guards and lifted one to his perch again, positioning him so that he looked like he'd merely fallen asleep. Then he pulled back the chamber of the gun, dropped the bullets into his hand, and placed the gun in the man's arms again. He swiftly did the same with the second man.

He looked over to me and I frowned. For I'd hoped it was Ronan or Niero.

But it was neither.

CHAPTER
14

I swallowed an oath. I didn't know whether to hope or be more frightened than ever.

The tall man crept to the next tower, wary of the other guards, pausing by the boss and carefully lifting the keys from his pocket. A woman lying in the crook of the big man's arm moaned and moved, even sat up, blinked heavily, and then laid back down, all while this mysterious visitor was right beside them. He moved closer to me, glancing at the guards, but he apparently decided to risk that they were sacked — or unable to shoot us if they awakened. He gave me a slow, idle smile that didn't reach his eyes.

"Here I thought it was going to be the bushy-bearded one that would come around for me," I said, forcing a cavalier tone to my voice. I hoped he didn't hear the waver in it.

He pocketed the key to my chains in his trousers, looked back at the camp and then to me. "I'm thinking you might be open to a deal," he whispered in my ear. His movements were smooth. Deadly.

I swallowed and tried to give him a casually interested look. "Oh?"

The hint of a smile tugged at the corners of his lips. I decided he wouldn't be terrible looking. If he wasn't a monster inside. And yet he was.

"What's your name?" he asked, his lips hovering near my ear, my neck. In all this time with the Drifters, not a one of them had asked that. I concentrated on that odd fact, rather than the man hovering near me. I didn't answer. His hands came to my waist, and foul, fetid darkness rolled out of him and into me. It took everything in me to remain still, to not react.

"No name?" he whispered, his lips near my temple, then my jaw. "No matter. There's a good dolly," he said, his hands beginning to move around to my back as he pulled me closer.

"You said you had a deal," I said quickly, and with some relief, his hands stopped roving.

He smiled then and drew a bit back, a small, thin-lipped grin on his face. "Why yes," he said, again in my ear, leaning in, his hands running down my back.

I closed my eyes. *Don't move. Don't move, Dri.*

"Here's the deal," he said in a breath. "I free you. And you give me a tumble around the corner."

I tried to gather enough spit to swallow and failed. "What's to keep you from returning me to these chains afterward?"

He laughed softly, lowly, and in that moment, I wished it was Bushy rather than this man. Even the boss. This guy was far more ruthless. "Nothing. But what's your option, dolly? I can have at you either way."

"True," I allowed. I looked him in the eye. "Unchain me,

quickly, and I'll see through your deal." I hoped I managed to give him the teensiest invitation in my look. Inside, all I could feel was revulsion.

Glee surged through him. He crouched down and slowly unlocked my right ankle and then moved to my left, his long fingers lingering on my calves. I knew that if I left this cave with him, I'd likely not return alive. But being free of at least two of my chains sent a wave of hope, strength through me.

He ran his hands up my legs and over my hips as he rose and I couldn't handle it any longer. Again, I acted on instinct, grabbing hold of the chains at my wrists, lifting myself up and kicking off of him, then wrapping my legs around his neck, squeezing with every bit of energy I had left to me. He writhed and struggled, clawing at my legs, too surprised to reach for his knife. But he was strong, and we went on in our strange death dance for long minutes, the chains rattling so loudly, his grunts and growls so frequent, I couldn't believe no one came to his aid. But I concentrated only on him, on his waning breath, his hatred. It was so dark, so all-encompassing, I began to draw back, loosen my hold, until I remembered Niero urging me to remember what I knew, rather than what I felt.

He is my enemy. He will use me and then kill me.

Dimly, as if I were twenty paces away rather than right there with him, I watched as the life faded from his eyes. And then, I felt nothing at all from him.

I forced myself to release him, staring as he crumpled to the ground, the key still buried in his trouser pocket. I glanced up to the chains that still held me. *Great, just great.*

I closed my eyes and tried to think. Was there any other way out? And what would happen, come morning, when the Drifters found this man dead beside me? Would they decide to use me and kill me themselves? Had I traded one horror for another?

But when I opened my eyes I saw that the man named Socorro was standing five paces away, his gaze shifting from me to the man and back again. I braced for his shout, the moment when he would awaken the rest of the Drifters. But instead, he crouched, fished for the key peeking out of the tall man's pocket and then came over to me. He lifted a hand, palm up. "I'm going to free you," he whispered.

I felt none of the menace from him that I had from the other, but I still stared at his profile as he reached up to the first lock. "What do you expect in return?"

His brown eyes shifted to me in surprise, and then thought. "Nothing," he whispered, moving to the next hand. And I believed him. There was a light within him, dim, like a lampshade covered in soot, but present nonetheless.

"Why are you doing this?"

"I don't know," he said, unlocking my other hand.

My arms fell beside me, numb. I took a step and stumbled, realizing that I was again trembling all over. Shock, I assessed distantly. Still, I forced myself to stumble over to the Jeep and look over the edge. Niero didn't move. Was he dead? With a tentative hand I reached for his neck.

He was alive. "Niero," I whispered, shaking his shoulder.

He moaned but didn't open his eyes.

Socorro came up beside me. "We have to leave him. You must be away. Far away, when they wake. Me too."

"No," I said with a sigh, remembering how the two big men struggled to drag Niero between them. Socorro and I were far smaller, but there was no way I would leave Raniero behind. The Maker would have to find me another way out.

"Listen," Socorro whispered urgently, eyes moving to the sleeping guards in the tower above us. "We will never get clear in time. Not with him."

"You go back to your bed roll by the fire," I urged him. "You've helped me enough. I'll see to my friend myself." I knew it was ridiculous, and I hoped he wouldn't let me try such a silly plan. But I had to give him an out. I knew what he did — we'd likely die trying to escape with Niero between us. And I didn't want this man's death on my hands too. Not a … friend.

Socorro sighed and looked up at the top of the cave, then out to the river a moment. He straightened, resolution and resignation twisting within him. He moved to the Jeep's back gate and opened it.

The click and creaks from the metal gate echoed about the whole cavern. Socorro and I froze like river reeds in deep Hoarfrost. I dared to scan the other Drifters, fearing the worst, but the only thing that seemed to move in camp were the small, dancing flames that remained in the fires, licking at the burned-out remains of logs that were mostly embers by now.

My eyes moved to trace the curving river, the beaches, disappearing into the depths of night. We had to get out of here. Fast. I pulled at Niero's body, putting my foot against the gate for leverage. He easily weighed twice what I did. *The Maker will make a way,* I repeated to myself, trying desperately to ward off my own doubt.

Socorro leaned his shoulder into Niero's other armpit, grabbed hold of his arm, and rolled his body across his shoulders. He was a slight man, not much heavier than I, and I could see him straining under Niero's weight.

"No," I whispered. "Let me help you."

"You lead the way," he said, ignoring my words.

"Where?" I whispered, already turning. "Where do we go?"

Behind us, a Drifter coughed and groaned. "Just go," Socorro said, and I readily agreed. All I sensed in him was fear, likely caused by thinking what the other Drifters would do to us, should they catch us.

There's a time for flight, and a time for fight, our trainer had told us. This was definitely time for flight. I supposed it didn't matter which way we went. The most important thing was to be away.

We moved down the river's edge, along with the current. I glanced back, to the cave fifty paces behind us, knowing that at any moment one of the Drifters would wake. See me gone. Cry out and wake others who were not totally lost to drunkness.

But no torch appeared at the mouth of the cave. Was it possible this would work? A tiny surge of hope spread through me. *Maker, have you made this way?* But despite my prayer of hope, I found myself glancing back again, fearing — almost expecting — the worst. A hundred paces. Two hundred.

Miraculously, Socorro kept his footing over the rounded rocks, and we continued around the riverbend, the cavemouth now almost out of sight.

"Do you swim?" Socorro asked, between pants for air.

"I do." Everyone in the Valley learned to swim as babes.

"Good. If they come," he grunted, staggering under Niero's weight, "Jump into the river. It will carry you down and away from them faster than they can run. Go deep and swim to the other side. Because they do not swim."

I nodded, even though he could not see me in the dark. "Will you dive in too?"

"No. I cannot. I do not swim."

I took that in. He planned to help me while likely sacrificing himself. "Why come to my aid? What am I to you?"

"I ... I couldn't look away. Couldn't stand aside and do nothing. Again."

I faltered and he pulled to a stop, panting. I wished I could see his face. But I felt the pain in him.

"The Maker urged you to aid me," I said.

Fear echoed through him and he glanced over his shoulder again. I caught a glimpse of his profile in the dark. "Shh," he said, pulling me forward, as if he feared that our conversation would be overheard by the very shadows. And perhaps it was. "You must not say such things. I don't know what it is like from where you came, but in the Desert, mentioning the Maker will get you killed."

We walked for a few minutes in silence, other than for an occasional gasp or moan from me when my foot caught and wrenched my knee. "I wasn't always a Drifter. Once I lived in a village, on the edge of the Desert. I think my father was a follower of the Way." He said the last of it so lowly that I wondered if the sounds of the river were playing tricks on my ears. Was I so desperate to find a trusted friend here that I would hear anything I wished? I decided it was likely.

"I have to stop," he said, "put him down." I hurried to his side and helped him lower Niero to the rocks. Socorro straightened, his back audibly cracking.

My hands ran up Niero's chest to his neck. His pulse was still strong, giving me hope again. And Socorro couldn't go on carrying him forever. "Niero," I whispered, shaking his shoulders. "Niero?"

But he didn't move, still unconscious.

"If you're caught again," Socorro said, sitting on a rock

beside us, "don't talk of such things. The Drifters won't like it. There was once a girl …" He faltered and then gave way to silence, apparently thinking it was best not to share.

But here in the wilds, I knew that knowledge was power. "What happened to her? Tell me."

He hesitated and dipped his hand into the river for a drink, and I did the same. Then, "They took her to Zanzibar to trade, like they planned to do with you. But she wouldn't keep quiet about the Way, the Maker. The Drifters burned her alive, as is decreed."

His words stole my breath a moment. It was the same everywhere but the Valley, we'd been told. No warlord tolerated competition from anyone. Even the Maker. "But the Drifters … they live by no decree. They have no ruler. Why do they care?"

"Everyone is ruled by someone. For us, it's the camp boss. And the boss both reveres and fears the Pacificans. They, above all, loathe talk of the Maker."

I thought on that a moment.

"Socorro, you obviously do not belong here. Come with us."

The offer was out before I'd thought it through. But wasn't he an example of who we were to gather or send to the Valley? A man responding to the Maker's call, his stirring? Even to the point of risking his life?

"I can't," he said, and I felt the regret deep within him. "I don't know how to swim."

I smiled. "I can teach you."

"No. I'm too far behind." He spoke not of swimming then, I knew, but of deeper subjects.

"It is never too late to begin on matters that matter."

"We'd best continue on," Socorro said after a moment. And together, we again managed to get Niero across his back and we walked along in silence, around the bend in the river and halfway around another. The clouds parted above us, and I saw stars — more stars in a wider space — than I'd ever seen before. In the Valley there were always clouds, or mist. Tiny breaks occurred at times, but never this sort of clearing. "Do you often see the stars here?"

"Most times, yes," he grunted.

"As far as the stars feel from you, the Maker can feel the same." He was listening to me. Intent on words my trainer had taught me, as the elders had taught him. "But even though he feels distant, he is right here." I patted his forearm. "Right with you. As close as Niero is, across your back."

"Even with a Drifter?" I heard the disbelief in his voice, as I felt the pang of loneliness, desperation within him.

"Everywhere. In the Desert, the Plains, Zanzibar, even beyond the Wall."

A movement in the dark to my right made me pause and I pulled him to a stop. But all was still, except for the rush of the water beside us. I felt him glance back in the direction of the cave, knowing he only wished to get farther away. We'd just begun moving again when everything came into motion at once — dark forms, shadows all around us.

I almost cried out as hands grabbed me, but my fear was immediately swallowed in a sea of victory and relief, and sweet, delicious surprise as they folded me into their arms.

My humming armband told me exactly who they were.

CHAPTER
15

They were my friends, along with others. I listed them as they neared me, finding relief with each name. *Ronan, Vidar, Bellona, Tressa, Killian.*

Ronan took Niero from Socorro and carried him to a wooden raft on a quieter part of the river. The rest of us clambered aboard in quick succession. Vidar bent to untie the raft, but I reached toward my new Drifter friend in panic.

"Wait! Wait! We can't leave Socorro! They'll kill him."

Vidar turned to him. "Come with us, friend. We will get you to safety."

Socorro hesitated.

"Is it not best to face the fear of the unknown," I asked, "than to face a known death?"

"Company's coming," Vidar said, "and Socorro's about the last we can fit on the raft."

We could see several torches bobbing their way down the

beach toward us, and I could make out five or six silhouettes of men beneath them.

"C'mon, Socorro!" I said sharply. "What's your alternative? They'll kill you, if they find you came to my aid. The Maker urged you to help me, now let me help you. Please!"

The Drifters were close enough for us to hear them shouting, even over the rush of the river. Soon they'd be close enough to shoot.

"We have to go," Ronan said, reaching down to untie the raft. "Make your decision, man."

At the last second, our rescuer stepped on to the raft, tilting it a bit, but I breathed a sigh of relief. Bellona and Vidar began moving quickly — Paddling? Using poles? It was impossible to see in the dark — but I knew we were getting farther into the river and farther down. Deeper into safety. Swiftly leaving those who pursued us behind.

"Ronan..." I said.

"I'm here," he said. He reached out and pulled me into his arms, and a wave of confidence and hope washed through me. "What happened to Niero?"

"He was shot. Hours ago. When we were captured." I hated the hopelessness in my voice. "He's lost a great deal of blood."

My new friend edged near, trying to get out of the way for those maneuvering the raft and bumping me by accident. I yelped and he immediately apologized, even as Ronan growled a "watch it."

"It's all right! It's all right!" I said, feeling like I had to ease Ronan down like a fierce guard dog. He was terribly edgy, perhaps because we'd been so recently reunited. I knew he'd be blaming himself, that I was taken. That he hadn't been there to protect me. "Ronan, Socorro helped me. Several times."

"I'm grateful," Ronan said, his voice tight.

"As am I," I said, reaching out to squeeze Socorro's forearm as he hunkered down on all fours. I could feel the tight pull of panic within him, probably as much from the fear of drowning as the *What have I done?* question that had to be roiling through his mind.

I understood his terror, even if I blessed every inch of water between me and the Drifter scum. Sometimes, when you didn't know better, you settled for filth, thinking it was the best you could hope for. "There's so much more ahead, Socorro. It will be better for you. Trust me. You'll see. We'll show you."

He said nothing, and I could only imagine what he was thinking by exploring more of what he felt. *Lost.* He'd just left everything he'd known, for me. For us. It made me determined to help find sanctuary. Peace. Maybe even a bit of joy, something the Drifters seemed desperately far from.

From the other side, Ronan secretly slipped his hand into mine, his touch nothing but pure, brotherly. But he'd not forgotten joy, at least tonight. It seemed to fill him from head to toe, our reunion. And aside from his anxiety over keeping me from more harm, his relief mirrored mine.

We reached the far bank, hitting rocks that caused us to spin, and then hitting against them again, nearly toppling us all into the water. Vidar and Bellona jumped off, each shouting orders at the other. Ronan stepped off when it was knee-deep and helped them shove us to safety, firmly against the bank.

As we made our way onto the sandy shore, two boys emerged from the woods, each carrying lanterns. They smiled shyly at me and my eyes went wide with surprise. The shepherd boys. The same boys that saw me arrive with the Drifters.

"How did you find them? How did … Did those two tell you where we were?"

Ronan helped me to walk toward them, his arm around my waist, partially lifting me. "Hoodites. They found us while we were in hiding. We barely avoided the Drifters by throwing them off our trail but we only became more lost. They found us and led us to you."

"How'd you get the bikes across?"

"A sort of ferry, much like this one. They don't keep them around, for obvious reasons. The Drifters loathe water, and the Hoodites prefer to feed that fear rather than give them the tools to conquer it."

I glanced back over his shoulder to the other side of the river, remembering the deeper dark I'd left behind. I shuddered, and he shifted me in his arms even as I lamented losing one of the bikes. How were we to move on? Three of us squeezed onto one? There'd be no way.

"How bad is it?" Ronan asked, bringing me back to the present.

"What?"

"Niero's wound. You said he lost a lot of blood. But how bad is the wound? Did the bullet pass through?"

"I don't know. One of them said something about it going clean through. But I never got a chance to examine him." Now that we were with them again, I was suffering a new sort of worry. Even if he recovered, how was Niero going to keep up with the rest of us? Ride on a dirt bike at all? Ride anything? This kind of injury put a person flat-out for weeks, months. He might never recover fully.

In the olden days, my parents told me, there were doctors who operated. Opened up and fixed broken bones, stitched up ligaments, tendons. Had medicines for pain, others for healing. But we'd long since lost the skill — and the supplies — to do such things. In our village, there was one woman of three decades and four years who'd slipped on the ice and broken both her legs. She never walked again, relying on her husband and children to bring her food, to carry her to the outhouse, to dress her. How had she escaped after the night the Sheolites came and murdered my parents? Had her family carried her away? To where?

The memory made me nauseated.

"The Maker will show us the way, Dri," Ronan said, as if reading my spinning mind. "Rest in this — we are together again. Safe for the moment."

Killian and Vidar carried Niero between them, and I thought about Ronan's words as we slowly made our way along the trail away from the river, through the trees, the fragrance of pine both making me miss home and yet allowing me to take the first full breaths I think I'd taken since we left. But my heart grew heavy, the more I thought about moving on without Niero among us.

The sun was rising. At first glimpse, up at the cliffs that surrounded us, I thought I might be hallucinating, giving in to the pain. For above me were a hundred or more rock formations, standing like giant, silent men watching us pass. *The Hoodites.* Appearing as they'd been described to us. As the sun rose, the soil that formed them turned color, from the pink of a girl's blush to an iron-enriched red.

Our child guides stopped as the sun crested the horizon and dropped to their knees, bending with arms outstretched until their faces touched the earth. "Praise to you, Maker," they said in unison. "Praise to you, who rules the day and night. Praise to you who will guide our steps. Amen."

Then they rose and continued on, leaving us in mute awe. Ronan smiled at them and then at me. Because we'd never seen anyone but Raniero and the elders worship and pray without concern, out in the open. We, the Ailith, had been raised to meditate in the morning and at night, but we did so in secret, away from anyone who might see us.

I found myself peering about, fearing they'd been seen, even though we were miles from the Drifters and likely anyone else. To be found praying to the Maker — or any god at all — was a subversive act, punishable by immediate death. And here, we Ailith — chosen followers of the One — were shown how it was done by two shepherd boys.

Vidar cast me a wide, toothy smile. "I'm likin' this new land. This is land a man can *breathe* in."

I huffed a laugh.

Ronan smiled again at me but then did a doubletake, grabbing hold of my chin and gently moving my head in one direction and then another, all grim intent now. With the light of day, my bruises had obviously been discovered. "What'd they do to you, Dri?" he growled.

"A couple hits, when they took us," I said, brushing his hand away. "It's to be expected. I'm fine."

"She fought like a true Ailith warrior," Niero said, his voice croaking out. All of us turned to him, laid out against a grassy bank.

"Niero," Bellona said, falling to her knees beside him.

"Niero!" I cried, falling to his other side, taking his hand in mine.

He took a deep, faltering breath and looked each of us in the eye. "I'm alive. Thanks to the Maker. And Andriana."

"And Socorro," I hurriedly added, my eyes wet with tears,

looking for my new friend. I made way for Tressa, who knelt beside Niero. By the light of the shepherd boys' lanterns, she'd prayed over him and dressed his wound, but now, in the daylight, she moved to unwind it and see if there was something else that could be done.

Niero caught her wrist and shook his head. "Not now. We must get to the Hoodites. Then, you may see to me."

Tressa paused and then nodded once. Vidar produced a canteen and Niero drank deeply from it.

A few minutes later, more Hoodites approached, and they carried a stretcher, woolen fabric stretched across poles.

"Let's get you in," Ronan said to Niero, gesturing to the stretcher. Killian waited on the other end.

"I can walk," Niero muttered. "If you'll just help me to —"

"We'll make better time with this."

"But I —"

"C'mon, Niero. In you go," Tressa said, urging him toward it. "With as much blood as you've lost, you're liable to faint dead away at any moment again."

"I very much doubt that," he said, still resisting. Was that a hint of pride within him?

But we all circled around, arms crossed, until he did as she asked.

We set out again, Vidar taking lead, his pistol in hand. I was behind him, with Ronan carrying the front of the stretcher and Killian the back. Tressa and Socorro were in front of Bellona, who brought up the rear, an arrow nocked on her bow. Vidar studied the cliffs that surrounded us, as if wary of an ambush. But all we saw as we hiked were the Hoodites giving way to a massive, smooth, silver-stone cliff, and all we heard was the thundering waterfall ahead. It was a long time before we finally saw the falls, and when we did, we paused to admire it. Where there was less velocity, it spread wide and ran down the face of the cliff at the edges, creating beautiful, painted colors beyond it on the rock — a natural painting of bright green, a brilliant aqua, and blood red in waves. In the center it spread in an even sheet, misting upward from the pool at the bottom.

"It's the color of your eyes," Ronan whispered to me.

"Hey, Dri," Vidar said over his shoulder, when we moved out again, his tone oddly hushed. Vidar was never hushed. He was a little short on breath too, by the sound of it. I opened my eyes wider, realizing that I was feeling incredibly drowsy, exhausted from the pain and trauma of the night. *Practically asleep on my feet.*

"Yeah?"

"Tressa told me … She said you said on the canyon rim that your gift is unfolding, growing?"

"Yes."

"Emotions now feel stronger to you, now, when you touch someone?"

"Uh-huh," I said, blinking slowly, forcing myself to take a step and then another rather than shuffle and likely trip.

"Mine too."

That got my attention. "What?" I forced my eyes open and stared at the back of his head.

"I mean, not emotions. And touching people. But my, uh, vision? My understanding of light and dark? That's changing."

"What do you mean?"

"I can see them, everywhere."

Ronan spoke up. "See *what*, specifically, Vidar?"

Vidar paused. "*You* know."

"Vidar," I said wearily. "We don't. What? Shadows and light?" What else did a man with the gift of discernment see?

"No," he said. *"Angeli e demoni,"* he whispered over his shoulder in what I guessed was an old language, as if he didn't quite dare to say it in our own. Vidar wiped his right cheek against the shoulder of his shirt, clearing it of sweat, and then studied the ridge. "Like up there," he said, "above us."

I looked up to the waterfall, then along the cliff, but I saw nothing. "On the ridge?"

"Yes. There are about twelve of 'em, I think, all along the ridge."

My eyes widened and I searched the ridge too.

I was about to tell him I didn't see anything, but then I reached out to lay a gentle hand on his shoulder and get a better read on his emotions. Fear startled me — but it was a *respect* kind of fear, not a *scared* kind of fear. Then awe. Wonder. And such a sure gladness ... it was almost as if I *had* seen them, through him.

"Angels, huh?" I said.

"You see them too," he said, hope lacing his tone.

I smiled. "No. But I can feel your emotion, brother. And your heart tells me what my eyes cannot."

There was a mixture of sorrow and gratitude that came from him then. To be understood, at least on one level, was a blessing; to not be able to share our gift, truly share it, was somewhat isolating. I knew it well.

"What do they look like?" Ronan asked.

I liked how he understood too, in measure. How he never doubted Vidar. Believed him from the start.

Vidar searched the ridge again and tripped over a rock, barely keeping his feet. But he didn't seem to notice, other than hurriedly holstering his pistol.

"I'm not sure. I can just barely make them out. But they seem to be waiting on us or something."

"Indeed," Niero said from his stretcher, looking up to the ridge. Ronan and I shared a look. Could *Niero* see the angels?

The closer we got to the waterfall — and presumably, the angels — the more my armband emitted a low, pleasing *thrum*. Vidar stumbled a couple of more times, and me behind him, so enrapt that Ronan yelled at us to pay attention to where we were going. It felt like he barely heard Ronan, and I understood why. I couldn't release his shoulder, so engaged was I at the wave of wonder and joy that washed through him, again and again. What would it be to *see* angels?

"They *are* here to watch over us," Vidar said. "Welcome us. We're right where we're supposed to be," he said, in such wonder that I felt warmed to the core.

I thought about that. About the Drifters. About the pain. Had the Maker used it all to bring us here? Was that his way? And why here?

And, Maker? Couldn't you have managed to direct us here without Niero getting shot?

The shepherd boys took us on a path that led *under* the waterfall, spraying us so thoroughly my entire front was wet, then led us deeper in, behind it, into a natural grotto that spread wide above and around us, and was covered with green moss at the edges. I smiled. *Sometimes you have to brave a little wet to enjoy getting dry*, my dad used to say. Memory of him saying it — and thinking of how he'd love it here — made me a little sad. All their lives, my mom and dad never left the Valley, their only thought to protect me. To raise me to take this journey, to answer this call.

Ronan led me to a roaring fire, ringed by stones that

warded off the damp chill of the cave. Tressa moved to Niero, sitting across the fire from me, but he again waved her away, toward me, whispering something to her as he moved off his stretcher and leaned back against a sloping boulder and closed his eyes. She reluctantly left him and came to my side, studying my face with the practiced eye of a healer.

Killian brought her a bag, and two children brought her a pot of steaming water and rags. She set to work on my face, gently washing away the blood that I hadn't known was there, then mixing a poultice together to pat across my bruises. She dipped a cloth into the steaming water, wrung it out, and then handed it to me. "Let it steam against that for a while," she said, her blue eyes looking into mine. "Do you have other injuries, Andriana?" she asked gently, under her breath.

I could feel the heat of my blush and quickly shook my head, knowing she had guessed the sort of treatment I had endured in the Drifter camp. "Thankfully, no," I said lowly. "But had not Socorro come to my aid ..." My voice cracked and I knew my blush likely deepened, judging from the fierce heat beyond the steaming cloth.

"Thank the Maker he did," she said, patting my arm, and in her touch I felt no judgment, only understanding, empathy, care.

People brought me water — and food, delicious food, trying to tempt me and nourish me, even in the midst of my weariness and distraction. Dimly, I acknowledged a portion of pink fish, cooked over the flames and handed to me on a stick. And with wonder I took what looked like corn from a young girl offering it to me. The tiny, beautiful, light yellow kernels were in perfect rows, and seemed stuck to what felt like a small rod the size of my fist. Flame-roasted leaves held it like a plate.

I looked from it to the girl, who had another in her hand. She giggled. "You haven't seen corn before?" she asked, biting into her own.

"Have you?" I countered, lifting it up to smell it. My mouth watered. "I ate some from a can, once. Long ago. This is almost too pretty to eat, in those perfect little rows."

She giggled again, and was about to take another bite when her eyes opened wide.

My armband began to thrum again, and for a moment I wondered if Vidar's angels — our angels — had entered the grotto. And as much as I wanted to take a bite of my corn, I wanted to see who'd arrived more. The people in the grotto — more than a hundred strong — parted to make way for a small woman, with dark hair shorn to just inches. She wore boots, pants, a sleeveless shirt, and what appeared to be a vest made out of some dark animal skin. Across her olive-skinned forehead she wore a braid of leather, but it was another braid that drew my attention.

Around her right forearm, she had the tattoo of an armband, exactly like our cuffs.

She took a skewer of fish from a boy who offered it to her and took a bite, even as she grinned at us Ailith, looking each of us in the eye. She moved to grasp arms with Niero, still seated, smiling down at him as if they were old friends.

Then she came to me and squatted. Without asking, she rested a gentle hand on my head and bowed her own, as if listening. My armband hummed with pleasure at her arrival, and my mind burned with a thousand questions.

At last she smiled into my eyes. Her own dark, sparkling eyes lilted in a cheery slant against her dark skin, reminding me a lot of Niero. "My friends," she said, setting aside her fish and giving us a regal, royal bow, then rising to look at us all again. "Long have I waited for this day. I bid you greetings in the name of Kapriel, true heir to the throne. I am Azarel of Pacifica." She spoke with a royal edge, crisp and yet full of depth. It was like nothing I'd ever heard before.

"You ... you know Kapriel?" Vidar asked. "You know where he is?"

Her smile faded and I felt her pain. "Not at the moment, though I've searched every path opened to me over the last year, which eventually led me here. Perhaps now that we've been joined, the Maker shall illuminate Kapriel's hidden prison. For we are to free him," she said with a single, confident nod, bringing a fist to her chest.

"You are Ailith?" Tressa asked, gesturing toward Azarel's tattoo.

"No. I am but Kapriel's servant, and now yours too." She ran a small hand over her arm, across the tattoo. "Kapriel dreamed of this mark, every night, for over a year. Together, we took the ink to commemorate the vision. When the Hoodite shepherds saw you," she said, looking to the children, then over to me, "captured and stripped, exposing your armband, we knew. We *knew*. The Maker had brought you to us. I've been here for weeks, waiting on word as to where I was to go next — but on and on, he bid me to remain. To be still and listen."

"The Maker speaks to you," Killian said flatly.

She cast him a curious look. "As he does to every one of his faithful. Have you not heard him? You, who travel with so many with high gifting?" Her brow knit in confusion.

"You speak of *hearing* him," he repeated, looking back at her as if she'd gone crazy. He shook his head, sending his blond dreadlocks bouncing about his shoulders. "As I hear you now."

She paused. "Yes. And no. It's more of a listening, deep

within. An understanding sort of ear. I hear him in bits, phrases. But it is enough."

"It is a high gift, like those of the Remnant," he said, looking at me, Vidar, and Tressa, eager to explain it away. "She must be Ailith."

"No. It is a gift, but for everyone of the Way," she said, crouching and biting into her fish. "Be at peace, brother. There is time enough to speak of such things. But tonight we must eat and decide where we are to go next."

"We heard of another, a follower of Kapriel, living among the salt caves north of here," Ronan said. He folded his arms. "A *man*. We were heading in that direction when we were confronted by the Drifters."

Slowly she looked away from Tressa to Ronan. "You've heard of our brother, Asher. He was living and ministering to the faithful there, true. Building a Community to serve the coming king, as I endeavor to do, everywhere I go." She studied him. "Apparently, the Maker's plans were different than your own, bringing you here, to me. Because I can tell you that Asher left the salt caves weeks ago. He was on his way to Georgii Post."

"Georgii Post," Ronan allowed, a shadow of challenge in his eyes. I knew what was irritating him. Her demeanor was overbearing, almost lordly. As if she was in on every secret. But I saw Raniero took her manner in stride, as if he was not bothered by it.

I bit into the corn and the creamy, roasted taste exploded in my mouth. It was so much better than what I'd even remembered.

Azarel laughed at my expression. "Delicious, isn't it? You must try the alpine strawberries and fiddlehead stew." She rose and went to a table, then brought some of each to me. Three tiny red berries and a bowl of creamy, green soup. Then she went to get more for my companions.

I tried the soup first, wanting to reserve the bright-colored berries. Whatever the green fiddleheads were, I knew I liked it. There were bits of dried meat and potato in the stew too. When my wooden bowl was empty, I set it aside and popped one of the precious berries — fresh, not dried — into my mouth.

Azarel laughed again, and I decided her laugh was like music, a bright, happy tune, which seemed to lighten her heavy bearing. She wasn't mocking me — only amused. "You don't normally eat the stem of the berry."

"I don't care," I said, still chewing, not wanting to swallow yet, because then the sweet, tart taste would be gone from my tongue. At last I swallowed. "Where did you get those? And the fiddleheads? Do they grow here?"

She smiled and nodded. "Along with leeks, kale, arugula, fennel, and more. Dagan, over there, can show you, when you're up to it." Her eyes drifted to where I still held the cloth against my poultice. Her eyes narrowed. "I heard you were taken captive by the Drifters. Did they hurt you quite badly?" she asked gently.

"Not in any way that won't heal," I said.

She nodded in approval, taking a sip from her soup bowl and studying me so intently, it made me skittish.

I glanced over to a reedy young man of perhaps two decades, the one named Dagan. He shifted and smiled shyly as if he was honored by Azarel's attentions, and a bit in awe of us.

But as I tossed the last berry in my mouth, feeling it ignite taste buds I hadn't known I had, it was I that found myself in awe of him.

CHAPTER 16

I slept soon after supper, exhausted from my trials as well as the relief in our rescue.

I awakened in the deep of night to the sound of the falls, the crackle of the nearby fire. I reached down and felt the stones from the fire they'd set around me, and they were still lukewarm. All around, the Hoodites and Ailith were asleep, reminding me of the cave full of Drifters last night, and yet so different. So very different.

The feel, the spirit of true Community. For the first time, I began to believe all I'd been taught from childhood on. That it wasn't just a time to come, a dream held for generations. I was living it, right here. I wasn't just a part of seeing the Maker's vision come to pass. I was a vital aspect of it.

A movement over by a pool of water that drifted inside the cave drew my eye, and I noticed Raniero. He was naked to the waist. Unwinding the bandages, washing the blood from his torso. I sat up and then gingerly stood, feeling every ache and pain of the battles and abuse I'd endured, and yet I also felt alive, so *alive* and free. Was it my escape? Or this place?

I carefully moved past Ronan, sleeping at my head, and between Tressa and Killian's mats, making my way to Raniero. He was trying to reach his back with a sponge, to wash away the dried blood there, and looked up at me when I neared, then away. Was I intruding? Was it too private? And yet, did he not need assistance?

I remembered the moment the Drifter's bullet struck him. How I had the sensation that he was broadening, stretching, to protect me. I'd felt the impact of the bullet as it struck him. The wave of his body, slamming against me, shuddering from the pain . . .

I crouched behind him. "Here. Let me," I said, reaching my hand out for the sponge.

"No, I'm fine, Andriana. Go back to sleep."

"I had to let you go, Niero," I said miserably. "Drop you off the bike. That moment . . . It was terrible. Please, let me. It will make me . . . feel better. To help."

He sighed and handed me the sponge. I rubbed it over the wide breadth of his bronze skin, frowning as the water illuminated scars across his back. A hundred battle scars, faint but present. Some of them were massive. I frowned. He wasn't that old. Only a few seasons older than we. How had he gathered so many wounds? Healed so many times? And in what battles?

I knelt by the pool and rinsed out the sponge, glancing over at him. "You want to tell me how you received all those scars on your back?" My eyes flicked down to his broad, sculpted, naked chest. I could see more there too, faint, raised, pale lines

"No," he said softly.

"Will you tell me anyway?"

"No." He stared back at me as I searched him, trying to get a read on his emotions. But he was blocking me again. He had to be. How'd he do that?

I returned to his back and finished washing him, being careful toward the top, where I knew the wound was. The bullet must've just missed a lung — a miracle in itself. But when I reached it, washing away thick, crusty blood, all I saw was skin beneath.

I blinked once, twice. Where the bullet had hit him, there was now just a small, puckered circle of scar tissue, directly over where I imagined his lung was. It hadn't missed it. How was he breathing? Whole?

I rose and looked at the front of his chest, where it exited. I put one hand in the center of his back and the other on his massive bicep, going back and forth and back again.

He smiled then, clearly enjoying my confusion, my awe, then gave me a little shrug. "I'm particularly good at healing."

"Did Tressa do this?"

He shook his head.

"Azarel?"

"No."

"You are ... This is a high gift?"

"Of a sort. The Maker's song is strong within me," he said, giving me a smile that made his dark eyes twinkle. He brought a fist to his chest as he said it, and I smiled back at him, amazed.

A man coughed behind me and I looked back, startled.

Ronan.

Belatedly, I saw how the two of us must have looked, and dropped my hands from Raniero's warm, bare skin and rose. "I was just ... I was just helping Niero clean up. He had blood on his back he couldn't reach." I knew I was blushing, looking guilty. And it made me angry that I felt the need to explain myself. I'd done nothing wrong.

Raniero pulled on a clean shirt, then crouched by the pool to wash out his other one, stained so thoroughly I didn't think it'd ever come out. So much blood ... When he received his wound, he'd been away from any Ailith, far from Community. He'd been unconscious in the back of the Jeep. And yet now, here he was, whole, healed. "Go and get some more sleep before the night's out," he said to us both, meeting Ronan's gaze of quiet challenge without flinching, without guilt. "Tomorrow's a new day."

I turned and followed Ronan back to our fire and settled onto my bed roll beside the stones, now just barely warm. Ronan was mad, his hurt and jealousy and anger practically shouting at me. But he knew what I did — he had no claim on me. None of us were to be attached to another beyond a sisterly or brotherly love. That was what the elders had told us. So for him to take issue with my intimate moment with Niero would be to admit defeat on that front ... and what?

Might Niero even send us home?

I closed my eyes and feigned the deep breathing of sleep, hoping to coax him back into slumber. After a long while, I heard Ronan finally give in. I slowly opened my eyes, peering at him from beneath my lashes to make sure he was asleep, then canvassing the cave to find Raniero again, curiosity burning within me.

He was at the mouth of the cave, kneeling, facing out, hands on hips, his body a silhouette against the wall of the water six feet out. The sun was rising, casting a coral glow to the water, and Niero lifted his arms as if in greeting, then bent in meditation.

For the first time, I wondered if he ever slept. He was always the first one up, and the last one to sleep. Was it his role as our captain, our leader, our ultimate protector?

Or something else entirely?

Abruptly, Vidar sat up, rubbed his face, and stared with sleepy eyes toward the waterfall. He blinked heavily, and then stared again. Surprise and wonder seemed to seep from his skin.

"Vid?" I whispered.

He glanced over to me, then to Raniero again.

"What do you see?" I whispered.

But Vidar shook his head and lay back down, already fast asleep.

I looked over to Raniero, and after a moment he turned his head sideways, his face in profile. It was almost as if he was listening, aware somehow that I was watching. Quickly, I lay back down.

And yet try as I might, there was no more sleep to claim.

■　■　■

The next morning, Dagan, the Hoodite farmer, led us out and down a trail that ringed the waterfall and past another string of Hoodoos — the limestone figures that looked like men, carved from ancient cliffs. "They were formed by erosion," he said, "eons ago."

"Even before the War?" Tressa asked.

"Far before the War. Thousands of years before. Hundreds of thousands before, maybe." He looked at her with shy interest. I decided that half the men in the Hoodite camp fell in love with her the hour we arrived.

I glanced toward Ronan, hoping he wasn't drawn to her like that. *Not that I have any claim on him. Completely out of bounds, Dri. Get it through your head, once and for all.*

He is not yours, and he never will be.

Dagan turned and walked over a small river, balancing on a fallen tree, and we followed. We entered a new trail through the woods, and minutes later exited to see a wide, south-facing plain, divided into neat rows.

My mouth dropped open. Because I was seeing something that I hadn't seen anywhere but in an ancient children's book that belonged to one of the elders.

A farm. Acres upon acres of a neatly tended, perfectly cultivated farm.

Killian stepped forward and pressed his hand against his dreadlocks, then looked back at Dagan in sheer surprise. "You? You did all this? Planted all this? How ˮ

Even as he asked it, I noticed the clouds gathering above us. How long until they broke loose and drenched us?

Dagan shrugged. "Ever since I was a young one, I was drawn to the task. The hope of tilling, planting, tending."

"But no one …" Ronan shook his head. "No one's truly *farmed* since just after the War."

Dagan waved his head to one side and then the other, and went to the nearest row of plants, digging up a potato and showing it to us. "That's true here, but not what I hear tell of Pacifica. It's simply a lost art to us out here, I think. Between the damp and the cold and the massive swaths of land lost to the wasting poisons …" He shrugged and moved to another plant, this one nearly a foot high, with a delicate, lace-like leaf. "Here near the Hoodoos, we have less rain. And even our

Hoarfrost isn't as cold as yours is, in the Valley, if I understand it right." I'd seen him talking last night with Vidar as they ate.

He pulled out the plant, taking out a knife to slice off the roots, then rubbing the bulb clean on his pants. He gave each of us a slice. "Fennel. In olden times, the bulb was big, as big as a woman's fist."

I tasted my slice. It was a little bitter, but with a warm flavor.

"You can use the whole plant, in soups or other dishes. And," he said, giving us a secretive look, "I've seen a bee."

"A bee!" Niero said.

"What's a bee?" Tressa asked.

The old fragments of Winnie the Pooh books came back to my mind. Pooh had always been after more honey, a golden, sticky, sweet substance that bees seemed to produce in trees.

Vidar was becoming more excited by the moment, pacing back and forth. He kept looking at the farm that spread before us, and to Dagan, as if he were a miracle-worker. I supposed, in a sense, he was. "Do you know what that means? What doors might open to us if we could coax the bees back?"

"No," Killian said, crossing his arms. "Enlighten us."

"Well, bees, uh ... bees do ..." He waved at Dagan, too excited to finish a sentence, and perhaps not entirely sure himself.

"Bees were the great pollinators, before the War," Dagan said. "Even before the War, there was fear because whole colonies died of disease. But it's due to bees that fruit trees could bear fruit. Nuts. At one time, there were over a hundred different crops that depended on bees. Some plants get pollinated by wind blowing it from plant to plant. Others need bees."

We stared at him as if he were speaking a different language.

"Where did you learn such things?" Ronan asked, bending

to clip a small bit of the fennel leaf off and chew on it. He spit it out, as if it were too bitter. He waved toward the neat rows of plants, some faring well, some clearly struggling. "How did you know how to create all of this?"

"My grandfather traded for an old book on horticulture from what was once our Great North. It's all about farming in cold climates," he said, looking around at our blank faces. "He said that our climate here, now, is more like the Great North was, before the War. They, too, had short growing seasons and difficult weather. While she had more sun during her Harvest season than we do here," he said, waving up at the clouds, "it was about as cold. A short season and similar temperature was reason enough for my grandfather to begin experimenting. My father picked up from there, and last year, when he died, I followed in their footsteps."

I looked up to the Hoodoos that lined the western edge of the farm. He was right; it was far warmer and drier here than in the Valley. Did the stones, the heat they retained, have something to do with his success?

Niero shook his head and paced. "But how did you get the seeds? How did you begin?"

"My father and I found the remains of a cabin near here. Even now, you can see the remains of fence posts here and there. It had been farmed before the War. And my grand-father ... " He gave us a sheepish smile and rubbed the back of his neck. "Others called him foolish. Crazy. But he spent his life trading for seeds. More books on horticulture. I guess I caught the bug."

"Or the gift," Niero said, gesturing forward. "This is extraor-dinary. A farm. A farm!" He laughed in awe and crouched, lift-ing a handful of dirt, squeezing it in his hand and staring at it as if it was from the Maker's land itself. "Between this ... and Ignacio's herd ..." He looked up at all of us. "Don't you feel it? The hope we might have, in this land? The Trading Union — if we could build upon what these two have started. We could build true alliances, and feed our people. Many people."

"Others must know of such secrets," I said. "We've traded for dried apples for years. That's a crop that demands sun and bees, yes?" I asked Dagan.

He nodded. "I think there are still orchards to our west. The crops seem to come from Pacifica."

Azarel hissed at the name. "He is right," she said with disgust. "Pacifica has retained the art. And carefully kept it from the Trading Union beyond the Wall."

"Why?" Even as I asked it, I knew the answer.

"Power," she said, pulling her head to one side, her lips curling into a sneer. "Greed too. But mostly power. They want to retain the secrets that everyone wants, so that ultimately everyone is beholden to them. Keallach wants everyone to come to him, wanting something only he can give." She looked to the rows of plants as the rain ceased again, then over to Dagan. "If he knew this was here ... that Dagan had discovered the way to till the soil and produce again, they would hunt him down. And kill him."

I breathed in sharply and Dagan frowned and looked to his fields, but clearly her words didn't surprise him.

"What of the Drifters, just across the river?" Ronan asked, one hand on his hip, the other in the air. "What if they discover it, and tell others?"

"The Drifters can't swim," Socorro said. For the first time I studied him in the light of day. He was about my height, with mezzo skin and round eyes. He was terribly skinny — had he not received his share of the food in that Drifter camp? I imagined his kindness keeping him from demanding, pushing, pulling for what was rightfully his.

"And for a decade now, the Drifters have kept to that side of the river, and we to ours," Dagan said.

"Until your people came to rescue us," I said softly, "and Socorro crossed with us."

Their dark eyes met mine. Dagan nodded once.

"We've compromised him then," I said to Niero. "Dagan has to be one the elders spoke of. One we are to save and preserve. With him with us, we're closer to providing for our people," I said excitedly, matching his pacing now. "Not just trading for food, but *producing* it."

Niero paused, chin in hand. "But we can't take our farmer out of the only land we know can produce. These crops — they would fail in colder, wetter conditions, right?" He looked back at Dagan.

"I assume so. My grandfather tried to plant in many places. It was only when we reached this place that plants began to take root, flower, grow." He bent and plucked several red strawberries from a short vine and handed them to Tressa with a shy grin.

Killian crossed his arms and frowned, towering over him. I smiled over his jealousy, but then thought, *Better Dagan than Ronan going after her.*

Inwardly, I chastised myself. *You're just as jealous, Dri.*

"They'll kill him," Vidar said with conviction. "Those who are against us. As soon as they know of it. Have you traded any of these goods?" he asked. "Any at all?"

Dagan shifted nervously. "A bit. With our brothers and sisters in the salt caves. But they would never betray —"

"Never betray us, no," Azarel said, shaking her head, looking as if she herself had been caught. Maybe she had taken the supplies herself and now regretted it. "Not on purpose. But it would only take a careless word at a trading post "

"Even now, word might be out," Vidar said, his entire body coming to attention, slowly searching the woods, the Hoodoos, as if reaching out to sense any darkness, hovering near.

"Others can see to your crops, Dagan," Niero said, regretfully. "We need to get you — and your seeds — to the Citadel to keep you safe. The elders have additional texts there that you can study. Perhaps experiment with what's still possible to grow in the Valley, given our heavier Hoarfrost. When all are gathered, when our mission is complete, you shall emerge and lead us, sustain us, with this gift."

"I'll take him," Azarel said, crossing her arms.

"You. Alone," Niero said, eying the small woman who had been a companion of Kapriel. "I don't think so," he added, walking away from her.

She scurried around him, gesturing to the bare, lean muscle of her arm. "I got here, didn't I? From Pacifica. *Alone.*"

He frowned down at her. "Perhaps it's easier to get from Pacifica to the Hoodites."

She laughed under her breath. "Brother, you clearly have *no* idea what's ahead of you."

"Nor do you know what's ahead of *you*. Unless you have some sort of foreknowledge gift."

She pursed her lips and sighed, crossing her arms. "Well then, how 'bout I share what I know, and you share your knowledge, and we'll both get where we want to go faster?"

"Fine."

"Fine."

I had to turn away, their attraction was so palpable. Was I the only one to read it in them? Killian saw it. He rolled his eyes and let out a scoffing breath.

"You should stay with them, Azarel," Socorro said, as we all turned to go. "I will take Dagan to the Citadel."

We turned back to consider him. "I know the Desert," he said with a shrug. "As well as the ways of the Drifters. I can keep him safe." He gave us a small smile. "Besides, I'd like to see your Valley."

Ronan said, "He might discover Ignacio and his grandmother too, along the way. Help them along, in case they've gotten waylaid."

Azarel considered him, arms folded, and bowed her head. "He's right," she said at last. "Dagan will be safer with him. It is as the Maker has seen."

"How do you know that?" Killian asked in irritation.

"Because the Maker has told me as much." She turned her dark eyes to the ridge, and then glanced at Niero and Vidar. She was troubled by something, as if she'd smelled something foul on the air.

"Right this instant?" Killian sneered. "The Maker said, 'Dagan will be safer with him.'"

"No," she said, squinting her eyes. "A moment ago." She stared at him. "Perhaps I am to travel with you Ailith for a time," she said. "It appears there is much you do not yet know about the Way. If you are to accomplish your mission "

"We have what we need to accomplish our mission," Niero said in irritation.

"Do you?" she asked.

"Yes."

"You're sure."

"If you are questioning our ability to …" His words faded as he watched her look to the trees, and slowly pull a bow from her shoulder, and finally an arrow from a quiver on her back. "Azarel?"

"You feel that?" she asked Vidar.

"What say we get back to camp?" Vidar asked nervously, falsely bright, eyes settling on the trees, hand reaching for the halberd on his back. I felt the cold fear within him and shivered.

"Vidar? Something coming?" I asked. *It wasn't fear. Terror. And worse, doubt.*

"Maybe. I-I don't know." His eyes met mine and I felt his shame. "My mind is on such hyper-alert, I seem to be sensing everything, both good and bad. So fast," he held his head, "so intense …"

"You're sensing something terribly evil, as well as good," Azarel said, putting her hand on his shoulder. "Your gift will settle in time. Become clearer. More consistent. All your gifting will be so," she said, looking at each of the Remnants. "But for now, we need every one of you to take up your weapons."

CHAPTER
17

They emerged from the forest in even segments — twelve of them in an arc about us, four of them dressed in the long, royal red cloak and hood that we'd seen on the one in Nem Post and Zanzibar. The others were in a darker, shorter red oilskin, the color of dried blood.

Four were trackers. Pacifica's elite. With scouts to back them up.

Vidar swore under his breath, and his hand trembled as he switched the halberd to his left hand and drew the pistol from a holster with his right. "Let me take care of 'em," he said.

"No," Niero said, lifting a hand in his direction, even while keeping an eye on the advancing men. "Only the weapons of old. I don't want the Drifters hearing gunshot and deciding that now is the time to come over."

"You think they don't know we're here?" Killian asked, unsheathing his sword. "Who do you *think* sent them our way?"

"No guns," Niero insisted.

"Trust me, the Sheolite elite cannot be killed by a bullet anyway," Azarel said, drawing an arrow across her bowstring. "You must not only take them down, you must cut out their heart or decapitate them."

"She's right," Ronan growled. "By all rights, I killed the tall one the last time we battled." I saw him then. Sethos, the tracker we'd first encountered at Nem Post and later in Zanzibar.

"Fantastic," Vidar grumbled, shoving his gun back in the holster at his hip and gripping his long halberd with both hands. "Next you'll tell us that their blood is green, right?"

I didn't even smile. What had Azarel meant? I drew my sword and wished I had time for a drink of water. My mouth was completely dry. Sethos and another were focused on me, their intent clear and cold.

"I don't suppose our angel friends are here now?" I asked Vidar. If nothing else, I thought their presence would comfort me.

"No," he said grimly.

"We must keep them from getting any closer to Dagan's fields," Niero said quietly. "Everyone understand that?"

"As well as away from the waterfall," Azarel added.

"But your priority is to stay with your Remnant," Niero said.

"Agreed," Ronan said, sidling slightly ahead of me as the Sheolite advanced.

"Agreed," Killian said, guarding Tressa and Dagan.

"Agreed," Bellona said, moving closer to Vidar.

"I am Sethos of Pacifica," cried the tall tracker in the center of our enemies. His voice was low, his tone confident. He tossed his braid over his shoulder and glanced over us, one to the next, taking measure. "You are outnumbered. We only want the Remnants. They are practicing the high gifts and must face a judge. You knights may go in peace. We'll call it a peace offering." He carefully set the tip of his sword on the ground and rested his gloved hands atop the hilt.

Ronan's chin lifted. "There is one Judge. And you are not him."

Sethos kept staring at me, ignoring Ronan. He lowered his chin and sent a wave of such dark intent that I took a step backward. Just like in Zanzibar, I felt bleak, empty *sorrow*, in its purest form. As if they took a thousand grieving children, bottled their tears, and then sprayed it from their very pores.

He laughed at my stumbling, lurching step.

Ronan growled and took a step closer to our adversary, essentially blocking me. Niero closed the gap from the other side. And I felt immediate relief from the intense pull of our enemy.

"And you are the lovely one that escaped us within the bowels of the city," Sethos said, pacing casually, his gaze moving on to Tressa. He shook his head as if amused. "How thoughtless of us not to search there. There you were, all that time, the rose growing among the sewers of men."

"Perhaps it would not have been quite as easy as you make out." Killian took a step forward, sword at the ready, jaw set, daring them to advance.

"And you two," the man said, ignoring Killian, glancing over to Azarel and Vidar. "You knew we approached, even though we were cloaked." He clearly spoke not of what they wore, but something else —

"You can't hide ugly for long," Vidar said, setting his halberd tip in the dirt as our adversary had with his sword. Bellona nocked an arrow and lifted her chin toward Sethos, legs spread-eagled, looking fearsome. Azarel stood ready, her first arrow already drawn and aimed at his chest.

"I am on royal orders from my ruler, Keallach. Those four," Sethos said to Niero, pointing at me, Vidar, Tressa, and Azarel. "Give us those four to face justice and we leave you to live. It is a generous offer, since anyone consorting with those of the high gifting are subject to immediate execution. I shall not offer it twice."

I quickly glanced at Azarel. Why would he include her with us? Was she a Remnant? Or was it because she was a consort of Kapriel?

"Keallach has no jurisdiction over us," Niero spit out, striding forward.

"You're wrong," said the man, matching his pace. "He shall rule all." They clashed ten steps ahead of us, the rest of us taking on our adversaries moments later.

"Stay with me, Dri," Ronan said over his shoulder as we ran.

"Right behind you."

Ronan and I had prepared for this, over and over. Our trainer's voice echoed in my head. *Keep your back to his, Andriana. Closer! Lunge, then draw away. He will protect your back, leaving you free to defend your—*

Two scouts and a tracker were moving directly toward us, even as Niero and Sethos engaged, swords clanging.

Ronan feigned right and surprised the first scout, plunging his sword into his kidney, then narrowly missed the second by inches. The third made it around to me. He didn't pause, driving toward me so fast, I bumped back into Ronan.

"Dri?" he grunted over his shoulder, his adversary's sword coming so close it sounded like it'd just missed my ear.

"I'm fine!" I grit my teeth and pushed toward my assailant

for several steps. While Ronan and I wanted our backs to each other, we had to have some room to move.

But then I saw that Tressa had the same problem as I — Killian had taken on two in front of him, and one had come around to her. Except that given her inability to fight, she could only lift a shield, blocking each blow, or jump his sweeping sword every time it threatened to slice through her legs.

I growled and turned in an arc, bringing down my sword down with such force, it surprised my attacker. It hit him on the shoulder just as he was driving his sword toward my thigh. His sword tip paused a hand's width from my trousers, as the man faltered, my sword still embedded between his shoulder and neck. He went to his knees, gasping, and I wrenched my sword free and turned away, hoping that not looking into his eyes would keep me from feeling more than the first tendrils of the man's fear now worming its way into me. I supposed I should bury my dagger in his heart to make certain he was dead, but I couldn't. I just couldn't.

I ran ten paces, taking on Tressa's attacker, one of the elite. "For men who claim they simply want us to speak with their king," I said, blocking his second strike, our swords paused above our heads, "you surely seem intent on killing us."

"We'll maim you if necessary to take you back to Pacifica," he spit out, turning and striking with enough force that I only barely held on to my sword. My whole body seemed to vibrate from the impact. "Continue fighting us," he said, his red face inches from mine, "and you may well die." He didn't stop, pressing and pressing and pressing me back from Tressa, as well as away from Ronan at the same time.

An arrow plunged through his shoulder, making him arch, its bloody point flashing in the sunlight. As he whirled,

Azarel's second arrow cut through his chest. But I only caught it in my peripheral vision, because Vidar cried out, and I turned to see him fall to his knees. "No!" I cried, seeing his attacker lift his sword to strike again.

Bellona narrowly saved him from the tracker's death plunge — a downward stab between his shoulder blades — by slicing the Sheolite's arm and then tackling him with a warrior's scream of rage. They tumbled over and over through the grass. When he rose, Niero cut his head off with his crescent-shaped blade and leaped over him to go after Sethos again.

Which was good, because I'd caught the tracker's eye again. I saw him behind the scout, already on the attack.

Ronan was still grappling with his two attackers, casting me a desperate look, wanting me to — what? Help? Run? He had no room to come to my aid.

The tracker advanced on me, calmly cracking the shaft of the arrow that stuck out of his chest and flinging it away. He did the same with the second. And then with a snarl he lunged with his sword, fierce and sure. I took the impact of his strike, again and again, growing weary, each parry more difficult to manage, each a little later, a little closer.

And then he slid his blade down mine, twisted, and sent my weapon flying.

My eyes went wide as they followed it, watching it turn end over end and then settle in the dirt. Even in exercises, it had been a year since my trainer had been able to do that to me. I had daggers at my belt, but he still had a sword. I needed some distance.

I turned and tore for the nearest trees, knowing he was right on my heels. If I could only get a ten-pace lead, I might be able to turn and fling my dagger with enough force to take him down. But even as I ran, I knew I was making a terrible mistake. Putting distance between me and every knight the Remnant had … And yet, what choice did I have?

I made it to the first copse of pines and rounded them, turning to see where my enemy was. As expected, he was right there, already plunging his sword toward me, a grim smile on his lips. I scooted left, narrowly avoiding its tip, but then he had turned, swinging his weapon toward me on the left. Again, I narrowly moved in time, and the edge of his sword cut into the tree trunk, momentarily immobilizing him.

I flung my dagger without pause. At the same time it hit him directly in the heart, an arrow went through his neck.

Azarel, I thought with relief. *Or Bellona.*

His eyes bulged, and horrible sounds came not from his mouth, but the bleeding neck wound. He choked and seemed to not know what to grasp at first — the dagger at his chest, or the arrow at his neck. Instead, he simply crumpled. His heart was still in his chest, his head still upon his shoulders, but I felt the tinge of death.

Quickly, I turned away, trying to break the bond of emotion between us. His final desperation, his panic, threatened to take my knees from beneath me as surely as a Sheolite sword would. I gasped and reached out for another tree trunk, leaning against it as nausea shook me. Try as I might, I couldn't shake this Sheolite as he faltered on the edge of life. It paralyzed me, what I felt then.

Emptiness. Darkness. Agony.

It was unlike anything I'd ever experienced. Was this what the Sheolites went on to in the afterworld?

I was repulsed and yet inexplicably drawn at the same time. I closed my eyes and listened, deep within, and it seemed as if I could hear whispers, words I couldn't quite make out … enticing me closer, closing in around me, opening up to welcome me in.

But then I could hear dim shouts in the distance too. My name. Frantic warnings.

I opened my eyes and looked directly across the field to Vidar, staring right at me, as were all the remaining Sheolites, still on their feet. The rest of the Ailith turned toward me too, confused, but Vidar was the one who seemed to understand what had happened. His lips rounded with the word *no*, his face a study of horrified alarm. What had I done? My cheeks flushed with embarrassment.

Sethos of Pacifica had his boot on Niero's chest, the point of his sword at his neck. But he stared steadily at me, the hint of a smile spreading across his face.

Another motion on either side of him caught my attention. Dark mist seemed to gather, incorporate, widen, lengthen, spreading among the Sheolites and stretching steadily toward us. It was so thick it blotted out the sun, and I blinked, trying to refocus on the task at hand, what I had to do to help us escape these predators.

Somehow, in concentrating on the eternal evil place, I knew I'd given our enemies a foothold. Some sort of crazy, internal foothold

But if I could do that, could I do the same for our side? I immediately knelt and lifted my hands, closing my eyes, my face rising to the blocked sun, as the elders had taught us, as the Hoodite children had shown us without pause. I did not fear the attack of a sword any more than I feared this dark, unnatural cloud that was steadily stealing through and around my people, my friends, Ronan.

Maker, forgive me. See me. Deliver me and my friends. Wash away this evil like a good rain. Make a way for us. For you are mightier than the sword.

I opened my eyes to the battle, renewed. Niero was again on his feet. I saw Sethos grimacing and stumbling backward. He looked furiously to me as if I were to blame. And then he tried the trick he had in Zanzibar, his hands becoming like claws, the tips pointing toward me, a scream so high — so eerie — emanating from his mouth that I wondered if it was real.

I covered my ears and leaned toward the ground, the sound of it echoing about my mind as if it were eating away at my memory, my ability to think.

Maker, Maker, protect me. Strengthen me! Drive them away!

On and on it went, each second pulling more strength from my bones, stealing my breath, making my head spin in a wide, slow, dizzy circle. I thought I saw Vidar running toward me, lifting his halberd for a fierce strike.

I couldn't think. Couldn't breathe. Couldn't call out.

It was almost as if I was on the precipice of death, of disappearing.

From far away, I thought someone picked me up and carried me. But I couldn't open my eyes to see who it was. And in that moment, I was too weak, too tired to care. Even if it was Sethos.

Because I felt like I was dying along with the tracker beside me.

And it took everything in me not to slip away to the dark, empty place that seemed to have opened a window in my heart.

CHAPTER
18

I came to slowly, shivering and trying to make sense of what was around me. Trying to remember exactly what had happened.

I took stock one sound, one sense at a time. The crack of resin from wood, spitting and hissing in a fire as it heated. Ronan's strong arms and the broad expanse of his chest. His hands rubbing my arms as if willing the blood to flow again. The prayers of Niero and Tressa and Azarel, each beside me, their hands resting on my legs. Farther out, the murmur of conversation around us. Fear. Concern.

I finally managed to open my eyes and looked around. Niero and Tressa were indeed beside me. Dagan, Socorro, Killian, Bellona, and Vidar stood around them, heads bowed, their lips moving in echoed prayer with them.

"Hey," I said, massaging my throbbing temples. "Quit acting like I'm almost dead. I don't give up that easily."

Niero's eyes sprang open first, and when he saw me staring

back he closed his eyes and rocked back in visible relief. "Oh, Andriana, thank the Maker."

"Andriana, what happened to you?" Azarel said. "I've never seen anything like that with the Sheolites." Her eyes darkened. "And I definitely did not like how Sethos was looking at you."

"How-how was he looking at me?" I remembered the scene far better than I liked. Every second seemed etched into my memory. I only hoped someone could put it into words.

"Both as conquest and enemy," Vidar said. *Yes. Like I was both solvent and acid. Poison and serum.* "It was as if when you reached the trees, you summoned him. I could hear you, somehow. Like you were calling us."

"Not just us. Sethos and his men too. What *was* that?" Ronan asked.

"I-I don't know." I squirmed then, wanting some space to breathe, think, no matter how sweet it felt to be in Ronan's arms. He let me loose, gently settling me to his side. But I felt warmth in my belly when I felt his arm still around my lower back. Still protecting me? Reassuring himself I was all right? *He's just being sweet, Dri. Just being your knight. Nothing more.*

They all remained where they were, waiting on me. "What happened?" I asked, trying to put it together. "After I passed out?"

"Every one of them turned toward you, as if they'd been redirected. As if they were called to you," Ronan said.

"And I could see them, Andriana, as they truly are," Vidar said, a shiver clearly running down his back. "*Demoni.* With scales that covered their temples and a ridge on their back." He paced nervously, wringing his hands, and I could see he was injured. "Right here," he said, gesturing behind his neck, right above the shoulder blades.

"I know," I said. I hadn't seen it as he had, but I had felt it.

We shared a long, miserable look. Neither of us was anxious to run across them again.

"There was something else," Vidar said, shaking his head. "Something in and amongst the men, later on. Like nothing I'd ever seen. Dark and whispy and barely visible."

"Wraiths?" Azarel spit out.

"No," he said, shaking his head. "More like dark angels, moving from spirit to body. Taking form right before my eyes. Is that possible?"

"You're asking me?" Azarel said. "I don't know! All we saw was that dark mist."

I nodded. I hadn't seen them exactly. But I'd felt them.

It was then that I noticed Niero's grim understanding. As if he'd expected this. Knew it as old knowledge while the rest of us were spinning.

"But at the same time, we weren't alone," Vidar said, eyes wide with glory, excitement. "The angels, from the Hoodite waterfall. I think they were there too. Wading in, fighting beside us. They came in when Andriana went to her knees."

"Yes. Yes," I said. "That's right."

"You saw them too?" Ronan asked, brown brows furrowed.

"Not exactly. I just sensed their presence."

Niero stared at me, hard, then set to pacing, chin in hand. We waited for him to speak, but he just kept pausing, looking my way, then pacing again.

"Whatever transpired back there, the Sheolite recognized this power in her too," Azarel said, shaking her head, poking a stick in the fire. "She summoned them, in essence. Those from both realms. This is not good. Keallach and his minions wanted the Remnants before," she said to Niero. "Now they'll be ten times as interested."

"Why?" Tressa asked. "Why do they want us alive? Are we not enemies?"

Azarel took a long, slow breath. "It's complicated. Both Kapriel and Keallach were raised with knowledge of the Ailith."

"There were elders among them?" Ronan asked.

Azarel shrugged. "I suppose. Kapriel never said. What he did say was that Keallach is interested in anyone who will assist him in obtaining ultimate power. Politically, monetarily, physically, spiritually. And he is well acquainted with the ways of the dark." Her eyes lifted to study me, and I felt a wave of her suspicion on the back of their collective alarm. "But they would only turn their focus on you, Andriana, if they *felt* the dark within you. Or such a pure stream of light they knew they had to take you down, and fast."

"That was it," Ronan said, his tone defensive. "She was praying. You saw her. We all saw her."

I met her gaze, steadily, as I rose, fists clenched. "No. It was the dark that evoked their interest."

The others frowned as I sighed, trying to put the pieces together like I had an old wooden puzzle with a notch in the wrong place. "While that Sheolite tracker was fighting death in front of me, and when Sethos focused on me too ... it was as if the dark opened up before me. I *felt* the dead place. And truthfully, I couldn't help but be intrigued. Curious." I bit my lip and tried to figure out a better way to say it. "It was like coming across a forbidden door, left unlocked, and just taking a quick peek in to see what the big secret was ... I couldn't seem to resist."

They all continued to stare at me in mute surprise. Even Ronan. I shifted, feeling the heat of a blush rising up my neck.

"And now?" Niero asked sternly. "Now that you've glimpsed what is behind the forbidden door?"

"I won't be nearing it again," I said, a shudder running through me.

"I think the difference," Azarel said, "is that you were able to open the door. Or as that Sheolite fought death, before you, you were able to follow him into the depths. I think that is what drew their collective interest. That unique power."

I nodded again, meeting her eyes, grateful for her understanding even if I didn't like what she described. For that was exactly what had happened.

"Until I ended him with my trusty halberd," Vidar said proudly.

"Andriana, the more and more you explore your power," Niero said wearily, giving Vidar a nod, then turning back to me, "the more you might be attuned to the dark and light. Potentially growing in your gift, as Vidar has. This will help you, and us as well. But you must take the utmost care, Andriana," he said, bending to put his hand on my shoulder. "Because, clearly, that sort of task is very dangerous. You-you almost …"

His words faded and he clamped his lips shut, as if he'd decided not to finish his sentence on purpose. What had he wanted to say? That I almost died? Disappeared behind hell's gates? A shiver ran down my spine again. Was that true? Could I really be lost in the darkness? Simply cease to exist? But when I studied his face, it was clear to me. He didn't fear that I'd die.

He feared I'd willingly give myself to the powers of darkness.

That I'd go against the Ailith.

Rage, hot and sudden, washed through me. *After all I'd been through, sacrificed ... After Mom and Dad?* I stood. "*You think* I would *betray* you? The Ailith? Our cause?" I shoved his hand from my shoulder.

"Whoa, Dri," Ronan said, rising and lifting his hands out to block me in case I attacked Niero. "He didn't say that."

"He didn't have to, Ronan." Some of it was guesswork, putting together his fear and anger — because he was tougher for me to sense than the others — but judging by his expression, I'd guessed right.

Niero looked sick, moving his head but not quite shaking it. "Andriana, no. You'd never do it on purpose. But this is really big. As your gift unfolds ..." He sighed and rubbed the back of his neck. "Power begets power. But most people think the greater the power, the surer the foothold. It's not like that. Think of a mountain peak," he said, putting his brown hands in an inverted V. "The greater the power, the more narrow the foothold, and therefore the more likely we are to tip either way on its precipice."

"You mean fall to the wrong side," Vidar said.

I looked to Niero, rage making me tremble, as he rubbed his temple as if in misery.

"I take it your elders never prepared you for something like this," Azarel said.

I looked to her, my anger fading as fast as it had come on. What was wrong with me? Why this sudden fury passing through me? It left me weak, shaken. And weren't they all simply asking wise questions? "No, they didn't," I said dimly, still staring at Niero, still wondering how he could think I would do anything to hurt the people I loved.

"Asher is wise and will know how we should negotiate

this," Azarel said, looking uncertain for the first time since we'd met. "He has spent much time with Kapriel. He was preparing to head to Georgii Post. Let's see if we can intercept him there. It's but a half-day's journey."

The rest conferred, and it was quickly decided to do as she suggested. It seemed the only true avenue open to us, and we had to reach a petrol trader soon.

"The trademaster at Georgii deals in fuel," she said.

"How are we all to get there on bikes anyway?" I asked, crouching, my pounding head in my hands. "We're already down one. And we need to send Socorro and Dagan back to the Valley, which would leave us two."

"Send them on mudhorses to the Valley," she said with a shrug.

"Bikes would be better than horses with Drifters about," Bellona put in.

"From here until you reach the Great Expanse, the Drifters shall dog you no matter how you travel," Azarel said. "Once you reach Castle Vega and the Great Expanse, all you'll have to dodge is Pacifica transports."

"Transports?" Bellona repeated.

"Vehicles that take Pacifica's people to Castle Vega. They come outside the Wall to engage in depravities of all kinds — depravities they pretend they don't have. And her merchants go to meet with those of the Trading Union. Because none are allowed on *their* side."

I tried to imagine what she meant about *depravities*, but then figured it was best to wait and encounter it when we had to — not spend time dwelling on it. Surely it couldn't be any worse than Zanzibar.

"Can we somehow get on one of those transports?" Killian asked.

"No," Azarel said. "Pacificans all wear an identity chip, embedded under their skin here," she said, rubbing her right shoulder.

"A chip," Killian repeated flatly.

"Something they can read with a device they wave over you. If you're found trying to enter the kingdom without one, you'll be immediately imprisoned."

"That wouldn't be great," Vidar said. "But hey, maybe that would lead us to Kapriel."

"Do you have one?" Niero asked.

"I did," she said. "Until I dug it out and destroyed it. If it stays in you, they can find you. Anywhere."

"So, if the Maker is leading us to Pacifica," Killian said, "and if Kapriel is held as a prisoner there, he's likely behind not one wall but two. How are we to get past the first?"

Azarel paused. "Across the Great Expanse. The driest, widest desert. They've walled everything else. They patrol the Great Expanse, but the only physical barrier is the land itself."

"Land a mudhorse can't cross," Niero said.

"A mudhorse could get you partway. But all the way?" She cocked a brow in his direction and shook her head. "Unlikely." She hesitated. "Although they might get you as far as the mountains that border Wadi Qelt."

"What is Wadi Qelt?" Tressa asked.

"A valley and the home of Keallach's Hoarfrost palace, on the western edge of the Great Expanse. He took over a sacred sanctuary, once inhabited by those that followed the Way."

Ronan grunted, his brow crumpling in confusion. "Why?"

"Keallach," Azarel said in a tired voice, "likes to preach

enlightenment. He declares we are in the new age of peace among all, so he didn't wipe out the monastery when he built his palace. The desert brothers and sisters still abide there. But do not be fooled," she said solemnly, looking about at us all. "It's only his twisted rendition of his early years of training with the elders. Kapriel understood truth and lives by it. Keallach lives to create his own truth."

We stared at her. Regardless of how it had turned out, nowhere had we heard of a king protecting anyone of any faith. Wasn't it a start, at the very least, in the right direction?

"I have to say, spinning his own truth is a mite better than cutting off their heads and mounting them on stakes for being a follower of the Way," Vidar said.

"There is that," Azarel said, giving in to a small, sad smile. "But trust me, it's more for show than any heartfelt belief. The Way was likely lost in that place many years ago."

"Belief has many layers," I said.

"Yes, but — " she began, frowning at me.

"Wait, wait, wait," Vidar said, holding up his hands. "You're saying that the only way past the Wall is through Keallach's own palace? We're a little thick at times, I admit, but isn't that idiotic?"

Azarel shrugged. "It's the only way. Pacifica's Wall is not like Zanzibar's. You must sneak through it or around it. And *through* is fairly impossible. Besides, Keallach won't be there during Harvest. It's weeks yet before he'd consider going."

"We'll face the challenges of this Wadi Qelt when we reach it," Niero interrupted, shaking his head. "*If* we can even reach it. We have three dirt bikes left. I don't like the idea of any of us trying to outrun the Drifters with mudhorses. We barely escaped them on bikes."

"My people," Dagan said. "When I was a boy, they tried to get a couple of dirt bikes running. They had several, using the others for spare parts."

"Did they succeed?" Vidar asked, casting him a hopeful glance.

Dagan shook his head, looking sorry he'd even mentioned it.

"Still," Niero said, "Vidar's good with engines. Will you let him see those parts?"

Dagan nodded and he and Vidar rose to go, Bellona right behind them. Tressa and Killian moved off to find us something to eat, while I remained with Azarel, Niero, and Ronan.

"So ..." I said, dreading asking. Knowing I had to find out. "What happened back there? After the attack? How did you drive them back?"

"We didn't," Ronan said, rising. "I mean, we did, to a certain extent. We could fight the Sheolites. We killed a few. Vidar took out that one tracker with his halberd. But they were strong, and gaining strength, as if edified by the dark ones who joined them."

"And?" I said when he paused.

"You began praying," Niero said, his dark eyes tender, searching me. "Calling out to the Maker. And when you did, we ourselves were strengthened. Sethos knew you were the key — he went after you. Straight for you, Andriana. We only narrowly stopped him."

"How? Did you kill him?"

"No," Ronan said miserably, as if he'd failed me. "Maimed him. It is as Azarel said — death must come thoroughly to such enemies."

"It's a wound which will not plague him for long," Azarel

said, her tone full of warning. "Trust me. The lizard grows a new tail."

"When Vidar killed the tracker that seemed to have you in that death grip, they sensed the tide was turning and disappeared the way they came, back into the forest."

I looked in alarm to the waterfall that served as our barrier. "Would they come here? Vidar?"

"He'd know," Niero said, nodding, when Vidar shook his head, telling us he didn't sense them anywhere near. "We can sleep here again but we must move on to Georgii Post come morn, not beyond. I do not want to invite further trouble for our Hoodite bretheren."

CHAPTER 19

We moved out at daybreak, Azarel riding behind Raniero on a patched-together bike that I feared wouldn't make it through the day. We saw no one all morning — not a Drifter or Sheolite — and we alternated between being thankful for the gift of it and holding our breath, certain we'd run across our enemies over the next rise. But we made good time across the bumps and divets of the salt plains and entered the red canyons by noon, a muddy river meandering to our left.

Killian first spotted the Georgii scouts, riding on horses along the curving ridges on either side of us. We slowed down, and lifted white flags to let them know we approached the post in peace. The nearer we drew to the fort, the greater the number of guards on either side of us became. They were still a fair distance away, and high above us on the cliff, but the canyon was narrowing the deeper we went, and around each bend they got closer and closer.

"Are they armed?" Killian asked, pulling to a stop on a well-worn road between two towers built of stacked flagstone.

"To the hilt," Azarel said, studying the cliffs.

A mirror flashed against the sun, directly in our eyes, and Azarel said, "All right, we've been given clearance. Move ahead. Slowly."

"What do you do when there's no sun?" Vidar asked.

"Pray the white flags are enough," Azarel returned with a grin, twisting the throttle, leading us out.

Around the next bend, we saw it, a walled fortress-post that ran from one side of the canyon to the next. It became clear that anyone who came this way had to come through the post, or circle for miles to get around it and on to the most direct road to Castle Vega. Eight guards came out on dirt bikes to meet us and take our papers. Unlike the guardians of the trading posts and Zanzibar, they didn't look twice at us women, which came as a huge relief.

"How long do you intend to stay at Georgii Post?" asked the leader, looking at Raniero and Azarel, then letting his gaze drift over the rest of us. He was about five decades. Lighter hair, tanned skin.

"Three, four days," Niero said easily.

He locked eyes with him. "Your papers say you hail from Nem Post. Where from, before that?"

"Here and there," Niero said casually.

"Where specifically?" the man said, his gaze hardening.

"Does it matter?" Azarel asked, sliding a packet out from under her vest. "We prefer to keep our business to ourselves. Care to help some travelers out?"

The man hesitated, then pointedly stared at the other men until they looked away. He grabbed the package from her hand

and unfolded it, peering inside. He quickly slid it inside his own jacket. "That'll buy you a decent amount of privacy. Go ahead," he said, gesturing to the fort gates. "Just see that you do not get into any trouble, or you'll answer to me."

"Understood," Azarel said, flashing him a small, charming smile.

We followed her and Niero again, well aware that there was likely a gun trained on every one of our heads as we passed. Up ahead, a drawbridge stood open, allowing us to cross up and over the river, which appeared to flow below the very city. Inside the high, thick adobe walls, I could see that the post was divided into a neat grid pattern, with two- and three-story buildings rising on the far edges, where the walls were the canyon walls themselves. Azarel led us directly east, and into what appeared the poorest sector. I groaned inwardly, thinking of the Zanzibian inn and the flea-infested mats. It looked like we'd be sleeping on our bedrolls again this night.

Children, barefoot and filthy, shouted as we passed, raising their hands and running after us as if we were exotic animals. They swarmed us as we stopped, begging for food, for coins, for a handshake, for any attention we were willing to spare at all. Never had I seen so many. I laughed and touched one's head, another's cheek, shaking hand after hand. A skinny, ragged man with dark curls emerged in the doorway of the nearest building, at first wary. Then upon seeing Azarel, he lifted his hands in greeting, a smile filling his face.

He pulled Azarel in for an arm clasp, then grabbed her head with both hands and kissed both her cheeks.

She laughed and yanked away, looking with some embarrassment at all of us. "Brothers and sisters, this is our brother, Asher."

He was shorter than I, dark in skin and hair, but there was a *lightness* about him that made it impossible to do anything but smile in his presence. He was jubilant that Azarel had returned to his side, tucking her hand around his arm as if escorting her, and staring at all of us in glee. But what was funnier was that she allowed it, shaking her head as if he were a troublesome kin. I never would've guessed she had such a soft side.

"My friends! My brothers and sisters," Asher whispered in awe, looking each of us in the eye. "Can it be true? Is it possibly upon us at last?"

"Let's go inside, Asher," Azarel said in a hushed tone, furtively looking up and around. "We can talk inside, where it's safe."

He reluctantly turned, and we moved into a building whose ceiling was so low that Killian, Ronan, and Niero all had to duck their heads. In the corner, two men and a woman were busily chopping vegetables and putting them into a huge kettle sitting over a low-burning open fire. Above it, a hole opened to the next floor and, presumably, to the sky beyond that. Inside, it was still fairly smoky, and it was with some relief I sat down on a cushion, down where the air was clearer.

A girl of perhaps a decade came around with a jug of water and poured us each a cup, then continued to fill our cups as we drained them.

"We're blessed with good, clear water here at the post," Asher said, "given the river passing below us. It's free of the parasite that plagues many." He passed a loaf of bread around and we each tore off a piece, trying not to shove it into our mouths too quickly.

"Are you settling in?" Azarel asked in surprise.

"For a time. There's much to do here. Much to do. The people are hungry for the truth."

"*Asher,*" she said, rising and going to the front entry, where she peered both ways before shutting the ramshackle, dilapidated door.

"Ahh, let them hear. The dark ones are deaf. But the right ears are always open." He grinned at all of us, and with mouth half full said, "Look at you, the called! Here in this very house!"

"Asher!" Azarel said in alarm, looking over her shoulder. "Do you wish to be hauled off and impaled? Do you wish for us *all* to be hauled off?"

"Ah, prison hasn't broken me in the past. And I am weary of the secrecy, Azarel. Aren't you? Especially here, with them?" He looked around at all of us in wonder. "I can hardly believe my eyes. The prophecies were true. The elders knew. They *knew*. And now … with you all together. The Ailith rising …" His brown eyes grew wet with tears. "How we've waited. Longed for, and waited for this. If only Kapriel …"

"What news?" Azarel said gruffly, pulling at his arm. "What do you hear of him?"

"Bah," he said, flicking out his hand. "Rumors. Stories. What are we to believe?"

"And what is the most consistent one of late?"

Asher looked at her and frowned. "That he's on the Isle of Catal."

Azarel dropped her chin and winced. "No," she whispered. "No."

"Where is the Isle of Catal?" Niero asked.

"An island off of Pacifica," she said, shaking her head. "The harshest prison anywhere. Impenetrable. Let us hope that story is a lie."

"And if it's not?" Niero said.

"Then we have to find a way to get in and out. Alive."

"Excellent," Vidar said, rubbing his hands together. "Finally a true challenge."

Bellona shook her head. "Really? Must you?"

"What?" Vidar said, looking puzzled.

"There are fifty ways to die on the Isle, as well as off her coast," Azarel said, any hint of smile in her eyes or voice gone. She paced to the small, dirty window and ran a hand through the short spikes of her hair. "It is where Pacifica sends her worst criminals."

"Why so surprised?" Niero asked. "Didn't you say that Keallach wanted him someplace no one would find him? Haven't you looked everywhere else?"

She shook her head. "It's simply impossible," she said, almost to herself, looking to the flames beneath the giant, flame-blackened soup kettle. "He promised. After everything else ... he promised."

"Don't tell me you believe anything that Keallach said," Asher said. "Not anymore."

"But ... Catal?" she said, rising in one smooth motion. She lifted a hand to him. "To his own brother?"

Asher waved his head back and forth as if formulating a response. "Where else? He still believes he can turn Kapriel. So why wouldn't he keep him there while he continues to try to break him?"

She stared out the window as if she were not in the room with us. Not seeing the street outside, full of the urchins. Seeing someplace far distant ... and clearly frightening. She loved him; I understood it then. Loved Kapriel as she loved Asher. They were like bonded kin to her. And she'd loved Keallach once too

I felt the doorway in my heart open to the dark. Just a sliver. For it was in there that this Keallach lingered. The man she'd loved once as a brother. Now missed. Was he the one who had sent Sethos after us? The Sons of Sheol? I searched that tiny opening in her heart — for Keallach, to know more of him, her connection to him.

Asher's cup clattered to the ground. "What? What is that?" he asked, looking wildly around the room, his eyes settling on me. "Stop! At once! Shut that door! Speak the name of the Maker!"

I stared into his eyes and repeated the name he'd just uttered — *Maker* — feeling myself pull back to the present. To my people. Here. Now.

Asher rose and walked over to me. Ronan rose too, his heart filling with equal alarm. I stared at Asher, unable to move. He looked around the room and then back to me. "She is Ailith? One of the chosen? Are you certain?" He reached down and pulled me to my feet.

Ronan grabbed his arm, trying to pull him away from me, but Asher held firm, and for a moment we were an awkward, jostling trio. My knight looked into my eyes, and then released me as if confused.

Azarel came up beside us. "Asher," she said gently. "We are in need of your counsel. Andriana ... Her gifts are complex."

He stared hard at me, then her, then back at me, and I felt the alarm in him. "You are certain she has not been turned?"

Ronan let out a scoffing laugh under his breath but Asher's tension didn't ease.

He took a long, deep breath, which seemed to steady him. "What were you thinking about just then, Andriana?" Asher asked, his brow wrinkling further in deep thought. "Tell me."

He took a step toward me, not to harm me, just to study me, as if he wished to see me better. But Ronan put a wide hand on his chest.

"Keallach," I said. I needed Asher's help. His counsel, as Azarel said. "When Azarel mentioned Kapriel, and his brother, I followed her emotions. Her memory of emotions. And it seemed to open a small door." I turned wide eyes on him, remembering his shouted commands. "How did you know?"

"That door must remain *shut*," Asher said, leaning toward me again while ignoring Ronan's warning hand. "Do you understand me?" He left me and went to the window, peering one way down the street and then the other. "Every time you even get close to that door within your mind, your heart, you call to the dark ones. Concentrate on it long enough and they'll know exactly where we are. It's almost as if you bear a chip under your skin as the Pacificans do."

I nodded, feeling fear inside me that echoed his own. "But how can I keep it shut?" I cried. "Ever since we met the Sheolites in battle, and I watched one die, I can feel that door. Like it's inside me, as if it's clattering in a stiff wind — as if it's about to fly open. And what's inside seems so important to understand. As if it will give me an upper hand at some point."

Asher put a hand on his head and heaved a sigh. "It is good we've crossed paths, my friends. Forgive me," he said. "You so alarmed me … But yes, I can help you. Great is the force of the dark, but greater still is power of the true light." He straightened. "First, we eat. Then we shall speak of such matters."

Asher not only fed most of us but also the orphans outside, and two couples across the alley who housed some of the children each night. As the sun set, women pulled the big pot off the fire and carried it between them to the alley outside.

The other couples that Asher had mentioned brought theirs out too, and together they fed the hundred or more who gathered in solemn lines, each with cups or battered bowls in their hands. Some were toddlers, clinging to older brothers or sisters. Some were well past their first decade. Most were boys.

"Where'd they all come from?" Bellona asked Azarel, arms folded. "Why so many?"

"Georgii Post is a crossroads station that's tripled in size over the last few years. A small city now, really. Some are the spawn of Drifters, abandoned here. Others are the children of subversives, taken. Many have lost their parents to the Cancer."

"Why here?" Bellona pressed.

She shrugged. "Georgii has decent weather. Less rain. Clean water. Food, that they can steal or are given," she said, with a nod to the lines. "Where would you go if you were a child outside of Community?"

I watched as Asher moved among them, touching every one of them, a hand on a shoulder, a tender stroke of his fingertips across a cheek, a pat on the back. Niero stopped beside me and observed him in silence too. "It's a gift, what he does. Not only feeding them, but showing compassion, love."

Niero said nothing, only smiled a little and watched Asher with those dark, keen eyes of his.

"I like being with him. Azarel too. They belong with us somehow. Or we with them."

"That's how it is," he said softly, "meeting others who know the Maker."

I looked back to Asher, now kneeling beside a small boy who was sniffling, tears running down his dirty cheeks. "How does he find the money? To rent this house? To buy this food?" The soup was meager, a thin broth with mostly chunks of potatoes in it, but it was something. And there was enough, enough for everyone in line, including us, it turned out, as I accepted a bowl. It was with some surprise that I smelled fragrant spices, and when I sipped from the edge, found that there was a tart taste that teased my tongue.

"His father, and Azarel's mother, as far as I can gather, were close to Kapriel's parents. They were raised beside the twins in the royal court." His eyes shifted from his bowl to Asher again. "They have lost and gained much in the years since Keallach moved against his family."

I frowned. "But he cannot still be a man of wealth. Not out here, not now. Not so far from Pacifica."

Niero smiled his little smile again. "Wealth is not always counted by the coins within your purse. Look at him." He thrust his chin out, in Asher's direction, and I took another sip and then did as directed. Asher was standing with two men, hands on either of their shoulders, laughing so hard his face lifted toward the rooftops above us.

"But how does he do it? How do they do? Buy what they need to continue out here?"

"Just as we do," Niero said, leaving me in order to speak to Azarel. "One day at a time."

Three children beside me were huddled in a circle, their bowls licked clean, and drawing something in the dirt at their feet. I turned to get a better look at it, and with some astonishment, saw that it was at first an A, then a B, then a C. The older child among the trio was teaching the others. "Where did you learn that?" I asked.

The boy looked up at me, a flash of fear running through him.

"It's all right," I said. "I am only curious."

"Asher taught us," he said. Then, with a look of warning at the others, the three dashed off. As if they doubted my assurances. I watched them go, musing over that. Even back home, in the village, only a select few were designated as "scholars" and given time to learn how to read and write. I'd been one of them, and each of us had been tutored by parents or a neighbor. I'd noticed it was the same among the Hoodites. Life was too difficult, too demanding, to allocate resources — time, energy, funds — to such things. It took every hour, every ounce of energy we had, just to forage for enough food and adequate shelter to survive. Learning was relegated to the evening hours, when those who were not designated as scholars were too tired to absorb much at all. Knowledge was mostly shared in story and discussion around the evening fire.

"But if we teach this young army to read and write," Asher said in a whisper after supper, gesturing out the doorway as a group of them ran by, "they might copy words of truth often enough that it will be written on their very hearts. The dark may try and steal it from their hands. Confiscate books and scrolls. But it still shall remain. And they shall carry it to the far reaches of the Trading Union."

"You are sharing the sacred word with them?" Azarel whispered harshly.

"I might be, here and there," he said with a mischievous glint in his eye.

Azarel shook her head. "It is a dangerous game you play, Asher. Every one of those children could be hanged. After they watch you get impaled."

He sighed and reached for her as if begging her to understand. "At least they die knowing truth, knowing hope. Having an awareness of the One who will welcome them home. And if they find their way out …" A smile spread across his face and the light returned to his eyes. "The Maker accomplishes his goals in mysterious ways, yes?"

It was Azarel's turn to sigh. "You condemn them doubly. Both the sacred word and teaching them numbers and letters? They'll stand out, rather than blend in."

"Bah. I bless them doubly. Better to live twice as deeply than to die in the shallows."

"You're already a marked man. Must you make yourself a bigger target?"

"If I am called to be so, how can I do anything but?"

Azarel turned to us. "You see, now, why I had to leave his side? He makes me crazy. I want him to *live* for our mission, while he seems bent on *dying* for it."

Asher smiled. "We've made it this far, haven't we?" He reached out his hand and she took it, the edge of her mouth quirking up reluctantly. "There is still much to do. So we must do it, yes?"

"Yes."

"Now, back to you, my friend," he said, turning toward me. "The Maker has blessed you richly. With gifts that must be cultivated, as must those within Vidar and Tressa, as well as in each of us." He smiled as my eyes narrowed in confusion. "Ahh, yes. We are *all* gifted among the Community. Your gifts only happen to be more pronounced."

"Asher," Azarel said, eying me carefully. "Back when we met Sethos, near the Hoodite camp, he spoke of not only wanting the Remnants — Vidar, Tressa, and Andriana — but of me. He seemed to think I was one of those he was to bring back to Keallach."

His eyes met hers for several seconds. He rolled an empty

cup in his hands. "It may be that he was sensing your connection to Kapriel and the Maker. Or because you are one of the most hunted subversives ever to escape Pacifica."

I thought about Azarel. And Asher himself. They both exhibited an awareness, understanding, that I'd thought impossible outside the elders in Community. And yet they were relatively young. Our age, or certainly no older than Niero. I could see, if one was sensitive to such things at all, how they'd be recognized as a force. And why Sethos would want them dead.

"Come, sister, and sit with me," Asher said to me, waving me closer. I sat down and he turned until we were knee to knee. He smiled into my eyes. "Take my hands. The rest of you, circle around us. As we move through this, I want you to be praying for protection. Seal us so that the evil ones cannot get close to our sister, Andriana, or sense our presence here, no matter what happens." He looked each one of the Ailith in the eye, waiting until each nodded, then turned back to me. "Come. Take your ease," he said with a grin. "This doesn't have to hurt."

I forced a smile to my face.

"Now, Andriana. Your primary gift is reading emotions, yes?"

"Yes."

"I believe what's happened is this: Your gift gives you access to the heart. To feel as others do, and therefore know them more clearly than any of us can ever hope to. In essence, you are experiencing what they are, yes?"

"Yes."

"This is a magnificent blessing," he said, squeezing my hands, "when encountering those ready to leave behind the lies they've been told." He shook his head a little and his dark curls bounced around his neck. "You will be called upon again and again in the days to come, because in you our people will see the Maker's heart. It is reflected in your beautiful eyes, like pools of water. It's a huge blessing," he said again, squeezing my hands again and smiling.

His face fell a little then. "But in opening such a sacred highway, you've discovered something else. You've accessed the inner realms — that doorway to the soul. And in our *enemy*, that doorway leads to a fearsome darkness. That is what we must teach you to keep locked, no matter whom you face and when."

I nodded. No one was more eager than I to do as he said.

"Andriana, I want you to first search me. Read me and my heart. Tell me what you find, no matter how intimate it might be."

"All-all right," I said. I had never done it on command before. He closed his eyes and took a deep breath, smiling a little, his face as open in invitation as his soul. I'd never had an easier time accessing another's emotions. "Welcome. Peace. Excitement," I said. "Those are first and foremost."

"Good. Continue."

"Kinship. It's as if we're already family."

"Indeed we are. As knit together as if we were born of the same father."

I smiled, responding to his joy, bubbling to the surface in pleasing waves. "You might be the happiest person I've ever met."

"Wait until you meet Kapriel," he said. "Continue."

I delved deeper, seeking fear, concern, stress — emotions we all seemed to face constantly within the Trading Union. But even deeper, I couldn't quite find them. My eyes popped open. "How do you do that?"

"What, sister?"

"Live without the negatives? Fear? Worry?"

His brown eyes opened and he smiled at me. "Fear and worry are the antithesis of faith, are they not?"

"I-I suppose they are."

"Every time I give in to concern about tomorrow, even my next hour, I rob *this* hour, *this* day of strength, peace. The Maker holds all my days. Do I trust him with them, or not?"

I drew in a long, deep breath, studying him, considering his words. Then nodded.

"Good, continue."

I searched him again, and besides a playful spirit I detected nothing. Anything else was too faint to register. "Hope. A pleasure in others. That's it."

"Excellent. Excellent. Now focus on those same emotions in your own heart. Consider your father. You had a male protector, yes?"

I swallowed hard. "I did. My dad."

He stared into my eyes, his brows lowering as he noted my pain, my hesitation. "He is gone now," he said softly.

"Yes," I said, feeling my throat tighten.

He didn't drop his gaze, and I knew his care and concern. "Remember, Andriana, the good things. Remember him holding you close to his chest, close enough to hear his heart, the warmth of his skin. Do you have such a memory?"

I remembered the day my father held me on the banks of the river as a little child while I tossed rocks into the water, the warmth of his chest behind me, the strength of his arms around me. I felt safe and yet free. I nodded, sniffing, struggling to hold on to the memory like a hug from Dad himself.

Asher squeezed my hands. "You have that image in your

heart and mind now? Of a papa and his precious daughter? Hold on to it. Now consider the one who is holding you, in just the same way, is the One who saw you before you were born, and sees you as complete, perfect, even now. Only full of possibility and promise."

I considered that

"Good. Remember this, how he will not let you go. Now, Andriana, go to the dark door. The door introduced to you by the Son of Sheol."

I turned inwardly toward where he directed, feeling weary, dreading it. I could almost see it rattling in the wind, a tornado on the other side

"As you approach it, tell me what you feel. Sense."

I forced myself to face it. Study it. "Fear," I said, chagrined to hear my voice tremble. "Cold. Danger. But also mystery."

"Go to the door but keep it shut. Do not allow it to open. It is sealed, because the Maker has sealed it. He will guard it. But you still have the power to open it. The dark within each of us wishes to pry it open, because behind it is power. Power that is not ours to wield, but yet entices us."

Even his words teased me, made me want to take a quick peek, even though I knew what would happen. It was a terrible pull. Like water rushing faster and faster, pulling me in the closer I got to it. I licked my lips. "How do I keep it closed?" I panted, as if fighting for breath, as if the dark waters were rapidly rising to my waist, my chest, my shoulders.

"You keep it closed by relinquishing your desire to control it. The Maker will guard the door, Andriana, if you allow him. Don't try to do it yourself. Imagine his hand, as strong and sure as your own knight's, against it. His shoulder against it. Imagine it small, and him far larger. There is no way they can enter. Not unless you tell him to move. For he gives you the ability to choose for good, and not for evil."

"I choose good. I choose to keep it shut." Even with those simple words, the door within seemed to gain a seal, weight, all the heavier and difficult to open. The rattling ceased in my mind.

"Say it again."

"I choose good. I choose the Way. I choose light."

"Good," he said. "Very good."

A weight slipped from my shoulders. Peace washed through me. I opened my eyes, blinking heavily. And Asher did the same. "You understand now. The Maker has given you the knowledge because you are strong." He pulled one of my hands into both of his, cradling it against his chest. "But he is stronger than any force you come against, if you will only lean into him for support. Remember that, yes?"

"Yes," I said. "I will."

CHAPTER
20

We slept well that night, close together all in one room, and for the first time in a while I didn't awaken with a night terror. I did, however, wake up inches away from Vidar, who had the most terrible morning breath. I tucked my nose under my sweater and turned to my back, listening to children whisper and rustle about upstairs. A baby cried and Asher rose, gesturing to a woman in the corner to lie back down — he would go up and fetch her. "She's probably just wet," he said.

I smiled and listened as he went upstairs, humming in a low tone. The little one quieted, but soon I heard others moving about. As the sun rose and coral light filtered in the dirty window, the entire household awakened, and we set about dressing, fetching water from the well a few blocks away, building cooking fires, and preparing breakfast. My stomach rumbled as the porridge began to bubble, and I was as guilty as the passel of children hovering near the pot. The young woman shooed us off, sending us off to do more chores. I was assigned market duty, to purchase the day's supplies. "I'll save you your bowl of porridge. Go and get your mind off of it," she said with a smile.

"Give the extra to the children," I said. "I'll find something in the market."

"I'll go with you," Ronan said, stepping beside me. Bellona and Vidar followed behind, unwilling to miss anything.

Niero handed us a few gold coins, and told us to buy enough to feed Asher's crowd for the whole day. We walked to the center square of the post, surrounded on all four sides by the most prosperous of merchants. In the middle, there were rows of tents, and people were selling everything from fresh vegetables to fabric to paper to meat. My eyes widened in delight. Never had I seen such a bounty. Men and women shouted out about their wares, especially those who competed with the same offerings. Locals bartered with them and tucked their goods into baskets.

We purchased loaves of bread and rounds of cheese. Meat for dinner, a whole roast. I couldn't wait for the children to see it, sizzling on a spit above the fire. Apples — fresh apples — and on impulse, some slates and chalk for Asher to use with his students. At least if we purchased them, I reasoned, his teaching might remain more of a secret. There were Georgii Post patrols, but they seemed friendly with the locals, not antagonistic, and I could see why Asher seemed so happy here. It was a good town in which to find your rest. As well as do good.

We passed the day in conversation — not all of it so intent, for once — laughing, eating, and resting. And after dinner, as we all settled in together in one room again, I wished we could stay for a few weeks. I wanted to know more about Asher and Azarel. More about Kapriel and Keallach. But mostly, I wanted more of this sense of normalcy.

"Take what you can get, when you can get it," Ronan said

when I confessed my wish in a whisper. "I'm thinking there won't be many stretches of 'normalcy' for a while."

But as he said it, he slid his hand into mine. When I looked to his face, wondering what he was feeling, he was already asleep. And the only emotion I felt from him was peace.

■　■　■

We were deep into slumber when I heard the screams, the wails of women, the shouts of men.

Asher hurried to the window, and in the passing lantern light of someone outside I saw concern in his face for the first time.

And in that moment, it was as if all the air had been sucked from the room. I gasped, and felt Ronan reach out for me. "Dri?" he whispered. He lifted me to my feet, even as I continued to fight for my next breath. "Andriana!" he said, taking my other arm and shaking me. "What is it?"

I could feel the fear in him, but more than that I could sense the fear that prowled the streets. The darkness. "They're here," I said, taking a quick breath as if the heaviness had been released from my chest momentarily, even as the cold chill spread through my armband. "The Sheolites."

"It's a reaping," Asher said to us, lighting a candle after pulling the drapes.

But what I saw in the light frightened me more than the dark. "Where are Vidar and Bellona?"

"They're on watch," Niero said. "On the roof."

We could hear children crying upstairs. One gave way to a full wail.

"A reaping?" Ronan asked Asher. "What sort of reaping are you — "

"The children," Asher said. "They've come for the children."

"What?" Killian said. "No!" I could hear the metallic slide of his sword from its sheath.

"Wait," Asher said. "They do not come to kill the children — they come to claim them. There is hope yet. Remember what I said? These children hold the Secret Words in their hearts now. There's no telling what impact they may have in the wider kingdom."

Azarel was pacing while clenching and unclenching her hands. "They cannot find us here, Asher. If there is a Sheolite tracker out there … If I am found with you, they'll know who we both are. In but a breath, they'll know. Our kinship betrays us. They'll figure it out!"

"Quickly," Asher said in response, lifting a trapdoor in the floor. "Down below, all of you." After a pause, he said, "Join my own prayers for protection for us all. That they only take children who will be given to good homes, a future. Not to the factories or mines."

I frowned in confusion. How could he relinquish any of them? His orphans — the children he so clearly cared for? Someone rammed on the door with a meaty fist, making me jump. The flimsy door rattled, and I glimpsed torchlight in the momentary gaps. The time for argument was over. I was the first one down the steep stairs to the cellar. The rest jammed in behind me. Ronan and Niero; Azarel, Tressa, and Killian: we all crammed together in the tiny root cellar, so close I fought to breathe. I squeezed into the corner, trying to make room for the others behind me, knowing that Killian must be folded in two, being the nearest to the top. I tried to match my breathing with Ronan's, who was cradled around me, concentrating on the rhythm of it so I wouldn't panic — either from claustrophobia or him, so intimately close — a crazy, embarrassing thought as men above us bashed their way into the house.

"Peace, peace," we heard Asher say above us. "What is it you require?"

"You are a known keeper of children," said a man. "By order of Georgii Post's boss and the king of Pacifica, we demand a review."

"I do my best to feed the children, give them places to sleep," Asher said. "I've applied for permission to look after them."

"But you did not apply for permission to *teach* them." We heard a scuffle and then a ram against the wall. Asher?

There were others tromping up the stairs already. What of Vidar and Bellona, on the roof? I closed my eyes and did as Asher had taught me, focusing on the Maker holding me, holding all of us. I concentrated on Ronan behind me, the way his body cupped mine. Comforted me. Held me. How his chest rose and fell behind me. The rhythm of his heart against my back. His skin releasing heat, comforting me. *Maker, my Maker, see us. Protect us. Let them not discover us down below. Protect Asher. And the children. Be with each of the children.*

A child screamed. "Ah-shee! Ah-shee!" she cried, obviously calling for Asher. I shuddered. I thought I recognized the voice of a small blonde girl who'd followed him around all afternoon, looking up at him in adoration. "*Ah-shee!*"

"Shh, shh," Asher soothed. "Not this one, sir. Leave her with — "

"You dare to ask for anything?" the man sneered back. "I could have this house burned to the ground this instant. You know you are not to keep the unwanted. Or *teach* them."

The child screamed.

"Don't fight them, sweetheart," Asher said, his tone tight, high. "It will be all right, child. Peace, peace —"

"Where are the others?" the man yelled at Asher, so terribly close again. Dirt from the floor above scraped from their boots and rained down on our heads, inches below. I glanced over my shoulder and saw each of my friends' faces, looking up, illuminated in the warm, dancing torchlight filtering between the floorboards.

"You've seen every child in this house!" Asher said.

I heard another child scream, two others wail, and my heart lurched. Terror filtered down to us, even two stories down. *Comfort them, Maker. Let them know they are not alone, never alone*

"The others! Newcomers to the city. They were seen entering this house."

"Yes. Friends I met among the Trading Union. They ate supper with me."

"And where did they go?"

"It is a big town, is it not? There are many places for a traveler to sleep among the post. I had no place for them here, what with all these children."

The man paused. A child whimpered, above us now. Another was sobbing. I could hear a baby then. No, two. Carried down the stairs, then directly above us.

"We shall take these children with us for the reaping," said the man. "Do you take issue with this, Asher?"

"Ah-shee!" screamed the little blonde girl again, weeping. I could feel her panic, her longing, and it made me want to scream myself. Ronan seemed to sense that, and held me tighter, across the forehead with his broad hand, across the belly with the heft of his arm, as if willing his steadiness into me.

Asher paused. "I stand for the innocents. These children

are not yours to take. If there was but some assurances given, some process —"

We heard the sickening sound of impact and then the heavy collapse of a body, rattling the floorboards above us. The soldiers departed, leaving the front door open, and we paused, desperate to burst out, but also anxious, fearing that others might still linger nearby.

I felt the chill in my bones before I felt the renewed chill in my armband this time. "Wait," I whispered. At the same time as I thought Niero did the same.

A tracker. It had to be.

We heard the heavy creak of the floorboards above us. The pause, beside Asher, then the movement onward. *Protect us, Maker. Blind them. Keep us safe. Keep the children safe. Keep Vidar and Bellona safe*

Ronan curled even more tightly around me, hugging me to him, shielding me with his back as our armbands grew icy cold and more entered the house. Because this time, it was the Sons of Sheol who walked through Asher's house, hunting us. They filtered through the room, up the stairs, and then returned to the main floor.

Asher roused above us, and we heard him try to rise. "Be gone from here, dark ones. Be gone!"

A man hissed, and again Asher was struck. I bit down on my finger, trying to stay quiet. Trying to focus on the Maker as he'd taught me. *Hold tight the door . . .*

But it was hard. So hard. The dark beckoned, called to me. It was as if those above me reached down between the floor-boards, like vines that grew before my eyes, wrapping around my neck, my arm, my chest, rattling the door within, prying at the seal . . .

"Andriana," Ronan whispered in my ear, so quietly I could barely make out the words. "Andriana, you are of the light. You do not belong with the dark. You are Ailith."

Everything went silent above us, as if the leader had held up a hand, listening, and everyone around him stilled.

But Ronan's words found their mark. They calmed me. Centered me. Helped me remember who I was. Whose I was.

"We are done here," said a man a moment later. "We sense their presence, but it is only an echo of their passage — they are gone. Let us continue the search."

They slipped out, and I felt Ronan ease an inch back from me while taking his first full breath in a long while.

After about a couple minutes passed, Killian said, "Go?"

"Yes," Azarel said, sounding like the rest of us felt — that she might burst if we were trapped here any longer.

Killian lifted the trap door and peeked out. The sound of crying children a floor above us was no longer muffled, and my heart keened in tandem with their pain. Sorrow seeped into me like a drenching, soaking rain, making me hug myself in an effort to fend it off.

"Where'd they take them?" Killian said as Azarel came out. "And what is this reaping?"

"A collection," Azarel said, helping Asher sit up, checking out the wound on his head.

"It happens in many cities," Asher said. "The women of Pacifica ... They suffer from a high infertility rate. Perhaps from living so close to the old war zones. And many choose to not bear children, fearing what it will do to their bodies. So they adopt children from the Trading Union instead. They send patrols to collect desirables every couple of years."

"Desirables," Azarel said flatly. "The reaping is nothing but a sanctioned mass kidnapping."

"Agreed."

Killian paced, hands on hips. "Those children were orphans." He gestured outward. "*Your* orphans, of a sort. But they did not have homes, parents. Will they be taken someplace better, at least? Offered love? Care? A future?"

"Oftentimes, in good measure," Azarel put in. "At least, as far as what Pacifica can offer." She shook her head and rubbed her neck. "It is those that are *not* chosen that I worry about most. Those that are sent to factories or mines to work."

"Slaves?" I whispered. "They enslave them?"

She met my gaze. "They're paid. Given food and a place to sleep. But it is far better for them to roam these streets than end up there."

"It is but one reason we must keep the Trading Union from falling to Pacifica's rule," Asher said. "One more reason we must free Kapriel so he can lead us. Unite all who can fight against them."

Vidar and Bellona, both bleeding and clearly hurting, came down the stairs then, children clinging to them, all snotnosed and weeping. "What just happened?" Vidar asked.

Killian ignored him, still focused on Azarel and Asher. "So that's it? We are to just stand aside and watch it happen?"

"Yes," Azarel said. "This is not a battle we can win. We are called to the greater war. And it is as Asher says — "

"Every war is made up of many battles," Killian said. He moved his head back and forth in a slow shake as if trying to sort through the messy details. "They do not ... They wouldn't take a child from a parent — "

"They do," Azarel reluctantly admitted. "When a child

is deemed desirable. Intelligent. And, as the captors claim, underprivileged."

Killian swore under his breath, met Vidar's eyes, and the two were out the door in an instant.

"Vidar!" Niero called. "Killian!"

But neither answered. Ronan sighed and went after them. He paused at the doorjamb, and looked back at Raniero.

"Yes," Niero said with a groan. "We must go after them." Tressa and Bellona took off, but I had barely moved when he reached out and grabbed my arm. "You sure you're ready for this?"

I nodded and he gestured out the door. The others were at the end of the block, peering around the corner. We hurried to meet up with them, and as we did my arm cuff began to vibrate.

A man shouted and a woman wailed a block away, back in the direction we came. We all shared a look and turned. Niero and I reached the corner first and peeked around. Two soldiers in gray uniforms had a man pinned to the wall, beating him. Another held a woman by the arms as two others came out the door with a tiny, beautiful babe. "We claim this child for the kingdom of Pacifica."

"No! Please," the woman begged, trying to wrench her arms from her captor's grasp. "Please, we are not underprivileged," she sputtered, finally free and falling to her knees. She raised clasped hands before her, begging. "We have food every day. Clothing. Please. He is our heart!" she cried, reaching for the soldier's leg as he turned from her.

It was agony, watching it. Feeling it. My heart seemed to tear in two. Thoughts of my own parents crowded my mind, threatened to steal my breath

We moved toward the family — between us now — and

Killian, Vidar, Bellona, and Tressa. The men continued to beat the father, even as other soldiers shoved the screaming mother back into the house. Two men were moving away, one carrying the child. The father faltered and fell to his knees just as one of the soldiers looked up and spied our approach.

He turned to face us, hands on his hips. Half a block down, over his shoulder, I could see the rest of our group stopping the men with the child.

"You there," the soldier said, "be on your way. This is no business of yours."

"I disagree," Niero said, leveling him with a swift punch across the face. The man spun away to the ground.

Ronan ripped the man from the doorway, away from the mother, and rammed him across the narrow alley, into the other building's wall. I flipped the third man as he tried to grab me, and Niero leaped on top of him. I turned to the woman, who stared at us with mouth hanging open.

"Quickly," I said. "Gather a change of clothes for each of you and anything of value. You must flee now, before the others learn of what's happened here."

She turned and moved, as if in a daze. Raniero brought the father inside the tiny apartment, his arm draped around his shoulders, and set him on a chair. "I don't know ..." he said, lightly slapping the man's cheeks, trying to revive him. "He doesn't look ready to move "

Through the doorway, I saw another soldier charge down the alley, probably at Ronan.

"I've got him," I said, bringing a cup of water to the man. "You go and help the others."

Raniero was out the door again, even as Tressa arrived, carrying the baby. She handed the sobbing child to her mother, who let out a strangled cry, and then joined me with the father. "Can you do anything for him?" I asked Tressa. I bit my lip. We had to get this family up and out of here. Now. Before an alarm sounded, and all of Pacifica's troops descended on us — for more reasons than one. If the father didn't come-to quickly …

Tressa knelt in front of the man and held his face between her palms. "Brother, brother! Awake! By the power of the Maker, I command you to awake!"

The man lifted his chin and blinked rapidly, focusing on her.

Vidar was in the doorway then. "With us making such a ruckus, that tracker is likely to turn back our way."

"Come," I said, helping Tressa bring the man to his feet. "We need to go." I looked over to the woman, still running around, stuffing things into her bag. "Leave it or you will lose your greater treasures!" I reached for her hand.

She hesitated, and in that moment, I felt her fear of the unknown, her attachment to the comforts of this town she'd called home.

"It's changed," I said. "What you had here. There is nothing but loss ahead for you if you stay. You must run."

Her wide, haunted eyes met mine, and then she nodded once.

Outside, Azarel gestured for us to follow and we ran down a street, then down an alley, then through a tunnel to another street. We climbed one set of stairs after another. Killian and Vidar came up and took hold of the man, carrying him between them. Behind us, we heard whistles. Shouts. Apparently, the bodies of the battered soldiers had been found. Or one had roused enough to call for help.

Worse, our arm cuffs continued to grow colder, proving Vidar's assumptions correct. The Sheolites were coming for us. Or worse, we were heading toward *them.* "This is the only way out for this family? With us?" I whispered to Azarel, pulling to a stop.

"Yeah," Vidar said, casting a long, unnerved look down the alley. "Because I sure don't think they'll like these guys in red ..."

"It's their only chance, yes," she said, looking furiously around at us. "I told you this isn't a battle we can win. Now if they find us, we're *all* lost." She clamped her lips shut and whirled, waving at us to follow. We turned left and went down a set of stairs, through another tunnel, and then up two more flights. We stopped by the well where we'd filled our buckets. Azarel turned to the mother. "Do you know how to swim?"

The woman shook her head, panic of a new sort rising within her. I looked down into the dark well and I could hear rushing, sloshing water, as if through a confined space. But there was no way to tell how deep it was. This was Azarel's plan? To send a family who couldn't swim out through an underground waterway? With a baby in their arms?

She met my gaze. "One way in or out of this city, and that's through the gates," she said. "I imagine there will be a few of our friends from Pacifica waiting on us there. The only *other* way is this," she said, nodding over the well wall.

I winced. Raniero and Ronan stepped closer as the whistles got louder. All of us felt our armbands begin to vibrate, and not with the deep gladness of approaching Ailith or angel, but with the cold, warning alarm of approaching demons.

"I'm up for a swim," Vidar said.

I considered him and then looked to Raniero. "Listen," I said. "You, me, Ronan, Vidar, and Bellona are all of the Valley. We are comfortable in the water. You and Vidar can take the parents. Ronan and I can take the baby. Bellona can lead the way and clear any soldier from our path, should the waterway be guarded. Good?"

"It's as good a plan as any," he said. He looked over to Tressa and Killian. "Do you two swim?"

"Somewhat," Killian said. "But we'll manage, together."

"Stay close to me," he said. A whistle blew, this time just a block away. We looked at one another in alarm.

Bellona leaped over the side, and we heard her hit the water a second later. We leaned over, waiting for a report. "It's pretty deep," she called up, "and moving fast. Going with the current " She was clearly ten feet downstream already. The well was little more than a funneling of the river that ran through the canyon, a place for the people of the post to dip in their buckets and carry water to their homes.

I turned and faced the mother, still holding her baby. "Give him to me," I said. "I'll keep him safe."

As she passed him to me, the babe curiously calm and quiet, I felt his mother's dread, her fear. I wished I could do something. There was nothing more dangerous than a person who was in full panic, believing they were about to drown. On impulse, I reached out and grabbed her arm, and focused on all the power of the Maker in me. I concentrated on hope. Faith. Belief. Peace.

She gasped and took a step away. "How did you do that?"

I smiled, opening my eyes. "You felt something?"

"Felt something? Y-yes." She took Raniero's hand and he helped her to the well wall, next to Vidar. "It's as if I believe I can do this," she said in wonder, looking down into the dark abyss.

"Uh, *people*," Vidar warned, thrusting his chin in the direction of the alley.

I saw the men pass the mouth of the well alley at a sprint,

capes flying, soldiers in gray behind them. But, thankfully, they didn't see us.

Vidar and the mother dropped in, and the baby in my arms began to cry, reaching out for where she had been a second ago. I glanced back at the alley, scared the wailing would bring the guards. Raniero picked us both up, placed us on the wall, and grunted, "Go, Andriana. Be safe." My last view was of Ronan and the father climbing the well wall even as we dropped.

I pinched the baby's nose and covered his mouth as we fell. My feet touched the bottom, and I shot up as I heard somebody else plunge in behind me. I shoved off, floating down the tunnel with the current, aware that the baby was trying to get enough breath to scream. I could feel his rage building, getting ready to bellow with everything in him. But a screaming child would bring the soldiers down upon us. Or worse.

I floated on my back and put the baby on his back against my chest, trying to calm him as I had his mother, concentrating on hope, assurance, peace.

I held my breath and grunted as I cleared the last post wall and entered the wider river, where a passing guard might spot us. But the baby stayed silent. I smiled in amazement. I exulted in the gift of it, then worried that the child was unwell. Choking on water, perhaps. I lifted him up, wishing I could see his face, and felt him wriggle and thought I heard him coo. As if we'd simply taken a bath. Played.

I laughed, lost in the wonder of it. What was happening here? Yet another rendition of my gift unfolding?

I could not only read emotions, but I could cast them too? As Niero seemed to?

CHAPTER
21

We washed out along the canyon a few minutes' walk below Georgii Post, her walls rising high above us like a black behemoth bent on chasing us down. Coughing and sputtering, we made it to the rocky riverbank, gasping for breath.

The mother, clearly half drowned, pulled herself away from Ronan and crawled over to me, reaching for her baby. "Oh, thank you. Thank you, thank you," she said.

"Thank the Maker," I said, sitting up and panting. "He delivered us all." The baby giggled, and I smiled and closed my eyes, rolling on to my back and putting a hand on my head, panting.

Raniero came out of the water behind me, practically hauling a bedraggled Killian and Tressa to the beach. After he caught his breath, he turned to Killian and Vidar. "What were you doing back there?" he thundered, grabbing hold of Killian's shirt in his fists, then casting a fierce stare at Vidar. "You could've killed us all, going after them!"

"We had to do *something*," Killian said.

"We *can't* help everyone we meet in need," he said, shoving Killian's shoulder. "We can't! We have to keep our eyes on the greater mission! Now what do we do? We don't even have our bags or the bikes!" He shook his hands in the air and stalked off a few paces. I knew he wore the remaining armbands in a leather bag at his belt, but I assumed our money was gone. As well as the bed rolls and provisions

I looked over to the small family, huddled together, sorry they had to witness this, even as I shivered with a bone-deep chill. But they didn't seem to care about Niero's words — they were lost in relief at simply being together. It made me swallow hard, missing my parents, knowing that I, too, would give up everything to see them again.

Raniero was calling out names in the dark, making sure everyone had made it. "Come," he said. "Everyone get to the top of this bank. We need to put some distance between us and the post. It won't take them long to search the river."

My teeth were chattering now in the pre-dawn chill, and I wished we had time to wring out our clothes, wait for day-break and maybe a little sun to dry them out. But we had no time. We had to be away in case those who chased us figured out how we disappeared.

I shivered as I thought about the Sheolites reaching the well platform and finding nothing, but sensing us.

"This way, Andriana," Asher said, passing by me, little more than a dark form against a darker backdrop.

"Asher! You came with us!"

"Via another well. And it was far better than facing the Sons of Sheol on my own," he said. He caught my hand and helped me up and over the rocks as if he'd walked them a thousand times in the dark.

"What will happen to the other children?" I asked.

"The couple across the alley will tend to them. The Maker has seen this day in advance. Let us find out together where he wishes for us to go next," he said, sounding curiously assured, even though everything had just changed for him. Again. Just weeks after he'd arrived here. I wondered if I would ever gain a measure of his peace, his assuredness.

When we reached the top of the rocks and joined the others, I pulled off my coat and wrung it out.

"Now what? Anyone have any direction?" Raniero said, pacing back and forth. "Feeling clear on where the Maker is leading?"

We were all silent.

"Are we not to go after Kapriel?" I said. My voice shook with cold, and Ronan wrapped his wet coat around my shoulders. I didn't know if it hurt or helped, but I appreciated the gesture.

Azarel let out a scoffing laugh. "We've gone through this. You can't simply walk into Pacifica. The way is long and difficult. And it doesn't end there. Once we breach the Wall, we have to cross Pacifica, reach the coast, and then the island."

"I thought you couldn't get near Pacifica," Niero said. "That they know your face."

"She shouldn't," Asher said. "She'll endanger you all."

"Well, I'm not exactly confident they can move on without us," she said. "Look what just happened! We didn't even have a night in Georgii!"

"Azarel," Asher said soothingly, with an edge of caution.

"What?" she said. Even in the dark, I sensed her shaking her head. She sighed and sat down heavily on a nearby rock. "I'm sorry. This is simply ... trying. How are they to make it without us? Beyond the Wall, especially?"

"Because they travel with the Maker. If he wills the Ailith to enter Pacifica, he'll make a way. Now, come. We know this much, yes? We must be as far from Georgii Post as possible, as soon as possible, yes? So that is our first step. Our best bet is to catch the daybreak trading train."

"But, Asher," Azarel said in agitation, "the train will be heading to *Castle Vega*."

"We have kin at Castle Vega," said the father of the little family among us. "They would welcome us and those who aided us."

"See there?" Asher said in delight. "Confirmation of your next steps. Let's see it through." His use of *your* wasn't lost on any of us — he didn't expect to be with us long.

He moved out and we fell in behind him, all silently miserable in our soaking wet, squeaking, clinging clothes. The baby began crying; I glanced back toward the post, wondering if sound carried across the desert floor or if it would be muffled. To my relief, the mother soon soothed him, perhaps putting him to her breast. How else would a mother comfort a soaking, cold baby out in the middle of a desert at night if she didn't have the high gifting of an empath? I had no idea. *That could come in handy if I'm ever a mother*

I looked up and saw the clouds breaking here and there, stars peeking through. Ronan sidled up beside me, his presence instantly settling my nerves. It was almost as if I grew warmer with him around. Or was it just the walking?

"Are you well, Dri?" he asked after a bit.

"Other than my wet clothes chafing me in a hundred places, yes. I think so."

"Believe me, I understand. But Andriana ... the Sheolites. They were close back there."

"Yes," I said, a shiver running down my back when I recalled how cold our cuffs became. "Too close."

"But it didn't ... I mean, it wasn't ..."

I smiled. "No, Ronan. No door opened. I think Asher taught me what I needed to keep it at bay."

"For now."

I considered his words, his tone. He didn't want me to get overly sure of myself. And while it irritated me at first, I knew he had just cause for his concern. "For now," I repeated.

Just as the sky began to lighten in the east, I made out the trader train, heading west from Georgii Post. A half hour later, the convoy of overpacked trucks and trailers reached us, with armed men on motor bikes surrounding them. I looked at the bikes with longing, wishing we could've brought ours. But what would we have done with the family we'd rescued? And weren't these people to provide us shelter in Castle Vega?

It was as Asher said: It was all in the Maker's hands. All we could do was take the next step.

Raniero flagged down the train and spoke with a guard, then the driver of the lead truck for a long while, and finally waved us in. Somehow, he'd talked the man into allowing us to ride. We climbed up and into the back of the massive truck, sitting atop crates and bales of goods, leaving the most level space for the Georgii Post family. Atop the cab of the truck was a man with a massive gun, surrounded by sandbags. He barely acknowledged us as we searched for the seats that would stay the most stable on the rough road ahead. Behind us in the trader train was another truck — what they called a bus — filled with so many people they could not take another, and then three Jeeps, each fully loaded. We weren't even all seated when the truck lurched forward.

Azarel thought of it first — peeling off her outer layers and folding them over one of the crossbars to dry in the wind. The rest of us quickly followed suit, we women ignoring the admiring grin of the driver behind us, who drew closer to get a better look as we were left in nothing but our T-shirts and long johns. I didn't care, I decided, hunkering down to get a good grip as the truck lurched and swayed. All I wanted was to be dry. And warm. Not to mention the guy wasn't getting a look at anything beyond what I would show in the bathing pools of any village of the Trading Union.

Still, Ronan made his way over and sat down, arms folded, back to me, directly in the line of vision between me and the driver. He folded his own oilskin and outer trousers over the bar in front of him, further blocking the man's view. I laughed under my breath. My protector and my guardian, in more ways than one. My heart swelled and I closed my eyes, experiencing all I was feeling for the guy. Day by day, there was a stronger draw between us. More connected. How was that possible?

"Penny for your thoughts!" Azarel said, holding on to the crossbar above her, the wind whipping her shirt around the taut, muscular, flat belly above her low-hung long johns. She was fiercely strong, almost as strong as Bellona. But the way she was looking at me was … soft. Friendly.

"What's a penny?"

"Sorry. It was a coin, back in the olden days — it's an old expression. You look … happy. And that is funny. Here. Now."

"I am," I said simply. "I'm surrounded by my people and not walking across this desert floor in wet trousers."

"Amen to that, sister," she said, offering her left arm.

I smiled and reached out my right, clasping her at the elbow as she did mine. She studied me, and in that moment I knew she knew that there were a few more thoughts beyond what that penny bought her. Her eyes flicked to Ronan and back to me, the wisdom in them making me look away.

"There's no time for that," she said, leaning close, nodding over to Ronan and meeting my eyes with warning in her own.

I glanced away. Was it really any of her business? It wasn't as if I was going to kiss him. It was only fun thinking about it.

"It could be used against you," she said, no trace of softness left in her face.

"I understand," I said. *Now leave me alone.*

She looked out to the rapidly passing scrub oak and tumbleweeds, doing their best to break free in the wind. There were no more bluffs, only endless flat. Up ahead were more mountains, rising from the desert floor, but not for miles yet. She turned back to me. "I loved a man once."

I glanced down at Ronan. Could he hear us over the wind and engine? Did I care if he did?

"What happened?" I asked her.

"He was taken by the Sheolites," she said, her brown eyes hardening. "They wanted Kapriel. Knew I knew where he was. So they cut apart the man I loved before my eyes, piece by piece."

I tried to swallow, but found my mouth terribly dry. I felt the grief within her. The deep mourning, like a dark blue, swirling pool. And the fury. The thirst for revenge.

She shook her head. "Don't ever let them know. No matter what happens, don't let them know," she said, gesturing toward Ronan. *Don't let them know he holds your heart.*

I held her gaze and nodded once, the only acknowledgment I'd give her that she was possibly on the right track and I appreciated her warning.

"How'd you do it?" I asked. "Endure it?"

She looked away for such a long while I thought maybe she hadn't heard me. But then she turned back. "Our strength goes beyond ourselves, Andriana. Remember that too."

We could see Castle Vega glinting in the periodic sun, breaking between the clouds a good hour before we reached her gates. She was perched in the foothills of the desert mountains, and built largely of white stones. When we got closer, we saw what reflected the sun — big spans of what Azarel called solar panels, made of glass and metal.

Soldiers in clean blue uniforms climbed aboard the truck, examining the boxes, opening a few crates, demanding our safe-passage papers. The family had automatic clearance, I found out with relief, given their kin within the walls of the big city. They merely had to show a beaded bracelet on their left wrists. Thankfully, Niero carried our safe papers in a waterproof oilskin pouch, alongside the remaining armbands, or we would've faced additional challenges. Only the edges were damp, and the guard seemed too harried among the throngs entering and exiting to do more than eye him curiously over its edge. Azarel and Asher entered with us, as if they belonged, and weren't stopped. Apparently this was a city that did not fear its visitors as others did.

After a while, we were cleared for passage and we climbed down from the truck, joining those in a large vehicle that pulled up to take us into the city. I soon found out that many came from Georgii Post daily to work in the city, employed in kitchens and as cleaning servants for houses and buildings bigger than I ever dreamed there could be. Each was practically a palace, competing with her neighbors, climbing high into the pale blue sky.

"One family lives in that?" I asked after a long walk from

the city gates, my eyes lifting to search four stories above me. At the top were guards. "Do they not trust their neighbors?"

"Yes, and no," Azarel said. "Castle Vega subsists in an uneasy alliance. She is largely owned by ten families, all of whom make most of their money off of those who come here from Pacifica to gamble and indulge in other ways." She looked like she loathed being here, and she seemed jumpy.

"Are you all right?"

"Yes," she whispered as a patrol of Pacifican soldiers passed us, forcing me to lean in so that I blocked them from seeing her face. "But I haven't been this close to Pacifica in over three seasons."

"Three seasons?" I repeated in surprise. "How long since … How long since you saw our friend?" I gave her a meaningful look.

"Four seasons," she said. "He was taken from me and Asher four seasons ago." She moved ahead to speak to Raniero, and I considered her words, even as I gaped at houses that I thought would only be found in fables of old. I reached out and touched the polished white stone and then rubbed my fingers together, finding the rock smoother than my skin.

I looked up and saw a small female child, blonde curls bobbing around her head and big ribbons tying each pigtail. She wore a beautiful purple dress, and stared dolefully at me as I passed, finally sticking out her tongue, pulling the prettiest doll I'd ever seen close to her chest.

Her action surprised me, and I fought the impulse to stick my tongue back at her. Did the people of Castle Vega teach their children rudeness?

Four seasons, I thought, going back to Azarel's words. So Kapriel'd been about a decade and five when she'd last seen him. Ronan and I'd only become accustomed to wielding a heavy sword, lifting a shield by then. It was so young to be taken captive, thrust into prison.

Did Kapriel even yet live? Might he have perished in the prison of Catal long ago? Were we heading deep into enemy territory, seeking nothing but a ghost? All this time, I thought Asher and Azarel had seen him far more recently than —

"Stay together," Raniero said, urging me to hurry and join the others. We were winding our way up the hill, now entering a market district — much bigger and more permanent than Georgii Post's — each stall or small store hawking different wares of old. Here a bookshop that called to me — Ronan took my hand and dragged me past — and then a cutlery store full of every sort of knife, fork, and spoon you could imagine. The next was full of dishes, the following an apothecary, with one shelf full of bottles of tonics and potions. It was Killian's turn to pull Tressa past that one. But my cuff grew cold as we passed a dark tent, with a sign outside offering fortunes told and another offering to summon the spirits of dead relatives and friends.

My attention turned to the people that milled along the streets, rather than on the shops and homes that lined them, and I began to pick out tall, thin, long-limbed women, so pale they looked ghostly, with their hair pulled back in severe buns, dark shadow around their eyes, and brown stains at their lips. At first I thought they were ill; soon I knew it was a look they aspired to obtain. They all wore long, draping gowns that flowed behind them, in various shades of ivory, cream, and pure white. The outer layer was almost translucent. The inner layer was nothing but a body-hugging sheath.

A shiver ran down my back as we passed a group of them,

each on the arm of a man in fine clothing. They were unnatural. Almost haunting.

"Who are those people?" I asked, taking Azarel's arm as we passed another pair of them.

"They are the people of Pacifica," she said, head down, moving quickly. "Do not let them see you looking their way."

"Why?"

"They only want their own kind staring their way. Anyone else is considered offensive. Rude."

I frowned and looked back into the tents as we passed. Again, I got a cold shiver as we passed another fortune teller. "Think we're almost there?"

"We must be," she muttered. "There's not much left before we hit the far wall of the city."

I breathed a sigh of relief as we turned a corner and climbed a new hill, stopping at the foot of what looked like a castle. "Here," said the man we'd rescued. "My father is a servant in this household. He will see that we have shelter for the night."

Azarel paused and looked up at the towering house, then to Asher, who shook his head. Fear washed through her, and in smaller measure through Asher. But it didn't feel quite like fear, I thought. It was more like *warning*.

Asher turned to Raniero. "This is clearly your next step, not ours, brother."

"No?" Niero said, forehead wrinkling as he looked up at the palace before us and then down the street. "Might there be another — "

"No," Asher said urgently. "Those within this house ... It makes sense that you have been brought here. You shall learn much. Try and avoid notice. Listen. Then escape before you are pressed to do so. It is a dangerous house, filled with dangerous people." He leaned closer. "But it shall lead you far closer to Kapriel than any other," he whispered.

"I don't like it," Niero said, frowning, leaning away, "if it will put my people in enough peril that you won't come with us."

"Nor should you. But sometimes we do things we do not like in order to win a greater battle, yes?" He reached out and touched Niero's arm. "Azarel and I ... There are many in this household and those who know them who may very well recognize us. We must be away."

"Even now we take great risk by standing here," Azarel said, casting a worried eye to the street and back.

"I understand," Niero said, taking her arm in his. "I confess it wearies me, thinking of carrying on without you two. You've eased my burden, for a time."

"You are strong enough for the task," Asher said, taking his arm. "The Maker has seen to it. I look forward to the day our paths cross again."

"Do you need money?" I asked carefully, finding myself wishing there was something to keep them with us. "Anything to see you through? How will you manage?" Asher had left everything behind. Not that we had anything to give ourselves. All our provisions were at Georgii Post — hopefully put to use by Asher's friends, rather than our enemies.

"The Maker will see us through, just as he will you. You'll see," Asher whispered with his gentle smile, looking at me and then the others. "There's a gift in traveling light. Be confident in him to see to your every need."

"We will continue to make preparations for the coming king," Azarel whispered as she took my arm and briefly pulling me closer, "here in the Union. Know that you are covered by our continued prayers."

"And you with ours," I said.

Asher lifted a fisted hand, shoulder high so as to not attract undue attention, as they backed away from us. "Until the next time, my sister," he said to me. "You remember what I taught you, yes?"

I felt our parting like a pang, but forced a smile in return. "Until the next time," I repeated, watching them go. In them was only hope, such hope for us.

But in me was loss, fear. Fear that we were weaker without them.

And therefore, somehow, infinitely more vulnerable.

CHAPTER
22

The small family's grandfather was overjoyed to see the loved ones we'd rescued, and quickly ushered us in through a servant's entrance of the grand house. All around us, the servants were running ragged, preparing, we were told, for a grand party that evening. Out of the fray stepped a man with a closely shorn head and curiously long facial hair on his lip — what I later learned they called a mustache — who introduced himself as Mr. Olin, the butler, and took Niero aside.

After their brief discussion, it was agreed that in exchange for food and shelter for the night, we'd join the rest of the staff in helping with the cleaning, cooking, and service. There was apparently a large party that evening, and Mr. Olin found himself shorthanded. "It will be the best disguise possible," Raniero said with a sly smile, "if our enemies from Georgii Post come hunting. They'll look for us in the tourist district, not up here, in the heart of the residential district. But you all keep your heads down. Do your work, and don't draw attention to yourselves. We'll work. We'll eat. We'll sleep. We'll gather information, as Asher suggested. And then we'll leave in the morning after breakfast, to find our way across the Great Expanse."

So we readily complied to Mr. Olin's demands. Not that we had much choice. It was as if we'd been spirited into an entirely different world, and I felt like I could barely keep up with all my mind was taking in, forced to focus on my immediate tasks in order to keep breathing. Men were separated from women — leaving every Knight and Remnant on edge — and we were led to the servants' preparation rooms. We stowed our weapons and coats there, hoping they would be safe, but were faced with few options other than to risk it.

Then we took what they called "showers" — a miraculous contraption that I decided I could rapidly become accustomed to — under warm water, with creamy soap that smelled of lavender. I did my best to keep my armband out of the flow, fearful that the heat would wash away the protective oils and the true brilliance would begin to emerge. Even the constant rub of our clothes had made a bit of the precious metal beneath shine through in places. I looked furtively around as I stepped out of the hot stream, hurriedly wrapping myself in a wide, white towel.

I was handed a brush and told to sweep my hair back from my face to dry. Our clothing had been taken away "to be laundered," and we were given new underthings and cream-colored gowns that made me pause. They seemed very similar to the white, flowing fabric that the fine ladies of Pacifica favored, but the lines of ours were far more simple. The neck was cut wide, meeting in the barest point at each shoulder so that it draped over my breasts and arms. I frowned at my image in the mirror, noting how it cut away in a slit down my arms before clasping in a loose loop at my wrist. The armband would be visible if anyone gave me more than a cursory look. A girl swiftly tied a black rope of ribbon around my waist, cinching it tight, and, after a nod of approval, left me. I turned slightly, looking at my reflection. I had never seen my whole length in a mirror. I'd seen bits and pieces, but not *all* of me at once.

And I looked … beautiful. Refined. And clean, so clean. Cleaner than I'd been in weeks.

I rotated and looked at myself over my shoulder. The skirt fell straight to the floor, the back dragging a bit on the polished marble tiles, but not so much as Pacifica's ladies' gowns. With my long, dark hair down behind me in a straight sheet, and the ivory gown skimming across my body, I looked foreign. I barely recognized myself.

Our feet were quickly scrubbed, the nails cut, filed, and buffed, as were our fingernails. We were to wear no shoes. "Are we to be servants or ladies of the house?" I asked as another woman brushed out my drying hair and put a braided ribbon of black leather around my head, leaving my hair down around my shoulders. It reminded me of Azarel's own brown headband — was it a Pacifican style?

"Oh, we are far from the ladies, with our hair down," twittered a girl. "But the ladies claim we offend their sensibilities if we aren't as clean as they are."

I was tossed an apron to keep my gown clean and set before a bucket of potatoes to be peeled. As I worked, I listened to the kitchen help discuss the master of the house and the last party he'd had. Apparently, he'd invited three different women to the desert palace for the party tonight, and the servants were laying bets on who might gain his favor. "He's past his second decade," complained a skinny, frowning kitchenmaid. "The master ought to settle down now."

"There's no settling that man down," said her fat counterpart. "Married or not."

When my peeling task was complete an hour later, I washed head after head of what I thought must be lettuce — I'd only seen it in books — and then basket after basket of small berries. It took everything in me not to sneak bites of everything I saw, because each thing looked more enticing than the last. My stomach rumbled, and the berries looked redder than they had a moment before, and the smell reminded me of Dagan's precious berries. Would these taste the same? Different? They wouldn't miss just one, would they?

I was reaching for the nearest one, a perfect teardrop of red, when the butler barked, "Girl!"

I snatched my hand back and looked over to Mr. Olin, once again taking in his short hair and facial hair across his lip. I'd never seen such a thing as his mustache without a beard — the men of our village preferred to shave, as had most I'd seen throughout our journey, other than the Drifters. And his mustache hung so low on either side of his mouth, I fear I stared at him for an impolite length of time.

He rolled his eyes and flicked two fingers over his shoulder. "Come," he said, already turning to go, obviously expecting me to follow. I looked over at Bellona, who was working on butchering meat two tables over, and she opened her eyes wide as if to say, *Be careful.* Tressa, folding napkins, gave me the same look.

The man paused at the corner and gestured impatiently for me to take off my apron and leave it on a peg beside a few others. Then when I stepped forward to go, he looked me over with a frown, paused, lifted a hand, and then flicked those fingers again, chin waiting in the air as he eyed someone behind me. "See to her hair," he sniffed. I shifted, wondering what I was to do. But then another girl arrived with a brush, and after ten quick strokes of it through my hair I was apparently acceptable in appearance, because he was in motion again. We paused in an enormous cupboard with stacks and stacks of fine plates, bowls, and cups, and he motioned for me to take up a stack of twenty plates — these made of delicate ivory rimmed in gold — as he picked up a similar stack himself.

The stack was unwieldy in height, but I was used to physical work and followed him into the dining room, sweating more over the value in my hands than the weight. But once outside the kitchens, I couldn't keep from staring in awe at the rich decorations surrounding me.

"Come, come, girl, close your mouth," frowned the butler, looking at me over his shoulder. "Look nowhere but to my back."

"Forgive me, sir," I said.

"You may call me Mr. Olin." He cast a dry look over his shoulder. "You look as if you've never seen a fine house before."

"I haven't. Not like this." It was out before I could think, and I immediately clamped my lips shut. But I'd caught his attention.

"Oh? From where do you hail? Most people in Castle Vega have worked in the noble houses at one point or another." He peered at me quizzically.

"Far from here, sir," I said.

"How far? Where specifically? Eh? Never mind. We get people from all over the Trading Union. I'm only glad you and yours arrived in time to assist this night. Lord Maximillian invited an extra twelve people!" he said under his breath, in a tone that sounded like a mix of admiration and frustration.

We turned into a dining room, which contained a table that was longer than my whole house back in the village. It appeared to be made of gold, or at least covered in it, and gleamed in the light coming through the wide windows that banked the room. There were seven pieces of silver at each place setting, and four crystal goblets of various sizes. I gaped at the extravagance. The opulence. The riches. What one set of that silver could do back at Nem Post ... the supplies we could purchase!

I briefly wondered if the Maker would choose to look elsewhere if I pocketed a few sets, but was distracted by Raniero passing through the room carrying a huge, stuffed chair. He was barefoot and in cloth similar to mine, his shirt flowing over his massive chest and almost glowing against his charcoal-colored skin. He gave me a small smile of reassurance and continued on.

I almost laughed aloud when I saw Ronan walk through with a table, so glad was I to see him, especially looking so clean and handsome. But when he paused, staring at me in return, I shifted in embarrassment.

"Andriana," he whispered, looking at me in open admiration.

I blushed, and then doubly when the butler looked from me to Ronan and back again. He snapped his fingers. Ronan and I hurried into action again. "There shall be no fraternization among the servants!" Mr. Olin cried after Ronan. "No fraternization!" I had no idea what the word meant, but I understood his tone.

But as Ronan turned and left the room, my heart caught, because I could clearly see his armband through the gossamer-thin fabric of his shirt, and he didn't even have a slit, as my dress did. I glanced down and saw that as my arms strained to keep hold of the plates, mine was all the more visible too.

The stack in my hands waved precariously off balance, and my eyes went wide as I quickly stepped to the side to bring them back into balance.

"Set them here, girl, before you drop them," said Mr. Olin, pointing to a side table. He pulled a small black stick from inside a pocket and took a plate from the stack, leading me to the table to give me instruction. "Now, I want you to take this stick and make certain the plates are equidistant between fork and knife, as well as this length from the edge of the table. Can you see that done?"

I nodded.

"Good. Your eyes are beautiful, but moreover they're *quick*. I hope my confidence in you has not been misplaced."

"No, I don't believe it has been, sir."

He gave me the tiniest of smiles. "Well, see to your task with care. If you do a good job this night, perhaps we will speak of further employment in the coming weeks. You are quite   comely. That will please the master."

"Thank you, sir. That would be an honor, sir." I looked down, not wanting him to see in my eyes that we would not likely share breakfast. But then, who knew? Maybe it'd take a while to figure out how to cross the Great Expanse, as well as gather some funds. Perhaps we were to sojourn here for a few more days, weeks even. Earn some coin as well as room and board to replace what we'd lost. It all depended on where we were led and when ... which was decidedly less than easily seen in advance, I thought with frustration.

When my protectors had told me that I was Ailith, that I'd been born to help save the world, I'd thought our path would be much ... clearer, *obvious*, than it was turning out to be. This felt more like muddling our way through from station to station than any clear-cut path to do the Maker's bidding. So far, all we knew for sure was that we were to free Kapriel. Somehow. Some way.

Mr. Olin left the room, and I stole glances at the fine fixtures around the plates. Gleaming silver candelabras, one between every four place settings. The four crystal goblets, in various sizes, above each plate. A thick, soft napkin that I couldn't resist running my finger across — I'd never touched such fine fabric! Above, on the walls that climbed high, high above, were pictures — vast oil paintings of foreign landscapes and people in odd costume, next to golden-edged mirrors. I forced my attention back to my task. It wouldn't do to have Mr. Olin return and see I'd gotten distracted.

I'd placed fourteen plates, carefully measuring from the lip of the table and then placing them as instructed, when I heard a woman singing outside the window.

I looked left and right, and saw both doorways were empty. *No, stay on task, Dri.*

I went and took three more plates from the stack and placed them as I'd been told. But the woman's voice — so high, so clear, so haunting — filled the streets and filtered up to the dining hall and through the slightly opened windows. The doorways remained empty as I returned for three more plates; no one else apparently was about. I took up more plates and was turning when I heard her voice, in haunting measure, each syllable floating up to me

"And upon the field, and upon the plain,
The Ailith rose where they were slain,
And forevermore, whene're she sang,
He wept and wept and wept again."

Had I misheard her? Or had she actually mentioned the Ailith?

I rotated back to the window and saw that the sun had broken through the clouds and streamed through them, down toward the palace and in through the window in dusty rays. I could see the outline of other rooftops, the edge of the castle wall … Unable to resist any longer, I hurried over to the glass and looked down. Below was a small courtyard surrounded on three sides by buildings — one of which was this fine house — and atop a small pedestal was the woman.

The singer continued to weave her song, each note higher and higher, while her eyes stayed focused on the window. My window. She seemed to be singing directly to me, staring but not seeing, with wide, glassy eyes. I listened hard, but her words seemed to be slurring, becoming difficult to make out. But surely her words, and one in particular, hadn't been my imagination! As I attempted to decipher more of her song, people gathered before her and rocked back and forth to the tempo, smiles across their faces.

It was just sinking in that my cuff was humming, along with dropping in temperature so that it chilled my entire arm, when a man said, "She has quite the beautiful — "

I whirled, and the center plate slipped from the stack in my hands. I tried to grab it, missed, and then all three were slipping in different directions.

"Whoa!" the man said, reaching out to grab one from the air and then another with lightning-fast hands.

Just as the last was about to hit the marble tiles, I knelt and caught it, inches from shattering. I let out a little breath of relief and wonder, then slowly looked up, along fine trousers, a wide belt, and a shirt of the finest silk, to the handsome face of a man of about two decades. Two young women trailed behind him. All three of them had honey-gold blonde hair, eerily similar in shade. Dyed?

Still holding the plates, he grinned down at me. "Girl?" he asked, lifting them slightly, as if to remind me of my task.

"Oh! Forgive me," I said, rising in a fluid motion. "Thank you so —"

"Girl! What a travesty! What were you doing?" asked the butler, sweeping in beside us. He bowed, and bowed again. "Lord Maximillian, forgive her. Forgive us."

Lord Maximillian. The lord of this house? One so young? He couldn't be more than two decades and two. The kitchen gossips' conversation came back to me and I eyed his companions. Where was the third?

"Girl!" Mr. Olin barked, frowning furiously at me. I hurriedly looked to the ground.

"Ease up, Olin," he said. I could feel his gray-green eyes studying me, examining every inch of me. And my armband was vibrating, the chill a stark warning. But it confused me. Because every other time it had grown so cold, I was around Sheolites. Men out to kill me. This one … wasn't. Was he?

"I startled her, Olin," he said, his tone warm and friendly. "It was entirely my fault."

I glanced up then, grateful for his intercession, and his smile broadened a bit. He had even, white teeth. Dimples. And that honey-blond hair that curled about his ears. I inwardly reached out, trying to read him, but got no emotion at all.

"By the cosmos, you're certainly beautiful," he said, staring back into my eyes. The women behind him, dressed in the manner of Pacifica, drifted away and out the door, as if excused.

I looked down again, embarrassed at his praise. Was that the way of Castle Vega? Such easy compliments?

"When did you come to work in my house?" he said.

"Just this morning," I said.

"You shall address Lord Maximillian as 'my lord,'" Mr. Olin snapped, cheeks reddening. He hadn't informed me, and I was apparently making him look bad.

"What's your name?" Lord Maximillian said in an easy tone.

"Andriana ... my lord," I hastened to add.

"Get back to your task, Andriana," Mr. Olin hissed, "with the salad plates next." I immediately set off, reaching with trembling hands for more plates and hurrying to the table.

But the lord of the house followed me, studying my every move. I gave him a darting look over my shoulder and tried to read him again — wanting confirmation of warning, clarification, anything — but could get nothing, nothing but confusion, flitting emotions impossible to pin down. He paused, and then smiled. I decided he was flirting, playing, not intending to do me harm. Perhaps the armband had been warning me of someone else, nearby. The chill in it *had* thawed a bit. I fought to control my breath, and dropped my shoulders and lifted my chin, pretending as if he weren't there.

"Have we met before, Andriana?" he asked.

"No, my lord."

"Are you quite certain?"

"Quite, my lord," I said, measuring the plate from the edge of the table and adjusting it a tad.

"Somewhere in the city, other than this house?"

"No, my lord."

"How? How are you so certain?"

He stood in front of me, blocking my way. I dragged my eyes up to meet his, trying to think of an answer that would send him on his way. "Because I just arrived in the city, my lord."

The young nobleman studied me, smiling with chin in hand and his eyes squinting, then waved the butler away. I felt Mr. Olin slip from the dining room behind me and felt twice as vulnerable. How I longed for my sword . . .

"Stand still for a moment, Andriana." I did as he asked; there was no getting around it. The lord's eyes ran from the top of my head, raked slowly down my body to my toes, then back to my face. I bent my head in shame, wishing I could take him down and choke him until he understood that I was to be respected. He'd never met a woman like me. If he only knew what —

"Do you play a game with me? Tell me the truth. Have we *not* met? You are terribly familiar. Perhaps in another district . . . one you don't wish to admit to."

I swallowed hard. It didn't take much for me to imagine what sort of district that might be, in a city that had no moral code. "No, my lord, I am not playing a game. Perhaps I only remind you of another." I waited, head bowed, and he finally stepped aside so I could continue my task.

"So you are new to Castle Vega," he insisted, trailing me. "Perhaps we've met elsewhere in the Union or Pacifica. From where do you hail?"

"Most recently from Georgii Post," I said, moving around him to retrieve more plates once he leaned against the cupboard counter, directly in my way. But as I lifted my arms, he caught my wrist with his right hand.

"Now what is this?"

I froze and looked at him, the Maker only narrowly

keeping me from twisting, turning, and flipping the man onto his back. Could he feel my darting pulse beneath his fingers?

His eyes moved from my flared nostrils down to my armband, well aware that I was alarmed, angry that he dared to touch me. Enjoying it. He casually lifted his left hand and ran his fingers up the slit, separating the fabric, peeking in. The humor in his green eyes faded. "Where did you get this, Andriana?" he asked.

My armband was icy-cold. It was as if he recognized the design. Because of the tattoo that Kapriel and Azarel shared? I remembered Azarel and Asher's fear when they saw whose house our Georgii Post friends had led us to, their refusal to enter. Was this young lord one they feared would recognize them?

Even with him touching me, I still wasn't able to read his emotions. But they were plain enough on his face. *Danger*, my heart screamed. *Danger, danger, danger . . .*

"A trinket," I said, gently but firmly pulling my wrist from his grip. "Given to me by someone dear. A simple reminder of my home, Lord Maximillian," I said, reaching up with my other hand, as if I might cover it, hide it, make him forget he'd ever seen it.

"A trinket," he repeated flatly, looking into my eyes. Staring hard. Penetrating as if he could reach through them and delve directly into my heart, grabbing hold of it and the truth within. I gasped and took a step back, as if he'd struck me, my hand moving to my heart. I could feel it pound beneath my palm, but it felt distant, foreign. My armband began to vibrate, so cold it felt as if it might shatter.

Several long seconds passed.

"Andriana," he said softly, as if mulling over my name,

breaking our gaze at last and moving to another tall cupboard beside a tiny window at the end of the storage room. I could no longer hear the singer outside. Indeed, it seemed as if her presence had been a dream. He opened a cabinet, pulled out a heavy, crystal bottle, and lifted the glass stopper off the top. He poured amber liquid into a thick, short glass and lifted it to his lips, sipping slowly. I waited nervously.

"You are new to this city. Do you know who I am, Andriana?" He took another long, slow sip, then looked over at me with deadly calm eyes. It was if he squeezed my heart as he said my name.

"L-lord of this house, Lord Maximillian Jala."

"Yes," he said, after a moment's pause. "That's a start. You may go, Andriana. We are done for now."

CHAPTER 23

I rounded the corner and leaned against the wall, closing my eyes.

Something had just gone terribly wrong. I could feel it, even if I couldn't put my finger on it. While Asher had seemed confident we'd been led to this location for a reason, clearly he and Azarel had never thought one of us would be placed anywhere but in the kitchen this day. But I had. And the master had recognized something about me, beyond the armband I wore. Did he know I was Ailith?

I took a deep breath and strode toward the kitchen, intent on finding the man from Georgii Post we'd saved. He could tell me more of what I needed to know. Once there, I ducked behind a tall clock as Mr. Olin passed to avoid having another task assigned, and searched through the thirty or more servants, all moving in different directions and on different tasks in the kitchen. The closer we got to dinner, the more crowded and bustling this room would become, I decided.

I glimpsed the man I sought on the far side of the kitchen, but by the time I got there he was gone. In frustration, I reached out and stopped a girl of perhaps a decade and five. "Please ..." I said. "Tell me. Who is the lord of this house?"

She stared at me in confusion, then mirth. "Why, this is the holiday house of Lord Maximillian Jala, one of the Six."

"One of the Six?" But before I finished my question, I knew of whom she spoke.

I stepped back from her and belatedly realized I'd brought a hand to my chest, as if alarmed, and dropped it.

The Council of Six. Pacifica's ruling body, formed to do Keallach's bidding. I'd heard Asher mention it in conversation with Niero. I turned away from the girl, so that my face wouldn't betray me further, but my mind was racing. I'd imagined the Six as old men, vile and menacing. Lord Jala ... I shook my head, remembering his warm green eyes and glossy blond hair. His quick smile — and his quicker hands, catching the plates. Saving me from disaster. And yet, would it not have been better for the plates to crash? For me to be summarily dismissed by Olin? Rather than have one of the Council of Six take note of me as he had?

But then, was this not just the sort of break we needed? To get closer to Keallach and his men? To find out how to get to the Isle of Catal and free Kapriel?

Men and women passed me in the kitchen, and I lifted a towel and plate, wiping it so I looked busy, hoping one of the Ailith would come by. I needed to talk to Raniero.

Now.

Setting down the plate and towel once the crowd had passed, I picked up a pile of clean linens and went out the door, as if Olin had set me upon another task. I walked down a wide hallway, then past one grand room after another, each with beautiful, polished stone floors and luxurious carpets, rich paint, and even fabric on the walls. Walking quickly through the house, I saw many servants but none of the Ailith, and the longer I searched, the more anxious I became. What if I ran into Lord Jala again?

I squeezed the linens in my sweaty hand, wondering at the heat in this part of the Union, and glad for my light gown and bare feet upon cool tiles. I heard the laughter before I saw them. Up ahead, the house opened up into a central courtyard, lined on all sides in a three-story portico draped with flowering vines. In the center, beside a curving pool tiled in blue, young men were throwing their heads back laughing, clapping one another on the back. I moved around a screen and peeked through the crack, watching as they drank from crystal glasses filled with amber liquid, just as Lord Jala had done.

Young women hung about them. These were not dressed as the women of Pacifica, but rather scantily, showing belly and cleavage as if they were in their underthings rather than clothing for the light of day. They draped their arms around the young men's chests from behind, tickled their ears, kissed their necks and jaws. But the men practically ignored them, concentrating on one man's engaging story from what he called "the front."

"The swine had taken up a farm!" said the man. I had a hard time looking away from him and the other men, they were so collectively beautiful. Like cousins of Lord Jala. Where was the lord of the house? Why was he not with these others, plainly his friends? I'd never seen so many handsome men close to my own age, in such a small space, in … well, ever. I was drawn to them, like one of Dagan's bees to the flowers.

Dagan. What had the man just said about a farm?

"You have to watch the simpletons every moment," said a tall man with a long, straight nose and sculpted cheeks. "They are far better off looking to us for everything they need."

"As are we, harvesting from their fields as needed," said another man, lifting a hand to stroke a nearby girl in the most unseemly fashion. My belly clenched. Were the girls with them by choice? Or were they slaves? Or purchased women, as we'd seen along the inner streets of Zanzibar?

"What'd you do?" said another. "About the Hoodite's farm?"

I sucked in my breath at the word *Hoodite*.

"We razed it. It was beautiful, in a way, seeing that fire stream out in such a vast swath," he said, waving his fingers as if seeing it again in his mind. He shook his head and pulled a girl into his lap, nuzzling her neck until she giggled, then looked back to the others. "We have to remain vigilant. We can't allow thoughts of independence to rise among the Union. The last thing the king needs is civil war. Not after what we've been through." He lifted his crystal glass wearily, as if he had fought each battle himself, and the other men raised their own to clink his.

"Not that it would last long," said another. "It'd hardly be fair. Us against the Union."

"True."

"What of those who planted the farm?"

The first man grinned and lifted one brow. "It was tricky, hunting them down. But our people in the field are there for a reason. I believe we took care of the problem." His smile faded a bit. "It's for the good of all, of course."

"Of course, of course," murmured the rest.

"Sethos will be here soon. He'll give you all further details."

Sethos. I tried to swallow, and found my mouth terribly dry again. *Sethos, Sethos. He couldn't possibly mean ...*

My eyes shifted back and forth across the paintings upon the room screen, thinking through his words. A farm. Hunting them down. Sethos.

The vision of a tracker in his elite, hooded cape came to mind.

No, no, no, no, no ...

I had to find Raniero.

I whipped around to go, but stopped abruptly.

"Hello, Andriana," Lord Jala said, taking a long, unhurried sip from his crystal glass. He was a foot away from me, leaning casually against the wall. "What are you doing here?" He lifted his eyebrows as if honestly asking the question, but it was clear he knew exactly why I was far from my assigned duties.

"I-I'm afraid I got lost, my lord," I said. "Your house is far more vast than I am accustomed to." I darted past him and scurried down the hall, but he kept pace with me.

"Perhaps you need a tour," he said jovially, setting down his empty glass as we passed a table. "So that you don't get lost and end up hovering behind screens, appearing as a spy."

"Oh! Yes! Of course you are right, my lord. I do not wish for anything like that to occur. I must ask Mr. Olin if that is possible. He is so busy, what with your dinner guests due to arrive so soon."

I turned right, hoping it was the way back to the kitchen. I was honestly so flustered, I wasn't certain. All the while, Lord Jala walked beside me, hands folded behind his back. "I think, Andriana, that I'd like you to be my personal servant tonight," he said.

"Personal servant, my lord?" I asked, pausing at another

junction. It was all feeling terribly unfamiliar. "I … uh … Forgive me, but I am so new to the household, I'm certain that I wouldn't know what to do and when. Mr. Olin would have a fit."

"Olin is always in a fit. Come now, it will be fun. And I can show you around. So you won't get lost again."

I looked back down the hallway, from where we'd come, and realized he'd let me wander into a far quarter of the house, not at all the way I'd wanted. My armband thrummed with cold warning. I stilled and straightened, trying to remember to breathe. "My lord, I-I am not like those other girls. With your friends back there." I lifted my chin and looked him in the eye. "I will serve you, if that is what is required. But you may not touch me."

His eyes widened in surprise and then he smiled. His smile grew wider and wider until he laughed. "Oh, my dear Andriana." He pulled his lips together and shook his head a little, as if I'd just become ten times more charming and quaint with that one statement. He lifted a wry brow. "A woman has never said such a thing to me, in all my life. Let alone a *servant*."

I wanted to slap him. Drive the side of my hand into his layrnx. Tell him that I was no mere servant, nor would I ever be. But the Maker intervened then. Clearly. In the way that Azarel spoke of.

And he told me to stand down.

My eyes moved to the ground as I tried to gather myself, trembling with twined rage and fear. "Forgive me if I offended you, my lord. Clearly, I am not your best choice for a personal servant."

Please let me go please let me go please let me go …

He stared at me so long, I thought he hadn't heard me, and I shifted uneasily.

"Come," he said, turning and walking down the hall. "I think it shall be most amusing, having you about this night, Andriana."

I forced myself to hurry and catch up with him, dread filling me. I reached out to try and read his emotions again, wanting to know if he was planning something evil. But again, I got nothing but a quick, alarmed glance from him, as if he'd felt my probing. My heart lurched, this time because I wondered if my gift was fading. If I was losing it somehow, because I was away from the other Ailith? Because I was in this house of the enemy?

He strode down the hall and then put a hand on a doorjamb, swinging around and into a massive bedroom, and giving me a waggle of the eyebrows as he did so. I hovered there, within a few feet of the entrance, as he moved into the room. There was a large, round bed at the center. Massive windows at the far end, showcasing a view of the city and the desert beyond. I could see the last vestiges of sunset on the horizon, and a storm building above it.

He pulled off his shirt and tossed it onto the bed, then walked over to the window with his hands on his hips. I looked around, at exotic artwork that lined the room. Simplistic. Graphic. Bold in color and texture. It was a relief to find visual diversion anywhere but in the half-naked man at the end of the room.

He turned partway, not looking at me but speaking over his shoulder. "You'll find my evening's choice on the mannequin," he said. "Bring it to me."

My eyes searched the length of the room and found what he

spoke of. A beautiful, densely woven silk vest and a fresh ivory shirt in the same fabric as I myself wore, both hanging on the wooden form of a man's torso. On the floor were slippers in a similar silk weave. I moved toward them, wondering about such extravagance, such silliness. When there were people who struggled to make it through the night, given the cold of every Hoarfrost! I remembered my parents piling me with skins, our breath clouding in front of our faces as we said our prayers.

I went to him and placed the slippers beside his feet, tossed the vest over my shoulder, then lifted the soft shirt up to him. My face burned. Was it as red as it felt?

"Slip it over my shoulders, Andriana," he said.

I clamped my lips shut, refusing to look into his eyes, and lifted the shirt collar up and over his head, carefully keeping my eyes on the window over his shoulder while thinking of ten different ways I could bring him to the floor, break his pretty neck, force him to beg me for mercy. He had a few inches on me, but I was fairly confident that I had years of death-strike practice on him.

He lifted his hands up idly, as if he was not two decades, but rather four seasons old, and I took a deep breath and pulled one sleeve over his hand and then the other. I took the vest from my shoulder and moved behind him, helping him into it.

He turned to me. "Good. Look upon me."

I looked him over, scanning the ensemble, but refused to look him in the eye.

"It is well?" he said.

"Well enough," I allowed.

He laughed. Lighter at first, then louder. He shook his head. "Oh, Andriana. How glad am I that you wandered in my doors this day. Life has been rather … dull of late. You are the perfect diversion."

My heart warred within me. I was both complimented and horrified. What did that mean? I seemed to be getting myself in deeper and deeper.

He reached forward and took my hair, pulling half forward over my shoulder, letting it drop, slowly, over my breast. I reached out and grabbed his hand before I could think. "I told you. You may not touch me."

He smiled. "Forgive me," he said easily, no apology at all in his tone. "I forgot myself."

But in that instant, I read him at last. It was as if in his utter surprise over my move, and my touching him, he was open for a moment. And what I learned made me grow cold.

He pulled his hand away from mine, his dark gaze hardening. "What did you just do?"

"What?" I feigned surprise, gaining strength as I gained knowledge. "Nothing, Lord Jala."

"Oh, that was far from nothing," he said, reaching out to my ear.

I shied away, thinking he was about to touch me again, but he brought out a flower. A dark red rose, the bud perfect.

It was my turn to shake in surprise. "How-how'd you do that?" I said, reluctantly accepting the stem he offered me. "Ouch!" I said under my breath, as a sharp thorn pierced my thumb. I let the gift drop to the floor and glanced up at him, concerned that he'd be dismayed by my action, but he seemed unconcerned, only watching me. Taking in everything he could about me, absorbing me, in a way.

I wondered if the thorn had embedded itself beneath the skin, it hurt so badly, as an orb of red formed. I lifted it closer to my face and squeezed to see if the thorn was still caught, needing to be plucked out.

"Hmm." He wiped his index finger across the rising blood on my thumb before I could move away. He peered at the red smear on his finger for a breath, then slid it into his mouth, watching me all the while.

I gaped at him, every cell within me beginning to freeze, along with my armband.

Clearly enjoying my horror, he walked away from me, toward the door. "Come along, Andriana." He walked out like some freakish prince — his slippers sliding on the tiles, making his feet pop up slightly — and rounded the corner. And given that I had few options, I followed, feeling as if I carried thousand-pound weights.

I followed him down the hallway, and he didn't look back again, turning left, then right, then down another hallway until we were facing the courtyard. I could hear the others laughing ahead, more raucous than ever.

We moved through wide doors to the portico now capped by the purple clouds of sunset, and the others greeted Maximillian as if he'd been gone for weeks, not minutes. Seeing other servants, I moved to their side, hands clenched before me, wondering what would be required next. If only Lord Jala would forget I was present, I might be able to slip out. I felt shame, then, finding myself wishing he'd find distraction in the girls that circulated out and among his friends. For a moment, I thought that it was what they wished. But within seconds, I knew their collective shame, their misery, their desire for escape. They acted. Desperately hoped that one more empty night of pretend might open a doorway to freedom

The sorrow threatened to overcome me. Choke me. My gift

had not disappeared. Lord Jala was simply harder to read than the rest here, before me.

"Wine, Andriana," Maximillian said to me, gesturing pointedly toward an empty glass and then the pitcher on a nearby table.

I picked up the goblet, went to the pitcher and poured, aware that most of the men watched me as I moved.

"Where did you find this comely creature, Max?" purred a man, coming closer to me as I set down the pitcher. I swiftly finished my task and tried to smoothly edge away, making my way toward Lord Jala.

"She wandered in this morning, seeking work, according to Olin." He accepted the goblet from my hand, but was blessedly distracted by the woman who came to sit on his lap.

His friend followed me back to the edge of the courtyard. He wavered a bit, clearly feeling the alcohol he'd consumed. "There is something about her "

Max looked over his shoulder, his eyes far more focused than his friend's. "You sense it too, Fenris?"

"Ahh, yes," said the man. Fenris, too, was little past his second decade. He reached up to touch my cheek, and I moved my head away.

He smiled, as if I played, and moved both hands up to touch my arms.

"Don't," I warned, looking him in the eye, and the other two servant girls looked at me in alarm. As if it wasn't allowed, refusing men's advances.

Lord Jala laughed, the girl kissing his neck as he watched us.

His brown-haired friend didn't share his amusement. He was tall, reedy, strong. And he clearly perceived my avoidance as challenge. Mouth in a line, he moved toward me, taking my wrist, and I could hold back no longer.

I did what I'd longed to do to Maximillian earlier: Twisting, turning, and pulling him over my shoulder. Slamming him to the ground, watching with satisfaction as his mouth widened in a gasp and his eyes rounded, belatedly feeling horror as my bare foot rested on his chest. My hands still clung to his twisted wrist, as if screaming my guilt.

What have I done?

I looked up to Lord Jala, waiting for the worst.

But he laughed. Laughed and laughed until he cried, his green eyes twisting in merriment as the other noblemen joined him. All except Lord Fenris. "Gentlemen," Maximillian choked out at last, wiping his cheeks free of tears, "meet Andriana, my new maidservant."

CHAPTER
24

I backed away from Lord Fenris, dimly hearing Lord Jala lackadaisically introducing the other lords of Pacifica — Kendric, Daivat, Broderick, and Cyrus — to me. They rose and moved to stand around me and their fallen comrade, as if we were a small theater act. None of them meant me harm but Fenris. They'd adopted Lord Jala's mode of thinking — that I was entertaining. And they seemed hungry for entertainment. Their longing for distraction, engagement, opened up and threatened to swallow me in a sea of empty need.

Fenris rose, brushing off his ivory shirt and tan, woven silk vest, his neck and lower cheeks flushing in fury. "Send her to the dungeon, Max. Such … insolence!" He leaned closer to me, and I didn't have to read him in order to capture a full serving of his loathing.

"What?" Lord Jala said, rising behind his compatriots at last, shoving the girl off his lap and coming closer to us. He patted Fenris on the shoulder, but the man shoved him away.

"Friend, don't you see? This is the most fascinating woman to cross our path in months!" he said, gesturing toward me. "The emperor will be utterly besotted ..."

"Don't waste your time," Fenris said, looking me over from head to toe. "She's not met her second decade."

"Ahh, but she's not too far off," Lord Jala returned, looking me over again. "Same as his highness, for that matter."

"It would be a boon, finding his mate from among the Union," put in Lord Daivat, giving me a quick glance. He crossed burly arms and scratched dark stubble on his strong chin. "Bind us together and all that."

"Bah. If he's to take a bride from the Union," another said, "it'd be best if she was the daughter of a trade post boss. Someone with true power." His eyes were bright and penetrating, an odd, light blue. I thought he was the one called Kendric.

"Power," Lord Jala said, tapping his lips. His eyes slid to my arm — to my cuff — and then away. He took a sip of wine. "It's been proven that the women of the Union do not suffer from the infertility rate as our own women do. And Keallach is bent on having his own blood heir."

My mind raced, even as my heart seemed to pause and then pound painfully. Was I gathering what I thought I was gathering? Was I surrounded by all six of Keallach's council? And were they honestly considering me as a potential mate for him?

I wanted to vomit.

"Our women do not suffer from infertility as much as the desire to maintain their youthful figures," the one I thought they called Broderick retorted. He was lithe, elegant in form, with dark brown eyes and hair. "It truly must end. For the health of the kingdom. And our future with the empire."

I frowned, my eyes moving between them. Throughout the

Trading Union and apparently the kingdom of Pacifica, the accepted age of matrimony was after a girl's second decade. But in Zanzibar we'd seen women married far younger. Was the emperor honestly seeking a bride? When he was but a decade-and-seven himself?

My stomach rolled again.

"My lords," Olin said, entering the courtyard and attempting to look utterly refined, even as he cast me an alarmed look, finding me encircled by the council. "Dinner is served. If you would kindly move to the dining room ..."

"Yes, Olin," Lord Jala said. "Thank you."

Olin paused at the doorway, gesturing for me to come with him, as if I'd absently wandered in and he needed to collect me ... as if I were a stray dog in the very heart of the palace. My heart leaped, and I was turning toward him, eager to make my escape. Any punishment he heaped upon me would be better than —

"No, Olin," Lord Jala said behind me. "I've asked her to attend me."

Mr. Olin pulled up straight. "Yes, of course. Very good, my lord." He hesitated. "But the girl ... she has not been introduced to the nuances of the dining hall, my lord," he said. "Perhaps after a few days of training, she might attend you?"

"Nonsense," Lord Jala said, passing by us. "Come along, Andriana. You've as quick a mind as you do nimble defenses. Let us see how you might employ it within the intricacies of the dining hall."

I groaned inwardly, waiting until the others filed out, and avoiding Lord Fenris's narrowed gaze as he passed. When the men had left, we servants followed, leaving the courtyard consorts behind, like garden statuary.

The two servant girls coached me as we went, whispering

instructions to walk three steps back and to the left of my charge, to keep my eyes on Lord Jala at all times so as to be ready to do anything he bid, to stay silent, to not fidget, to hold a pitcher of wine and refill his goblet any time it reached half full, to hold an extra napkin and trade it out after each course — draping it across his lap from left to right — to pretend as if you were not listening to the conversation, but listening enough to be aware in case your master had need of you ... On and on they went, sending my head spinning.

"Dri," whispered a man as we passed. I looked over my shoulder. Raniero!

"I'll catch up," I said to the girls. They shared a look of alarm but moved on without pause, clearly more bent on protecting their own necks than worrying any further about mine.

Raniero pulled me into the narrow hallway that appeared to lead to a servant's entrance. "You all right?" he said.

"Yes. I mean, no! Niero, do you *know* where we are?"

He nodded at me grimly.

"Do you know who *that* is?" I gestured down the hall. "Lord Jala! And he saw my armband! He seemed to recognize it! And those others?" I grabbed his hand, fear at last bringing tears to my eyes. "Niero, we're surrounded by Keallach's entire Council of Six!"

Niero drew slightly back. I watched as he swallowed hard. "It is as the Maker has foreseen. He wants us here for some reason. We must see it through."

I shook my head at his mad words. "I have to go. If he turns and finds me gone — "

Niero stared down at me with his dark, intense eyes. "Jala is Keallach's right-hand man. Incredibly dangerous. We need to gain what knowledge we can and then get out. By daybreak at the latest. I'm securing some mudhorses."

"Mudhorses? They'll never make it across."

"Do you have another idea?" he whispered back. "I need to get you out from under Jala's nose ... as well as the rest of them."

I couldn't argue with that. Between the man licking my blood as if he could *taste* me and considering me as bridal material for Emperor Evil, I couldn't get away fast enough. But if they caught us, or caught up to us ... I remembered Fenris's look. That man would delight in bringing me pain.

"There's something else, Andriana," Raniero said, and I could sense his next words would be painful.

"What?" I said pausing at the corner.

He peered around the corner. "Sethos and some of the others arrived."

"What?" I squeaked out. "Already?"

"They appear to be heading in for dinner. That's why I came to find you. I didn't want him to surprise you."

"Raniero," I said, my panic rising, "I'm to attend Lord Jala. In *there*. In the dining room!"

He put his hands on my shoulders. "Look at me. Andriana. *Look* at me."

I was breathing hard, and it took everything in me to turn my wild eyes to his.

"Concentrate," he said, speaking peace into me, filling me. "Concentrate on the power of the Maker within you. No matter what you face in there," he said, "you must remember all we've discussed. To not give in to the feelings. To rely on what you know. To utilize what you've been given." He squeezed my arms. "Keep the door in your heart shut. We'll do our best to distract them." He gave me a small smile. "What better place to hide than in plain sight?"

"Easy for you to say." I made myself move down the hall, practically running to meet up with the others, just as they met the dining room doorway.

Fifty people were being seated, and I moved to the end of the table, to Lord Jala's left. My armband was thrumming, hurting me, it was so cold. I wished I could turn it off. Shout at it, *I know, I know.* When Lord Broderick stood up to formally greet the nobles, raising his delicate crystal glass in a toast, I stole a glance down the table. Sethos was partway down on the left, flanked by two other Sons of Sheol, and I was thankful he was partially blocked by other guests. He turned his head, as if he'd picked up my scent, and I quickly centered my mind on the power of the Maker, praying he would protect me.

It surprised me that Sethos and the others wore white, as the other nobles did, rather than red. That the Sheolites ate food. Drank water. Wine. I concentrated on that. If they ate and drank like humans, they would bleed like humans. Reminded myself that I'd seen them die. Such remembrances made me breathe a bit easier. We'd killed the scouts the night of our Call. We'd killed that one tracker and a couple of scouts near the Hoodite farm. No matter how it seemed, they were not immortal. Fearsome, but no more powerful than me within. I was more powerful really, with the power of the Maker flowing through my heart —

Lord Jala shifted in his seat and Mr. Olin shot me a wide-eyed look. I started and moved forward to refill his half-empty goblet, my hands trembling so much that I feared the red liquid would spill across the white linens and ivory plates. All so terribly white and the wine so red, red, red …

I only dared breathe again as I moved back, hoping that I'd not drawn Sethos's attention.

Killian and Ronan came in with several other servants, carrying enormous trays. Mr. Olin nodded toward them, and I went to retrieve a small plate full of lettuce and onions and nuts and berries, with the most delicious-smelling oil drizzled across it. My mouth watered as I carefully set it before Lord Jala and backed away, wondering if and when we were to eat.

Perhaps they leave the scraps for us, I thought darkly. *Like dogs in the alley.*

The conversation turned to progress up north, a rebel queen proving to be dogged in her resistance against Pacifica. I wished other conversations would fade so I could hear better, and I fought the urge to step forward, cock my head in order to learn more. A rebel queen? I had to appear as if I didn't care, that I only was thinking of my lord's needs, not his topic of conversation. But he turned to me and said, "What do you think, Andriana, of the rebel queen to our north?"

"I-I beg your pardon?" I said. "My lord," I added belatedly. Several guests shared glances of surprise. But the entire table fell silent.

"You are just in from the far reaches of the Union, are you not?" Lord Jala said, his eyes merry. But it wasn't merriment I saw in them, only cold calculation. "Who better than you to give us the people's perspective." All eyes were turning toward me. I kept imagining that I could feel Sethos's cold stare and shifted on my feet, trying to keep guests between us so that he wouldn't get a straight view of me.

"You honor me, Lord Jala. But I know little of what you speak. There is a rebel queen?"

His green eyes narrowed as he stared at me. "Come, come. Everyone knows of the rebel queen of the north."

"Forgive me, Lord Jala. I have not yet heard of her."

He pursed his lips and turned away, back to his guests. But Sethos had caught me. I felt the heat of his stare. From the corner of my eye, saw his nostrils flare. Slowly, he rose. "My Lord Jala," he said, lifting a finger at me. "You have a rebel beside you *now*. Step away from him," he hissed, pushing aside his chair in his haste to move toward me.

My heart leaped. All was lost. I slid one foot slightly back, and was beginning to lift my hands when I remembered this one was no match for the Maker, or me, a child of the Maker. Did I believe it or not? Was I willing to risk it all on what I believed? Because if I fought at this point, I'd surely die.

I centered myself, concentrating. Concentrated on my breathing remaining even, my pulse steady. The door that this enemy had opened now remained completely shut, held in place by the Maker. I concentrated on my gifting, of casting emotions as well as reading them, and did my best to think of nothing but *peace, peace, peace.*

"My lord," I said, dropping into a slow dip toward Sethos, head bowed. "I wish nothing but peace on this room."

"Peace on this room, but what about peace on this house?" He reached out and grabbed my chin, lifting it. I stared into his eyes, fluttering my lashes and wrinkling my forehead to appear as innocent as possible. *You do not know me. You are mistaken. Confused. You feel only peace. Pleasure.*

He dropped my chin as if I'd burned him. His eyes registered confusion. "You are the girl from Zanzibar, from outside the Hoodites. You are *Ailith*." His words were more certain than his tone.

"No, my lord. You are mistaken. I am Andriana, of the Valley," I said, dipping my head again. "Not of the Hoodites. Perhaps I appear like one you once met."

"Of the Valley ..." His brow furrowed at the center.

"Come, Sethos," Lord Jala said, waving him back. "Leave the girl alone. You may interrogate her later. *After* our dinner, yes?"

Sethos stared at me for a long time, and I continued to will confusion and doubt into his mind. Again, he stepped back as if he'd been punched, and his frown deepened. Clearly, he didn't know what to make of me — and was feeling the effects of the emotion — but now he wasn't going to let me out of his sight.

But he was retreating for now. Giving up.

As he finally, reluctantly, sat down again and conversation resumed, I took a long, slow breath through my nostrils, staring straight ahead, trying to focus on what I was to do as a maidservant while my mind roiled with warrior tasks. And I tried to not cry.

It was going to be a long, long night.

Hours later, my feet ached and my stomach rumbled as the dinner guests finally finished their desserts. They'd had so much to drink that their conversation had come down to little more than laughter and slurred commentary. Watching them, thinking about the amount of food and drink they'd consumed, and how it would've sustained my whole village for a week — or by value alone, for a month — I thought, *This is why the Maker has called us. They wish to rule us, use us.*

We must be free. To be independent. To make our own way. Let them live as they wish, but not on our backs. No longer.

It was as if in that moment I knew exactly why I'd been brought into the world, been made an Ailith. For this moment of clarity and understanding. Because these people had not only become accustomed to much — they'd become dependent on keeping others down in order to maintain that level of comfort. Sucking the Trading Union's people dry of blood. Her women. Her children. Making her rely on them for resources so that we wouldn't fight them. Keeping us blind, beyond the Wall, so we didn't glimpse possibility. Opportunity. Keeping us from speaking freely. Worshiping our Maker as we wished.

They wanted us to remain in ignorance, trapped by our difficult condition and isolation.

And it would take everything in us, working together, to make a way for change.

Surely this wasn't a coincidence, us coming to this house, in this place, at this point.

I'd been told since childhood what my mission was. But in that moment, I *felt* it too. The Maker had brought us here so that we could live, learn, and fight for the change we so desperately needed. To get us back on track. To build a world like he'd envisioned it. To treat one another with honor and respect and love and grace —

"*Andriana*," Lord Jala said.

I belatedly saw he'd been gesturing to me and I hurried over. He was holding on to the table, as if he felt dizzy. "Help me to my room, girl. I've had a bit too much to drink." He threw his arm around my shoulders and I staggered under his dead weight, almost falling, and automatically clasped his waist. We moved out of the dining room, the others tossing terrible comments after us, insinuating I would attend him in more ways than one. But I wasn't afraid. I was getting angrier and angrier by the second. And that anger gave me strength.

We lurched down the hall for a bit, until I saw Ronan coming our way. He grimly took the nobleman's other arm over his shoulder. I sighed in relief, wondering if he'd been hovering, waiting to assist me.

"Who are you?" Lord Jala said, staring at Ronan as if puzzled. "Are you new too?"

"Ronan, my lord. I thought I could help you get you to your quarters."

"Quite right, Ronan. Quite right. But once we're there, you'll need to leave me and the lovely Andriana alone."

"Certainly, my lord," Ronan said, casting me a look behind his shoulders that said *over my dead body.*

"I have some questions for this one," he said, pulling me closer, as if in a hug. He looked over at Ronan. "It'll be best if she tells me. Because Sethos won't be so kind."

"Yes, Lord Jala." We turned the corner and made it to his suite. I opened the door, letting it swing wide, and we moved inward. Maximillian was almost asleep on his feet, his head hanging down, his eyelids lifting slowly, one at a time.

"He didn't have that much to drink," I whispered in confusion to Ronan, as we dropped him on the bed and pulled him straight. I knew; I'd been pouring, and carefully waiting for my half-full moments.

"No, but what was *in* his drink was powerful," Ronan whispered, lifting a conspiratorial brow.

I let out a small laugh under my breath. "You didn't."

"I did," he said, moving over to shut the door and returning to my side. "I didn't like how he was looking at you. And while you were chatting with Raniero, Bellona and I saw to his carafe."

I cast him a wondering look. How had he managed to watch me across the far reaches of this sprawling estate? But somehow, I knew he had. "Feeling a bit protective of your Remnant, are you?" I whispered.

"Hey," he said, with his own smile and a half shrug, "it's my job." He pulled off Maximillian's slippers and set them aside, looking askance, as if they smelled.

I laughed and pulled up the covers over the man, watching as he snored. I was so relieved. Remembering him before we'd left this room, earlier in the night … A shiver ran down my spine. He'd been careful to not imbibe too much throughout the evening, even as his companions gave way to it. Why? As Ronan suggested, had he had thoughts about toying further with me? Or because he practiced more self-control? He was the emperor's right-hand man.

"I don't like it, Ronan," I said, feeling a wave of excitement from Lord Jala as my fingers brushed past his wrist. "There's something off."

My armband was growing colder again, a rhythmic *thrum* emanating from it. I was going to ask Ronan if he felt his doing the same, but he lifted a hand to his own and looked to me in consternation. Wordlessly, he took my hand and we hurried to the door. But when he opened it a crack, it slammed backward, ramming him in the face. He fell to the ground and was up immediately, trying to get back to me.

But Sethos and his men already had me trapped. He leaned closer to me, inhaling through his nostrils as if he liked how I smelled, and I tried to punch him. He caught my hand and twisted it, pulling me around and against him so I'd be forced to see what was transpiring. Two others held Ronan and a third savagely struck him. I couldn't bear to watch, Ronan's pain captured me in a way that no other's had.

"Ronan!" I cried. Not for help, since I knew he couldn't rescue me. But because it hurt. Ached. With each strike he endured, I felt it too.

Sethos studied me from the side, his quick, dark eyes beginning to make sense of my response. "Fascinating," he whispered. "Hold!" he cried to the other men across the room from us. A man paused, his fist in the air behind him, and looked over at his boss.

Lord Jala sat up and casually walked in between us, clearly as sober as I was. *He'd been faking*, I thought, with a sinking heart. Heard everything. Pretended, in order to get information ... "What'd you discover, Sethos?" he said, coming closer to me.

"Watch, my lord," he said, pulling a handful of my hair back so I was forced to look upon Ronan across from me. My knight stared at me in utter misery — both because he couldn't get to me, free me, and because he guessed what was to come. "Now," Sethos said to his man.

I imagined I felt it, even before he struck. Bent over, losing my breath from the pain, as if the man had driven his fist into my belly instead. He struck again, this time at Ronan's face, and I wrenched to the side.

Lord Jala laughed soundlessly. "Utterly intriguing," he said. "They're linked?"

"It appears so, Lord Jala. At least in some fashion." He pulled my other hand behind me and swiftly wrapped my wrists in terribly strong tape. "I'm wondering if it isn't these bands ..." Sethos ran his hand down my arm, hovering over the cuff, laughing scornfully when I struggled, as if I thought I could get away.

"Come now, Andriana," Lord Jala said. "Where will you go? We've rounded up everyone dear to you."

That made me grow even colder. They had everyone? Raniero? Tressa and Killian? Vidar and Bellona?

"I believe a bit of experimentation is in order," Lord Jala said. "Take them down below, to the dungeons. The emperor will want a full report." He reached out and grabbed my arm as Sethos pushed me past him. "Unless you'd like to simply tell me that you are who I think you are."

I stared back into his eyes, hoping he saw my furious desire to see him die.

He threw his head back and laughed. "Ah, yes. Such a warrior spirit! We'll see how long that lasts. Be advised we don't take kindly to enemies of the empire." He lifted his chin, as if a thought had come to him. "A moment, Sethos. Let us confirm we are on the right track."

To my horror, he gestured for a man to bind my legs. Then, slowly, carefully, so I would feel the full force of my powerlessness to stop him, he bent and ran his hand all the way up my right leg, exposing skin to the hip bone. To my birthmark, the one all Ailith shared. A perfect crescent moon. He stared at it for several breaths. "She is beautiful, is she not, Sethos? And what an intriguing birthmark . . ." He took hold of my hips and leaned close. "Do you know who else has a birthmark like that, Andriana? The emperor," he whispered.

I tried to reach out and bite him, my teeth clicking as they clamped together, narrowly missing him.

"Temper, darling, temper!" he cooed.

Sethos laughed, a low rumble in the broad chest behind

me. "Search him too," he said to the men who held Ronan, and they pulled down the waistband of his Pacifican trousers just enough to expose his birthmark too. Ronan stood stock-still, but I could feel his gathering rage. "Bring him," Sethos said, turning and bending to flip me over his shoulder.

We moved down the hallway, Ronan held between two strong guards with others before, between, and behind us. I relaxed, as if I had no more fight left in me, wanting them to relax, just looking for the right opportunity, as did my knight. Ronan and I had practiced this many times with our trainer. All we needed was just the tiniest diversion …

We turned the corner and I saw Raniero dive into the two guards in the middle, taking them to the floor. Vidar leaped on top of the back of one, ramming his head to the marble floor.

"That'll work," I muttered, wrenching so hard that Sethos faltered. Bellona charged us and we went to the ground. I looked back to see Tressa cut loose my hands and feet, then rammed my foot into the nearest guard beside me, carefully avoiding eye contact with him. Ronan was shouting and roaring, driving one man into the wall with brute force, audibly cracking his ribs, then doing the same to the next.

We still had three men who fought to hold us, including Lord Jala and Sethos. Lord Jala grabbed me and slammed me against the wall, leaving me stunned and woozy for a moment, then pulled a long, fearsome knife against my neck and my body across his as a shield. I panted, trying not to move, because each time I did, the knife bit into my skin.

"You just get more and more fascinating, Ailith girl," he whispered in my ear.

He'd known from the start. Since … when? When I looked familiar? Or when he saw my armband?

He wrenched me toward Ronan as my knight turned his attention on us, his hands still bound. Jala made a warning sound, sidling backward, pressing the knife against my skin so hard I felt a warm trickle of blood.

A dagger came singing through the air, and I saw Bellona, on her knees, still pointing at us after the throw. I winced, thinking it was about to hit me, but it struck Lord Jala in the flesh of his arm that held the knife. I rammed backward against him, even as I felt his pain wash through me, touching me as he was. We hit the wall, and he dropped the knife and fell, apparently dazed from hitting his head. Sethos let out a seething, snake-like sound and twisted as Bellona and Vidar ran toward us, screaming in defiance, Raniero right behind them. Sethos turned and turned and then disappeared, leaving nothing but his black cape.

Ronan stepped on it, to make certain it wasn't an illusion. "How ...?"

"A sorcerer," Raniero said, joining us.

Bellona sliced Ronan's bound wrists apart, and he reached for Lord Jala's lapels, clenching them in his fists as he stared into his green eyes. "Tell your people the Ailith have arrived. And everything is about to change." With that, he shoved him into a room with two guards, slammed the door, turned the key and slipped it in his pocket. He took my hand.

And then we ran.

CHAPTER
25

The Georgii Post family had alerted my companions to our plight, and therefore made it possible for us to escape. Downstairs, they shoved our stowed weapons and clothes, still damp from the washing, into our hands. As shouts and screams sounded above us, they led us out of Lord Jala's home and through the alleyways, then into crates set inside the beds of a trader truck and outfitted with escape hatches beneath. Apparently we weren't the only ones who used the route to enter or exit unseen. The father pressed a sack of coin in Raniero's hand. "We are eternally grateful. As is my father. Thank you, brother, for saving my family."

"Thank you for aiding mine," Niero said with a grin, glancing over at the rest of us.

"I was only able to secure four mudhorses," the man whispered, nodding to those in the back of one of the trucks. "The smugglers will get you partway." He looked nervously over his shoulder when someone shouted. "And hopefully the mud-horses will make it the rest. I'd better be going. Be safe."

"You as well," Niero said, clasping his arm.

Four soldiers in gray ran down the street, yelling. Hurriedly, we settled down into the crates, two in each, and three men set about hammering shut the tops.

"If they come looking for us," Ronan said, grasping my arms, "it will make it look more like cargo. They'll be less likely to pry them open."

I nodded.

Ronan took my cheek in one hand and seemed to try and see my face in the slivers of light that came through the crate slats. I could feel his worry.

"I'm fine, Ronan," I said, answering his unspoken question. "He didn't hurt me. But if it's all right with you, I'd very much like it if you held me for a while."

He didn't answer, but I knew his relief, his pleasure. He sat back against the wall of the crate, legs akimbo, and I curled up against his chest. He wrapped his big arms around me, cradling me close, stroking my arm, and my armband hummed with warmth. I knew Niero wouldn't like it, this intimacy, but I didn't care. The day had taken my very last bit of energy. Negotiating my time with Lord Jala and Sethos had sapped me dry. And here, nestled against my best friend in the entire world, hearing his heart beat, steady and sure ... Well, it gave me hope. Strength.

We spent the night listening to soldiers blow whistles and sound alarms, shouting at one another as they madly sought us out. Holding our breath when they came near. Somehow, comforted by Ronan, I managed to sleep. I hoped he had too.

By morning, I was so antsy for the trader to get rolling, to leave Castle Vega's walls behind us, I thought I might scream.

I rose and scrambled back to the far side of the crate, rubbing my face, pushing my hair back into a quick knot that wouldn't hold without a strap or pin. Ronan watched me, moving his legs as if they were stiff, his green-brown eyes calm. I envied his ease, even in the face of such awkward intimacy.

"I wish you were the one who could cast emotions," I whispered.

A small smile tugged at the corners of his lips. He had nice lips, I decided. Full and inviting

"I gotta get outta here," I said, widening my eyes and stretching out my hands as if they were electrified. I reached out and touched the side boards of the crate that confined us.

"Soon, Dri," he whispered. "Hang in there." But his head was turned as if he were listening to something outside.

Violet pre-dawn light infiltrated our crate, and we could hear the traders exchanging jibes with another. Then, at last — at long last — we were finally moving. The wagon jostled us back and forth, and the crate creaked in protest. I thought of the others in the crates around us, and it gave me comfort. We were leaving this dreaded place at last.

Of course, we moved deeper into enemy territory. But at the moment, the *prospect* of facing our enemies in the future versus being seized by them now seemed like the lesser of two evils.

There was little cover left to us anymore, anywhere, now that the Council of Six had a clear vision of my face, as well as most of my companions. We needed to move, and fast, if we wanted to accomplish the most we could.

Pacifica was bent on keeping the Trading Union captive; we had to somehow break free of that bond, and to do so it seemed clearer than ever that we needed to infiltrate her borders and free Kapriel. We needed a figurehead. A leader that all would recognize. But Pacifica would be wary of our approach, making certain no Ailith entered past her wall. Lord Jala knew we wore the armbands now. He was certain to alert every guard on every transport inward.

The trader truck pulled to a stop with an ear-splitting screech of brakes, and I caught the low tones of conversation. The back gates were opened, and I could hear a couple of guards move in and around us, tapping on the boxes nearby and trying to lift our crate lids. I closed my eyes and thanked the Maker that the traders had thought to nail them shut. One, a woman, spoke lowly to the mudhorses tied inside, sounding as if she was petting one. Moments later, the guards hopped out, giving the driver clearance to move forward. Perhaps the hours between our escape and now had made them all think that we were long gone.

How I wished we had been able to leave hours ago.

But there was only one way for us to enter Pacifica at this point — through a barrier most considered insurmountable, the Great Expanse. We drove for a long while, bouncing so hard that sometimes Ronan and I hit the lids of our crates. The light became peach-hued and warm, dust motes dancing in the air between me and my knight. We sneezed and coughed, choking on both the dirt in the air and the exhaust from the truck wafting about us, thicker and thicker.

At last we pulled to a stop, and the traders came and freed us, offering us canteens of water, even as a boy led our mudhorses down the ramp.

I gaped at what I saw as I stretched and paused at the edge of the truck bed. I'd thought the Central Desert had been desolate, but it did not prepare me for what it was to be in the middle of the Great Expanse. In a daze, I took Ronan's hand and walked down the ramp to the cracked earth, turning in one direction and then other other. In the distance, I could see the tiniest hint of buildings, waving in the heat rising from the ground — what I assumed was Castle Vega. To the other side, I thought I could see bits of mountains, what the traders gestured to and said in a vague tone, "Pacifica." They didn't want to know where we were going or why. They'd received their payment; now they wanted as much distance between us as possible.

The driver climbed into the cab of the truck then, leaving us with nothing but several tanks of water, four mudhorses, and a casual point west. "Good luck," the driver said, leaning an elbow out of his cab.

"The Maker watches over us," Raniero said, looking up at him. "We don't need luck."

The driver gave him a startled look. "Don't let those people hear you say that," he said, gesturing west with his head, toward Pacifica. "They'll tear your fingernails from your fingers, force you to recant. Before they slice the skin from your body, to prove you are mad when you scream."

"We cannot be stopped," Raniero said, straightening, facing the man. "Tell everyone you meet. War is coming. The Ailith will lead you. It is time for the oppressed to be set free."

The rest of us stilled even as the driver whistled lowly. "Well, I'll think on that. I'm right attached to my head staying on my body. And what you're suggesting I share, brother, is punishable in all forms of death."

He drove off, and I saw then that he was flanked by two Jeeps with massive guns mounted on back, presumably his protection against Drifters. We all circled slowly, taking in the wide, desolate plain again. Our mudhorses were clearly on their last legs, probably given up as good as dead already, so why not send them off across the impassable desert? The traders had brought us miles north, in order to avoid any soldiers or transports crossing the desert to our south. I shivered, thinking of the driver's comment about death, and then squinted up to the sun in the midst of a cloudless sky.

Never in my life had I seen a sky without cloud. Never in my life had I known a day without rain at some point.

But I was about to.

Hour upon hour, we crossed the endless Great Expanse, following what we believed was a black market trading trail, the barest of smoothing in an otherwise uniformly wind-blown field.

I couldn't believe how little precipitation we encountered over the following days. Clouds gathered and then dissipated above us, leaving us vulnerable to the sun's merciless beating. Back home, I had never *not* wished for more sun. Nor had I *not* wished for the clouds to go away. But now I prayed for the opposite, craved the protective covering of gray, the relief of rain.

We wished we had our dirt bikes back.

Wished we were through this dreary, dry landscape with mountains that teased us ahead, always ahead.

Wished we'd received more water from the smugglers.

Wished we'd come across any water, even if it might be impure.

Wished we could steal our sister's or brother's water without feeling guilty about it.

Wished they had any left for themselves, even.

Wishing upon wishes. Prayers lifted, dust upon our dry tongues.

By the third day, Bellona and Vidar's mudhorse collapsed

beneath them and died moments later. They walked beside us, moving almost as fast as our weary, dehydrated horses. An hour later, our mudhorse gave way too, his front legs folding beneath him, as if he hoped to still rise for a long moment but then gave up and rolled to the side, his tongue hanging out, thick and discolored. I felt a wave of guilt as I stumbled aside, as if I'd killed him. Perhaps I had, riding as long as I had.

And yet I'd had no choice.

It was either him or me.

"So, boss," Vidar said with a dry cough, pausing beside our horse, lifting a hand to Raniero. "This whole saving the world thing is gonna be tough if we die of thirst in the desert."

Raniero looked over at him and then ahead again. "Keep the faith, Vidar," he said in a weary tone, "even when it looks dire."

I made a slow turn, keeping an eye out for Drifters, knowing we'd be vulnerable here if they came upon us. It was unreasonable to fear them more on foot than on the back of a mudhorse, but I felt it just the same. But it seemed even the Drifters had abandoned this part of the desert, perhaps fearing patrols from Pacifica. Which gave me another reason to scan the horizon.

My lips cracked, and I had not even the saliva to moisten them for a moment. I hadn't urinated in two days and felt no need to now. *That can't be good.*

Up ahead, I watched Niero's mudhorse falter, then collapse. Niero awkwardly jumped away, narrowly avoiding getting pinned.

The only mudhorse remaining was Killian and Tressa's. Hours ago, Killian had jumped to the ground and led the mare forward, Tressa still on its back with her fair skin sheltered by an oilskin cape that had to be holding in all kinds of horrible heat.

But it was as if the sight of Niero's horse going down gave this last one permission to do so too. Killian pulled Tressa from the horse's back as she fell. They stood to one side, staring at the horse, her tongue hanging out of giant, yellowed and cracked teeth.

We thought about burying the mudhorses, but it would've taken too much time and left us exposed for too long, so we left them where they fell. Our time was limited — of that we were certain.

We carried on, walking as a disjointed group, each one only managing to put another foot forward, lacking the energy to care how close they were to the others. The only one who paid attention to me was Ronan. He walked behind me, too weary to constantly turn and see if I was keeping up or wandering. He stayed silent, until I faltered or slowed. Then he'd put a gentle hand at my lower back and pushed me onward, saying nothing.

We had to be close. Had to be. We'd walked more miles than we'd been told it took to cross the Great Expanse, hadn't we? Barely slept. Barely ate.

Tressa stumbled and couldn't rise; Killian paused beside her, begging her to keep moving, cajoling, yelling in moan-like fashion.

We kept on going, knowing if we stopped, we'd collapse as well. The only choice, if we wanted to live this day, was to press on, Niero said, when he first recognized we might not make it. *Press on, no matter what happens to the rest of us. If any of us can get to the end of this infernal desert, they will round up help and send them to collect the rest. Understood?*

His words rang in my head like a dim, hollow memory. Almost a dream. Had it really happened? Had he really said that? Advocated us leaving one another when all along, that was the last thing he wanted us to do?

Survival instinct seemed to have a way of messing up any plan.

On and on we trudged forward, frequently stumbling, others coming to our side, awkwardly helping us rise and continue. I was barely able to keep track of them all — barely able to focus my eyes on Niero, before me, Vidar to my right by about ten paces, and the vague sense of Ronan, still behind me. I thought I ought to turn around and make sure he was still trailing me — be certain nothing had happened to him — and spot the others in the same motion, but even the thought of that was too much. Anything beyond one step after another was too much.

I fantasized about the Hoodite waterfall, spraying us with its mist. Standing before it after a meal of grilled fish and berries and corn, after diving deep into a pool and drinking all I wished. I daydreamed about the river that separated the Drifter's camp from Hoodite territory. I longed for the rivers and falls of the Valley, the springs that dotted every acre, bubbling up, delicious and cold. I thought about them so much that I thought I could almost hear one. Could practically taste the minerals and sweetness upon my tongue.

And then I was sure I did. I stopped, hands splayed, cocking my head, listening.

Ronan tried to urge me on, as he had so often these last days, but I pushed away his hand and urged him to shush, his trudging, dusty feet covering the sound.

He came alongside me, listening. Dimly, I recognized his face was covered with a sheen of sweat, and dust caked to every pore. Then he turned sharply to the left, where we could see a flurry of red boulders from a nearby hill, apparently dislodged in a slide. At the bottom, there was a telltale sign of new growth, and the closer we got, the scent of water.

Until that moment, I didn't think water could have an odor. Other than stagnant pools, filled with rot, or lakes lined with dark peat moss, of course. I didn't think water, fresh from the ground, spilling over rocks, *smelled*.

But oh, it did. *It did.*

The scent of delicious, liquid, mineral *life* filled my nostrils. I think I cried out, as Ronan did; a partial moan, a partial victory yell. We stumbled forward, half of us not wanting to believe it, in case it wasn't real — a *mirage*, Niero called it — half of us exulting in relief and unable to fight off the glory.

It was a desert spring, cut open by the rockslide. A miracle.

Ronan reached it first, hesitantly dipping in his hands, acting like it might disappear if he touched it. But it didn't. He pulled his cupped hands to his face and drank every drop he could, wiping the rest of it over his sunburned skin, even as I cupped my hands beneath his to catch the falling droplets. We took turns, greedily dipping and drinking, and it took everything in me to back off and give the others a chance too, when they reached us. It was as if my body had become layers of paper, thin and dried in the desert wind, almost ghostlike, a see-through version of my true self, and the only thing that would bring me back was to drink and drink and drink and drink.

I knew the others were as dehydrated as I. If we'd been Drifters, we might have drawn weapons for the right to drink until sated. But we were Ailith kin. And so, we reached down deep and practiced respect, even in the midst of our desperation.

It took an hour for us all to finally sit back, bellies full of water, faces and hands and arms washed in the delicious, clean water.

Niero saw them first and let out a low sound of alarm, hopping to his feet, knees bent, crescent sword drawn.

We lumbered to our feet too, still exhausted, even if we were no longer thirsty.

I saw then what had caused Niero's alarm. Men and women with shaved heads, dressed in robes the same color of red as the rock, helping them blend in. Each carried a staff in one hand.

"Be at peace, brother," said one to Niero, letting his staff fall a little farther from his body. "You have made it across the Great Expanse. Come and abide with us. We offer you sanctuary for the night."

"Who are you?" Niero called.

"We are your brothers and sisters," he said, obviously no sort of answer at all. With that, he turned to begin climbing back up the rocks, the five others following after him.

"Where do you abide?" Niero called, chasing after them, pausing at the hill's ridge then looking back at us. We followed, hesitantly, not sure that this was at all wise.

"Be at peace," said the man at the top beside him, just before he disappeared over the remains of the rockslide.

"Are we in Pacifica?" Niero persisted, as we topped the rockslide too, then picked our way down the other side. Ronan reached up and took my hand over a tricky jump. I allowed it not out of need, but of pleasure. In the crate, being so close to him ... I thought for a moment.

"Pacifica, yes. But there is a time to walk, and a time to talk," said the man, glancing over his shoulder at Niero, interrupting my dreamlike, fuzzy thoughts. "This is a time to walk. Be at peace. We will talk in time."

We frowned, but followed. Perhaps this was but more of the Maker's provision, a chance to rest. Recuperate, after our harrowing crossing. Our armbands felt neutral — neither warm nor cold. We followed the desert dwellers across several rocky hills, then down into a valley that grew cooler with each step. We could hear water again, and as we turned a bend in the trail I noted that we were on the edge of another small canyon, with a creek at its bottom. But halfway down was a channel, dug into the cliffside and carrying swiftly flowing water. An aqueduct?

I think that was what it was called. I remembered my parents teaching me about such things. The Romans had built many of them, shifting water to dry cities across hundreds of miles. Farmers had used them once in our own lands to water fields. I glanced up at the strange, light clouds, wondering again about the lack of rain. In all my days, I'd never experienced such dryness. Even the eastern desert grasses had been lush and clumpy in the damp sand, in comparison to the occasional, stubborn cactus here on the western edge, the soil dry and biting at our skin. Memory of my thirst made me want to dip into the aqueduct, now beside our trail, but I feared it would be rude. I also feared that I'd have difficulty stopping again — part of me wanted to get *into* the narrow trough, feel it wash over me, reassure me that my thirst was over.

We continued down, down, down into the canyon, each step blessedly cooler. We were almost beside the small riverbed at the bottom — so much blessed water after the dry abyss — and continued to follow our red-robed guides at a steady, unrushed pace. When we rounded the next bend, Niero stopped short and I almost ran into him.

"Niero?" I asked. But then I saw what had drawn his attention. Ahead, above and on the other side of the river, was a long, sloping ramp leading to a palace that seemed to have been carved from the cliffs themselves. Room upon room, with small balconies, boasting baskets of well-watered flowers and deep green vines, in bright contrast to all the rock.

"It's Wadi Qelt," he hissed over his shoulder. "We've stumbled into Wadi Qelt."

A shiver ran down my back. Wadi Qelt? Where Keallach's Hoarfrost palace was? Asher had spoken of desert fathers and mothers, a sanctuary ...

Niero actually took a step backward *into* me, as if he intended to turn around and leave. But as I looked up and around, I saw another group of robed monks among the cliffs and trail behind us. Were they peaceable? Even if they were, if we tried to leave now, would it draw undue suspicion?

Three ahead of us turned and looked back, puzzlement on their faces. "Please, come," said one, gesturing forward. "There is nothing to fear here."

I concentrated on his face, hard, to see if I could detect anything evil about him, but found nothing. No scales, no spooky, misty darkness around. I glanced to Vidar, and he gave me a little shrug. But he looked concerned too ... as if he couldn't get a read on them at all. All I could determine was that they seemed rather innocent. Mindless, even.

"It's okay," Niero whispered as he passed by me. "Keallach isn't due here until Hoarfrost."

I nodded, but my heart was pounding. We needed to enter this sanctuary, eat, refill our canteens, and get out as fast as possible. That much was clear.

We crossed a small bridge and then proceeded up the path toward the sprawling palace, made partially of adobe and timber in order to blend into the cliff. But it was elegant, refined even in its rustic splendor. We entered through two wide, tall, fortress-like doors, noting the twenty-foot wall that seamlessly surrounded the palace, where the cliff did not provide protection. Inside, thick-beamed porticos with lush, winding vines and fat, purple blossoms gave us shade.

"You must bathe before you are invited in to the master's table," said our guide over his shoulder. "Most travelers enjoy it very much."

"I would imagine," Niero said carefully. "Is your master here this day?"

"No. The master is in Pacifica. But you are still welcome at his table."

Niero smiled, saying, no, just a bit of food for the road and good water for our canteens was all we needed and then we'd be on our way.

The monk insisted that food was only distributed at the table, and all those who came to the table had to be clean.

I was trying to stay quiet, obedient.

While alternately wanting to scream of our imminent danger from our mortal enemy and my need to get rid of the last three days' worth of grime and sweat I wore as a second skin.

To sleep. Even the word, *sleep*, called to me. Sang to me, like a lullaby ...

Our guide agreed to give us new supplies, then led us under the portico and through a small, rounded tunnel that opened up into the most perfect outdoor bath I'd ever seen.

A long, rectangular pool stretched before us, gloriously blue against the red rock, and at the end, it opened into a small circle. From above, a tiny waterfall moved down the rock, emptying in the circle like it'd been divinely bestowed upon the palace. And five feet away was a separate steaming pool that seemed to enter a cave.

"Another spring, like the one you found, feeds this small

waterfall," said our guide, studying me with wise eyes that could clearly see my desperation to dive in. I looked around guiltily at my companions, but realized I wasn't the only one who was literally salivating over the waters before us. I longed to swim the whole, lovely, long length of the pool and then sit in the circle, feeling the gentle spring water falling down, washing through my hair. Just ten minutes would give us so much more energy for the rest of our journey ...

Niero, hands on hips, looked up and around at the cliffs that surrounded us, as if determining the risk, then at all of us and sighed. "All right. Just a quick dip and then we — "

We were immediately setting our weapons aside, pulling off our sand-caked, grimy boots and our socks, the dirt on our skin making a line above them. I'd never been as hot and dirty for so long as I'd been in the last days, and here, *here* it seemed we'd find relief.

As fast as I was moving, the young men were in first, diving into the pool in nothing but their long johns, and we women followed in our leggings and camisoles. The water was divine, the pool deeper than I was tall, even with my arms stretched upward. I knew this because I tried, releasing all my held breath and sinking to the bottom, delighting in the sensation of being immersed in total. Of swimming, truly swimming for pleasure, for the first time since, I didn't know ... forever? Even back in the Valley, any extra hours were meant for training. Or meditation. Or helping my parents. And the few times Dad and I'd gone swimming, it had been a hurried exercise, the water so cold it set our teeth to chattering within minutes.

Still, I remembered hiking with him once, the afternoon uncommonly empty of rain and warmer than usual. We'd come across a pool, a widening in the stream, and with one quick look, raced to pull off our boots and jackets and jump in, clothes and all. He'd taught me to float on my back that day, his hands gentle, reassuring, beneath my thighs and between my shoulders.

Dad, I thought, floating on my back now, slowly making my way to the circular pool and my companions. *Mom*. How distant they felt from me now. How long ago our life together felt. They'd sacrificed everything, their very lives, to get me here, to this place. For this time. For this purpose.

To save the world, somehow. To gather the faithful, to prepare for the future. For change. For hope.

Were we getting closer to that vision?

For every step forward, it seemed we took five back. But that was a thought that would take a night's sleep in order to process fully.

I turned, dived deep, and came to the end of the pool, the small falls sounding like thunder beneath the surface. Ronan was waiting for me there, as I figured he would be. He smiled. His freshly scrubbed skin, hair — long and loose and fanning behind his neck in a black mass — along with water droplets clinging to his long eyelashes, his nose, the soft lobes of his ears   all of it made me look away, quickly, because never had I seen him look so incredibly ... clean. And more, of course.

"M'lady," he said, smiling and offering me something cupped between his two palms, like a valuable treasure.

And it was.

Soap. More of that delicious, creamy, lavender-scented soap of Pacifica.

I barely stifled a shriek and then hurried to the waterfall, to scrub my hair and neck and face and shoulders. I paused and then pulled out of the stream, submerging my shoulders. I edged a glance downward. *We'd forgotten our cuffs!* Looking about, I saw that Niero had not joined us, electing to keep watch over our weapons and clothing — as well as the two monks who seemed to have settled into a peaceful meditation, sitting on either side of the long pool to wait for us. I felt sorry for him, that he wasn't with us, and then I felt latently guilty, knowing I'd seen his displeasure and ignored it, even as I dived in.

Carefully, I looked down at my right arm, then over to Ronan as he leaned against the edge of the waterfall pool, waiting for me to climb with him into the next. Both our armbands still seemed to retain the protective oil and grime the elders had rubbed into them, even after the soap and water. But what of the others'? I cast a careful look over at the nearest monk, but his eyes were closed now, his face utterly at peace. Was he praying? He looked a lot like the elders in the Citadel. Or even like Azarel when she prayed.

As I scrubbed my hair, I kept stealing glances at Niero. Then, as I rinsed out the suds, I closed my eyes and reached out toward him, seeking to find what emotions he was feeling, wondering if he was still uneasy here. Or if he was picking up something dangerous. Or glorious. *Something.* But I got nothing. I frowned and lifted my head out of the stream of water and really concentrated, reaching out with my mind, my heart, the way I read anybody's emotions these days.

Again, I got nothing.

"Dri?" Ronan whispered.

I turned back to Ronan, planning on telling him to let me be for a moment, but in my searching state, his emotions rocked me.

My mouth dropped open and I stilled, staring at him.

Because he wasn't hard to read at all. Concern. Care. Desire. Delight. And . . .

CHAPTER
26

Are you ... are you *reading* me?" he asked. I didn't have to continue to search his emotions to know he was irritated. His face told me as much.

"No," I said, moving toward him, to the side of him, lifting myself out of the cool water and padding over to the hot pool, focusing on the steam rising above it.

"Liar," he said softly, rising and following me. "That's *my* gift. I can tell when you're telling the truth. And when you're *not.*"

I ignored him, since all I could read from him now was anger. Indignation. I looked at him in confusion, trying to discern what I knew I'd felt.

"One of us should go relieve Niero," I said with a sigh to the others, dipping my foot in and then pulling it back quickly. It was incredibly hot. "How are you people *sitting* in there?"

"You get used to it," Vidar said, leaning his head against the edge, looking utterly relaxed. "Trust me. You want in here."

"I tried to talk him into a swim," Killian said. "Niero wouldn't budge. Truly. You have to feel this water, Andriana," he said, reaching up to help me climb in. "It melts away every aching — "

I gasped, staring at his arm. He saw his cuff then too, and quickly yanked it below the surface of the water.

Ronan edged past me and crouched down, helping to shield the other Ailiths as they checked their cuffs.

Each band was gorgeous. Glorious. Pristine. As perfect as the day it was given to them.

"The minerals in this pool ... or the heat," Vidar said in a low voice, turning his to and fro in the torchlight. "Something took off the protectants."

I turned to go after their clothes and nearly screamed when I found a monk, a head shorter than I, right behind me. "Are you finished bathing, friend?" he asked. He held out a red robe to me in one hand, a long sheath of a dress.

Had he seen Vidar's band before it was submerged again?

"Please, it is our custom here in the canyon to dress as the earth herself does," he said. "For a sense of continuity. We can wash your clothes and return them tomorrow to you as you journey onward."

"Oh," I said, lifting my hand. "There's no need to go to such trouble. We must be on our way this night anyway."

His thin brows gathered in a frown. "But the day is almost done. You must wait until dawn to leave. The city of Pacifica is still three days' journey away, through rather treacherous paths. It is not wise to try to travel at night."

I glanced over his shoulder at Niero, who frowned as he drew closer. But I took the brick-red robe from the monk, seeing no way around it. Even if we left it behind as we sneaked away.

"Tonight, you dress as we do." He gestured to one side of the pool, toward a small building I assumed served as a dressing room. Had we offended them, so haphazardly stripping down to bathe, mad to get into the water?

Niero stood where we'd left him, watching us warily.

I reached out to take the robes from the monk, glad I could shield my friends from his sharp eyes, while at the same time hoping he didn't see my trembling. "Here, let us hand out the rest for you." Ronan was there, then, beside me, helping me lift the robes from the men's arms as well as help block their view.

"Thank you," I said to the monk, refusing to move, as the man's dark eyes shifted left and right. I felt a bit of suspicion rise between us, and then nothing. What was it about these monks that made them so difficult to read? Only the Sons of Sheol were more difficult ... and Niero.

"You will dress in there," he said carefully, nodding toward the small building.

I hurriedly nodded. "Forgive our ill manners. We were so keen to dive into your pretty pool, I'm afraid we didn't stop to think."

"You are not the first weary traveler to do so. Think nothing of it. Dinner shall be served in an hour's time. Zulon," he said, motioning to his small companion, "shall escort you to your quarters for the night."

"Thank you," I said again, copying his slight bow. He padded away, and I wondered if it was all in my head. Had I become so jaded, so guarded, that even these monks who were practicing such peaceful ways — generously offering us nothing but kindness and hospitality — set me on edge?

Which made everyone's growing concern all the more overwhelming and frustrating. Who cared if they saw the bands?

These people were not Drifters. They did not strike me as the sort who would kill us for the treasure we wore. They wore nothing of substance on their person. In fact, they all wore the same red robe, the same hemp belt, and nothing on their feet.

But wealth was wealth, I thought grimly as I shut the small changing room door, yanking off my wet underthings and pulling on the red robe, grimacing as it pulled taut over my breasts and hips, clinging, then finally reaching my ankles. I was glad for the secondary piece, an evening cape that cupped below my shoulders and crossed in a band over my upper arm. I almost shouted in relief. "You won't believe the Maker's provision," I said, coming back around and looking up in glory at Ronan, Vidar, and Bellona, who stood next in line.

I flushed at the reactions I immediately could feel in the men. Apparently, I looked ... *good*, really good, in this borrowed clothing. "Look," I said grimly, gesturing to my arm, willing them to get back to the most important thing — disguising our cuffs.

"Thank the Maker," Vidar said, sidling past me. "For more reasons than one," he said, giving me a long, head-to-toe look over his shoulder.

"Vidar! Stop!" I was mad at him, but he also made me laugh when I needed it the most.

"It's hard to stop," Ronan said, crossing his arms and looking me up and down too, but now with a more distant, detached manner. "You looked very fine in Castle Vega, but here ... You look royal, Dri."

"Thanks. I think."

The others emerged, one by one. Tressa looked perfect, her smaller form not making it cling at all. Bellona looked like a warrior princess, and she was none-too-pleased about it.

The men looked even better, given that there were no formed shoulders or cut-outs at all in their capes, allowing them to more completely conceal their bands.

When we were all finished, we went back to Niero, who was now stripping down to his long johns and T-shirt himself. "Apparently, no dunking, no dinner," he said to us, and nodded over to two monks who stood behind him, staring dead ahead, staffs out at an angle in their right hands. They looked like really relaxed guards. But also very serious about their work.

I was just reaching out to try and read one of them when Niero dived in.

"Hey, Raniero," Ronan called carefully when he emerged, halfway down the long pool. Niero turned over on his back and looked back at us. "Just get your dip done. Don't take time to go in the hot pool. I'm hungry."

We all stared in his direction, willing him to get what Ronan was really saying. I didn't know if he did, only felt relief when he nodded once and dived down again. As he bathed, one by one we lifted our swords and small shields and daggers, placing them on our person.

"You will not be allowed to take those inside the palace," Zulon said quietly.

"I'm afraid I don't go far from my sword," Killian said.

"Then you shall not be entering the palace. You may sleep out here," he said, gesturing to the smooth stones around the pool.

Killian stared down at him.

He stared back, unwavering. I could detect no fear within him. Again, I could detect nothing at all.

"There is no need for weapons here, friend," Zulon said simply. "You are in no danger."

Niero came up behind us and then between us. "Leave them," he said tiredly, and we all followed him and Zulon back into the palace, pausing by the door to place our swords, shields, and daggers in a small armory locker. I suspected every one of my fellow Ailith did as we had been trained — and kept at least one dagger strapped to our legs. We were never to be completely unarmed. It had been drilled into us from the start. When I was just short of my first decade, I could hit a three-inch target with a dagger from ten paces. Now I could do it from twenty.

So it was that when we entered the peaceful rooms of the monks' sanctuary, we felt more vulnerable and ill at ease than when we entered Zanzibar.

CHAPTER
27

Vidar paused beside me. "You all right?"

"Yes. Why?" I asked, irritation still lacing my tone, and now focused on him.

He gave me a searching look and then turned away with a shrug. What was that about?

Ronan eased me forward, a hand on my lower back.

"Please," I said, sidestepping away and trudging on. I wasn't sure why I was so agitated. *Maybe I'm just hungry. And tired. I'm so tired. I'll be fine after a few hours' sleep.*

We turned and stared down a long, low table that dominated the dining room, lined with men in red robes. It struck me again that the women we'd met on the desert's edge had disappeared. Perhaps they had their own quarters, or were not allowed as part of whatever holy order they belonged to. *It figured. The king of Pacifica advocates some sort of religion ... but it doesn't allow women.*

But at the moment, I couldn't bring myself to care much

more about it, since the food smelled delicious. The last thing we'd eaten was a bit of bread the day before. We hurriedly sat down in a line together, each taking a separate, wide cushion on the floor and crossing our legs as the monks did. As soon as we did, servants came out — appearing like young monks in training, just past their first decade, dressed in the same red robes — and set a small bowl before each of us. It smelled delicious — a clear broth with onions and some other sort of vegetable floating within it.

We waited for our hosts to begin, and when they each took a sip we hurriedly did the same. But whereas they took their time, setting their bowls down, we had a hard time stopping. Within seconds, I was sure that every one of the Ailiths' bowls were empty, our mouths burned by the delicious, hot broth. We quietly waited, hoping there would be second helpings, or something else offered, because that had barely taken the edge off our collective hunger.

Happily, the servants appeared again, clearing our bowls, followed by others delivering a plate full of steamed rice and some sort of white meat, and even more curious, a bright orange vegetable.

"I think they're carrots," Ronan said, thoughtfully chewing his second bite. We'd only seen carrots in books.

"And the meat?" I whispered back.

He shrugged. All our lives, we'd had lots of meat. Mostly mudhorse. And mostly dried. This, soft, light, moist meat, never dried, was a wonder in my mouth. Where had they gotten such a treasure? And enough to serve so many? I suspected it might be indicative of the wealth ahead of us in Pacifica.

I ate every kernel of rice, rolling the last over the roof of my mouth to memorize the size of it, the texture. I'd only had rice twice before, and it had been years. They passed a platter of fruit afterward—I could identify apples and oranges and what I suspected were bananas. Fresh, not dried, they looked decidedly different. But there were several pieces I put into my mouth that exploded with sweet, tart, acidic flavors, though I had no idea what they were. In the end, I took a deep breath and resituated myself on the pillow, exploring the feeling of my full belly.

All, my life, it was understood that every meal was a gift, and it was never assumed we'd have three the next day. We never took more than our share, and never as much as we wanted. Breakfast, lunch, and dinner, we took a modest portion, then found in sitting, talking, and laughing, we were fine. We'd had enough. But tonight I'd experienced fullness in a whole new way. It felt vaguely uncomfortable. And yet wonderful too.

Tea was passed, cups ceremoniously filled. No one looked at one another. No one spoke. When everyone had had adequate time to finish their tea, the two men at either end of the long table rose, bowed, and pivoted on their heels to exit. The others followed, and we did as well. I hoped we'd be led to our quarters, because now I was outrageously weary, thinking I could stretch out on the dining table behind us and be perfectly happy until morning.

Zulon stopped in the hallway, bowed to us when we had gathered, and then led us to a corridor with open door after open door. He gestured two of us in at a time, frowning a bit as men and women entered together. I prayed he wouldn't take issue—because there was no way our knights would leave their Remnant here, in this foreign palace, regardless of how tranquil it seemed. Not after what we'd experienced at Castle Vega. Bellona and Ronan could've switched places for the night, I thought, but that would still leave an odd couple. And the rooms were clearly meant for two. Only Niero entered alone.

Ronan and I looked about and then to the doorway on the hall, which held no door within the gap. I supposed they wore their red robes either by day or night, and lived communally, so they felt no need for privacy. There were two narrow beds, one on either side of the small room, and on the other side, a wooden door between two windows. I opened it and peeked out, then smiled, exiting fully onto a narrow balcony, which perched over the river below. We were on the second of what appeared to be twenty such balconies on this floor. To my right, I could see the falls. To my left, the curving slant of the canyon wall — the way we'd entered.

Above the balconies was the floor of another, not as deep as our own, but covering the whole width and beyond it. Perhaps a deck of some sort off a larger room above us. A shiver ran down my spine when I imagined it to be Keallach's, then I shook the idea away. Surely his quarters were in an entirely separate part of the palace.

But still. I stared up at it. What if … What if he'd built this place, allowed these monks here, because he felt the call of the Maker? He'd been born as we were, on the seventh day of the seventy-seventh year. Did he not have the same call upon his heart? Was he wrestling with it, even if he'd become misguided?

Ronan joined me at the balcony rail and leaned down, forearms on the wall. He whistled softly. "It's beautiful. Utterly peaceful," he said in awe.

"Agreed." I peered over the edge and watched as the water flowed past; even its pace seemed relaxed. "I could stay here a long, long while. A daily bath. Food. And a bed. Ronan, a *bed*."

He smiled at me and let his eyes rove over me a moment

too long to simply be friendly. They held a hint of Vidar's open admiration, and again, I felt pretty in my red robes. The first time I'd felt like that in days ... since Vega. I bit my cracked lip and turned away, feeling every inch of my skin come alive with awareness. Not wanting to delve into such thoughts and feelings — thoughts and feelings that inevitably left me feeling lonelier than before. *Ronan and I can never be together. Never. Keep your eyes on the bigger prize, Dri. Conquering the world for the Maker. Setting things right that have been wrong for so long.*

I turned and took my bundle of clothing from a monk, curious how he knew which was mine but thankful for the distraction. My only clothes from home — and the Pacifican gown — were in a simple burlap bag. As I set it on the floor and pulled them all out — ostensibly to repack it to be ready for tomorrow — I wondered if any of us were truly clear on any goal besides surviving the following day. It increased my agitation, thinking about that. Of going from place to place, trying to stay alive and keep my friends alive. It seemed impossibly far, our ultimate goals. Of freeing Kapriel and making a way for a coming king. Of saving people who could put our world back into some semblance of order again. Of building a society that would honor the Maker. There was too much in the way. Too many against us — and the farther we got from home, the more daunting our call became.

CHAPTER

28

I need to walk," I whispered, abruptly standing.

Ronan looked over at me, and rose, leaving only half his profile visible in the flickering lamplight.

"No," I said, lifting a hand to him. "I need to go alone."

"I don't think so."

"Ronan. We're surrounded by a couple hundred peacable monks. They're probably all asleep by now. We'll be out of here come morning. Can you give me a break? Rest? A little alone time? I've been surrounded by people for weeks."

His lips clamped together. Then, "I can give you the *illusion* of time alone. Twenty paces. But I go with you." When I opened my mouth to argue, he crossed his arms and shook his head.

"Fine," I said, acting irritated, but secretly glad. I turned and walked out of our room, then down toward the dining room and out to the wide verandah, well aware that Ronan trailed me as he'd said he would. The sun had set, and the clouds rolled in, thick, and, by the smell of it, heavy with rain at last. But there was just enough light to see the rolling paths that moved around the palace, beneath more trellises heavy with flowers and beside other greenery all along the way. I thought I'd never seen anything so lovely, so pristine and refined, and preferred it to the showy wealth of Lord Jala's home.

It was far more earthy. Real. As if it was a place blessed by the Maker's hand itself.

A monk moved along, lighting small lanterns, and at the end of one path I discovered a tiny garden cupped by a high, wide wall. With no way out but to go the way I came, Ronan paused, retreated ten steps, and then sat on a low wall to wait for me. But I was in no hurry to leave. I walked past benches, letting my hand drift through the tall, waving, exotic grasses and flowers, smelling their perfume in the air. I circled three times before settling on the bench and looking up, watching the clouds, ready for the rain to fall—almost wishing to feel its well-known, cold drops on my face. But after a while, the clouds parted and stars sparkled against a deepening blue sky.

"You've chased away the rain," said a voice.

I jumped and sensed Ronan rising at once, but my attention was on the far corner, where the newcomer approached. I'd not sensed another's presence at all. Was there a hidden gate there?

"Forgive me," said the young man, smiling shyly as he entered the light. He lifted his hands and stepped forward, and I could see he was in the red robes of his brother monks. "I didn't mean to startle you. Or your friend," he said to Ronan as my knight hovered, now five paces away. The stranger's face was open and friendly. And handsome. A *layered* face, with depths that begged exploring. And his eyes ... There was something about his eyes that made me want to stare into them.

I searched him and found no threat within, only curiosity.

And I immediately relaxed. Even if he was the most strangely attractive monk I'd ever met ... he was still a monk. There was a sense of familiarity in the air, welcoming, and I took a deep breath as he sat down across from me and looked up to the night sky.

"We'll leave you," I said, rising. "We are obviously intruding on your space."

"No. There is no place within the sanctuary that isn't meant to be shared. Will you not stay?" He looked up at me, and his expression was hopeful.

I paused, confused. None of the other monks had seemed interested in chatting. They appeared to largely live in silence.

"There is room enough for us all, yes? Enough to share and yet still find tranquility in our own small sphere. That is the exercise of this place."

"I-I suppose so," I said, tentatively taking a seat again. Ronan sat down again too, but this time on the end of the wall, closer at hand. Our new companion didn't seem to mind. Again, all I read in him was warmth. Friendliness. My armband only elicited a warm hum, so I settled back. Perhaps I could gain good information, if this monk was willing to talk.

"Do you make a study of the stars?" he said, staring upward, hands tucked beneath his thighs. He looked to be about as tall as Ronan, broad and strong across the shoulders. His profile was regal.

He looked to me and I hurriedly stared toward the skies again.

"I do," I said, agitated. "But I've only seen them a handful of times. Where we come from, it's rare."

"Oh?" he asked, his curiosity spiking at the same time I read Ronan's displeasure in the space between us. "Where are you from?"

"Far from here," I hedged, daring to study him again in the flickering candlelight when he looked to the stars again. Straight nose. Wide eyes, rounder than Ronan's, the hint of a smile at his lips, as if he were playing a game. I thought I sensed glee from him for a second, but then it was gone. My eyes narrowed. Was he toying with us? "Have *you* always lived here?"

"Me? No," he said, shaking his head. He leaned forward, arms on knees, and met my gaze without blinking. "But where I am from, the moon and stars come out nearly every night to welcome those beneath them."

"That must be lovely," I said, looking up again. "Does it not rain where you are from?"

"Come Hoarfrost, yes."

"Then you are from Pacifica."

"Indeed. It rains, but not as it does in other areas of the Trading Empire." I let his words rumble around my head. Not Trading *Union*, but Trading *Empire*.

"How long have you abided here?" I asked.

"Off and on, throughout my life, really."

"All your life?" I blinked in surprise. Perhaps he'd been like one of the younger monks in training we'd seen earlier.

He nodded and looked up. "Do you know your constellations, new friend of the Valley?"

Again, I moved in surprise. So he'd guessed exactly where I was from. But he didn't seem to be gloating. Or intending to use it against me in some way. What use was it anyway? What harm would it be for him to know? "How do you know that? Where I'm from?"

"Your accent," he said easily, still staring upward. "See there to the west, just over the edge of the canyon? Gemini. And over there, Pleides, or the Seven Sisters."

I squinched my eyes and peered at the sky, trying to make out what he was gesturing toward. "I have no accent."

"You do. It's a gentle, rounded, warm tone you of the Valley share. I'd recognize it anywhere. I had a tutor, once, from your lands. Do you see Gemini yet?"

I shook my head.

"Here," he said, rising. "If we put out this torch, we'll see all the better." I felt Ronan draw closer as the monk moved, felt his wariness. But the monk only sat down again, a dark shadow now. We looked up, and I knew he'd been right; it was far easier to see now.

"There, to the west?" he asked gently.

"Maybe ... I think so."

"Do you know the story of the twins of Gemini?" He lifted a hand to the sky.

"No."

"Zeus desired a woman named Leda, and seduced her in the form of a swan the same night she lay with her husband, Tyndareus. From that night, two eggs were created, one bearing two sons, and one bearing two daughters. The girls were Clytemnestra and Helen."

"Of Troy?"

His eyes met mine in surprise and delight. "You know of Greek mythology?"

"I know some," I said. "But I'm not familiar with that story."

"It's a good one," he said, rubbing his palms together, then lacing them behind his head and looking upward again. "Helen of Troy was supposedly the most beautiful, but her sister had many, many suitors of her own. But when you are possibly the daughter of Zeus, half immortal, perhaps that makes you all the more enticing, wouldn't you think?" He was looking at me again; I could tell from the sound of his voice.

"Perhaps. But they're nothing but stories. Fanciful tales to entertain the masses."

"Perhaps," he said, as if setting aside my comment. "The boys were Castor and Pollux. Some say that one was immortal and one was not. When Castor died, Pollux begged Zeus to make him immortal, and they were reunited in the heavens." I felt a brief pang of sorrow within him, but as quickly as I identified it, it was gone. Sorrow over the ancient gods? It made no sense. Perhaps I'd imagined it.

"You still don't see Gemini, do you?" He rose, presumably to point it out to me, and Ronan got to his feet as well, sidling closer. "Easy," the monk said in a reassuring tone to Ronan as he came to my other side. "I'm only going to show her." He paused, as if waiting on Ronan's permission. Then he edged even closer, slightly behind me, and pointed upward, so close now that the inside of his elbow brushed my temple. He smelled of sandlewood and juniper. My skin tingled at his proximity. Again, there was a brief sense that I knew him from somewhere. A familiarity.

"There, beside the V of Taurus, and the three stars of Orion's belt?" he said, his breath washing over the bottom of my ear lobe. "Trail eastward, and there you have it, Pollux and Castor."

I could feel Ronan's agitation. "Got it," I said, moving away from the monk and closer to my knight. "Thank you. How did you learn so much of the night skies?"

"I find them fascinating. And the stories behind them even more so." His tone was like a shrug, as if he worried I might decide he was silly.

What was wrong with me? I was paying far too much attention to this stranger. But there was something about him that drew me. Swiftly, I took the bench again, feeling the need to gather some information to justify my actions. Otherwise what would I say to Ronan tomorrow? Or Niero?

I felt the curiosity from him, this time lingering and open, as he walked languidly around the tiny garden to take the bench opposite from me again. I breathed a bit easier, given the space between us. Because with this one ... Well, I'd never had my pulse jump around a guy other than Ronan. For good reasons. Lord Jala was another matter.

"What is your name?" I asked.

"We all go by 'brother' here," he said, "none of us with greater stature than the two elders that lead our community."

"Ahh, I see," I said, vaguely disappointed. *But what about Zulon?* Maybe that one had broken some rules, mentioning his name.

"And you, my friends of the Valley? What do they call you?" He struck a match and lit a candle between us.

"Andriana," I said simply.

"Andriana," he repeated, as if relishing the name, then his eyes flicked to Ronan.

"You can just refer to me as 'brother' too," Ronan said quietly, the first he'd spoken. I felt his anger and frustration again, but I ignored him. His emotions were lost in the face of the newcomer's curious desire for connection, and my own pull to meet him, read him, for more than a moment.

"Brother, can you tell me what religion you practice here?" I said, plunging forward. "It was my understanding that no religion is allowed to be practiced anywhere in the Trading Union."

"Ahh, but sister Andriana, you are now in Pacifica." He looked up at me, and his dark eyes sparkled in the candlelight. He nodded gravely, arms again on his knees, hands together.

"This is an experiment of our brother, the emperor," he said. "A new religion in which we practice living together in peace, harmony. Our hope is that it will entice the earth to return to her normal rhythms, and she will be restored."

I stared at him, deciding to plunge on, even as I remembered the trader's warning of a crime punishable by death and felt Ronan's rising agitation. "What god do you pray to?"

He gave me a gentle, confused smile. "We do not pray to one god. We are but stewards of the earth, and we've been poor stewards at that. We endeavor to try and change that. We wish not to control, but to make a way for the energy to flow through us. To model to others that a way of peace is the way to happiness."

I nodded, wanting to appear amiable. And really, did not some of his words make sense? Weren't we ourselves striving to let the Maker work through us, through our gifts? Wouldn't we all rather lay down our weapons and live in peace with others? "There is much to be done to get our world back in order. Have you, by chance, met any Drifters?"

He laughed, the sound of it warm and pleasant. "It takes a long time to help heal a planet so desperately wounded. But we believe it's possible to take steps toward that healing, and that in time all people will come together. Even the Drifters."

We shared a smile. He was highly educated — that was clear. He looked older than I, but *felt* about my age. Did they study here as part of their religion?

"And you say — you say the emperor advocates this religion?" I said.

"It is not a religion, per se. It is a way of life." He lifted his brows, full lips pursed. "Though none would dare argue it with him."

"I have to say, that is quite brave of him. To advocate a way of life that even echoes of religion."

"It took some time," he said, looking up to the stars, "but eventually, they saw his way of thinking. None of the high gifts are allowed, of course," he said casually. "Nothing that would elevate one brother over another. Here we are all lowly. Close to the earth, even an extension of the earth itself."

"I see," I said, dry-mouthed. We sat there for a moment in silence, and I knew it was time to go. I was just gathering the skirts of my robe to rise when he leveled a gaze at me. "Do you yourself follow a god, Andriana of the Valley?"

I frowned in confusion, feeling caught between my desire to speak the truth and the desire to stay alive. "I am terribly weary," I said lightly, rising. "We have been on the road for weeks. Perhaps we can continue this conversation in the morning?" *As in, after I'm long gone?*

He paused, and again I wondered if I detected the slightest wave of irritation. "I shall look for you after breakfast," he said. Now there was nothing but friendliness and intrigue emanating from him. Had I imagined it? The irritation? "You too, brother," he said to Ronan.

Ronan lifted his chin in silent answer and then reached for my elbow.

I took a few steps and then turned back. Our new friend remained where we'd left him, looking up to the stars, his hands on either side of him on the bench.

"Brother?" I called. He looked at me, as if he knew I couldn't leave without asking another question.

"Why haven't I seen any sisters since this afternoon?"

His face held no emotion for a moment, and my heart rate picked up over his pause.

"There are other things that call to our sisters," he said, as if it pained him to say it. His eyes were on the ground, then slowly lifted, traveling the length of my body so slowly and so thoroughly that I felt myself blush and Ronan's hand tighten around my elbow again. His flicker of desire left me a little shocked, cold within, not like the burning embers that Ronan's own desire had set aflame within me. "We find sisters within the sanctuary ... distracting," he said. "Only sister travelers are allowed to abide here. Our own depart come twilight."

He forced a smile again and I ceased to be able to read any emotion from him at all, much like the other monks. They had either blocked me — or been utterly *empty*. "Forgive me. I've unsettled you, Andriana of the Valley. Please," he said wearily. "Go to your room and rest well. Even with your guard, it is best that a beauty on the level of Clytemnestra or Helen not be found wandering about in a community of men, holy or not."

His words shocked me. One, that he would pay me such a compliment, and two, that he intimated there might be some threat here. I nodded uncertainly and walked with Ronan quickly down the path. I knew he was angry. I was angry at myself. So much had been shared in that conversation. And yet so little. My mind roiled with a thousand questions. I knew I'd disclosed too much, that the monk had garnered more information than Niero would prefer, but one had to share knowledge in order to gain knowledge, did they not? And was it not fascinating — that Keallach advocated religion at all?

Perhaps he was not the enemy we feared. And even if he was, was it not classic advice to know one's enemy?

We entered our room, and I knew if we'd had a door, Ronan would have wanted to slam it. He looked at me in fury, his hands waving as though he wanted to shake me. "What was *that*?" he whispered fiercely.

"That was a conversation. Fact finding," I whispered back.

"Fact finding? I'd call it *flirtation*."

"Oh, it was not."

"Wasn't it? I've never seen you so interested in *stars* in my entire life."

"Ronan," I said, crossing my arms and staring up at him, wanting to throttle him as much as he wanted to throttle me. "We're leaving in the morning. I only thought I'd find out a bit about this place. About Keallach."

"And in turn tell that *brother* all about you? You know nothing about him!"

I pursed my lips and took two deep breaths before responding, searching his eyes. He was jealous. And fearful. Trying to protect me on several levels. "He knows my name. Where I'm from. Don't you think the clothes we arrived in screamed that we're from the Valley? That word spreads, even among these silent brothers? I've not seen another settlement yet that wears clothes quite like ours. And really, there's nothing to get so worked up over! I'll never see him again."

His river-green eyes searched mine, going back and forth, until he lifted his head, angrier than ever. "Quit *reading* me." He shook his hands as he turned away, as if shaking out a silent scream of rage. He walked out onto our balcony, leaned his arms on the wall, and hung his head.

I sighed and then padded out after him. "That's not fair, Ronan. Telling me to not read you. Don't you try and read me all the time? Even if you don't have the gift? It's just part of our nature. That desire to connect." After a moment, I wrapped a hand around his arm, feeling the lovely strength and steady pulse under my fingertips and more. He was a swirl of emotion.

"Andriana, you can't," he said, almost as a moan. "It's not fair. I'm trying everything I can ..."

I swallowed hard, the hint of his struggle against his attraction to me right there at last.

I knew of what he spoke. The incessant need to be close, and yet to stay adequately apart. To not give in to our attraction. To not disobey the elders — elders who'd set down this rule for a reason. I knew he'd give his life for me. But if we were entwined further — if I held his heart and he mine, we might make decisions not for the good of the Ailith as a whole, but for each other.

But oh, how the admission thrilled me. It wasn't my imagination. It wasn't one-sided.

He felt it too.

I made myself drop my hand, not wanting to torture him. But as my hand left his arm, he straightened and caught it in his. He ran his palm against mine, separating my fingers, weaving in his own. We stood there for several long moments, frozen by our wordless admission, staring out, holding hands, simply feeling the glory of skin against skin.

Not just a friendly hold, but a hold that spoke of so much more.

He turned toward me, and his forehead fell against mine, giving in. His warm breath flowed across my cheeks, my lips, feeling like a kiss in itself. "You *are* beautiful, Dri," he whispered, speaking words that no one in the Valley ever did. At least in public. "He was right, that brother." He lifted a hand to my cheek and I looked up at him, wanting him to grab hold of my face and kiss me. Barely moving, afraid I'd mess it up again. That we'd miss another moment.

He touched me, but his hand was feather-light on my cheek, as if didn't quite dare more contact. "Like Helen. Like Clytemnestra," he whispered, "but far finer. *Andriana*."

I swallowed hard, waiting. I took his other hand in mine,

wanting to will the invitation and courage and recklessness I felt within me *into* him. That he might give in, act at last.

"We should go to sleep," he said softly, and I knew the grief within him, the cost of it, to utter those words of honor, loyalty, integrity, so different than my own traitorous heart was speaking. I didn't care what our trainer had drilled into us. What our elders decreed. This, *this* could not be wrong ...

"Morning will soon be upon us," he said, his voice sounding strangled.

"Yes," I said, not moving away, lifting my chin up, offering him my lips.

His breath was ragged, a war raging within him, but after a moment he turned and pulled away. The separation felt like tearing, and I swallowed a cry. I longed to move backward in time. For him to take my hand again. For us to stand together where we'd been, all night. We didn't have to move. We didn't have to kiss. But if he would only hold my hand like that again ...

He went to the doorway, looked both ways down the hall, clearly trying to gather himself as much as perform the duties of a watchful knight. I settled on my bed, feeling dejected, and rolled to my side, pulling my knees closer to my chest.

With heavy steps, he came over to me, and my heartbeat picked up, wondering if he was having second thoughts —

But he only reached down to take my robe, shake it out, then pull it across me. Then he took a thin blanket and laid it across me too. His tender gesture was both touching and aggravating. "Good night, Dri," he whispered. I felt a sharp stab of fear from him, pain, until he backed slowly away.

I rolled over, one arm beneath my pillow, watching him in the nearly pitch dark.

Then he went to his own pallet and sank wearily down

upon it, turning on his side toward me, staring across at me, even though I couldn't see them.

And that's when I felt it. The first time I was absolutely certain of it.

Love.

He loved me.

Ronan of the Valley was sick with misery, helpless in his love for me.

Not as his sacred charge. Not as his friend, although that was there too. But as a man loved a woman.

He loves me loves me loves me loves me . . .

I couldn't help it. I smiled, even as sudden tears were in my eyes, my heart overcome with emotion. My laugh of joy came out in muffled huffs through my open, smiling mouth.

"*Dri,*" he moaned in helpless frustration.

"But don't you see?" I whispered, unable to stop myself. "It's all right, Ronan. It's all right. Because I love you too."

"We can't, Dri," he said, desperation in every syllable. "We can't. Our mission —"

"No," I said. "We can't stop what is. Only what might be. And this . . . Ronan, this-this thing between us, *is*. It's *always* been." I took a breath. "Hasn't it?"

He stilled, his eyes unmoving, caught in my statement of truth, unable to deny it. Then I thought I could see a tiny, pained smile, the flash of teeth. Or perhaps I'd only felt it. The joy. The relief of admission. "Good night, Andriana," he whispered.

"Good night, Ronan," I whispered back.

CHAPTER
29

I wasn't certain either of us slept much that night. But apparently I slept enough, because when I awoke as the rising sun turned the cliffs outside a warm, rosy pink, there was a beautiful, purple blossom on my pillow, inches from my face.

I smiled and then looked over at Ronan, face still lax with sleep, his eyes moving beneath those dark-lashed lids, clearly in the midst of a dream. When had he sneaked out to pick it? I couldn't believe I hadn't awoken. I slowly sat up, not wanting to rouse him, then ran my fingers through my hair, weaving it into a quick braid. I stole a string from my burlap satchel and secured the braid, then tucked the flower behind my ear, waiting for him to wake.

I cast a nervous glance to the hallway. If any of our companions saw me with it there, like an adornment, they'd chastise me. It was not the way of the Community to do such things. To call attention to oneself. We had higher goals in mind. Or we were supposed to, anyway.

But I couldn't help it. I wanted the first glimpse Ronan had of me this morning to be with his gift in my hair. Before we were reclaimed by our fellow Ailith and drawn back into the madness of our life. For one brief, shining moment, I wanted him to see me, with love in my eyes, and to look upon him, knowing he loved me too.

He thought me beautiful. *Beautiful*. But it was he who was beautiful, I thought, staring at him. The thick mass of dark, shiny hair, half covering his face. The slope of his cheekbone. His solid chin, and above it, those lips   What would it be like? For him to kiss me?

Wake up, Ronan, I thought, hoping he'd somehow hear my thoughts. *C'mon, Ronan, wake up ...* I moved the skirt of my robe, hoping the slight sound of fabric would bring him out of whatever dream had him so entrapped, then looked up, aware I was no longer alone.

My eyes moved to the hallway.

The young monk I'd met in the gardens last night stood there like he'd stopped in his tracks, staring at me. His eyes searched mine for a long moment and then he gave me the slightest smile and moved on past.

"Dri?" Ronan said sleepily, rising to a sitting position as if he regretted it. He rubbed the back of his neck and blinked weary eyes at me, then to the doorway, then back. "You all right?"

"Yes," I said, suddenly feeling silly. Exposed. I waited for him to recognize the blossom, and a breath later, he did, smiling as if we were sharing a secret about last night. "You look pretty," he whispered.

"Thank you," I whispered back, grinning.

He nodded, yawning and rubbing his neck again. "Did you pick it this morning?"

I stilled.

"Y-you … You didn't pick it?" My heart seemed to pause, then pounded.

"No." His happy expression rapidly turned to concern. "Dri. Where'd you get it?"

"It doesn't matter." I rose, pulling it from behind my ear, irritated when the sap from its stem stuck in my hair, pulling several strands with it. I yanked them out, just wanting it off of me. Away from me. Feeling oddly defiled, poisoned, I tossed it to the bed and went to my satchel, pretending I was looking for something among the few things there.

"Andriana," he said, putting a hand on my shoulder and crouching beside me. "Where did you get it?"

I took a deep breath and sighed. His fears were rapidly building into something bigger than the truth. "It was on my pillow when I awoke."

I could almost feel his head jerk to the balcony, as if wondering if it had blown in. Then he strode toward the doorway and looked both ways, a hand on either side of the jamb. "Did you see who it was?" he whispered over his shoulder.

I shook my head. "Whoever did it was really quiet."

But we both thought of the same person. I dug into my satchel with renewed fervor, not wanting Ronan to see my face at the memory of the young man staring at me, happy that I wore the blossom in my hair.

Rising dread filled me. Why did it scare me so? The attentions of a monk we'd soon leave behind forever?

Cold fear, warning, caution rushed through me. My armband felt frigid, so much so that I rubbed it as if it were an appendage I could circulate blood within again.

Ronan lifted his hand to his cuff too and frowned at me. "Dri..."

"We have to get out of here," I said, meeting his gaze. "Now."

He nodded and rushed over to his pack as I lifted my own to my shoulders.

Niero appeared at the door, every inch of his face shouting alarm. "Ready?" I glimpsed Bellona and Vidar behind him, yanking their burlap straps over their shoulders.

So they'd felt it too. Where were Tressa and Killian? I felt the fear rising up all around us, as if the palace walls themselves were climbing, then closing in. *A trap, a trap, a trap ...*

We moved out into the hall, just as Tressa and Killian emerged, our armbands practically zapping us with sharp, cold dread. Was it this place? The monks? Or approaching Sheolites?

All I knew was the Maker's firm command, clanging in my mind as clearly as a giant, round bell. We hurried down the empty hall toward the patio where we'd been forced to leave our swords and other weapons.

Niero carefully peered out and then led us forward. We all moved as we'd practiced in the wood ... even Tressa and Killian utterly silent, nothing but skin on adobe and stone. In seconds we reached the racks that had held our weapons, and in one glance saw it was empty.

"My friends, you must have breakfast before you are off," said Zulon, behind us. He gave us a smile, seemingly unaware of our alarm. "It is ready," he said, gesturing back down the hall. "Just as soon as my brothers are done praying, they shall join us."

Niero paused. I knew his conundrum. For us to walk out of here, without our weapons, might be a different form of suicide. But to stay here ... The mounting pressure made me feel like we might all implode at any moment.

"Zulon, we must be on our way to make the most distance in the coming day. Might you tell us where our weapons are stored?"

The small man paused. "I am sorry. But the master has not yet said it is time to go. You must wait for him to dismiss you."

"Master?" Niero said in confusion. "I thought you were all but brothers."

Zulon gave him a patient smile. "We are all brothers, yes. But there are elders. And there is one master."

"Who is your master?" Niero asked, giving him a hard look.

"Emperor Keallach, of course," he said.

I held my breath so long I felt faint. Could it be? The young man we'd met in the gardens last night? The one I saw this morning? The man taken with the story of Gemini's twins, and their cruel parting? My eyes shifted to Ronan's, and knew the same dread in his heart.

Niero slammed Zulon up against the wall, his big hand at the man's slender throat. "Our weapons. Now."

Zulon wriggled, clawing at Niero's hand. "Storage locker…" he choked out. "Around the corner."

Niero released him and Zulon dropped to the floor in a crouch, any peacable look about him disappearing, hate filling his heart. Ronan dragged me away, but I was stunned at the transformation I sensed within the monk; within seconds he went from empty, emotionless friend to savage foe. How had he cloaked such hatred at all? We turned the corner and ran to the end of the vine-covered portico, near the pool. All around it, monks were chanting, heads bowed, their staffs beside them in neat, tidy lines. For the first time, I didn't see the staffs as an aid for hiking the rough trails around their homes — I knew them as weapons.

Bellona, Killian, and Ronan formed a defensive arc around the rest of us, and Niero kicked in the wooden cabinet holding our weapons. It took two tries, and the chanting of the monks ceased as Niero wrenched aside the splintered wood and tossed each of us our blades, shields, bows. The monks turned toward us as one, but remained where they were, on their knees. Niero grabbed hold of his second crescent-shaped sword and said, "C'mon," leaving us, leading us in a sprint.

We'd almost reached the doorway to the monastery again — intent on running through the long, abandoned corridor to the other end — when a man shouted, "My Ailith kin!"

I knew his voice. The monk from last night. *No, it's not possible —*

"Don't stop," Niero said, reaching for the door. "The Maker wants us —"

But the door was locked from within.

Niero tried the door again, shaking it, as we sensed the monks rising behind us. "Around the building! Quickly!"

He knew what we all knew now. We could sense Keallach as a fellow Ailith, feel the hum within our armbands, even though he'd been somehow able to partially cloak his presence before. That was why I'd felt drawn to him, pulled. He was Ailith! But to pause, to give him a chance, or to try and fight our way through all the warriors at his side — either might prove deadly. The push to flee was so strong; it almost made me blind with panic, and I fought to remember my trainer's words, his methods to fight the fear. My eyes caught Vidar's and I imagined angels all about us, unseen but protecting us. The comfort was soon lost, but it gave me room to breathe at least.

"They're coming!" Bellona shouted from the back of our group.

"We'll have to divide!" Niero cried. And while I knew it was likely our only opportunity to all avoid capture, it increased my fear that he felt compelled to separate us — the last, most desperate thing we were trained to do.

It was an admission that some of us would surely be lost.

"Ronan!" Niero called.

Ronan turned and narrowly caught the leather bag our captain had worn tied to his waist. The one with all the remaining arm cuffs.

"See that it isn't intercepted by anyone but us!"

Ronan nodded, but I felt sick. He'd only give up the armbands if —

"Meet up in the mountains to the west!" he hissed. "*Go!*"

He paused and turned, lifting one crescent-shaped sword and shield as a group of monks swarmed him, surrounded him, their staffs in their hands and glee on their faces. It gave us a momentary reprieve. We were running, only twenty paces away. We'd caught some of the monks' attention, and they turned as one to chase us. "But Ronan ... Niero! We can't leave him!"

"We will do what he told us to, Dri," Ronan grunted, grabbing hold of my arm, yanking me onward when I dared to pause.

Above Niero, on a wall, I glimpsed Keallach — indeed the man from the garden last night and the hallway this morning — as he took position as leader. But what I felt in him stopped me cold, even as Ronan practically wrenched my arm from my socket, his fingernails tearing at my skin as he belatedly let go.

I paid it little mind. My eyes were on Keallach. My Ailith brother.

One of *us*.

And his were on me.

CHAPTER
30

My eyes dragged to Niero, who was below Keallach, surrounded.

"No!" I heard myself shout, as if listening to someone else. The monks were attacking our leader from all sides, swarming him. He defended himself well, but he was taking one blow after another, visibly weakening. Worse, two Sheolite elite trackers appeared on either side of Keallach. And one of them was Sethos.

Both jumped from the ten-foot wall and landed in a crouch to either side of Niero. The monks split and made way for them, as if in deference. In but a moment, Niero lost one crescent blade and drew the other, even as the second tracker struck his shield.

"We will find a way to free him," Ronan growled in my ear, wrapping his arms around my chest and wrenching me backward. "But we can't do that if we're captured too. C'mon, Dri. It's what he wanted."

Still, I stared back, torn by my desire to wade into the fray now, but knowing we were hopelessly outnumbered. There was a reason Niero told us to divide; he'd known this would be the way. Our only chance.

Keallach looked across the red-robed masses, and I knew the moment his searching eyes found us again. A jolt of clear chill ran through me, from my neck down my shoulders. But the combination of what I felt left me almost paralyzed.

Both hatred and love.

Yearning and revulsion.

Pull and push.

"He's confused," I murmured. "He doesn't know — "

"C'mon, Dri!" Ronan yanked me forward, and I knew he was right. We had to sort it out later. For now we simply had to escape.

Ahead of us, we saw Bellona and Vidar hop the wall and jump ten feet below, apparently deciding to try and dive into the river and swim their way across. Killian and Tressa followed, but I knew they'd likely make for the bridge and up the cliff on the other side — preferring to risk a death from a fall than another chance at drowning.

Ronan ran close to me, and I was glad I'd always been as fast as him. We were still searching for an alternate route out, without pulling more of the monks who chased us toward our Ailith brothers and sisters. Raniero had been right in his assessment; if we were caught, our only chance was to fight a much smaller group of monks than those en masse.

We passed the far end of the monastery and ran down the sloping road, and I glimpsed the horses. "Think we can make it to the corral?" I panted, and Ronan saw what I intended.

"I'll hold 'em," he said. "You go, Andriana. You hear me?" he cried as I continued to run. "Do not turn back!"

But I had other things in mind. I became aware of the two red-clad monks a hundred feet above, now scrambling at an angle toward me using a tiny goat trail that criss-crossed the cliff, as well as two others that had managed to get past Ronan and pursued me. The monks above picked up rocks and threw them at me, coming terribly close. I dodged and wove, watching as one after another hit the stone path only to crack and roll.

I reached the corral and yanked open the gate, relieved that they ceased heaving rocks — probably because they feared hitting their horses. I grabbed the reins of one gelding that still had a bit in his mouth and shooed the others out through the gate, not wanting to leave any in easy reach for a chase. I climbed the rails and leaped on the horse's back, drawing my sword as the two monks on the ground reached the corral and attempted to trap me inside. I leaned down and rammed my heels into the gelding's flanks, shouting out a warrior cry so fierce I surprised myself.

The horse rammed the closing gate with his right shoulder and shied left. I swept my sword down at the nearest monk and he released the gate, bending back to avoid my strike. The other swept his staff down on my wrist, so hard I almost lost my grip on my sword.

But I didn't. I kicked the horse again and leaned low, fixing my eyes on Ronan ahead of me and then spying the road below him. The monks kept coming, past the monastery. If I could pause to grab my knight, and we took the road down below them, much of it was too far for them to jump. And the road led … away. I wasn't sure if it would lead out of the canyon. But it would get us out of immediate danger.

The horse galloped up the cobblestone road, the two monks from the corral in pursuit. I paused near where I thought Ronan had stopped, above me. I could hear the grunt and cry of men fighting. "Ronan!" I screamed. "Down here! Ronan!"

Two, three seconds went by, each one bringing my enemies closer. A monk peered over the wall at me and shouted, and other heads appeared. Then a moment later, Ronan came flying over the wall, without as much as a look before he leaped. He landed in a crouch, took a breath, then turned and swiftly killed the first monk who was after me. As he yanked his sword free, the other struck him squarely in the back, making him arch in pain. I gasped, feeling it with him, as well as a fury I didn't know I had in me. The second monk didn't pause. He hit him again and again, moving so rapidly with the dreaded staff that Ronan didn't have the chance to respond — only bear up against the next strike he was to take.

I let out a growl and whipped the horse around, pulling a dagger from my belt. I sent it flying as the monk continued to attack my man, and it circled in the air — blade over handle — before landing between his shoulder blades. He stopped, stunned, and then his knees crumpled beneath him. Ronan looked up at me, panting, holding his belly, and then wearily stood to sheathe his swords on his back, climb onto a rock, and take my arm as I passed.

His weight nearly unseated me, but I managed to swing him almost all the way on. The horse pranced beneath us, unnerved by the second body upon his back, but as soon as I felt Ronan settle behind me, his arms wrapped around my torso, I kicked at the gelding's flanks and we were moving again, up the road, back toward the pool-end of the monastery high above us.

We rounded the bend, and I felt a breath of hope when I saw that no red-clad monks stood in our way. The farther we went, the higher the wall was above us.

And then I saw him again in the distance. Keallach, on a new section of the wall. Dimly, I realized that Niero was gone, but I could only concentrate on Keallach.

"Brother," I breathed as we galloped closer, longing to reach him, pull him back from whatever dark bindings held him. I willed the Ailith call — the thing that bound us all as one — toward him. Reminding him. Begging him to turn back from the abyss.

"Keep on it, Dri," Ronan moaned over my shoulder as I eased our pace. "It's our only chance!"

Keallach stood there, hands on hips, dark hair and red robe flying in the dry breeze, watching us from his perch. We'd have to pass right below him, just twenty feet away.

I pulled up on the reins, and the gelding circled in agitation, one way and then the other.

"Dri, no!" Ronan cried, clumsily trying to reach around me for the reins, but hurting too much to do much good.

Keallach held no weapon in his hand. No stone, no bow and arrow, not even one of the staffs. I felt pain from him, longing, as if he'd heard my Ailith call. But then Sethos stepped up beside him, blood glistening from a wound at his cheek, and that decided me. I dug my heels into the gelding's flanks and drove past them, before the tracker might leap again into our path.

Sethos did move as we passed, as if he intended to try and intercept us, but Keallach lifted a hand and grabbed him. The tracker snarled at him, his eyes betraying his confusion. But

Keallach only looked at us. *Fierce protection. Hope. Kinship* came at me in waves as we passed.

He was one of us.

And yet not.

It made me sick to my stomach, the confusion, the roiling indecision within him.

We raced down the road below them, toward what I hoped was freedom, as well as clarity on what had just happened. Why would he just let us go?

Unless we were heading to a dead end and he was simply playing with us.

But there was nothing to do but move down the road ahead. Gradually, it began to slope upward, out of the canyon like I'd hoped. But behind us, an enormous gong sounded an alarm so loud and deep in tone that it felt like it filled the entire canyon. And as we turned another corner we spied a small post, with six monks keeping watch on the road. A guard gate was visible just beyond them.

I pulled up on the reins again, and we hastened back around the corner and dropped to the ground. Still, there were no others giving chase. Why? Because they were concentrating on the others? Because they still hadn't rounded up the other horses? Or because Keallach played some odd game with us?

Ronan, still clutching his belly, edged against the wall to take another look. He grimaced and looked back at me, then beyond me to the road we came down. "Guard gate," he said with a wince, glancing down to his stomach as if he expected to see blood. How badly was he injured? "I'm betting they have weapons beyond wooden staffs in their arsenal. And the trackers arrived — did you see them?"

"Yes," I said, wishing I hadn't. If Sethos had rejoined

Keallach, that meant that Niero was down, or captured. I swallowed hard, looking back up the path, wondering if we were supposed to go back to him.

"We can't free him, Dri. Not today. Not just the two of us. And we have to get rid of these," he said, lifting the leather bag, shaking it like it was an added curse. He leaned against the cliff and looked up, as if hoping the Maker himself would show up.

"Can't go forward, can't go back," I muttered, pushing my hair back from my sweating face. I looked across the riverbed, over to the cliff on the far side, riddled with hermit caves.

Ronan did too. He slapped the gelding's flanks, sending him shying down the road on which we'd come.

"Ronan, what are you *doing*?" I cried.

"Creating a diversion. C'mon," he said, reaching for my hand and tugging me toward the river.

I saw it too, then, and felt the hope, the relief in him, even as panic threatened to overwhelm me. He meant for us to climb. Up, up into the caves. Or worse — to the top. But time was short. The gong continued to thrum, so loud it resonated in our chests as we reached thigh-depth in the river, trudging across. Ronan's arm came around my back, and we pushed against the water that now covered our waists then slowly receded as we came out on the other side. Still, there were no monks in pursuit.

"Quickly," he growled when I hesitated, practically tossing me onto the first ladder that led up to the nearest cave. I forced myself to scramble upward, the ladder rocking as he came up behind me. Was it strong enough to hold me? Hold us both? I fought back against the idea of us both falling to the ground.

We reached the first cave and slid into the dark, both panting, watching the road.

"Let's do another," he said, already moving toward the cave mouth. "The higher we can get before they —"

I grabbed hold of his arm and yanked him back to me, hearing the clatter of horse hooves approaching. We stood there, clinging together, watching as guards from the gatehouse came tearing down the road we'd left minutes ago. As soon as they passed around the bend, Ronan lifted the ladder up and into the cave, and we hurried out and took to the second, leading to the next level. I didn't wait for him to cajole me onto it — there was no time.

Thankfully, the next cave was empty too, and we moved to the third, each time removing the ladders behind us. But on the next one, the bottom rungs were missing, and I made the mistake of looking down. Ronan grabbed my chin and forced me to look him in the eye. "Just like the trees, Dri," he said, releasing me and leaning down and give me a leg up. "Say it," he grunted.

"Just like the trees," I bit out. I clambered upward, fighting to concentrate on one handhold at a time and not give in to my utter panic. He made do on his own, somehow right behind me, just as we used to in the Valley's trees. He'd always been able to make the first limb — the hardest part for me. Well, that and coming down.

We were almost to the top of still another ladder, three-quarters of the way up the cliff, when we heard more horses approaching from the monastery. We couldn't see our enemies, but we could hear them now, shouting, steadily nearing us. They were moving efficiently, smartly, trying to find where we'd left the road. We froze, and for a moment I wondered if they wouldn't see us clinging to the ladder, but then knew that was a false hope. Undoubtedly, they were well used to climbing, and they'd likely make the first level, even without the ladder. How fast might they overtake us? We could hold them off for a time, given our superior position, but for how long, without food or water or sleep? We were hopelessly outnumbered. And now trapped.

"Dri, to your right," Ronan said, and my eyes traced the rocks. I saw what he did — a shallow ravine, sloping inward, but the rocks on which we'd have to climb were far apart, terribly slim. "You can do it. Go. Now."

His tone brooked no argument, and I reached out a trembling hand for a handhold, then a foothold. I'd always followed Ronan in any climbing exercise. Not led him. It helped me to concentrate on what he was doing, then reflect it. Here I was exposed, as high as most trees in the Valley, liable to fall and take Ronan with me.

Everything in me told me to go back to the relative safety of the ladder, but I knew that would ultimately lead us to death, rather than only the *possibility* of death on the rocks, so I forced my other hand and foot from the ancient wood and set to scrambling right, into the shallow ravine and hopefully out of eyesight. Seconds later, Ronan followed suit.

The sounds across the water carried, making our enemy seem impossibly close. I waited for them to spot us and shout, even as I made myself concentrate on finding the next handhold, the next toehold. "Go," Ronan whispered.

"I'm going!" I bit back, reaching overly far for my next step. My toe missed it and I gasped as I felt nothing but air.

"It's okay," Ronan said, hand at my back. "Easy. Easy."

"'Go,' then 'easy,'" I griped, and I felt his rueful smile even though I couldn't see it.

"Go, as quickly as you can and still remain safe," he said.

"Got it. No problem."

The moment of a shared smile — the sense of normalcy, humor, in the midst of terror — gave me the extra measure of calm I needed. For a time, we moved upward at a steady pace, and my heart leaped when I saw the top come into view.

Ronan grunted as one of the rocks to which he clung gave way, clattering down the cliff below us, then down the crack toward the river. We stopped, stock still, waiting. Slowly, Ronan turned his head, back toward the river. I could see nothing, his body blocking mine.

But I didn't need him to turn back to me for me to know — we'd been spotted. "Hurry," he grunted, already moving upward beside me.

Our only chance was to make the top of this cliff.

Because they were coming.

CHAPTER
31

Blue sky widened above us. Ronan chose an alternate route, made the top of the cliff first, looked around, then reached down for my hand. I grabbed hold, wrist to wrist, and he lifted me to the top. We stood together a moment, arms around each other, panting, turning in a slow circle, then seeing we were alone, and temporarily safe, we separated, hands on knees, each trying to gain our breath. Immediately to our west were the towering, gray mountains, disappearing into a ring of clouds that we'd glimpsed when we crossed the Great Expanse. To the south was another desert.

"I've had enough with deserts, haven't you?" I panted. Raniero had told us to head to the mountains, likely knowing we'd find safety, familiarity among the trees. But the first of the forest was a good mile away. "Think we can make that?" I asked. "Before our enemies find their way up here?"

"Think we need to try," he said.

"Let's go." We set off in a steady jog. Within five minutes, we knew the mountains were farther than a mile, and I looked over my shoulder anxiously.

"Eyes ahead, Dri," Ronan said, grimacing through his obvious pain, repeating what our trainer had taught us to do. *Focus on the goal,* he'd always said. *See yourself as reaching your goal, rather than concentrating on what lies between you and what you seek.*

We ran a mile, then two, then three, I guessed, slowing only when we were close enough to smell the trees. Even then we walked briskly, Ronan turning to scan the dry fields, but there was no one in pursuit. "Why is he not after us?" I said, turning a slow circle. "Surely Keallach has the resources —"

"He let us go," he said, as troubled by it as I. "He must have chosen to let us go."

"And where are the others?" I said, my voice sounding strangled with fear. Niero, Vidar, Tressa, Bellona, Killian. We kept expecting to see a pair of them behind us, even in front of us, waving from the edge of the woods. But there was no one.

"Vidar and Bellona jumped into the river," he said grimly.

I looked to the left, knowing the current led that way. "They'll come out near that other desert."

"Probably."

But Killian and Tressa had crossed the bridge and begun climbing from the start. That should've put them closer to us.

"They're fast," Ronan said, obviously thinking along the same lines. "Killian and Tressa — maybe they're already ahead of us. Making their way toward the mountains through that ravine over there, where we can't see them."

"I hope so," I said. "Because I don't want to tackle what we have ahead of us alone, Ronan."

Dread filled him. "Nor do I."

"What do you think happened to Niero?" I dared to ask. I wanted him to tell me that he thought he'd escaped, that he —

"I don't know. But he's strong, Dri."

Stronger than you would believe, I thought, remembering the man's naked back, the scars from a hundred wounds, his ability to heal … It gave me hope. Hope that we'd see him again.

We reached the first trees and turned, gripping hold of them as if the slender trunks might infuse strength into us. We looked back across the dry plain and still saw nothing. Just tumbleweeds blowing across the prairie leading to the desert. "C'mon," he said, taking my hand.

But that is when we heard the metallic click of a gun hammer, then another.

"Stay where you are," said a woman.

"Raise your hands to your head," said a man.

Ronan and I shared a *what now* glance, slowly put our hands to our heads, and turned. I reached out, trying to get a sense of these people, but all I could gather was fear, the desire to protect themselves. My cuff registered nothing, neither hot nor cold, remaining completely still. I wanted to slap it, as if it might be asleep when I most needed it, but I didn't want to call attention to my adornment, or those Ronan carried at his waist.

"Who are you?" bit out the woman, sliding the barrel of the gun under my chin as the man put his against Ronan's temple.

"We mean you no harm," I said, looking at the dark-haired, olive-skinned woman at my side. Her round eyes were narrowed in suspicion. She was shorter than I, but strong, dressed in what appeared to be animal pelts. "I am Andriana, of the Valley. This is my friend, Ronan."

"What'd you say your name was?" said the woman, pressing the gun harder.

"An-Andriana." Wanting to add that it was hard to talk with a gun barrel under your chin.

She turned so she could get a better look at my face and then glanced over at the man.

"What are you doing here?" the man ground out.

"We are running," Ronan said honestly, "from the monks that inhabit that canyon to your east." I understood his methods. There was no point in lying. The monks could show up any minute and these people would know the truth; our only hope was in sharing a common enemy.

The man and woman shared another meaningful look and then lowered their weapons. "Then you'll be needing shelter for the night," the man said, resting his rifle across his shoulder. "Those monks are the worst at night. They like to try and surprise those they hunt in their sleep."

I shivered at his words, remembering the flower on my pillow — the silent entry and exit of the man I now knew as Keallach.

But the pair had already turned and took to a small trail through the woods. It was as if they expected us to follow, and if we didn't, they didn't care. They were concentrating on getting away themselves. After about fifteen minutes' climb, they paused beside the carcass of what I recognized as a deer, even though I'd never seen one myself, and the man took a machete from his back and swiftly hacked the doe into four quarters, gathered the entrails in a sack, then wiped his blade in the mossy bank to his side. "Each of you take one," he grunted, then lifted his portion and set off again.

The small woman followed suit, with me right behind her. I grimaced as blood dripped down her back, staining her leather shirt, but then I saw it was the most recent of many layers. These two were clearly hunters, and headed back to what I hoped was a village, with some safeguards from any enemy who tried to infiltrate them. The doe's hide felt wiry in my hand, the hoof and leg like a club, the meat heavy on my shoulder. All my life, I'd eaten mudhorse and mutton, but we'd never seen anything like this deer in our Valley. They'd long since been hunted out.

We climbed and climbed until my thighs ached in protest. Then we headed south along a slippery slope of rock scree, which set us sliding, again and again. We rounded the mountain an hour later, and paused on a small saddle, looking out and down to miles and miles of green, rolling hills and smaller mountains, their peaks about level with us now. In the distance, I thought I spied horses running down a valley. In another was what I thought was a sprawling farm, with neat, green rows that went on for miles, a thousand times larger than Dagan's field near the Hoodoos.

We turned and entered a small cave, turning sideways to squeeze through, one by one. The farther in we got, the darker it became, and the man who led us paused to strike flint and then blow on a pile of brittle dry grasses. Quickly, he set a torch into it, and immediately the entire cavern was illuminated.

Ronan's hand slipped around mine as we gazed upward. Directly above us were countless stalagtites, eerie in the dancing shadows cast by the torchlight. But before us was a massive, flat wall, covered in ancient paintings and words and dates from as far back as the War. There were quotes and maps and names, all mishmashed together, a collective wall of village memory, by the looks of it. But then my eyes settled on more of the words, reading them, really reading them. *Whoever dwells in the shadow of the Most High will rest in the shadow . . .* They were sacred words. Words I'd been taught as a child, passed down from one generation to the next but never, ever written down. Not as Asher had taught his little children. Not as these cave dwellers dared to do.

"Yo-your people," I stammered. "They've been here since the War?"

"Since before the War," said the man, picking up his quarter of the deer. "Since before things became ... *adverse* for people of the Way. My people could see it coming and fled." He looked directly at me. "We rise now because we knew you were coming."

My armband warmed to his words and the flame of his torch seemed to grow brighter. Whatever they meant, I knew then that we were among friends. If they would only agree to aid us.

"Come along," the man said, turning to go through a tunnel on the far side of the cave. The woman followed me and Ronan.

The tunnel dipped and rose, curved and curved again until I had no sense of how deep into the mountain we were. But my armband hummed the farther we walked, encouraging me onward. We heard the laughter before we reached the next chamber. Women singing, working side by side, pounding out some sort of paste in rounded stones with pestles. In a smaller room, children sat in a half circle around what appeared to be a teacher, writing letters and numbers on a wide, flat stone with a white-chalk rock. Men and women worked together on stretching hides across wide rings, perhaps to dry them out. In the corner, two men wove together strands into some sort of net.

But one by one, as they spied us in the doorway, they quieted and then rose.

The women were first; an older woman tentatively came

closer. She took my hand. "Can it be? Are they as he has foreseen?"

"Only one way to find out," our guide said, nodding. Now my armband was thrumming with the joy of a fellow Ailith nearby, and Ronan squeezed my hand, hope and excitement filling his heart. Every one of the people from the cave followed behind us.

We went through another tunnel and smelled the trees before we exited the rocks and could see them. We paused, in shock. In front of us was an entire village, spread through the limbs of trees larger than I had ever seen, trees that had to be a millennium old. Small houses nestled among them, connected by suspended bridges. I gasped as a small boy took to a rope and swung over to the next house, a hundred feet from the ground.

But Ronan was staring at another young man, in a small house at the edge of the settlement. He was on a narrow bridge, arms akimbo, staring our way.

As if he had expected us.

"Dri..."

"I see him."

The hunter looked from us to the young man and back again. "As he's foreseen you."

My armband seemed almost hot as we took to the first bridge and moved toward our brother, and he toward us. He moved like he had spotted family, and even at a distance I could read the joy, the warm recognition in his heart. He had to be Ailith. He had to be!

We rounded a huge tree that was bigger than my house. I tried to not look down, terrified by the height and meager rope that stood between me and a fall that would surely kill me, instead choosing to concentrate on the brother ahead of us.

And then he was there, across the bridge. Ronan grinned back at me and headed down to greet him, seemingly unaffected by the bounce and sway of it. I waited near the relative safety of the tree, wringing my hands in agitation. The men met midway, clasping arms immediately and smiling. Then the other one turned and followed Ronan back to me.

He was as dark as the huntress who had found us, and thin, shorter than I but clearly very strong. He took my arm and smiled into my eyes. "You are Andriana."

"I am," I said, gaping at him. "How did you know?"

"Because the Maker had given me your name years ago." Ronan hovered beside us. "And your eyes ... Andriana, I would've known your eyes anywhere."

"He told us," said the male guide who had led us up the mountain. "We have long been on the lookout for an Andriana with blue-green eyes."

"My sister," the Ailith said, grinning at me. "My brother," he said to Ronan. "I am Chaza'el. And we have much to discuss."

CHAPTER
32

But first," Chaza'el said, "you have traveled far, and you are weary, injured. You will rest over here, in that house," he said, gesturing to a tree house a couple hundred feet away. "You'll find everything you need. Bathe. Eat. And then come and see me in our gathering place, back in the cave. My people like to learn of new things, and new friends, together."

"Chaza'el," Ronan said, "the monks from the Wadi. I fear they will track us to the mountain and — "

The small man shook his head. "But they will not get farther. They've tried again and again through the years, but our hunters are adept at hiding their tracks. Never have they made it to the cave dwellings, let alone this far side of the mountain. Rest. We will make sure you are safe."

"Forgive me, brother," Ronan said, rubbing the back of his neck. "But as Andriana's knight, I must insist that we see your Ailith mark. I mean you no offense."

"Of course," he said with a bright smile. "As my people must see both of yours. They are very protective of me. Wear something that allows it when you come, yes? They will be delighted to see another of my visions coming to pass." He turned to go.

"Where is your knight, Chaza'el?" I called, looking over my shoulder at him. "Every Remnant has a knight."

"Indeed," he said, and the grief I felt from him then sent me seeking Ronan's hand. "She died last year." His eyes met ours. "To save me."

Ronan's fingers entwined with mine, a surge of protection running through him.

"I-I'm so sorry."

"Yes," Chaza'el said, "we all lost a sister that day. Perhaps you felt it, even from afar?"

"I-I don't know." I didn't remember it, if I had.

"I see," he said, his dark brows lowering, as if our lack of recognition deepened his sorrow. As if she had deserved at least that much respect. He looked outward. "We are on the edge of Pacifica," he said. "Terribly near our enemies. We are safe here, but down there ... We must take caution."

Ronan and I nodded and Chaza'el turned to go. We walked down a bridge — me clinging to the ropes on either side all the way, forcing myself to take one step after another — around another tree, then to the second bridge that led to the house where we'd been sent. Ronan opened the small door and walked in, waiting for me to enter before closing the door behind me. I leaned against the innermost wall, closing my eyes and panting. "Trees," I said. "Why'd Chaza'el have to live in the tallest trees we've ever seen?"

Ronan chuckled and lifted the pack from my shoulders. "We're inside now. Pretend like you're in the most solid, grounded house you've ever been in."

"Sure. No problem."

"Try, Dri. Try. It looks like we've found a refuge in enemy territory, and I, for one, could use a night's sleep."

"Me too." I took his hand and looked up into his face. "How is that wound, Ronan?" I asked, gesturing to his belly.

"Oh, not as bad as all that," he said. "Come." He led me forward, holding my hand. And it felt so good to touch him that I had no choice but to follow. Not if I didn't want to tear my hand away ...

We inhaled the scent of fresh-hewn lumber. Then we walked around the circumference of the giant tree, the bark on one side, open windows on the far side. There was a small shower — with a tank warming in the afternoon sun above us — three hammocks, and two small chairs beside a table laden with bread and nuts. We each took up a small round of bread and ate, swallowing as fast as we could. Then a handful of nuts — an odd, curving shape. I didn't know what kind they were; I only knew they tasted delicious.

A girl knocked at the door, clothing in her hands. "Chaza'el thinks these will fit you," she said.

"Thank you," I said, taking them from her small hands. She pranced down the bridge away from me, not even grasping hold of the ropes on either side. I shivered and pushed shut the door, then turned to look at Ronan, and past him, to the treetops outside the window. Suddenly, I felt like I was back in the Valley with him, somehow, and that Mom and Dad were within reach. That Niero might be nearby, watching over us.

I swallowed hard, feeling foolish. But I couldn't stop the tears.

"Dri? Hey, what's this?" he asked, coming close, then

cradling me in his arms. I leaned against his chest, and the tears came faster as he stroked my back and hair.

"I just ... for a moment ... It's all been a little much, you know?" I said with a breathy laugh.

"A guy doesn't have to be an empath to agree. It's all been a *lot* much. You've done well, Dri. So well. It will be okay. Somehow, it will all be okay. In time."

I hugged him close. "You think we'll see Niero again? And the others?"

"I do," he whispered, kissing the top of my head. It made me smile, both his hope and his tenderness. After a while, my tears ended.

"Now go on, take a shower," he said. "It'll make you feel better. Just don't take all the water."

"Agreed," I said, hurrying forward. I closed the curtain behind me and quickly stripped out of my clothes, covered in dirt and stains, and out of my underthings. I looked up to the rope, attached to the bucket above me, half closed my eyes, and pulled slowly, experimenting. The mouth of the bucket opened wider, dousing me with a steady stream of lukewarm water. I let it shut and took a bar of soap, thick with the scent of pine, lathering from top to bottom, working quickly, given the goosebumps spreading across my skin. I thought longingly of the warm pool in Wadi Qelt, then got angry at myself for thinking of anything pleasant at all in that place.

And it led me back to thinking of our Ailith kin. Were any still trapped there? Prisoners now? Had any escaped? Been hurt? *Niero ...*

I thought of Chaza'el's words about his dead knight, and shivered over more than cold, wet skin. Gently, I pulled the handle and rinsed off. The water and suds ran down the wooden slats beneath my feet and out through tiny holes at the base of the tree. I reached for a rough cloth on a peg outside the curtain and quickly dried off, then peered out carefully to reach for my clothes. Ronan was not in sight.

I yanked the soft doeskin downward and over my body. It was almost a dress, with sleeves that curved over my shoulders and reached my elbows and a hem that stopped mid-thigh. I pulled aside the curtain, feeling shy, as I looked for pants that must go with it. *There.* I unfolded the soft fabric to discover it was a skirt that wrapped around and tied at the side, and slid it around my waist.

"Ronan?" I called as I finished the knot. "You can take yours now."

He was rounding the corner as I said it, and stopped short when he saw me as I smoothed the top back over my hips. His reaction set my heart hammering in my chest. He seemed to remember himself, how he was supposed to be acting even if he was feeling otherwise, and hurriedly moved past me. "Saved me some water, did you?"

"Did my best," I said, handing him a towel, then reached for a wide-toothed comb fashioned from some sort of bone and began to work out the tangles. He hovered, his hand on the curtain, as if intent on getting on with his shower, but I could feel his eyes on me. I smiled, finding rest, distraction in his emotions. Joy at being this close to me. Sharing a rare private moment. Knowing he loved me. And I loved him.

It was a delicious little secret. The worst kind of secret. The most forbidden kind of secret. And all the better because of it.

He stared at me and I lifted my eyes to stare back, then looked to the windows, knowing we were being too obvious. But then here, on the outskirts of the tree house village, there was no one looking in. Our view stretched a hundred miles, over hills and plains, fields and forest. There were no eyes possibly watching us, for the first time in … almost ever.

I wondered again what it would be like to kiss him. To be held by a man who loved me, who would die for me. He'd held me before, but not for long, when I knew he wanted to kiss me. Touch me.

We were blessed.

We were doomed.

When he finished his shower, dressed in his own soft doeskin pants, I turned toward him. His long, dark hair still dripped down his chest, and one lock fell over his right brow and cheek. He was pulling on a shirt, but it clung and crumpled on his wet skin.

The spreading bruise at his belly gave me something to focus on in my sudden nervousness. "Oh, Ronan," I said, frowning, moving toward him. I looked down at it, reached out to touch it, but he grabbed hold of my hand.

"No, Dri. Don't."

"It hurts that bad, your wound?" I asked, pretending I didn't understand the real reason for his reticence. Chattering, nervous. "Do you have a broken rib?"

"It's fine," he muttered, still holding my wrist, his eyes intent on mine. "A few days and it'll be fine."

"It doesn't look fine. Maybe Chaza'el has a healer here — "

"Dri," he said, his tone tortured. My name was like a lament on his lips. "We can't do this." He dropped my wrist as if it burned him.

"Can't we?" I whispered, refusing to move away from him.

What are you saying, Dri? I wanted to shake myself for being an idiot. For hoping that it might be possible, despite the odds. And staring into his eyes, the color of a mossy river bank in deep shadow ... I felt a surge of hope within him too.

Ronan stepped forward, so close now he could wrap his arms around me. His feelings were so intense, it was almost as if he was ... But he wasn't. He just stood there, looking utterly torn. Overwhelmed. Full of both need and fear, as conflicted as Keallach had been.

"I was so scared back there," he whispered, his voice raspy. "I've been so scared, all along, that something would happen to you." He lifted a hand to touch my cheek. "If anything happened to you, Dri, if I was the cause ..."

"But you won't," I said, staring back at him. "You would never hurt me. Ronan, how could love ever hurt either of us?"

I was delirious, falling from one possibility to the next. There was something perfect about us falling in love. In a way, we always had been, since the first day I laid eyes on his secretive smile and easy mannerisms that so seemed to fill and fit my own. Our trainer had practically *told* us to fall in love when he told two stubborn, independent thinkers that we could never, ever do such a thing. It only made us want to find a method to surmount what he deemed insurmountable obstacles. To prove him wrong. To prove love right.

I made myself turn to step away, feeling everything he was, but doubly—both his desire and my own. Both his guilt and my own. But he reached forward and caught my hip and I turned back, half terrified, half glad.

He pulled me close then—fierce, fast—raw masculine power, and stared down at me in both pain and pleasure. "Andriana," he whispered, his breath labored. "What are we doing?"

"What we should've been doing all along," I said, looking up at him.

He frowned down at me, his breath still ragged as he wound his fingers in my hair, searching my face as if he couldn't believe I was real. "The Maker hasn't answered my prayers."

"No?"

"No," he said, shaking his head a little and reaching down to pull me closer. "I asked him to take it away. My desire for you. For me to love you, but not *love* you."

I slid my arms up and around his neck. "Oh, Ronan. Don't you think ... don't you think that this *is* a sort of answered prayer? Love? Like ours?"

He leaned in, nuzzling close, his breath warm on my face. Sweet. "Is that what you think?" he asked, his lips brushing mine with the barest touch.

"I think," I said, lifting up on my tiptoes to bridge the gap.

He kissed me then. Carefully, so agonizingly careful. Then, as the minutes wore on, harder, more urgent. He pulled away but I followed, kissing him, demanding he return to me, having waited so long for this ... so, so long.

He complied for a while, drawing my body close, then pulled his head back and stroked my cheek, searching my face as if he couldn't get enough of the sight of me, as if he couldn't believe what we were experiencing was real. "What have we done?" he whispered, his voice raw, rubbing his thumb across my lower lip, swollen from his kisses. "Andriana, what have we done?"

"What we couldn't *not* do," I said. "I was always yours, Ronan. Always. I love you."

"I love you too. Maker help me, I love you Andriana, with everything in me." He bent to kiss my forehead, my cheeks.

Then finally, my lips again, for a long moment. He pulled back and his eyes opened wide. "It's impossibly fantastic, love. And excruciating too. I feel as if I've been turned inside-out."

I smiled back at him. "Me too. Believe me. Twice over." I settled against him, resting my head against his shoulder, feeling the steady beat of his pulse, the rise and fall of his chest. I had the craziest desire to stay right there, in that tree house, and wish the world away. "I wish we'd been born somewhere else," I said. "To other parents. In another time. When we could just be. Together. Be in love."

He paused. "I don't." He pulled slightly away and cradled my face in his big hands, his eyes holding so much love that they filled with tears of intensity again. "This is where we were meant to be, Andriana. Here. Now. If we'd been elsewhere we might have missed *us*. No matter what comes, no matter what happens, Dri, know that I wouldn't have ever traded this moment for anything."

We stared at each other for a long moment, lost in the intensity, the relief, the admission.

"I wouldn't have traded it either, Ronan," I said at last, tears dripping down my face. I wasn't sure why I cried. Because I feared that this was all we'd get? A stolen moment? Or because it was so perfect, our final admission of love, when we'd worked so hard to avoid it?

I decided love was like that. Utterly perfect, no matter when, where or how it rose.

Or how forbidden and impossible it might be.

CHAPTER

33

Chaza'el had the gift of visions. Foresight as well, to a certain extent, though his visions and foresight seemed to be in bits and pieces. He indeed shared our crescent moon marking on the right hip, and already knew of Kapriel and Keallach being Ailith brothers. When the others in his village saw our markings, they clapped and laughed in wonder.

"What of the other Ailith?" I asked, trying not to sound as desperate as I felt. "Have you seen them? Will we be reunited soon?"

Chaza'el's brown eyes connected with mine and he gave his head a sorrowful shake. "All the Maker has given me is a vision of us all together, and I'm not even certain where we were."

We described each one of the Ailith — Tressa's red hair and blue eyes; Killian's blond dreadlocks; Vidar's dark and stocky appearance; Bellona's tough persona and long braid. And Raniero's tall, broad-shoulders, his sparkling black eyes.

Chaza'el rose and walked to the fire, staring into the flames. "All those except the one you call Raniero."

I swallowed hard, remembering him behind us, swarmed, surrounded by our enemy. And we had left him, abandoned him. We had to find him, be reunited, especially if we were to go after Kapriel on Catal —

"Dri, he told us to," Ronan said, taking my hand in his. "He *told* us to."

"I know," I said, shaking my head. "But I can't help wondering …"

"No. If we had stayed, fought beside him, we might not be here either." He lifted his hand to gesture to Chaza'el. "Clearly, the Maker wanted us to escape so we could find our brother. Right?"

"Right," I muttered. I could not deny the utter peace of us being here. But my heart also wondered after the man who had sent us here, to the mountains to the West. What would happen to us without him? Our leader? I looked over at Chaza'el, and thought about his armband. He needed it, needed the ceremony. He already had the gift, but if we were able to complete his entry into the Ailith fold, how much more powerful would he become? We needed every ounce of his ability on our side. But did we need Niero to do that?

"Do you think …" I began, looking to Ronan. "Do you think it's possible for an Ailith to take his armband without all the other Ailith with them?"

Ronan's keen eyes searched mine and widened in understanding. He looked to the fire and then shook his head. "I don't think so. There is something holy, even sacred, in those bondings. I think the other Ailith kin had to be present for the gift to fully … breathe."

"What do you think his gift really is?" Ronan asked me. "Keallach? I didn't see him use any in battle, or before, did you? Wouldn't that have been a good time to move objects, to stop us?"

"He has powers we haven't seen in anyone else," Chaza'el said, his eyes dull, his face slack. He looked up and around at all of us as we held our breath. "But they are held in check without the cuff."

"Miraculous powers?" I pressed, forcing the words out.

"Power like none other. What I've seen …" Chaza'el said, lifting his round face to the trees. He shook his head, as if he just didn't have it in him to continue. And we were too weary from the battle to press him. There would be time enough to come to terms with his gifting.

We were all silent for a while.

"What if," Ronan began slowly. "What if those monks captured one of the Ailith?" He swallowed hard. "What if Keallach gets his armband?"

"I think he needs us," I said. "For the ceremony. It's as you said. The cuff probably wouldn't adhere, his gifts won't *mature*, without Community about him. Without the Ailith. Without the Maker's blessing."

"Which is good," Ronan said dully, poking at the fire, "and really bad. Because if he needs us …"

"Chaza'el saw us all. Every one of us, except Niero, in that vision. Keallach won't have an armband if we can help it, right?"

He nodded, then we moved on, finding comfort and distraction in telling Chaza'el of every step of our journey, everything we could think of to help bring him up to date with us, hoping the knowledge would feed his comprehension of what was to come. The fire had burned down to embers, and our words were coming out slurred, we were so weary, when Chaza'el looked with compassion at us. "My friends, it is enough. You must sleep. You will be safe in the tree houses this night, with us on watch, so slumber without fear."

I rose on legs that felt weak and followed Ronan and our brother out of the cave, trailed by the others in silence. Across the bridge, the people separated, all going to different homes among the boughs and branches. After we were across, the bridge that extended between the side of the mountain and the first giant tree was lowered and drawn up for the night, a form of drawbridge over a "moat" that was nothing but a hundred foot drop.

"We have been safe here for over a century," Chaza'el said, putting a calming hand on my shoulder. "No enemy has scaled this mountain or come near our village for five decades. And if they do, our people are skilled at hunting. No word of our existence has escaped. Ever. We are like ghost people. The Pacificans fear us as such, spreading tales over the generations, and therefore shy away from our mountains."

I smiled as he waggled his eyebrows. He saw us to our own tree house, and promised to wake us in the morning — earlier if he heard any word about Raniero, or any of our Ailith kin. His brown eyes moved between me and Ronan, clearly seeing something we could not, then he nodded his good night.

Ronan shut the door and I turned toward the first hammock, then back to him. I hurried into his arms, and for a long time we clung to each other, not kissing, just holding the other. He rubbed my back, and we breathed in unison, simply enjoying being together. But I was so, so weary.

He seemed to sense it, and bent down and picked me up in his arms. Then he carried me to the first hammock and settled me gently inside it. He reached for a soft skin blanket and covered me with it, kissing me slowly, gently on the forehead. "Good night, Dri."

"Good night, my love," I whispered.

And with a devilish smile over the surge of emotion I felt back from him, I curled up and promptly went to sleep.

We awakened to bird calls through the trees, and Chaza'el burst through the door without knocking. "Rise!" he cried. "They're here!" He disappeared, leaving the door open.

I practically fell out of my hammock in my haste to get out of it, landing on one knee and wincing, even as I laughed. They were here. Here! Who? Who had made it?

Ronan landed neatly on his feet and laughed under his breath, helping me up. I was too excited to take offense, rushing to the door and down the bridge. We saw them as we crossed, over by the mouth of the cave. Vidar and Bellona. Tressa and Killian.

But no Niero.

They raised their fists in greeting, and I could see Vidar's white smile, even from where I stood. Hurriedly, we rushed around the tree and onto the second bridge, then waited on the platform as men and women hauled up the drawbridge that would allow us to reunite. It seemed to take forever. But as soon as Chaza'el gave us the nod of permission, we were running across it — even I didn't hold the ropes — concentrating only on reaching the other end. To our brothers. Our sisters.

I leaped into Bellona's arms, and Ronan hugged Tressa. The knights clasped arms, grinning in the glory of our glad reunion. "What of Niero?" I asked each one. All of them just shook their head, fear and concern wafting off of them like a foul odor. But I was so glad to be with them again, so happy that most of us were together, that my smile quickly returned.

We introduced them all to Chaza'el, and together entered the cavern to have some breakfast and share what we knew. Bellona had a bandaged wrist, having taken a fierce hit from a monk's staff, and I could see that Vidar had a long cut at his temple. "He almost had me, the little spider," he said, referring to the enemy monk. Spider was an apt description for the Wadi Qelt soldiers, who had spread and surrounded us so quickly, like a nest of babies burst forth all at once. I shivered at the memory.

"How'd you find us?" Ronan asked.

"The Maker guided us," Bellona said. "Our armbands grew warmer with every step we took to this place. And when we were off-track, they grew colder."

"So what now?" Bellona asked, tossing her heavy brown braid over her shoulder. "Onward to the coast? To try and reach Kapriel? Or behind us? To try and free Niero?"

Chaza'el stilled. "You intend to free Kapriel? From the Isle of Catal?"

"At the first opportunity," Vidar said with a wide grin. He lifted his hands. "I don't suppose you tree people have a boat ..."

But Chaza'el didn't return his smile. His brown eyes were wide and distant, his pupils dilated, as if seeing something else entirely in the dark. I bit my tongue when I wanted to say his name, not wishing to break whatever was happening. My cuff seemed to hum ... warmed as we watched our new brother.

He blinked and straightened, then seemed to see us all again, but still, we waited. Around us, his fellow villagers had stilled, as if they knew well this cycle of vision and sharing. Collectively, we all took a deep breath, like we'd all been holding it.

Chaza'el gave us an embarrassed grin, and impulsively, I took his hand. "Tell us, brother. Of your vision."

"It was of Catal. Kapriel's prison. I ... I've never had a vision of such clarity."

"Welcome to the company of the Ailith," Vidar said. "Just wait until we get you your armband."

Bellona shook her head at him. "But, Chaza'el ... Did you see the way in? How we might approach Catal?"

"No, but I saw our prince deep within her tunnels. He is unwell. Suffering."

I frowned. Kapriel was ill? And if he was suffering ... might Keallach pounce upon his weakness?

"That's not so great, Chaz," Vidar chided. "Can you redo your vision-thing again and see if you can figure out our route to him instead?"

Chaza'el smiled, recognizing Vidar's humor. "If only I could."

"Yeah, well. Let's work on that. Somebody get this guy an armband!" he yelled, as if summoning a tavern maid. And with that, some of the tension melted as we laughed.

■　■　■

We packed supplies and hiked all day, slept in a valley — taking turns keeping watch — then hiked all day the next. When we reached the saddle of the next ridge of mountains, Ronan and Bellona stood waiting, eyes alight, glee emanating from them.

The rest of us, weary but curious, joined them and looked out. There, in the distance, was something impossibly huge. A blue band, curving with the horizon.

"The ocean," Bellona said, as if she thought we didn't

understand what we saw. And to be honest, it wasn't until that moment that I did comprehend what the word could mean.

"It's so big," I said, shaking my head. "So vast."

Our mountain friends shared another look. "You've never seen it before?" said the huntress.

"Never," I breathed, still staring. It was simply so much bigger than I had imagined. And in comparison, I suddenly felt frightfully small. Tiny, on the edge of it.

Never had our charter seemed farther off, less possible, than now. To save the world. When it was turning out to be so big. It was one thing to think we could battle the evil that menaced her when we were in the Valley — when the world felt more contained, more known. Standing here, now, looking upon the vast waters, thinking of others beyond it, I realized just how much I didn't know about my world, and laughed aloud.

Ronan took my hand. "The goal, Andriana. Just the next goal, not everything in between," he reminded me softly.

I looked up at him and gave him a rueful smile. "It's so immense, Ronan. Our task. This world. And what the Maker has sent us out to do."

"But the Maker holds it all," he said.

"That he does," Vidar said in satisfaction, staring outward.

"To the end and back," Chaza'el said, putting his fist in the center of our ring. His new arm cuff glinted in the sun. "I'm with you, Ailith kin. As I've always been with you, from the start. From birth, strengthened by the hour of our Call, and wherever the Maker takes us next."

Slowly, we each placed a hand on his, one atop another.

"To the end and back," I repeated, looking every one of them in the eye — Vidar, Bellona, Killian, Tressa, Ronan, and Chaza'el.

"To the end and back," they said together.

NOTE FROM THE AUTHOR:

So often I get email from readers, wondering about correct pronunciation about names. My character names are carefully chosen, since a name evokes a persona in my mind. Many of these are warrior names, with unique nuances that tie to who the characters are. Some I just liked, even if their meanings made no sense. But I do hope they are names you can pronounce in your head! Here's how they sounded in MY mind ...

~LTB

PRONUNCIATION GUIDE:

Ailith: A-lith ("noble war"; "ascending, rising")

Andriana: An-dree-ana, or Dree, for "Dri" ("warrior")

Asher: Ash-er ("happy one")

Azarel: Ah-zah-rell ("helper")

Bellona: Bell-oh-na ("warlike")

Chaza'el: Chazah-ell ("one who sees")

Kapriel: Kah-pree-ell (variant of "warrior")

Keallach: Key-lock ("battle")

Killian: Kill-ee-un ("little warrior" — though he's not so little in my novel!)

Raniero: Rah-near-oh ("wise warrior")

Ronan: Row-nun ("little seal"; I know. Not as cool, right? But he was named Duncan at first draft and I had to change it due to publisher request, and "Ronan" sounded like a medieval, cool warrior name to me. I overlooked the real translation in favor of the man he became in my story. And that guy, to my mind, is more like a warrior, with the spray of the sea upon his face as he takes on the storm — which is a little like a seal!)

Tressa: Tre-sah ("late summer")

Vidar: Vee-dar ("forest warrior")